WHAT THE HEX

✳ ✦ ✳ ✦ ✳

JESSICA CLARE

BERKLEY ROMANCE
NEW YORK

Berkley Romance
Published by Berkley
An imprint of Penguin Random House LLC
penguinrandomhouse.com

Library of Congress Cataloging-in-Publication Data

Names: Clare, Jessica, author.
Title: What the hex / Jessica Clare.
Description: First edition. | New York: Berkley Romance, 2023.
Identifiers: LCCN 2022033394 (print) | LCCN 2022033395 (ebook) |
ISBN 9780593337585 (trade paperback) | ISBN 9780593337608 (ebook)
Subjects: LCGFT: Romance fiction. | Novels.
Classification: LCC PS3603.L353 W47 2023 (print) | LCC PS3603.L353 (ebook) |
DDC 813/.6—dc23/eng/20220715
LC record available at https://lccn.loc.gov/2022033394
LC ebook record available at https://lccn.loc.gov/2022033395

First Edition: April 2023

Printed in the United States of America
1st Printing

Book design by Daniel Brount

PRAISE FOR
GO HEX YOURSELF

"*Go Hex Yourself* is one of *those* books: the ones you read even though you should be getting ready for work; the ones you cannot help telling your friends about; the ones that make you giggle out loud on the bus; the ones that are so addictively charming, engaging, and cinematic, you just cross your fingers and hope someone will turn them into a movie. And that's because *Go Hex Yourself* is a romantic masterpiece, and the sexiest, most bewitching take on enemies-to-lovers I've read in ages. I want to live in the worlds Jessica Clare creates, and I cannot wait for her next book."
—Ali Hazelwood, *New York Times* bestselling author of
The Love Hypothesis

"This whimsical witchy rom-com absolutely sparkles with humor and charm. Its vibrant characters, unique magic system, and smoking-hot romance will keep readers enthralled. I found myself compulsively turning pages, laughing and swooning all along the way. A spellbinding delight!"
—India Holton, national bestselling author of
The Wisteria Society of Lady Scoundrels

"A magical rom-com with both literal and figurative sparks aplenty."
—PopSugar

"The snarky banter and paranormal elements make for a fun, otherworldly romance with plenty of heart."
—Washington Independent Review of Books

"This is a super fun paranormal romance with an interesting magical system. It's written with fans of the enemies-to-lovers and grumpy/sunshine tropes in mind, and has entertaining side characters. Definitely pick this up when you're in the mood for a lighthearted romance with a few laughs and some steam."

—Book Riot

"Jessica Clare knows her way around 'the other world' when it comes to romance." —Barnes & Noble

"In this breezy paranormal rom-com from bestseller Clare, an intense young woman trying to pay off family debts finds a job with unexpected erotic side benefits. . . . Fans of Katie MacAlister and Annette Blair will be pleased." —*Publishers Weekly*

"A lighthearted and fun romp." —*Library Journal*

TITLES BY JESSICA CLARE

HEX SERIES

Go Hex Yourself
What the Hex

WYOMING COWBOYS

All I Want for Christmas Is a Cowboy
The Cowboy and His Baby
A Cowboy Under the Mistletoe
The Cowboy Meets His Match

Her Christmas Cowboy
The Bachelor Cowboy
Holly Jolly Cowboy

ROUGHNECK BILLIONAIRES

Dirty Money
Dirty Scoundrel
Dirty Bastard

THE BILLIONAIRE BOYS CLUB

Stranded with a Billionaire
Beauty and the Billionaire
The Wrong Billionaire's Bed
Once Upon a Billionaire

Romancing the Billionaire
One Night with a Billionaire
His Royal Princess
Beauty and the Billionaire: The Wedding

BILLIONAIRES AND BRIDESMAIDS

The Billionaire and the Virgin
The Taming of the Billionaire
The Billionaire Takes a Bride
The Billionaire's Favorite Mistake
Billionaire on the Loose

THE BLUEBONNET NOVELS

The Girl's Guide to (Man)Hunting
The Care and Feeding of an Alpha Male
The Expert's Guide to Driving a Man Wild
The Virgin's Guide to Misbehaving
The Billionaire of Bluebonnet

For Kristine, whose edits are always *chef's kiss*

WHAT THE HEX

WILLEM

S ir?"

I look up from the book in my lap, annoyed that one of the servants has bothered to disturb me in my study. Putting aside the treatise on the casting benefits of various types of dried beetles as spell components, I eye my housekeeper. "Is there a problem?"

She gestures feebly toward the front of the house. "It's happening again."

My annoyance disappears immediately, replaced with surging anger and frustration. I jump to my feet, racing out of my study and down the hall. "Where?"

"M-mailbox," she calls after me. "Dorothy found a dead bird in your mailbox."

I storm out the front door and into the neighborhood. My house is in a little suburban community of other witches and warlocks, because it's easiest to have neighbors that won't call the police on me at all hours. I scan my lawn and the driveway. Nothing seems amiss, but the mailbox is hanging open. Biting the inside of my cheek, I manage to keep a bland expression on my face as I stalk toward the curb. One quick glance inside the mailbox shows that Dorothy did not lie. There's a dead dove inside, nestled atop my mail.

That *weasel*.

I knew he'd come after me, especially after I'd just stolen his prized library. It's an affront that can't go unrecognized. Still, to frighten my housekeeping staff feels petty. He's lucky they're well aware I'm a warlock . . . even if they're not aware that I'm a stifled one.

I pull out the dove, irritated. The breast of the dead bird has been painted with runes, and I'm sure if I opened it up and examined the contents of its stomach, I'd find laurel leaves and a pebble from a hero's grave. It's a specific sort of spell that my nemesis is casting, one designed to break my wards and make my house vulnerable to others. This isn't the first time that my old master Stoker has tried this sort of stunt. Ever since I left his service, he's tried to have me killed.

However, it *is* the first time he's cast a curse at my current house. The house I'd had built to my specifications ten years ago, after I'd been forced to move from the last one because Stoker had found me again. He wants to make my life hell.

And since I can't cast to protect myself, the only thing I can do is avoid him.

In retrospect, I probably shouldn't have stolen his books.

Ten years ago, I thought moving would solve my problems. My enemies would no longer have my address, and I'd finish the rest of my probationary period out under the radar. It's clear that Stoker won't rest until he finds me, and it doesn't matter how many times I move. The man's held a grudge for 250 years. Of course he's going to attack me while I'm vulnerable.

Well, no more. I'm not retreating. I'm done hiding. I made the

first move, so I shouldn't be surprised that he's retaliating. Still, a
dead dove is a little . . . over the top.

I take the dead bird inside with me and hand it to the housekeeper, who makes a sound of protest. "Get rid of that."

"But, sir—"

"I'll be in my study." I head for the bathroom, wash my hands,
and then walk back to my study, locking the door behind me. I
want to go down to my laboratory, but I never go when the help
staff is here. No one can know about the secret door I've had built
that leads down to my lab and my trove of stolen spell books. For
now I have to wait.

I take a deep breath, thinking through everything I need to
get done. New wards around the house—that's the first priority. An obfuscation spell to hide my address from anyone looking
it up online. Each spell will wear me out for at least a week. All
of them together and I'll be out of action for well over a month.
Without a familiar to act as my power source, I'll be forced to
rely on my own limited pool of energy. That means everything
will take twice as long to cast and will leave me vulnerable. I
can't pay another witch or warlock to do it for me, because they've
been forbidden to assist in my casting. It's part of my "punishment."

Only ten more years to go.

The thought is a dismal one.

Maybe I should start out with scrying, I decide. See what exactly Stoker plans—

A loud chirp echoes in the room.

My eyes snap open, and I look at the "mailbox" atop the mantel of the fireplace. An envelope is inside, delivered by mystical
means. It's the only way my old master—my *other* old master, the
one that's not trying to kill me—communicates with me. I stride

over toward it and tear the wax seal off the back of the envelope, reading the contents of the letter.

Stoker is on the move. Be aware.

—Abernathy

I crumple it and toss the notice to the ground. "Thanks for nothing, but you're a bit late."

PENNY

There's nothing better than a well-established routine.

I love knowing what to expect. I love everyone playing their individual part, and watching it all come together. Maybe that's me romanticizing even the mundane aspects of life, but the best kind of progress happens when the system works like a well-oiled machine. That's why I don't mind the weekly meeting of the Society of Familiars. Some people might find it boring, but I love it.

Well, *most* nights I love it. The current president of our society is . . . a bit difficult to listen to for long periods of time, if I'm being honest. I stifle a yawn as Derek Chapman bangs a gavel on the meeting table and then drones on. "Any other news to discuss before the society?"

It's silent.

"Anyone? Anyone?"

I glance out at the gathered audience. There are twenty people here tonight. There should be all fifty of our local members out there, but a lot of them lose faith and stop attending, or they come around just enough to renew their dues and then disappear again for another year. I'm doing my best to make coming to society meetings more fun, but sometimes it feels like an uphill battle since no one else is putting in effort. I don't blame them for feeling down about things. It's hard to keep being positive when year after year, there's no opportunity to apprentice. But I believe in positivity, and I'm sure our situation will change at some point. We just have to keep on.

"Anyone?" Derek drones out again.

Derek doesn't think he's part of the problem with the Fam, as we call the Society of Familiars. It's an ironic name, because none of us are actually familiars. We're the pool of candidates *in waiting* to become familiars. We're here because we have the bloodlines and the inclination, and we're just waiting for a witch or a warlock to come along with an opening for an apprentice. Until that glorious moment happens, all we have is the Fam.

And Derek isn't exactly a dynamic leader. He's dry and boring. He reads in a monotone from manuals instead of learning the information and speaking about it from the heart. He hyperfixates on tiny things about the society, like dues and attendance, and focuses less on the people themselves and what they bring to the group. As a result, our attendance numbers keep dwindling. You don't have to attend all the meetings to be in the society, of course, but as someone that loves to be part of the group, it's hard for me to watch everyone peel away under Derek's lead.

"This is your opportunity to speak up," Derek continues in the same colorless voice. He rubs his nose rather wetly, examines his fingers, and then peers out at the group. "Might I remind you that attendance and joyful participation will be considered by some warlocks and witches as a sign of enthusiasm."

Ugh. Please. There's a hierarchy to our group. Names are put on the list in order of how long we've been waiting and rarely get shuffled. The warlock or witch then pulls from the top candidates.

It doesn't have anything to do with "joyful participation." That's just Derek being, well, Derek.

I raise my hand and bounce to my feet, clutching my notes. Time to save the day. "I just wanted to say to please remember to bring your cookies for next week's baking swap! All cookies, cupcakes, and brownies are welcome, but remember that if you use known allergens or rare spell components in your baking, to please label your goods accordingly." I glance around the room, smiling at everyone as warmly as I can. "I also wanted to get volunteers for the car-wash fundraiser for Abby this weekend, and a reminder that several of us are going out for drinks after this. Everyone is of course invited!"

"Thank you, Penny," Derek replies, his monotone drowning the shot of fun I just tried to inject. "Any other familiar business?"

No one speaks up. There's a polite cough in the back.

"Then I'd like to close the meeting—" Derek begins, lifting his gavel like he's a judge.

"Wait." Someone in the audience stands up. It's Cody, a good friend of mine. We're about the same age and in the same situation—as in, we're both from a long line of familiars, and yet we have no one to serve. "When are we opening up membership again?"

I look over at Derek, who frowns. "We're not."

In the audience, Cody looks unhappy with this bit of information. "Why not?"

Derek blinks. He's elderly, and for a moment, I wonder if he's forgotten where he's at, and my heart squeezes with pity. Poor old thing. But then he turns to me, a hint of confusion on his face. "Why not?"

I have to answer? I stammer for a moment, then try to frame it in as positive a light as possible. "Right now we're focusing on our existing members to give them the best opportunity for familiarship possible."

"So in other words, we're not letting in new people because it'd make things too competitive?" Cody crosses his arms, his pose challenging. "Doesn't that seem a little unfair?"

I look over at Derek, but he's still watching me, so I bite back a sigh of frustration and keep a bright smile on my face. I shouldn't be surprised that Derek is making me do part of his job. I kinda end up doing it anyhow. "Membership being open or closed is voted upon at the annual meeting. If everyone feels really strongly about opening up for new applicants, we can take a vote then. Or you can send a formal request to have it added to a future agenda—"

Cody waves a disgusted hand at me and sits back down.

Oh. Well then. I keep smiling and look over at Derek. I guess it'd be impolite to point out that not only did Derek propose that we close enrollment, but he's supposed to be the one enforcing it, not me. Then again, if he's having trouble remembering where he's at, I guess I shouldn't be surprised he's forgetting this, too.

Derek bangs the gavel. "Business concluded for this evening. See you all next week."

"Drinks at the Alehouse around the corner," I call out cheerily. At least now it's time for my favorite part of meeting nights. "We'd love to see you guys there!"

✳ ✳ ✳

DESPITE MY WARM invitation, less than half the group migrates over to the Alehouse. I buy a few rounds of drinks to encourage people to stick around, and sip my amaretto sour as my friends talk about nothing in particular. Darcy is complaining about her job at a bookstore, and Megan just broke up with her boyfriend. Nathan asks if my job is hiring, but he always asks that. We're never hiring for my part of the job, unfortunately. There's a guy that works weekends at the front, but for spell component fulfillment? It's just me. I get why he asks, though. Of all of us in the Society of Familiars, I'm the only one that has regular contact with any witches or warlocks. The rest of them just sit back and . . . wait.

I head for the bar once my drink is gone, ready to order another round. To my surprise, I run into Derek. He's sitting at the bar instead of with the rest of us, and I feel a twinge of pity. I put a hand on his back and tap it to let him know of my presence. "I didn't know you were here! Why didn't you join us?"

He waves an irritated hand at me. "No one wants to sit with an old man like me."

Oh dear. Derek's words are slurred. I frown at the cluster of empty beer glasses in front of him. "You're not old," I say cheerfully. "You're just distinguished."

"I'm seventy-eight." He leans over toward me. "And I never, not once, served a witch."

"Because you've made your life all about the Society of Familiars, right?" Derek moved here recently from out of state, and ever since, he's been determined to be involved in our local group. I'm thrilled that someone's showing interest other than me, but I just wish he were a more dynamic leader.

But Derek just shakes his head. "No one wants an old familiar. I'm never gonna get to serve." He peers over at me through beer-glazed eyes. "You're gonna age out soon, too."

That stings. Ouch. "I just turned thirty. There's plenty of time for me yet."

"Yes, but there's always someone younger," Derek says in a lofty voice. "You're like me. The society is gonna be your life." He nods sagely and then taps my arm. "Play your cards right and you can be where I am someday."

I smile politely and grab the tray of drinks from the bartender the moment he sets them on the bar, practically flinging down my tip. Somehow, I manage to keep smiling as I make my way over to the table again, even though Derek's words are ringing in my ears like a death knell.

The society is gonna be your life.

Do I even want that? I'm here because I want to learn witchcraft. I'm here because I want to serve as a familiar. I want to grow in my own power and live hundreds and hundreds of years, and I can do that only if a witch or warlock takes me under their wing and teaches me. But the problem is that because most witches are so long lived, they don't like swapping out apprentices. They don't like change. So anyone that apprentices can expect to be serving for a few decades at least before being taught to go out on their own.

There's just not a lot of turnover in the familiar job market. They're positions that people wait years and years to get, and even if the witch—or warlock—is an absolute nightmare, you don't give up your coveted spot. In return for your service as a familiar, you get to learn spellcraft. You get to become one of the elite. It's what I've wanted all my life. Both my parents serve witches, and I've always wanted to follow in their footsteps.

It's just . . . I'm so tired of waiting.

The society is gonna be your life. Gods, I don't like that thought. Not one bit.

Lost in thought, I swig my drink and fish the cherries out of the bottom of my glass. Maybe I need to call it a night. Derek's words shouldn't bother me so much, and I work in the morning. With that thought in mind, I grab my purse and say my goodbyes to the group, promising to hang out longer next week. As I get up,

Cody follows me. "Hey, wait," he calls, bounding over to my side. "Are you catching the bus?"

I shake my head, giving my phone a little shake. "I'm going to call an Uber."

"I'll wait with you." He grins down at me, and the interest is clear in his eyes. Oh. Huh. For a moment, I contemplate what it'd be like to go home with Cody. We've flirted at past meetings, of course. I think everyone close to the same age has flirted, and a few people hook up from time to time. He's cute, though. He's got bright blue eyes and a bit of beard scruff, but it looks good on him. He's short, which I don't mind, since I'm short, too, and he dresses like a crunchy hipster. He's even got the sweetest little man bun at the back of his head, which I kinda dig. He moves out near the street with me but keeps his hands in his pockets, making no effort to call his own ride. "Wanna hear some gossip?"

"Oh em gee, do I ever," I squeal. I love gossip. Maybe I shouldn't, but what's the harm?

Cody leans in, and I can smell cinnamon schnapps on his breath. "I heard that Caliban Magnus stole his aunt's familiar, and to make matters worse, that familiar isn't even in the society."

I hide my disappointment. That's old gossip, and it's not even correct gossip. "I've met Reggie several times," I tell him. "She's a lovely person, and Dru recruited her directly. Reg didn't know anything about the society, so I can't really blame her for skipping out on membership. As for Mr. Magnus stealing her, he didn't. They're dating."

He gives me an incredulous look. "You know them?" Then his expression twists a little, and I can't tell if he's amused or sour. "Wait, of course you do. You know everyone through your job."

"Not everyone," I say uncomfortably. He's making it sound like I have an edge over everyone else somehow, and that's not the case. If anything, my working at CBD Whee! actually hurts my chances of becoming a familiar, because I'm good at my job and my boss finds me irreplaceable. If anyone asks Vivi about my apprenticing availability before they ask me . . . well, I suspect I know what her answer would be. And while I love that I'm so good at my job, I never wanted to be so good it would hinder me from realizing my dreams.

Boy, this night sure is turning depressing.

"They're nice," I promise Cody again. "I don't feel like Reggie's taking someone else's spot. Ben Magnus never has apprentices. It's not like he would have grabbed someone from the society. He never does."

"If you say so." He reaches out and brushes a lock of my hair behind my ear, giving me a smile. "I think you're nice, Penny."

Oh, that's definitely flirting! I'm not the most self-aware girl, but even I know he's into me tonight. I have to admit, I do look cute. I always try to dress up for our society meetings, just because I want others to find them as big a deal as I do. Cody leans in toward me, and I'm pretty sure he's going to kiss me. Do I want to kiss him back? Do I want to invite him back to my place for a no-strings-attached make-out session? It's been a long time since I've hooked up with a guy, and I probably have spiderwebs on all my girl bits from disuse.

For some stupid reason, I hear Derek's voice in my head again. *The society is gonna be your life.*

That kills my ladyboner fast. I slide away from Cody, giving him an apologetic look. "My ride will be here soon."

"I can ride with you," Cody says, not taking no for an answer.

I bite my lip. "Maybe next week? I need to type up these notes, and I have to feed my squirrel."

"Is that innuendo for something?"

Knitting my brows together, I shake my head. "No. I mean, I literally have to feed my squirrel. His name is Pipstachio, and he'll get cranky if he doesn't get his dinner before bed. He's kind of a tyrant with the sweetest bushy tail. I swear I'm not making this up."

Cody chuckles, pulling me close for a one-armed hug that squishes my face against his chest and probably gets makeup all over his shirt. "I like you, Penny. Maybe next week, then?"

"Maybe next week," I agree, hugging him back. Maybe I need some mindless kissing with a guy rocking a man bun to take my mind off just how stagnant things in my life are. Cody's a guy that's clearly a good time, not a long time, and as long as I go in with that in mind, I can't get hurt.

Maybe I need a fling to liven up my life a bit.

* * *

WHEN I GET home, Pip is clinging to the bars of his cage, chittering angrily at me. His food cup is turned over in the sawdust at the bottom of the cage, the edges chewed on. "I'm sorry," I apologize to him, opening the cage and extending my hand so he can climb up my arm. "I didn't realize how late it was."

Pipstachio immediately moves to my shoulder-length hair and nestles in it, grunting his distress.

"Right, right, dinner," I promise my squirrel. I love Pip, but he knows the routine. Wednesday nights are society nights, and therefore I get home late. I head to the kitchen downstairs, not surprised to see that neither of my parents is home. They never are. Mom has left a note on the fridge.

Aurelia is casting. Won't be home tonight, might not be tomorrow either. Don't wait up! XOXO—Mom

Dad didn't bother with a note, but his work schedule is taped up on the fridge. His witch likes to run her business like she's a corporation, and Dad has a set schedule, along with accrued vacation time and everything. Sure enough, Dad is working until midnight tonight with Diana, and then back at it again all day tomorrow. I pull out a bowl of diced veggies that I keep for Pip, and set it on the counter. "Here you go, baby."

Pip immediately scrambles down and begins to eat, this time his grunts happy ones. I open a container of pecans and add a few to the veggie mix to give him some variety, and then decide to make sandwiches for myself, Mom, and Dad. I've been more or less on my own ever since Mom started apprenticing with Aurelia fifteen years ago, so I know how to cook and clean and take care of the house. I really am excited for my parents. Getting to work with a witch or a warlock as a familiar is the dream of anyone in the society. Right now there are far more aspiring familiars than there are trained witches. It means that we're all waiting for a hopeful slot to come open. And not every familiar looks at their apprenticeship as a step to becoming a witch or a warlock on their own. Some just view it as a long-term job and are perfectly content to remain familiars all their lives.

Me, I want to become a witch. I want to be able to cast on my own. I want the independence and power that comes with being a caster. Right now, though, I'm not even an apprentice yet.

I sigh, looking around the dusty kitchen. Since I'm the only one without a witch, I normally do all the kitchen chores and the laundry, and I see my parents more in passing than anything else. It's almost like we're roommates more than family. Normally that doesn't bother me, but I guess I'm more down about Derek's comment than I thought. "At least I have you, right, Pip?"

The squirrel ignores me, eating a pecan and turning it in his tiny paws as he does.

With a sigh, I finish making two sandwiches, and I bag them up for Mom and Dad and put them in the fridge, then make peanut butter and jelly for myself. I sit on the counter across from Pipstachio and pull out my phone, checking social media and then my email.

I have an email from Reggie. Subject line: Can we meet? We need to talk!

Ooh, that sounds deliciously ominous. Excited, I click on it and read the contents.

Hey! So we've got a weird sort of proposal for you. I can't mention it in email but do you want to go for coffee at lunch tomorrow to talk? I'll call you in the AM!

—Reggie

PS—Nick says we're on for cards Friday night if you're game!

Ooh, cards and intrigue! This day is getting better already. Pip moves to my hand and nudges my fingers, a sign that he wants another pecan. Normally I wouldn't give him more, because he's kind of greedy, but I'm feeling generous. I pluck two more out of the can and hand them to him, typing my reply to Reggie's email with my thumb.

Yes to cards on Friday!! I have a new birds deck I can't wait to try! And also yes to coffee tomorrow! Just come by the office! LYLAS! Penny

Reggie immediately replies via text message. I'm just about to head to bed. What the heck is LYLAS?

PENNY: LYLAS = LOVE YOU LIKE A SIS. Didn't you pass notes in school?

REGGIE: No! And LYLAS to you too! :)

Night! I text back, grinning. Tell Ben I said hi.

He's coming with me tomorrow, she sends back. See you then!

Ooh, even more intriguing. I nibble at my peanut butter and jelly and wonder what on earth is going on that both Reggie and Ben want to talk to me about and can't send via email. Curiouser and curiouser, as Alice in Wonderland said. Maybe my life isn't so regimented after all if I'm going to be pulled into an exciting, top secret sort of warlock intrigue. I think about Cody and feel a little guilty that I get to interact with someone outside of work that's as important as Ben Magnus.

Maybe I have hit the pinnacle of what an apprenticing-to-apprentice sort can expect.

That's a depressing thought.

3

PENNY

Work the next day is incredibly busy. Floralia is coming up—a big springtime festival in the witch community—and that means everyone is putting in requests for spell components. Most of them are fairly generic and crop oriented, but there are so many orders that I spend all morning packing up components in the back and sell only one vape pen up front. It makes the time go by fast, though. I listen to bubblegum pop and dance as I pack order after order of raccoon whisker and thistle cap, and enjoy my day.

I just finish packing up a shipment when the door at the front dings and the computer monitor with the scrying spell on it shows the enormous, lanky body of Ben Magnus and the smaller form of his girlfriend, Reggie.

"Be there in just a sec!" I call cheerfully and toss the package on the scale, then head out front, wiping my hands on my ruffled apron. "Hi, you two!"

The sight of Ben Magnus with my friend Reggie always makes me happy and reminds me that anyone's life can change in the blink of an eye . . . and you can find love even in the strangest of places. Ben has a terrible reputation among warlock-kind. House

Magnus is known for its quirky bloodline, and Ben Magnus is legendary for his surly demeanor, his ruthless spells, and the fact that he never takes an apprentice. He's extremely tall, with dark, shaggy hair and overlarge features. I'd say he's definitely more "magnetic" than handsome. Reggie, on the other hand, is the sweetest thing. She's taller than me and athletic (but still dwarfed by Ben) and has the brightest, most genuine smile and cute freckles. Her brown hair is pulled up into a messy bun atop her head, and she's wearing jeans and a ratty T-shirt. Her familiar cuff is prominently displayed on her wrist, a sight that fills me with envy. The only cuff I have is one for the Society of Familiars, but it doesn't mark me as belonging to anyone. Just that I'm a wannabe.

Reggie beams that big, cheery smile at me. "You look nice today, Penny. Hope you didn't dress up for us."

"I just like wearing pretty dresses," I tell her, pulling off my apron and fluffing my shoulder-length black hair. Today I styled it in a flip so the ends curl up before they hit my shoulders, and I have it clipped back from my face with a tiny pink bow above one ear. My pink gingham dress matches, a retro-cut rockabilly style with a tight waist, a flaring skirt, and off-the-shoulder sleeves. Even in my low heels, I'm nowhere near Reggie's height, much less Ben's. "You two sure are tall today!"

Ben just blinks at me. Reggie giggles and moves forward to give me a hug. "Come on. Let's get some coffee, and I'll tell you all about our proposal."

I flip the sign on the door to *BACK IN 1 HOUR* and lock it behind me. Reggie and I have gone for coffee many times in the last couple of months. The good thing about CBD Whee! is that the strip mall the store is located in is fairly quiet, which means I can leave during the day and it's not as if it truly affects the flow of clients. Most people would probably wonder how a CBD store with a bad location manages to stay in business, but only those who are part of the witchcraft community know that it's actually a front for a spell components store, where we make the bulk of our money. As long as I get those orders out on time, my boss doesn't care if I disappear for hours on end.

This is the first time that Ben has ever come to lunch with us, though, and I admit I'm a little nervous. Between that and the whole "we have a proposal for you" sort of thing they keep bringing up, I'm wondering if our friendship is about to get strange. I hope not. I adore Reggie, and it feels weirdly good to have friends that aren't in the Society of Familiars. It reminds me that there's life outside of my small circle, and that's something I didn't realize I needed until I met her.

We walk a couple of blocks over to the coffee shop, a small chain store tucked down a slightly busier street. Reggie keeps the conversation flowing between us, with Ben silent as he holds her hand, and me on the other side of her. It isn't until we get our drinks and pastries and sit down at a table that Reggie gives me a sly look. "So, like I said, we have a proposal for you."

"You're about to ask me to participate in a threesome?" I guess. I mean, it's weird, but if we can all stay friends afterward, I suppose I'm down. It'd be something different in my life at least. Derek's comments last night must have really rattled me if I'm considering a threesome with my best friend and her boyfriend just because I'm bored.

Ben spits coffee all over the table. Reggie rears back in surprise, her mouth hanging open.

"Not that, then?" I ask.

Reggie's mouth snaps shut. "Penny, no! Why would you think that?"

"I don't know," I say defensively. "You showed up here with

your boyfriend and kept talking about a strange proposal for me! Double-yew tee eff, right?"

They exchange a look. "It's not about that at all," Reggie says. "You tell her, Ben." She nudges him with her arm. "He's your friend."

"He's not my friend," Ben mutters, but he gets a napkin and wipes down all the coffee he spewed on the table. When she nudges him again, he sighs and looks up at me. "An acquaintance of mine is in need of a familiar."

Oh my god.

Oh my god.

This is my moment. This is happening. I'm no longer going to be a spell component gopher working for a witch who never wants me to leave the cash register. I won't have my parents giving me pitying looks on holidays as they race off to take care of their witches and ignore their daughter. I'm going to be part of someone's life. I'm going to be important. My dream is coming true. I take a few gulping breaths, fanning myself with my hands. "And you thought of me?" I squeal. "That's amazing! That's—"

Both of them reach over to shush me, casting nervous looks around the coffee shop. "Penny, quiet," Reggie hisses. "Listen to the whole situation."

Uh-oh. There's a catch. My excited visions of the future pop like soap bubbles. "Go on."

Reggie glances over at Ben again, and he toys with his paper coffee cup. "So the warlock in question is . . . forbidden from taking a familiar."

I gasp. As the secretary of the local Society of Familiars, I'm responsible for all record-keeping. In addition to dues and meeting minutes, we have a list of warlocks and witches that we are forbidden to serve. For this particular area, there's just one warlock on the list. "Willem Sauer?"

Ben nods once. "Have you met him?"

I shake my head, wordless. Oh em gee. *Oh em gee.* Willem Sauer wants a familiar under the table? And they're asking me? I'm just about the worst person to be considered for the job. I play by the rules. I don't color outside the lines. I do everything by the book, and the book very specifically says "do not touch" when it comes to Willem Sauer. "Is he nice?"

"He's a dick," Ben says abruptly. "But I owe him a favor, and that's why we're asking."

Reggie raises a hand in the air. "Before you panic, just know that all we agreed to do was ask around. Please don't think you're obligated to say yes in the slightest. But he wants someone to help him, and he wants someone on the sly. I know you've been waiting for a while, which is why I thought to ask you first."

I swallow hard, thinking. I should say no. Of course I should say no. The covenant of the Society of Familiars states explicitly that we're not to work for anyone without going through the society for permission first. That it all has to be orderly and by the book. As secretary, I'm bound to uphold those rules, maybe more so than anyone else.

But then I think about Derek's words. How I'm just like him and how I'm reaching the end of my shelf life and how I'm going to end up being in the society all my life. Always a bridesmaid, never a bride. I've had a chance to sleep on it, and the idea is still horrifying. I'm realizing that if I continue on the path that I'm on, that's exactly how I'm going to end up.

And I hate it.

"I'll do it," I tell them.

Both Reggie and Ben look surprised. Reggie leans in, whispering, "Don't you want a bit more information first?"

I'm not sure there's anything they could tell me that would change my mind. I desperately need a change of pace, and even though this goes against everything I am as a law-abiding aspiring familiar, it's something I need to do, or I worry my life is going to pass me by. That I'll end up like Derek, shepherding a bored crowd of wannabe familiars through the system without ever getting to experience it myself. "Tell me about Willem," I say firmly. "Then I'll decide."

Reggie glances over at Ben.

Ben shrugs again. "He's a dick."

His girlfriend gives him an exasperated look and turns back to me. "What do you want to know?"

Willem Sauer isn't nice, if he's been banned from having a familiar. But I think about my mother and her witch. Aurelia is a stone-cold bitch, according to my mom. She's mean and ruthless, but she's really good at spellcrafting and Mom is learning a lot from her. She has an agreement with Aurelia that after twenty years of being her familiar, Aurelia is going to get a new familiar and Mom will be educated enough at that point to be a full-fledged witch. Twenty years of a tyrannical boss doesn't seem like such a bad deal if you know what you're getting into. Heck, Mom leaves her job as a familiar in five more years, but I can't apprentice with my mother. A witch has to have at least fifty years of casting experience before they take on a fresh familiar.

Witches live a long, long time, too. Some of the oldest ones date back to the Roman Empire, which would make them about two thousand years old. If you live for two thousand years, twenty years is just a blip. I can do twenty years if that's all Willem Sauer wants from me.

I've already decided, but I go ahead and ask the basics. "Is he married? Single? Children?"

Ben rears back, a strange look on his face. "You're not dating him. You're going to be his familiar."

"I know," I say patiently. "But my mother is apprenticing with Aurelia Snowthorpe, and Aurelia has two young children. Mom's been Aurelia's familiar for fifteen years, but she's spent the last five years nannying as well as apprenticing. I want to know what sort of family situation I'm getting into so I can find out how many people I'm having to help out."

"Your mother helps Aurelia raise her children?" There's an odd look on Reggie's face, and I realize it's a mixture of sympathy and pity.

Oh. Reggie gets it. I nod, letting the old ache wash over me. Reggie knows how abandoned I feel. I've more or less been on my own since my parents both started apprenticing. I look after myself and clean the house and try not to be bitter that my mom is spending more time with other children than she did with me in my teenage years. "Yes. That's why I'm asking."

"It's just Willem," Ben says, finishing his coffee and leaning back in his chair. He crosses his arms over his black henley and practically scowls in my direction. "Not married. No children. No one else can stand to be around him for long."

Not a great sign. "How old is Willem?"

"Two hundred and some odd change. Not yet three hundred." Ben shrugs. "Old enough to know what he's doing."

It's a decent age. At two hundred, Willem would definitely be skilled, but not so old and set in his ways that he'd be impossible to work with. I've heard some of the oldest warlocks and witches are extremely sexist. It's hard to break sixteen hundred (or more) years of misogynistic habits, I guess. "Any idea what sort of casting he does? Is he a specialist?"

"Not a specialist. And I imagine most of his casting has been minor or infrequent due to the fact that he's without a familiar."

"But you didn't have a familiar for a long time," I point out.

Ben gives me a smug smile. "He's not me."

Hmm, all right, then. Not a specialist, not too old to be impossible, just kinda a jerk. "He's not allergic to animals, is he?" I ask, thinking of Pipstachio. "Because that's a deal breaker for me."

Both Reggie and Ben look confused. "We didn't ask," Reggie admits. "You can always ask him about it when you have your initial meeting with him. Feel him out. See if he's someone you'd like to work for."

I really don't need an initial meeting. I already know I want to do this. I want to swap my useless society bracelet out for a familiar cuff. I want to do something with my life. I want to move ahead instead of stagnating. I don't want to be waiting in the wings forever. "I just have one more question," I say. "Why is he forbidden from taking a familiar? We're told not to work with him, but no one said why."

"Oh." Reggie looks over at Ben. "That's an excellent question, actually."

Ben rubs his jaw. "Do you remember Y2K?"

I laugh, because it's such an absurd thing to think about. The whole "all the computers are going to crash once the year rolls over to 2000" thing that people were so worried about back in 1999? "I mean, vaguely? Why? Was that him?"

"Yes and no." Ben glances over at Reggie, his gaze lingering on her as she nibbles on a pastry. "I believe he was working with a young warlock at the time, a guy by the name of Dorian Winters. I knew him. He was very much an ass-kissing sort, always looking to get ahead through whatever means necessary. I couldn't stand him."

"You don't like anyone, baby," Reggie reminds him.

"Right. Anyhow, he was working with Dorian. They were pooling their resources and actually going to do a corporate take-over of some kind. Show the Society of Warlocks that they were a power to be reckoned with. But then the other warlock vanished."

My brows go up. "Vanished?"

"As in . . . poof?" Reggie flicks her fingers.

"As in, cement shoes," Ben corrects. "No one ever found the body."

Yiiiikes. "And they think Willem Sauer did it? Oh em gee."

"Actually, they don't. That's the sticking point." Ben shrugs. "Willem's old boss accused him of being responsible, and a bunch of investigative castings were done. Nothing was proven, but nothing was disproven, either, so Sauer was put on probation. He's not allowed to have a familiar for thirty-three years. It's basically a slap on the hand as far as punishment goes, but the Council of Warlocks takes a murder accusation seriously."

"And so now he wants a familiar under the table. He sounds like a rules breaker." I don't know if I like that. I'm kind of a stickler myself . . . Well, except for the part where I'm considering becoming the familiar of a warlock banned from having an apprentice.

"What's ironic is that he's normally not," Ben says. "Willem actually loves the rigmarole of warlock society. He loves spellcasting and books. I think he has a bigger library than most warlocks that I've met, and he's very proud of his collection. It's strange that he'd be the one to break the rules so flagrantly. Something must have been going on behind the scenes, but Willem won't talk about it. Not to the council, not to me, not to anyone." He shrugs. "You don't have to worry, though. He's a prick and a half, but I'm confident he didn't do it."

For some reason, I feel like this Willem might be a kindred spirit. Maybe he's like me, and he believes in following the rules and just got pushed into breaking them this one time, and he got caught. Now he's stuck doing embarrassingly small castings because he doesn't have an apprentice. For a warlock used to working on bigger spells, that must be hell. My heart is full of sympathy, and hearing this decides me. "When can I start?"

4

WILLEM

I'm glad the Zoom meeting I'm on is a view from just the waist up. Above the waist, I look impeccable. My deep green Dolce & Gabbana suit jacket looks excellent on camera, my crisp shirt and narrow black tie a good, solid contrast, and there's not a hair askew on my head. I look calm and poised, a row of books artfully lined up on the office shelf behind me to give my background a distinguished air.

Under my desk, however, my foot won't stop twitching. My leg jiggles incessantly as I wait for Felix Atticus to make a decision. To spit out the answers I need. This could be the break I need, the inroad back to the higher echelons of warlock society.

When Atticus remains silent, I take the bait and speak first. "You know I'm the best one for the position. I want it. It should be mine."

"It should be, yes," Atticus says in an austere voice, his lined face tight with displeasure. "It's a shame you're tied up with a small business at the moment."

"The people you're hiring now aren't nearly as qualified as I am," I practically snarl. "We've had an excellent business relationship for over a century. I don't understand your hesitation."

Atticus peers down at me over his wire-rimmed glasses. He doesn't need them—he could easily cast a spell to enhance his eyesight—so I have to assume they're for appearances only. "I'm afraid that the job is a demanding one. My oil contacts will need regular dowsing spells, market cursing, scrying upon competitors, the works. The pay and prestige will be excellent, but I'm afraid it will also be impossible for someone with your limited capabilities, Sauer."

"Limited?" I sputter, indignant.

"Limited," Atticus agrees. "What's on your casting roster this week? Prove me wrong."

I'm silent, my mouth flat with tension. My hands are clenched tight in front of me on the desk, and it's either that or I'll start punching holes into the wall behind me. It's a blatant slap in the face. Atticus knows that without an apprentice to channel power through, I have to cast small enough spells that I'm only slightly drained. I don't have any fucking clients. I'm busy trying to keep my head above water as it is. Instead, I point out the obvious. "I only have ten years left on my ban."

"Then talk to me in ten years," Atticus says. He terminates the call, and I'm left staring at a black screen.

Furious, I get up from my desk and start pacing. I hate this. I hate that I'm trapped in this ridiculous limbo state. I hate that I've been hobbled and neutered by my inability to procure a familiar to act as my power supply. I don't need the money. At 270 years old, I've got millions stashed away. It's the thrill of casting that makes my blood sing. The rise of power between my hands as I call on the gods. The ecstatic sensation of a spell's aftermath. Gods, I miss casting. Not the piddly shit I've been stuck with for the last twenty-odd years. *Real* casting. *Real* warlock business.

Not locating missing cats or predicting bingo numbers for the few patrons I have left.

And Atticus has the perfect corporate warlock job, and I can't even throw my hat into the ring. With a fit of rage, I grab my tablet off my desk and fling it against the wall. It makes an unsatisfying thud and crashes to the ground, leaving a black mark on the pristine gray wall. Well now, that's just irritating.

I huff and storm across the room to pick up the tablet. Sure enough, the screen is broken. Even Fortuna, the goddess of luck, isn't smiling on me today. Scowling down at the shattered display, I see a window has popped up. I click on it—at least that still works—and a distorted view of a text message opens.

B. MAGNUS: Remember that thing you asked me about?
I found you one.

B. MAGNUS: If today is not a problem, I can have her
come by.

By.
All.
The.
Gods.

Ben Magnus, that moody, arrogant son of a bitch, has found me a familiar. I take back every bitter word I've ever said about my rival-slash-frenemy. He's found a familiar willing to work outside of the rules set down by the Society of Familiars and the Society of Warlocks both. It's a big risk. If we get caught, we'll both be expelled and forbidden from casting.

That someone is willing to take such a risk thrills me. I quickly type in my address and then rush into my laboratory, pulling out an offering bowl. I toss a sprig of herbs down to Janus, since he must always be given an offering first. Then I slice my finger and drip blood into the tiny silver bowl, pulling out my wallet. "Thank you, Fortuna," I say, unfolding a couple of hundred-dollar bills and then using a lighter to burn them. As the ashes drift into the offering bowl, I murmur a prayer of thanks to the goddess, in case she's watching over me after all. I burn another hundred-dollar bill for Abundantia, the goddess of prosperity. Then, because the other gods are jealous and capricious, I do a general offering of incense, followed by another sprig to Vesta to close out the ceremony.

The gods haven't forgotten me. Magic itches and wells up under my skin, the need to cast almost orgasmic.

I'm ready.

This familiar had better be ready to cast, because I'm going to put her through the wringer, as the mortals say. I've got more than twenty years of puny spells to make up for. I'm going to make Stoker suffer. I no longer have to be on the defensive at all times.

I can be back in the game.

✳ ✳ ✳

A FEW HOURS later, I've sent home the cleaning staff early and I sit in my office, drumming my fingers on my desk as I wait for the apprentice to show up. I've been told that her name is Penny Roundtree (such a bourgeois name, but not entirely unexpected) and that she will be by before seven tonight. I set out a bottle of the finest white wine in my cellar, display the charcuterie board that my cook arranged for my guest, and change into a more sedate navy-blue jacket and slacks.

My nerves flare with anticipation when the perimeter spell around the house chimes, and I head for the door. Normally I'd let the housekeeping staff handle things, but since this is supposed to be top secret, I don't want anyone asking questions. I race for the door like a breathless *Schüler* and open it wide before she can ring the bell.

The woman on the step is . . . not what I expected Ben Magnus to send over.

I've known Magnus for approximately 250 of my 270 years. The types of apprentices and witches he's consorted with in the past have all been of a singular sort of personality—strong. Efficient. Understated. I suspect a lot of this is simply because Magnus himself doesn't like attention, and he certainly doesn't like explaining himself. I thought anyone he would send in my direction would be the sort of familiar he would take himself.

Instead, I find myself staring down at a tiny woman who can't be more than five feet tall. She's wearing an excessively pink-and-yellow dress with a round white collar, and her black hair is in an old-fashioned flip. She has a round face with a snub nose, and when she beams a smile in my direction, it's so wide that her eyes practically disappear under her bangs.

"Oh em gee, hi there!"

It takes me a moment to realize she's speaking English.

"I'm Penny! You must be Willem!" That face-swallowing smile of hers gets even wider, and she lifts her shoulders, as if she's about to happily squirm on my porch like a puppy. "Can I come in?"

Wordless (and slightly aghast, if I'm honest), I step aside and let her in.

As she crosses the threshold into my house, I notice for the first time that not only is she dragging a garishly pink rolling suitcase behind her, but she has a large square birdcage in her other hand. It's covered with an obnoxiously floral linen, and my nostrils flare in distaste at the realization that she's brought a creature into my house. "Please tell me that's not a bird."

The woman laughs like a lunatic. "Of course not, silly. It's a squirrel."

"I'm sorry, did you say *squirrel*?"

She nods, staring up at the ceiling. "His name is Pipstachio and he's very well behaved, I promise. Wow, you live in this place?"

"No," I snap sarcastically. "I broke in and decided to answer the door for the owners. Of course I live here. Why wouldn't I?"

Penny gives me an odd look. "It was just a question." Her sunny smile returns a moment later. "Ben told me that you chase everyone off. I thought he was exaggerating, because he's kind of quiet himself, but I promise not to take anything you say to heart."

"My goodness, thank you," I say acidly. "God forbid I should harm your tender feelings." I glance back at the open door, hoping—praying—that this is a mistake and that this candy-colored smiling woman is somehow the wrong person. That I've misinterpreted or she has the wrong address.

But no, Penny is the only one here . . . and Ben Magnus sent her.

That bastard. He knows how much I hate loud, obnoxiously happy people. And now he's sent me one with a varmint in a cage? If I had the energy to curse someone, I'd curse his ass right now.

Closing my eyes, I take a deep breath. It doesn't matter. All I need is the well of her energy. As long as she's vaguely compatible for the job, I can use her. It doesn't matter if I like her or not. As her employer, I can set the terms. I can do this. Even if she grates on my last nerve with her presence, I can just cast enough to keep her sleeping all the time. It's not permanent. It's a means to an end.

Right now it's the only option I have.

"Oh em gee," she breathes again, staring up at the ceiling molding. "Why is everything here gray?"

"Because gray is a soothing color."

She pauses in front of the large Jackson Pollock I have in the entryway to my house. "This doesn't look very soothing—"

"This is my fucking house," I snap, buttoning my jacket tightly, a nervous habit. "And I like an elegant, neutral color. I like gray. I also like modern art that eschews tradition. I realize these are terms you clearly don't understand, but you'll simply have to make do when you visit this place. Follow me to my study and let's discuss the rules of your employment, shall we?"

I don't wait for an answer. I head down the hall and expect her to follow. After a moment, I hear a muttered comment and then the clack of her patent leather shoes on the floor. I unbutton my jacket again and sit down at my desk, glaring down my nose at her. She really is all wrong for me. I'm going to murder Ben Magnus with my bare hands. Behind my desk, I'm in the position of control, and I give her an imperious glance as she wanders in, staring at my library.

"Holy jeez," she whispers, eyes wide as she gazes upon the neatly organized shelves of encyclopedias. "Have you read all these books?"

"I am two hundred and seventy years old," I point out. My answer sounds petulant, even to my own ears, so I add, "But no. I haven't read them all. These books are for decor. My real library is . . . elsewhere."

She keeps staring at my bookshelves, fascinated, and slowly wanders over to the seats across from my desk. There, she sets the cage (and it takes everything I have not to snarl when she places it) upon a pale gray cushioned seat and sits down in the chair next to it. Her face squeezes up into that enormous happy smile again. "I think your office is bigger than my parents' house."

"Are your parents paupers, then?"

That smile drops, and I feel as if I kicked a puppy, which just makes my mood worse. "No. They're both apprenticing with witches. I still live at home, though."

I study her. After living for centuries, it's difficult for me to tell the ages of people. She doesn't look like a schoolgirl, but if that's the case, why is she living at home? "Your age?"

Her cheeks flush. "I'm thirty, actually. I thought I'd live at home for a few years after high school while I was waiting to apprentice." She bites her lip and fiddles with her skirt, smoothing it over and over again. "Just didn't think it would take this long."

"Mmm." Well, it sounds like she's as desperate as I am. Perhaps that's why Magnus sent her my direction. "Are you still interested in the job? Even knowing that you'll be working with me? I'm sure Magnus filled your head with how vile I am."

Penny's chin lifts and she gives me a resolute look. "It doesn't matter how bad you are if you can teach me how to use magic. I'm tired of waiting for a chance. I want to learn."

I nod and extend my hand over my desk, palm up. "Before we go any further, I'm going to need to see if we're compatible or not."

She glances down at my hand and then drags the heavy chair a little closer to the edge of the desk. My bulky square desk is intentionally enormous so the person on the opposite side feels intimidated, but I'm inwardly wincing at the scrapes on the flooring as she moves forward. She doesn't seem intimidated, just inconvenienced. With a beaming smile, Penny practically smacks her hand into mine and gives me an expectant look.

I notice again how tiny she is. I'm tall and lean, my hands long fingered and pale thanks to my coloring. Penny's fingers are short, and her palm small. It's the first time I've held a woman's hand and felt like she was fragile, and it's surprising for me, considering I don't have mitts like Magnus does. I notice a thick, unadorned cuff on her wrist—for the Society of Familiars. It looks like cheap garbage, if I'm honest with myself. No familiar of mine would wear such nonsense. I glance up at Penny and notice that she's gotten out of her seat to lean over my desk so our palms can touch, and as she leans, she's displaying a good amount of cleavage via the neckline of her dress. She closes her eyes, an intense expression on her round face, as if waiting for something.

I deliberately avoid looking and concentrate on the hand in mine, sending a tendril of arcane power into her, seeking out the well of her personal *sanguis vitae*. Every person has a well of power, and some have a deeper well than others. It's what separates the good witches from the great ones, and even the most talented spellcaster needs a familiar with a deep well of power or their witch won't be able to cast properly. Even before I tap at Penny's well, I can feel the hum of it. I send my tendril of magic deeper, sinking into her essence. It's a bit invasive, my method, and one I learned from Stoker. But since I can't go to the Society of Familiars and demand rigorous testing until they find someone that meets my criteria, this will have to do.

Penny shivers, her hand in mine, her brow furrowing. Does she feel my magic? That's unusual. I push deeper, trying to descend to the bottom of her magic pool to determine the size of it. As I continue prodding, I'm impressed by the size of her untapped power. I continue down. And down. And down. My eyebrows go up, and I give another shove of magic.

Her face contorts, her eyes still closed, and then I hit the bottom of her magic pool. For a moment, I revel in it. Jove's bloody testicles, this woman has an immense reservoir of magic that can be drawn upon. Her *sanguis vitae* is far larger than mine, and I'm impressed . . . and slightly covetous. Even if she's obnoxious and loud, I'm imagining all the spells I can cast utilizing her strength. She's absolutely going to be my familiar, I decide. I'm surprised another warlock or witch hasn't snapped her up already. I give one last push of magic into hers, as if staking a claim.

Stoker is so fucked. The thought fills me with glee.

She gasps, snatching her hand out of mine, and stumbles backward.

"Sorry," I say, my tone implying that I'm anything but. I straighten my jacket and lean back in my chair again. "Did I frighten you?"

"Huh?" Penny blinks, her face flushed. "No. No, I'm fine." She thumps into her seat, and the cage at her side rattles and something chitters inside it. "Quiet, Pip."

I frown at her. She looks rattled, but it's also clear she doesn't want me to press her on it. "You seem to have a sufficient *sanguis vitae*."

"A what?" She fans her face a little. "Is it warm in here?"

"It is not." With a look of distaste, I explain, "*Sanguis vitae*. Blood of life. Your well of power."

"You mean like my magic pool? Like in the card games?"

I shrug dismissively. "Whatever. I wouldn't know. But yours is sufficient."

She beams at me, tossing her hair back. "Well, of course it is. My parents are both familiars, too."

"Yes, well, I'm not going to apprentice them, am I?" I give her a thin smile. "Which is why I checked you. All right. If we're going to do this, I should like to lay a few ground rules."

"Excuse me?" she asks. "Ground rules?"

"Yes." I study her, crossing my arms over my chest. "While there isn't an official dress code for familiars, I really do prefer somber shades in my surroundings. And no patterns. That thing you're wearing? I never want to see it again."

Penny looks down at her clothes. "I'm sorry, are you referring to my dress?" At my nod, her expression turns indignant. "I love this dress!"

"I don't, and I'm going to be your employer. Also, the squirrel needs to go. I won't have it around me. I abhor vermin. Also, I don't want you to be loud when I'm trying to concentrate . . ." I trail off as she gets to her feet and smooths her skirts. "We're talking here. Where do you think you're going?"

"You're talking," she tells me with a sweet, sunny smile. "I'm done, though. You're not going to tell me how to dress. And I'm keeping my squirrel."

I sputter at her impudence. "Who is the employer here, chit?"

PENNY

S o . . . this is awkward.

Mega, super awkward. I smooth my skirts again and pick up Pipstachio's cage, calling his bluff. Willem Sauer may be a warlock, but he needs me and I'm not going to let him bully me. I'm not going to get rid of my squirrel or change how I dress. And I'm sure not going to tell him that I orgasmed the moment he "reached" into my magic.

Because that was incredibly weird and I'm not sure how I feel about that. Neither of my parents have ever said anything about a spell or a witch causing them to, like, *come* when their magic pool was accessed. I'm not sure if that's supposed to happen. Then again, I've never asked my parents that. Crestfallen, I realize I still can't ask them, since this is supposed to be a secret. Well, poop.

I cast a beaming smile over at Willem Sauer, the big jerk. "It was lovely meeting you."

His handsome face contorts in surprise.

He jumps up behind the desk, following after me. "Wait. Where do you think you are going?"

"I'm leaving," I sing out gaily. I'm not, of course, but if he's going to be an utter prick in our meeting, I'm going out the door. "You were seeing if we were going to work out. It's obvious we're not, so I'm heading out the door. Lovely to meet you, sir."

To my delight, he races in front of me, moving to stand in front of the doors. "You're not listening to me."

I tilt my head, pursing my lips at him. Since I'm in control of the conversation now, I take a moment to look him over. He's about as far from Ben Magnus as a warlock can get, I think. While Ben looks like an overgrown, broody goth who leans into the whole "emo warlock" thing, Willem Sauer looks more like he just stepped out of a business suit catalog. He's tall and slender, his deep green suit expensive and cutting edge without being too trendy. Willem has very pale skin and bright carroty-red hair that speaks of his northern European ancestry. His face is angular and proud, and his eyes are a light green that would probably be attractive if he wasn't such a jerk. Doesn't matter. He's not my type. "I'm afraid it's you who isn't listening to me, Mr. Sauer. We are both risking a lot by agreeing to do this, and I'm not going to let you treat me like an inferior when I have just as much to lose here as you do. Either we're equals and partners, or I'm heading out the door."

He sputters, and I can't help but stare at his immaculately groomed orange hair. His part is so straight I wonder if he takes a ruler to it. Not a hair is out of place, either. This is a man who's very into appearances, I decide. Then he should understand why he doesn't get to have control of mine. "We're merely setting boundaries," Willem protests. "These are preliminary talks."

"Okay, then. Talk."

The frown he lobs at me is fierce, but after a moment, he spits out, "I should prefer if you dressed sedately in my presence."

Well, he can prefer it all he likes, but it doesn't mean it's going to happen. "Noted. And my pet?"

Willem's lip curls. "Is it rabid?"

I blink at him, because that's a ludicrous question. "Why would I have a rabid squirrel?"

"Why would you have a squirrel at all?" he shoots back.

That's a fair point. "I found Pipstachio on the ground when he was a baby and fed him by bottle until he was old enough to eat on his own. He's very tame and he's never been outside in the wild. He has no diseases, and he's a delightful pet that will cause no problems." I level a cool glance at Mr. Sauer. "And he's absolutely not up for discussion. If you take me, you take my pet."

He makes a face and waves a hand at me. "Just . . . I don't see why he has to be here at all."

"Well, because I'm going to be living here."

The look he gives me is downright incredulous. "You're what?"

Oh dear lord, has this man not thought anything through? It's a good thing he's landed me, then. I give him an exasperated look. "Mr. Sauer, how exactly did you propose we were going to do this? I have a very full life already. I have a job. I have clubs that I'm a part of. I have friends. How are we going to mix that with me being your familiar?"

Willem crosses his arms over his blazer and scowls at me. "I'm not seeing why it has to mix at all."

Honestly, some people. He's lucky I'm the type that shows up prepared. Resisting the urge to roll my eyes, I go and sit down across from his desk again, settling my skirts, and give him a patient look. It occurs to me that suddenly I'm the one in charge of the meeting, and I have to bite the inside of my cheek to keep from snickering. I cross my legs and fold my hands over my knee as he stalks back to his desk. "Let's think this through," I say, keeping my tone practical. "Because we need to have all the logistics figured out before we jump into this."

"I'm listening," he says in a practically bristling tone.

"Spellcasting takes a lot out of someone, right? A familiar has to sleep to recover their strength. I've heard that from everyone. That's true, isn't it?"

He grunts.

"Okay, well, I work Monday through Friday until six at night. On Wednesday nights, I have the Society of Familiars meetings. Friday nights, I have an ongoing meetup with friends for cards. On Saturdays we usually have some sort of Fam get-together—"

He interrupts me, an irritable look on his face. "What does this have to do with me?"

"I'm saying we'll have to schedule your spellcasting around *my* schedule because I'm going to need to sleep after each casting. So either I'm sleeping here a lot, or you're coming to my house and casting there." I give him a triumphant look. "It makes a lot more sense for me to be living here, doesn't it?"

Willem rolls his eyes. "Jove help me, but it does. Fine. You can stay in one of the guest bedrooms." He points a long finger at Pip's cage. "That stays in the basement, though."

I ignore that part, just like I'm going to ignore the part where he told me to wear somber colors. "Okay, then we need to figure out the rest of this. We need a cover story. No one's going to believe that I'm living with you unless we have a really valid one. So we need to make it ironclad."

"Who exactly do you have to convince? What business is it of anyone else what we do?" He frowns, looking so dour that I want to reach across the desk and just smack that look of dismay off his mouth. He might be 270, but he looks to be about the same age as me. Maybe that's why I'm not intimidated by him and his fussing.

"People are going to ask questions. My parents, for example."

"So don't tell them," he retorts.

"Don't tell my parents? Then they'll really know something is up." I shake my head. "Or what about the Society of Familiars?"

"Leave it."

"I can't leave! I'm the secretary! I've been part of the society for nine years! You think that won't be a red flag if I move in with you, quit the society, and then you start casting again?" He narrows his icy eyes at me. "Like I said, we have to think this through. Luckily for you, I have the perfect solution."

Willem huffs. "I can't wait to hear this."

"I think we should pretend we're dating and in love."

His orange brows shoot up.

I raise a hand into the air. "It's not my first choice, either, trust me. But it would explain why we're suddenly together all the time. It would explain why I've moved in with you. My parents would think I'm in love and wouldn't ask too many questions. My friends would probably think I'm fucking you for the prestige of dating a warlock, but I can handle that. Your friends wouldn't question why you suddenly have a woman moving in with you. It really is the perfect cover story."

Willem just stares at me, aghast.

Like he's some prize. He's such a snob that I'm going to have a really hard time selling this to anyone without making myself seem like an idiot. The guy's an utter jerk so far, and I'm going to be the one that ends up looking bad if I tell everyone we're dating, but he's acting like I'm the one that's using him. I tamp down my irritation. "Unless you have a better idea for a cover story."

He's quiet as he stares at me. In fact, he's quiet for so long that I begin to feel uncomfortable. It won't do to squirm in my seat like a child, so I keep my hands clenched on my knee and wait. If he tells me to leave, that he's not doing this, I'll be a little sad, but also relieved. I'm the one that's taking all the risks, after all. If he gets banned from taking a familiar again, he loses a few more years. I lose my dream entirely. I'd probably lose my job, too, and I'd be kicked out of the Society of Familiars.

I'd lose everything. So we absolutely need a watertight cover story. I keep my face calm and my expression determined.

Willem eventually softens. He picks up a pen from his desk and taps the end of it on the surface. *Taptaptaptaptap.* "No one's going to believe that you want to be with me. No one likes me."

That almost makes me feel sorry for him. Almost, except he's been a humongous prick since I walked through the door. "Look, if I'm going to have to pretend that I'm in love with you, you're going to have to pretend to be lovable. Understand? This is going to require a bit of work from the both of us."

He gives a jerky nod. "And you still want to do this? Knowing that if we get caught, the consequences are dire for both of us?"

"I'm the one that's probably going to get in trouble, not you." I manage a crooked smile.

"Unfortunately, no. I've made some enemies in the past that would be more than happy to see me expelled from the ranks forever at another transgression." Willem's gaze grows thoughtful. "I should probably wait out my ten years."

"Probably."

"And you should probably wait for a witch to request a familiar."

"I probably should."

He goes quiet, those pale green eyes fixed on me. "You still want to do this?"

I think about Derek and his sad life. I imagine myself waiting, waiting, waiting to be selected, all the while getting old and never getting anywhere, while my parents remain young, trapped in the ageless bubble of spellcasting. Do I want to keep going like this for another twenty years? Thirty? Do I want the Society of Familiars to be my life and nothing more? I swallow hard. "I'm tired of sitting on the sidelines."

To my surprise, Willem flashes a very naughty smile in my

direction, one that takes his face from scowling aristocrat to something almost boyish. "Then let's get started, shall we?"

"Wait," I blurt as he jumps to his feet. "Don't we need to make more plans? What about a nondisclosure agreement?"

But he's already up from his desk and moving, rubbing his hands with excitement. "We'll begin with a double-ended curse. If either of us breaks the agreement not to speak of the truth, then we'll end up with the French pox."

"The what?" I yelp.

"Too much?" he asks. He thinks for a moment. "It needs to be sufficiently dire in order for us to keep it." He turns and holds his hand out to me.

"You don't think me risking my entire life that I've built to be your apprentice is sufficiently dire?" But for some reason, I take his hand and get to my feet. Two seconds after I do, I remember that the last time he held my hand, I came. I jerk but somehow manage not to snatch my fingers back out of his grasp. "I was thinking more of just a contract on paper—"

"I'm a warlock. I contract in curses." And he looks thrilled at the thought of doing one. "How about whoever speaks of our agreement has to forfeit their savings to the other?"

"Yours is probably bigger than mine," I warn.

"As long as it hurts for both of us, I'm satisfied. Come on, I'll take you down to my laboratory and show you around—"

I slide out of his grip. "If we're doing this now, I need to get ready. I have to feed Pip and change my clothes. Can you show me to my room and we can agree to meet in a half hour?"

The look he shoots me is full of impatience, but he nods and heads for the stairs. "Follow me."

6

PENNY

The second the door to my room closes and I have a moment alone, I sit on the edge of the bed and collapse. I open Pip's cage to let him out, and then flop back on the bed, my head spinning with everything that's going on.

Pip chitters at me and races across my stomach, sitting up and sniffing his surroundings before dashing off again to explore. I rub my hand over my face, taking a deep breath.

Okay, I'm doing this. I'm really doing this. In addition to working under the table for a super-cranky warlock, I'm apparently going to fake-date him as well. I must be insane to agree to all of this . . . but at least I won't end up like Derek. With that thought circling in my head, I sit up and look around my room. I'm not surprised that the walls here are gray, the bedding gray, and the furniture sleek and minimal. Willem really does not like clutter. Or color. There's a small table at the far corner of the room with a spindly-looking metal chair at its side, a piece of gray-upon-gray art hanging over the bed, and a small square mirror on the far wall. The room's a good size, and when I take off my shoes, my feet sink into the extra-thick, plush (gray) carpet. I peek in the closet and then head over to take a look at the en suite bathroom, which is decorated in gray and white. If this were a hotel room or an apartment, I'd be pleased at how clean and nice everything is. But it's not, and I can't stop thinking about Willem down below and how I've just agreed to work for him.

I'm not sure if I'm making a mistake. All I know is that I need something in my life to change, and right now this seems like the best path. I unpack my suitcase and plug in my laptop. I go to plug my phone in, too, and then pause. Should I text my parents? Leave them a note they probably won't even look at for days, providing they come back anytime soon? Dad's practically living with his witch at this point, and Mom only shows up to switch out her laundry most times. The lunches I make them go uneaten more often than not, and I'm left to my own devices. I'm not sure they'll notice I'm gone for a while.

That might not be a bad thing. It'll give me time to settle in, for us to get our story rock solid.

In the end, I text Reggie instead.

PENNY: Hey pal! Just letting you know that I had my meet & greet and it went well. I'm doing it!

REGGIE: Are you sure???

It's a little gratifying that Reggie's text comes back right away. Someone was thinking about me at least. I smile fondly down at the text, feeling better already. Reggie's got my back. She and Ben will help me if I need anything. I'm not in this alone.

PENNY: I'm sure. We're still on for Friday night cards right? I'll be there and I might even bring a plus-one!

REGGIE: Uhhhh

REGGIE: Do I even want to ask?

REGGIE: I mean of course, yes, we're on for cards.

REGGIE: But okay, I'm going to ask anyhow. Is your plus-one who I think it is?

REGGIE: Because I'm not sure how I feel about that!

PENNY: Yes it is, and I promise he'll be on his best behavior. I think it'll be good for people to see us together.

REGGIE: Okay, now I'm really confused.

PENNY: I'll explain it all to you when I see you tomorrow! xoxoxo

I lock my screen and plug in my phone. I could text Reggie an entire book of feelings right now, but we have to be careful. So I cuddle Pip and give him some love, then shake out some seeds and nuts on the table in front of his cage for his dinner. I change into a pair of comfy unicorn pajamas and some fuzzy slippers, remove my makeup like I'm heading to bed, and then head back downstairs to meet my warlock for our first spell.

I can do this. I can.

WILLEM

I'm practically euphoric as I watch the clock in the study, tapping my pen as I wait for the minutes to tick past. I didn't show her around the house or give her a tour, and I probably should have. I'm far too impatient to get into casting. I've been stuck with tiny cantrips and charms. I want to enchant something. I want to transmute something. I want to curse the absolute shit out of something. I want to make an entire table full of *defixiones* tablets.

I want to *feel* my magic again.

For the first time in decades, I have something to look forward to.

Possibilities float through my mind. I could curse every asshole that's mocked me in the last twenty-three years, and they'd never suspect a thing. I could scry on my enemies, who wouldn't know to put up a shielding spell. Potions. I can make so many damned potions.

I can defend myself against Stoker's microaggressions. The little things he does to pick apart my spirit and make me doubt myself. The chipping away he does at my life until I'm drowning in misfortune. All of that can change if I can cast enough to protect myself and even go on the offensive.

The sheer enormity of what's being opened up to me again makes me want to laugh aloud with delight.

There's a knock at the door to my study, and I jump to my feet, twitchy with anticipation. "Come in."

The familiar—Penny—steps inside. To my surprise, she's wearing a pair of garishly bright pajamas covered in cartoon horses and rainbows. Her makeup is gone and her hair is pulled into two short tails at her neck, and she gives me another one of those face-scrunching happy smiles. "I'm ready."

I pause, feeling I should state the obvious. "You're in pajamas."

"Well, yeah. I have to work in the morning. I figure once you're done casting, it'll be bedtime for me." She shrugs. "Casting really takes a toll on an apprentice, right?"

"It does," I admit reluctantly, somewhat rattled at the sight of her in sleepwear. Does she think this is a slumber party? "You should quit your job."

Penny looks around eagerly, ignoring my suggestion. "So are we casting here or somewhere else?"

"We'll cast in my laboratory downstairs. And I mean it, quit your job. I'll pay you wages. I'd rather have you on call at all times." I head out of my office, showing her the way, and I notice she's wearing pink fuzzy slippers, because of course she is. "It's necessary for what I want to cast."

"I'm not quitting my job," she says in an even tone. "The boyfriend I love wouldn't ask me to quit."

"Then it's a good thing he's make-believe," I retort tersely. "But fine, suit yourself. Run ragged. See if I care. As long as I can cast, that's all that matters." Stubborn brat. She'll change her tune after a few days. I know how much casting can drain a familiar and she doesn't.

But the look she shoots my way is eager as we head down the hall, toward my laboratory. "So what are we casting first?"

That alleviates some of my irritation toward her. We're in this together, I remind myself. She wants magic as badly as I do, and so we're both breaking the rules. I glance over—and down, because she really is short, especially without her heels on. "I thought we'd stick with the classic *defixiones*."

"That's a curse tablet, right?" At my nod, her eagerness bubbles up. "I've seen one up close, but I'm dying to know what it feels like when you cast one. They look so benign, but you can just feel the magic brimming inside them."

"When did you see a curse tablet?" I ask, curious. We cut through my kitchens and head to the back of the house, to where I have the stairs down to the basement. My basement is, of course, set up like a media room, but it's got a false wall that hides my laboratory behind shelves and shelves of Blu-ray Discs and vinyl. "I thought you haven't cast before."

"I haven't," Penny agrees. "But Ben is starting up a school for familiars to teach them the basics so when we apprentice with someone, we're not completely useless. He showed us a few tablets and some scrolls. I only got to attend one class so far, though." She grimaces. "Most of them happen during my work hours, and my boss thinks the class is frivolous, so she'd rather I work instead."

I agree with her boss.

"Speaking of Ben, we need to exclude him and Reggie from our curse spell," she points out. "It can't be a blanket curse on us, because clearly we are going to bring it up to them at some point."

I grunt, a little surprised that she's been thinking of the ins and outs of the work we're about to do. "Excellent point."

"That's what I'm here for," she chirps. "To make excellent points."

"Funny, I thought you were here to blind me with your clothing and bring rodents into my house," I mutter. She gives me a wounded look and I ignore it, surging ahead. "My laboratory is behind here. Come. I'm anxious to get started."

Penny follows behind me, but the cheerfulness on her face has been replaced with a vague distaste. I don't care if she likes me. I'm used to no one liking me. That's not why I strive for excellence, for power. It's not to make friends, and I remind myself of that yet again. I move to the media case and flick the hidden latch. "I don't want you coming down here without me," I say. "You could get into something dangerous."

"I'm not a dog," she protests. "I know not to touch things."

The wall slides open, revealing the staircase down to my basement laboratory. Most witches tend to hide theirs behind walls or in secret rooms. I'm sure it dates back to earlier times when we were persecuted, but the practice continues today simply because it's a lot easier than trying to explain away a room full of bat guano and dried aardvark tongue to a mundane sort of visitor. I head down the stairs as casually as I can, though my heart is pounding with anticipation. It's been so damned long since I cast anything of note. I'm craving it.

Penny sucks in a breath as we make it to the bottom of the curving stairs and my lab comes into view. I'm rather proud of it myself, the books neatly organized and all my components shelved and labeled in the correct spots. Several workstations are set up in the room, along with a computer for online research. One wall is full of shelves that hold the largest equipment pieces, an altar to Fortuna, a crystal ball, and various glassware. And covering one entire wall is my gorgeous, one-of-a-kind library of spell books. Some I stole from Stoker, some I acquired after the fact, and some I've written myself. They're my pride and joy, and I practically beam with pleasure at the sight of their leather spines and the gilded, tooled artwork on the fronts. "Impressive, isn't it?"

When I turn to look at her, she has a sleeve pressed to her mouth as if trying to stifle laughter. "More gray?"

"What's wrong with gray?" I snap, irked. Did she not even notice the absolute library of spell tomes I've acquired? Any other witch would be beside herself with pleasure at the sight of them.

This girl just gives her hair a toss. "You're allowed to have some color in your life, that's all I'm saying."

"You've got plenty for both of us." I head across the room, toward the storage cabinets that hold archival information. "I believe my last apprentice left her apprentice cuff here."

She follows behind me. "There's a lot of cabinets in here."

There are. There's another floor of storage cabinets below this one, but I don't point that out. I save everything and keep it in its proper place. Stoker always said—

Well, fuck him, actually. I don't want to think about him right now. I move to the drawer that houses jewelry and pick through the spent amulets and broken torques until I find an apprentice cuff. "Here we go."

When Penny says nothing, I turn around to find that she's got a worried look on her face. "If I wear this, won't someone notice it?" She twists the society cuff on her slim wrist. "That'd kind of defeat the entire purpose."

She's not wrong, but I'm two steps ahead of her. "Once you have it on, the second spell we do will be an illusion spell. Anyone that sees this cuff will think you're wearing that one." I point at the one on her wrist right now. "Problem solved. If anyone asks why it feels like magic, tell them you dropped yours and lost it in a parking lot, so I put a finder spell on it."

"I guess." She twists her cuff again. "It just doesn't sound like me to lose something as meaningful as my cuff, though."

I bare my teeth at her in a snarl. "Maybe you were distracted by how much you love your *boyfriend*."

Penny makes a face at me. "That's even less believable."

We glare at each other, and then I mutely hold out the bracelet, practically daring her to take it from me. This is who I am, and I'm not going to gloss over it or clean it up to try to woo her to my side. She has to take my personality with the job.

She stares at the cuff I hold out to her and then sighs, reaching out to snatch it from my hand. "Isn't there a ceremony of some kind? Something to make this feel more important?"

"Sorry to disappoint. I should warn you, once you put that on, if you take it off at any point, it will break the bond between us, and you can never put it on again. Understand? So you need to be certain."

Penny immediately takes off her Society of Familiars cuff and puts on my bracelet with a defiant glare. "I knew what I was getting into the moment I showed up here. You're not scaring me off."

And she holds up the cuffed hand defiantly and then extends her middle finger.

I snort with amusement at that, opening my mouth to retort something equally sharp, when the invisible tether between us snaps into place. My eyes flutter closed, and the feel of her deep well of *sanguis vitae* washes over me. Power hums in my veins. It feels so good I actually shiver like an idiot.

She's watching me curiously. "Do you feel something?"

"Yes. You don't?" When she shakes her head, I'm not surprised. She's not my first apprentice, though it's been a while. "I always forget that a familiar doesn't feel the same rush the warlock does. No matter. You'll get plenty out of this." I rub my hands together and gaze at my lab full of spell paraphernalia with ill-disguised glee. "Let's cast."

PENNY

It's weird to see Willem all charged up like this. He's been a sneering, aloof prick ever since I arrived, but now that I've got his bracelet on, he's wired. His eyes are practically glowing with anticipation, and I sit on a stool, watching as he races around his lab (which looks as bland and boring as something out of *The Office*) and pulls together components. I'd offer to help, but he's made it clear he doesn't want me touching anything, so I just wait patiently.

In a way, it's nice to see him happy like this. It lets me know that no matter how much of a jerk he is to me, he still has a softer side. He races past me, snapping his fingers as if he's just remembered something. "Goat's milk. I need goat's milk."

"For the spell?" I ask. "There's some at my job, but it'll take me an hour to get there and back. I don't mind going, though."

Willem shakes his head again. "We'll have to improvise. We'll make the tablet with hair of goat and regular milk, and if Sancus accepts it, I'll do a larger offering of goat's milk tomorrow to appease him." He crosses his arms over his chest, his expression thoughtful. "I think that should work. The other components are easy. Snake scales and meteorite."

To someone else, that might sound ridiculous, but I actually know what he means. Thanks to my job at CBD Whee! and the spell component fulfillment I do, I know that a lot of witches and warlocks carry a good supply of components at all times. Someone like Willem would absolutely have a few flakes of meteorite on hand. Fresh goat's milk, however, is harder to find. "I guess powdered wouldn't do?"

His lip curls as he looks over at me, as if just remembering that I exist. "Rule number one, apprentice. You always, always give the gods the best you can. If it's edible, you use fresh unless specified otherwise."

"I know that," I say defensively. "I work in spell component fulfillment." I mean, I didn't know that specifically about goat's milk, but I hate that he's trying to make me feel stupid. "So this tablet is going to be dedicated to Sancus? Why not Minerva or Jove or Mercury?"

Moving to one of the cabinets, Willem picks through a few containers and then plucks one out. "Sancus is the god of oath-keeping. Some people find that it's perfectly fine to cast and request power straight from the most important gods, but I find that the more drilled down and specific you can get with who you are targeting, the more power a spell will have."

That's interesting, and it strikes me as rather smart. "Is power important in a curse tablet? One between us, that is?"

"Not necessarily, since it will be a simple deal between you and me." He rushes past my stool, setting the tiny box labeled "Meteorite" on the table beside me. "But consider the next time I cast and offer up to Sancus. He might remember my well-thought-out offering and that I approached him first, and give it a little more oomph."

"So we're brownnosing the gods, then?" I joke.

Willem gives me another withering look. "You know what? Just stop talking."

"You talked to me first," I protest. Whatever. I didn't want to talk to his cranky butt anyhow. "Oh em gee," I mutter. "Pissy much." I'm silent as he gathers the rest of the components and then races upstairs, returning a minute later with a glass tumbler full of milk.

He carefully sets it down on the table, then lines up all the components he has compiled. From underneath the table, he pulls out a shiny lacquered offering bowl that looks as if it's homemade pottery. I want to ask if he made the bowl himself, but he'll probably just snap at me again, so I keep silent. Willem must be caught up in working the spell, because he retrieves the lead tablet— which I recognize—for the curse.

Since I work with spell components at my fulfillment job, I'm well aware of how curse tablets work. Some of the lazier witches have blank tablets sent to them rather than cutting their own, so I've had to create lead tablets myself before. They're sheets of thin, flattened lead, and I can't help but notice that Willem's stack is all uniformly sized, which tells me he cuts his own. I know I definitely wasn't quite so careful when I made them myself. With a pointed metal stylus, he starts scratching words into the tablet. "Excluding Ben Magnus and Reggie Johnson," he says as he writes. "This curse will apply to you and I. If we discuss our agreement with anyone outside of those two, we . . . what. You frowned on the pox, right?"

He turns and leans on the table, glancing up at me, and he's been running around so crazily that his impeccably gelled red hair has gotten mussed. One lock hangs over his pale forehead, just begging to be pushed back into place. I ignore it and focus on his words. "Yes. We're frowning on the pox. Let's make it monetary or unlucky or something. I'm not planning on breaking the curse, but let's also not go crazy."

Willem thinks for a moment, tapping his mouth with the end of the stylus. "Sneezing."

"Excuse me?"

"Uncontrollable sneezing for a full year if someone should break the curse. That way if we veer close to breaking it, a good sneeze will warn us."

Well, that's certainly creative. I've heard that witches like to think outside the box, but at least sneezing is better than the pox . . . which I'm pretty sure is something I absolutely do not want under any circumstances. "Unorthodox, but you're the man in charge."

It's like he's been transformed now that we're working out the details of the spell. Gone is the surly, aloof asshole from earlier. His pale cheeks are flushed with excitement, and when he glances over at me, Willem grins. "The trick to cursing an immortal," he says, lifting the stylus into the air to gesticulate, "is that you have to pick something that applies no matter the modern technology. In twenty years if we're no longer putting money into a bank, it won't apply. Sneezes are timeless." He pauses. "Annoying, but timeless."

I smile, because I actually didn't think of that. It's a good tip. "I'm not immortal, though."

"You will be soon," he says, not looking up from the tablet, where he's now scratching words into the lead surface.

Pleasure blooms through my chest. He's right. I agreed to do this and in exchange, I'm going to stop aging. I'll be frozen in time just like all the other immortals who practice magic. Well, they're not completely ageless—but witches and warlocks age much slower than normal people. I'm not going to complain about having two thousand years to practice magic instead of seventy-odd. "You're right."

"Of course I am," he says arrogantly. "Now watch and learn."

So I do. I watch as he pulls out a book and turns to the page he wants. He slices open his thumb, smearing blood at the bottom of the bowl, and then begins to murmur an incantation in Latin. I watch as the bowl begins to smoke and he adds the milk and goat hair, then the scales, and finally the bit of meteorite as he chants. I want to ask specifically what he's doing, but of course I know better than to interrupt a spell midcast.

He closes his eyes, places a hand on the tablet, and waits. A moment later, the tablet glows and the scent of charcoal fills the air. I bite my knuckles to keep from gasping aloud, because this is so darned cool. Here I am, at a real warlock's side, watching real magic. It's everything I dreamed of. Fascinated, I keep my gaze glued on the glowing tablet, riveted as the letters sizzle and flare with power as the spell itself takes hold. Oh wow.

Oh . . . oh dear.

I press my thighs together, because that intrusive tingle is start-ing between my legs again. Surreptitiously, I glance over at Wil-lem, but he's casting without even looking at me, one finger on the page of the book while the other drips blood into the snake-scale-milk-goat-hair concoction in the bowl. I try not to squirm, even as the sensation builds. Shit. It's definitely an orgasm. Shit, shit, shit. I clench harder, trying to push the unwanted feeling away, but it keeps spiraling and growing greater as the tablet continues to glow, the writing lighting up as the spell activates. I watch in a mixture of horror and fascination as the last line of wording lights up—and everything inside me squeezes in a fierce, breathtaking orgasm. "*Unh.*"

It takes everything I have not to gasp aloud. I do contort in the chair, though, my back arching as the breath leaves my lungs.

Willem looks over at me in surprise. "Are you all right?"

Oh em gee, the humiliation. "I'm fine," I choke out. "Just hit me by surprise, that's all." Is it . . . Am I supposed to come every time he casts? I honestly don't know, and I don't have anyone to ask right now. I'm sure not going to ask Willem.

"You look sweaty," he points out, his aristocratic voice displeased. There's a fierce frown on his angular face. "And flushed. Casting can drain a familiar quite a bit. Do you need to lie down?"

I need a cigarette is what I need. A cigarette and a chance to catch my breath. "I'm good."

"Then you won't mind if we move ahead and cast the illusion spell on your bracelet?" He holds his hand out to me.

Oh. Right. I'm so rattled I start to pull it off, and then stop when he yelps in alarm, grabbing my hand. "Sorry," I breathe, and it sounds husky and far too turned on. "I'm just . . . having a hard time concentrating . . ."

I get to my feet and immediately sink to the floor, boneless.

Willem catches me, an arm going around my waist. "I warned you," he says in a peevish voice. "Casting takes a lot out of a familiar. Just because it doesn't hit you all at once doesn't mean it won't hit you. Can you stand?"

"Yup." I clutch the countertop, trying to pull myself to my feet . . . and fail. "Actually, no."

He huffs in irritation, helping me back to my seat. "Wait there. I'll be right back."

As if I can go anywhere? We've just proved I've got noodles for legs. I slump in my seat, watching as he heads up the stairs and back out of the laboratory. The pulsing between my thighs seems to be setting up permanent residence, and I want to shove a hand into my pajamas and rub out another quick one in the hopes it will stop. I need to talk to Reggie, I decide. I need to find out if this is normal, or if it's something that goes away the more familiar I get with his casting. Mercy, I hope it goes away. I don't know how to act around him when he's trying to cast and I'm quaking like my vibrator's on its highest setting.

I chew on the oversized cuff of my pajamas, anxious. Do I say something to him? He was so stoked to cast that I'm not sure he's aware of what's going on with me. You would think Reggie would have warned me if this sort of thing happened, right? I could ask my parents, I suppose . . .

My nose tickles, and I fight back a sneeze.

Right. Okay. I didn't want to ask them anyhow. If I found out they were orgasming every time their witches cast, I think I'd be pretty horrified. It's better if I don't know anything at all.

I consider standing up again, but I'm surprisingly tired. I'm sure the orgasm is part of it, but I really do think I could fall asleep in this chair. My eyes drift closed—

—and I wake up as someone jostles my leg. It's Willem, returning from upstairs. He's got a glass of milk and a plate of cookies with him, and he sets them down on the table. "I want you to eat and drink."

"Thank you," I tell him, surprisingly touched. This might be the nicest thing anyone's done for me in a long time. How long has it been since someone's taken care of me and not the other way around? Even with the Society of Familiars, I'm the one integrating new people and handling dues and basically running the show. At home, I take care of my parents more than they take care of me. It's foolish to feel gratitude over a simple snack, but I almost feel like crying at his thoughtfulness. I pick up one star-shaped cookie and nibble on it. "This is really nice of you."

Willem recoils as if he's offended. "I'm just keeping you healthy. It does me no good if you're violently ill after just a single casting." With an irked look in my direction, he straightens up his casting table, putting away the book and replacing the unused components back in their spots, then cleaning the ashes out of the casting bowl. I must have missed the part where the components burned, too lost in my orgasm. Awkward. Very awkward.

I pick up the milk, hope he didn't add goat hair to it, then eat another cookie. "So what now?"

"Normally the tablet would be buried somewhere that neither of us would typically be able to locate it. However, seeing as how only you and I are supposed to know about it, we can't exactly hide it from each other." He drums his long, pale fingers on the table, thinking.

"We could bury it in the backyard and plant a bush over it," I suggest. "That way we'd both know if it was disturbed."

He gives me a look of disgust. "Manual labor? I think not." He stares down at it, thinking, and then snaps his fingers. "We'll lock it in a cabinet and throw away the keys."

I shrug. This is starting to feel like a lot of effort, and I'm getting sleepier by the moment. Yawning, I say, "It's fine. I don't plan on breaking it. I want us to work together."

"Me too." Willem carefully picks up the tablet and wraps it in cloth. "It can wait, though. Are you up to doing your bracelet? We need to get it handled tonight, or you're going to have to stay in until we can get it bespelled." He gives me a look that's trying hard to be insouciant, but I can tell just how badly he wants to cast again.

He's totally jazzed by this. It's like his energy is growing while mine is dropping. And I'm learning from him already. I'm not ready for this evening to end. I want to soak it all up. "I can keep going."

Willem flashes me a brilliant grin. "Excellent. Now, hold your wrist out while I gather the components."

I lean over the edge of the table, stretching my arm out. It feels so comfortable that I close my eyes, just to give it a moment . . .

* * *

I WAKE UP the next morning in a strange room, and I feel like I've been flattened. Yawning, I look around, sitting up in bed, and realize that I'm in my unicorn pajamas, tucked under unfamiliar gray blankets. The clock on the wall shows it's early, which means I'm not late to work. That's good at least. I smack my lips and squint at my surroundings. There's Pip's cage, and my suitcase is tucked against the wall. This is my new room in Willem's house, but I don't remember how I got here.

All I remember is laying out my arm so he could enchant my bracelet, and I must have fallen asleep. I look at the cuff on my arm, and I'm disappointed. It doesn't look like it's been magicked. It looks like my regular old Society of Familiars cuff. I run my fingers over it, but it even feels like my old cuff. I'm not supposed to take it off, though. Hmm. Maybe I'll find Willem and ask him before work.

I feed Pip and cuddle him for a bit, then let him race around my room while I get ready for work. The moment I head into the bathroom, I see a note stuck to the mirror.

Try not to pass out on me next time. Eat protein and make sure you drink electrolytes. We're casting again tonight. Be ready.

—Willem

Postscript—Do not fucking touch that bracelet. It's the right one.

I snort. I guess I should be thankful he carried me up to bed? Willem is definitely a prickly sort. I don't get the impression we're going to be friends by the end of this. We might actively hate each other by the time another month passes. But . . . I've already learned from him, and I suspect I'm going to keep learning. It's worth it.

With that thought in mind, I pack Pip into his cage and head downstairs. I don't see Willem anywhere, and I don't want to wander around his mausoleum-like house without permission, so I head off to work. I'll deal with him later. For now, it's business as usual.

8

WILLEM

I drum my fingers on my desk, irritated at the email glaring at me on my screen.

> Atticus & Partners regrets to inform you that we have
> found another candidate more suitable for the job.
> We thank you for your enthusiasm and wish you well.
> Please feel free to apply again in the future.

Apply again. I'd rather burn the entire place to the ground. Atticus can go fuck himself. Scowling, I hit delete just to get it out of my sight, and glare at my surroundings. Of course Atticus & Partners didn't hire me. They think I'm hobbled in my casting, restrained by the lack of a familiar. They think I am Stoker's broken tool, useless now.

My world is open again, and the possibilities are endless.

Well. Vaguely endless. I still have to work under the table, due to the fact that no one can know about our situation. I have to keep pretending to be powerless. Everything I do has to be on the sly.

If Stoker were to ever find out that I can cast fully again, he'd come after me and Penny both, and he'd do whatever he could to destroy our lives. I regret that I stole his books recently. It was a power move, and a big one. How the fuck was I to know I was going to get a familiar under the table just a few short weeks later? Now everything I do is going to be obsessively scrutinized, and it's going to make things tricky.

I'm momentarily frustrated at the realization that I'm still hampered. In the eyes of the world, I'm still a hobbled warlock. That's the wrong way to think of this, I remind myself. Instead of focusing on what I cannot do, I need to focus on what I can.

And what I can do is get revenge on everyone that's fucked me over since my ban. I can curse them, and they'll have no idea it's me behind it. I can hex them and cast the evil eye and make their businesses tank, and I'll never be suspected.

Dastardly, but no more than they deserve. All I have to do is make sure Stoker never finds out about Penny. I can fight a silent war against him and make him regret he ever fucked with me in the past.

Pleased with the thought, I decide to create a list of my enemies. Stoker's name is at the top of the list, and I add Atticus under it. The list consumes my afternoon, and I'm still focusing on it when the doorbell rings. One of the staff enters a moment later, a confused look on her face as Penny follows her in. "You have a visitor, sir," the housekeeper says. "She says she lives here?"

I wave a hand irritably. "Yes, yes. It's fine." I eye Penny's garishly bright clothing. Today she looks like a lime. Her dress is the most headache-inducing shade of green I've ever seen, accessorized with a string of pearls and a purse that's shaped like a star. Her hair is pulled back into a high ponytail, an equally lime-green headband just behind her thick bangs. She always looks well coordinated, at least. I can appreciate that about her appearance, even if I can't appreciate the way she goes about it. I study her, noting the bags under her eyes. "You look dreadful."

Penny flinches. "That's really rude."

"Tired," I correct, because she's probably right. I'm not used to having to be polite. If anything, I go out of my way to be abrasive to others. "You look tired. Are you up to more casting tonight?"

She sinks into the chair across from me, not nearly as perky and eager as yesterday. "We can't. Tonight we're playing cards."

"We're what? I'm not doing any such thing." Tonight I think I'd like to start with a scrying spell. A nice juicy one. I want to see who Atticus hired for the position I wanted.

"As my boyfriend," she stresses, "you need to meet my friends so they'll believe we're madly in love and we've moved in together. Speaking of which, we should probably iron out our story."

"You can go play cards after our spell," I tell her, getting to my feet. Already, I'm working through the scrying spell. A crystal ball, since I'm rusty. I'll divinate to Mercury, since he's a nosy sort and loves secrets more than the rest of the gods. For offerings, I'll have to find something that won't leave a trace for another scryer to find. Foodstuff is probably best. Perhaps I should check what's in my refrigerator.

"You're not going to come with me?" Penny asks, getting to her feet as well. She's frowning up at me. "We need to be seen together."

"I have things to do." My enemies list to flesh out. Spells to add to the list of castings. "I hope you've been loading up on electrolytes for tonight."

Penny shoots me a frustrated look. "Are you even listening to me?"

Soft cheeses? Expensive wine? Wine, I decide. I think I have a bottle of chablis that would be a good offering—

Lost in thought, I don't notice her until she comes up and taps me on my sleeve. She glares up at me with that round face of hers, eyes sparking with irritation. "If we're casting tonight, I have to cancel on my friends. I don't mind doing that, but I need you to go with me to the car wash tomorrow, then."

Car . . . wash? "What?"

Her small nostrils flare, which is almost comical on her face. "I told you my schedule, *boyfriend.* Tonight is cards, and tomorrow is the car wash with the Society of Familiars. It's to raise money for one of our members who has some medical bills." She crosses her arms over her chest and gives me a mulish look. "You have to do one or the other, or people are going to start talking. I mean it. I was down fifty percent on my workload today, and my boss wondered what was going on. I told her I was feeling under the weather, but we can disguise a lot of this with us just being wrapped up in a new relationship. It's not going to work out if you avoid all my friends or if I suddenly start canceling everything."

"Fine. Whatever."

"Not fine. Not whatever. Do you want to play cards tonight with my friends, or do you want to go to the car wash tomorrow?"

Ugh. Both sound revolting, but perhaps I can get out of both if I'm lucky. "Let's do the car wash tomorrow." *And I will pray for rain.*

A smile blooms across Penny's face, transforming her round features into utter joy. She's not traditionally pretty, I decide, but she really does have a warm smile that tempts me to smile back. Almost. "All right. I'll tell my friends I'm tired and staying in, and tomorrow we'll do the car wash." She pulls out her phone and starts to type. "Do you need me to change?"

I shrug. "If you think you'll pass out again, it might be a good idea."

She heads upstairs, typing on her phone as she goes, and I head for the wine cellar. I find the chablis and then pluck a few artisanal cheeses from the refrigerator. If Atticus has any sort of obfuscation spells on him to hide his doings, we'll have to work around them. I'm looking forward to the challenge, actually. I enjoy a good puzzle. I open the door to my laboratory and head down, leaving it ajar so she can follow me.

A short time later, Penny returns, still texting, and the rodent is on her shoulder. I groan at the sight of it. "Really?"

"Really," she says firmly. "He can't stay in his cage all day. He's used to having more freedom."

"He's a squirrel. Put him outside."

"I'm ignoring that," she says, thumping into the seat next to my worktable. "I just told Nick that I have a stomach bug and can't make it to cards. He'll pass it along to the others."

That makes me pause. "Nick? Boyfriend?"

"Nick has a boyfriend," she tells me, and then reaches out to pat my arm. "You're my boyfriend now, remember?"

My lip curls in distaste at the thought. A pretend relationship. She's lucky her magic reserve is so damned strong. "Whatever. Tonight I'm casting a scrying spell. We're going to take a look at what one of my rivals is up to." I hold up the bottle of wine. "And we're going to bribe the gods."

PENNY

Saturday morning, I feel like a squashed bug with a hangover. I throw sunglasses on, shower Pip with apologetic kisses, and then get ready for the car wash. I go for a relaxed look, with a concert T-shirt knotted at the waist and a short, casual skirt over some sandals. I pull my hair into two pigtails high on my head and skip jewelry, since I don't want to scrape it on anyone's car. I'm going to be covered in suds soon, but it's for a good cause.

Now to go round up my "boyfriend."

I peek into six different rooms before I find Willem. Despite my reminders that we're doing the car wash today, he looks like he always does. He's wearing a deep blue sport coat and a pressed white shirt underneath, the collar open only a fraction. He's got on camel-colored slacks that look like they cost more than my car, and the brown loafers he's wearing have bright red soles, which means they're impossibly expensive as well. "Double-yew tee eff, Willem. I thought we talked about this?"

He holds his place in his book with a finger, frowning up at me. Even every strand of his red hair is waxed into place. I don't think a tornado would budge it. "What are you nattering about now?"

I gesture at his clothing. "You're supposed to be going to the car wash with me! As my boyfriend!"

He glances down at himself. "I said I was going, and since it's not raining, I don't see how I can get out of it. Is there a dress code for your boyfriend that I'm unaware of?"

I make a wordless sound of protest. "You can't wash cars in that!"

Willem closes his book and gets to his full height. He has to be at least six feet tall, and considering that I'm barely scraping five feet, he's doing a great job at looming. "No one said I was washing cars. I'm showing up as your paramour. No more, no less."

Hands on hips, I study him. Other than the scowl, he does look rather nice. Overdressed, but nice. "Fine. But you have to be sufficiently boyfriend-y when we get there, all right?"

He snags my hand in his and lifts it to his lips. "I can pretend with the best of them."

Flustered, I watch as he brushes a kiss over my knuckles. Oh. Okay. I guess he *can* pretend with the best of them. "Right. Shall we head out, then?"

"Fine, but I'm driving."

"You don't know the way. I'll drive. Plus, my car needs a washing."

Willem's lip curls and he releases my hand as if burned. "I refuse to drive anywhere in that death trap you call a car."

Is he picking a fight? "What's wrong with my car?" It's a perfectly acceptable Mini Cooper.

"It has a hatchback."

"So?"

"So, I'm not pint-sized like you. We'll take my sedan." He pauses. "And we're only staying for an hour."

"Oh em gee, you really are going to pick a fight over this," I exclaim. "Seriously? I've done everything you've asked so far, and you can't do this one thing for me? Is this how things are going to be between us? You just deciding things and me being forced to follow along because you're being impossible and we're both tied up in this vow?"

"What's wrong with that?"

"I signed up to be your familiar, not your doormat!" I might be shouting. Just a little.

His eyes blaze down at me. "And thus by being a familiar, you are automatically subservient to *me*," he enunciates. "The important one."

"Oh, is that so? If you're so fucking important, why don't you cast on your own? Oh wait, that's right, you need your power source." I shove a thumb in my direction. "That's me, you big jerk!"

"Don't you mean 'jay ee ar kay'? Since you like to spell everything?" he sneers.

I gasp. "Maybe I just spell when I'm excited. Excuse me for living. Don't worry, you won't hear it *again*," I shout, my hands clenched at my sides as I yell at him. "*Because nothing about you is exciting!* You're the rudest, most distasteful warlock I've ever met. No wonder you can't get anyone to be your damn apprentice. No one in their right mind would give you a minute of their time!"

"Then I guess that makes you crazy," he roars back at me.

Shoulders heaving, I glare at him furiously. I can't decide if I want to punch his face or burst into tears. "You. Are. Awful." I choke the words out one by one. "And this is obviously a mistake."

Turning, I head back up to my room, storming up the stairs. I'm going to pack my bag and forget all about meeting Willem Sauer. If we can't get along over a car wash, how are we ever going to work together? If he won't bend even on this small thing, how does he think he's going to teach me magic? It's just not going to work.

I sniffle, pleased that I manage to hide my tears of frustration until I get into my room. Then I let Pip out of his cage, carry him over to the bed, and have myself a good cry as I snuggle my squirrel.

WILLEM

The nerve of the girl.

I'm still fuming ten minutes later, pacing in the music room. She hasn't returned to apologize or even stormed down the stairs to continue the fight. I keep waiting, and my irritation rises all over again. I've texted Ben Magnus, letting him know that he's an absolute bastard for setting me up with such a loathsome creature as a familiar. He hasn't replied, which tells me that he doesn't care.

Prick.

Scowling, I glance up the stairs and then decide I'm going to confront the chit. Just get it over with, and we can go about our day. I had plans for this afternoon. I wanted to cast something. Anything, really. I just need to feel magic singing in my veins. I'm an addict that's been given his first hit in years, and it's not enough. I need more. So I straighten my coat, run my hand over my hair, and head up to the guest room. The door is shut firm, and it's silent inside.

I knock, trying to bite back my impatience.

"Go away!"

I have never met a more frustrating female in my life. "Did you want to do this stupid car wash or not?"

"I do not. Go away now!"

She's determined to get under my skin. "I'm not going to apologize, because I'm not wrong!"

From the hall, I can hear her storming toward the door. She flings it open and glares up at me, her face tearstained and her eyes red, but vitriol still absolutely brimming under her skin. "I don't care if you're wrong or not. You're a jerk! You're mean and you make fun of the way I talk, and you're not even willing to do the smallest thing to sell the fact that I'm living here with you. So I'm done here." She stomps back toward the bed, where I see her squirrel sitting on one side of her suitcase as she folds clothes and packs them away. "This isn't going to work. You can find yourself another familiar."

Wait, what? "You can't leave," I protest, following her inside. "We've barely even started."

"I don't want to stay here if you're going to be a monster." She folds a garishly pink blouse without looking at me. "You don't listen to anything I say, and I've been giving and giving for the last few days and all you're doing is taking. If you're this bad now, you're going to be worse later on, and I'm not going to stand for it."

I'm appalled. Not just over the fact that she's leaving, but that I've made her cry. Even now, she sniffs as she folds clothes, and I feel like . . . well, a monster. I'm used to people like Magnus, who gives me just as much shit as I give him. Or Stoker, who made me feel as if I were a turd to be ground beneath his heel. I'm not used to soft, pink familiars with smiles that light up their entire faces and who want me to actually be *nice*.

I'm not entirely certain I know how. It's not a skill set I've had the luxury of cultivating. Stoker would say that kindness is weakness, and weakness must be stomped out. Then he'd take his cane and give me twenty strikes across the shoulders just to make his point.

Rotten old bastard.

But Stoker isn't here, and Penny is, and she's crying, and I feel helpless. Helpless because I've had a secret familiar for two days and I've already fucked this up. "I . . ."

She looks up at me, her mobile face absolutely miserable.

"I don't know how to be nice," I say after a moment. "I'm not used to it. I'm not good at it. But I would really like it if you would stay." I bite back a sigh and offer, "You can drive to the car wash."

Penny looks up at me, blinking. Her dark lashes are spiky with wetness, and the sight of her unhappy makes me feel like an incredible ass. Normally I don't care if people dislike me or if my presence makes them miserable. I actually get a little thrill out of it. But Penny is such a vivid, happy person that crushing her pleasure feels . . . wrong.

"You want me to stay?" she asks, her voice wobbling.

"I should like that, yes." The words come out of me with difficulty, as if everything inside me is far too tense to let my mouth move properly. "I'm not an easy person to live with. But I ask that you give me a chance."

Her eyes shine with fresh tears. "You're not giving me a chance. This has to go both ways, Willem. You have to meet me in the middle."

For some reason, I'm fascinated by the way she says my name. Most everyone just calls me Sauer or Mr. Sauer. Willem implies intimacy. Friendliness. I need to be her friend if this is going to work. "From now on, if I'm too abrasive, you have to tell me." The urge to tell her about Stoker, about his training methods, about how he raised me, bubbles up inside, but I quell it. No one wants to hear a sob story. They just want to hear solutions. "If I yell at you, yell back. No tears."

"I'll try not to cry." She manages a small smile, but it's not one of her Penny smiles, one of the ones that contort her whole face, and I know she's still upset.

"I'd much rather you threw things," I admit. "I know how to handle that."

A watery chuckle escapes her, and she leans over her suitcase and scoops up her squirrel. She pets its tiny head and hugs it to the front of her shirt. "You're sure you want to do this? Go to the car wash? It's going to be full of familiars, and they're all going to be extremely curious about us."

"Can I yell at them?" I arch a brow at her.

"I'd prefer you didn't, but it might be on brand for you," Penny admits. She moves across the room, her hips swaying as she puts her squirrel back in its cage, and I find myself watching her backside. I don't know why. I'm not attracted to her. She's not my type. I like tall, svelte, fashionable women. Aristocratic women. Not tiny things in neon clothing with vermin pets and snub noses. Ghastly, all of it. She turns and wipes her face, giving me another smile. "If anyone asks, I was crying this morning because we had a lovers' quarrel."

"Right." I can't believe I'm actually relieved that I'm going to be going to this accursed car wash with her. "Lovers' quarrel, and you won."

"There's no winning an argument with the person you love," she says, shaking her head at me. She pauses and touches her bracelet. "I'm glad I didn't take this off yet."

I am, too.

PENNY

It wasn't exactly an apology, but I think Willem is trying. To me, that means more than the words. The distressed, uncomfortable look on his face as he told me he was an unlikable person? It told me that he doesn't know how to have friends. He doesn't know what to do when a situation turns ugly. No wonder Ben and Reggie warned me that he's difficult. He's probably used to looking down on everyone and then getting his way.

I'm glad he tried, though. It makes me feel warm inside, even if I'm already exhausted by the time we pull my tiny car up to the parking lot of a local burger joint that is graciously letting us hold our fundraiser there. Two of the newest Fam have cardboard signs and are standing on the side of the road, waving them and encouraging people to pull in. Others are busy scrubbing cars and playing songs on the radio, laughing and having a great time. Well, everyone except Derek. Dull Derek is sitting underneath an awning, slurping a soda and trying to look busy (but isn't).

I park nearby and get out, brimming with excitement as Willem unfolds his long legs from my car and looks at the scene with a mixture of distaste and fear. "Okay," I say to Willem as I approach him. "Remember our story. You came into the store to buy spell components and we argued. You were impressed that I stood up to you, and asked me for coffee, and we've been all over each other ever since. That was a month ago, and we've been keeping things secret and just now decided to move in together, all right?"

He grunts. I can't tell if that's agreement or if he's just digesting what I said.

"Please," I whisper. "Please try to act vaguely boyfriend-like, okay? We have to sell this."

Willem's gaze focuses on me. He lets out a low, slightly irritated huff and then extends his hand out to the side.

It takes me a moment to realize he wants me to hold it. Oh. Delighted, I slip my hand in his and beam up at him. He's got good instincts for the boyfriend game, at least. I'm even more delighted—and surprised—when he leans over and plants a kiss atop my head. "I shall be an absolute buffoon of a boyfriend," he murmurs. "Don't worry."

I bite back a laugh. I'm just so relieved that I can't stop smiling, and it's not hard to sell a relationship when you're holding the hand of someone and grinning ear to ear, even if that someone is the irascible Willem Sauer. Everyone's staring at us now. All the familiars have stopped to watch us as we cross the parking lot, heading over to join the festive group.

"Hi, everyone," I call out chirpily. "Sorry we're late."

"We?" Cody gives me a smile, tugging at his wet shirt and gesturing at Willem with a dripping yellow sponge. "Who's your plus-one?"

Willem takes a step back, away from the sponge, and grimaces in distaste. "If you get that anywhere near my clothes, I'm going to murder you."

"No, he's not," I say cheerfully, putting a hand on Willem's chest. "Everyone, this is my boyfriend, Willem. We just moved in together. I wanted him to come here today and meet the crew."

Silence meets my announcement. I totally get why they're a little weirded out. It's been a long time since I've dated anyone, and never outside of Fam circles. My last two boyfriends (okay, *only* two boyfriends) were from nearby society chapters. And warlocks? They never, never date random familiars. It's not forbidden. It's just . . . weird. I think it's because a lot of them don't view us as equals. And after knowing Willem for a few days? I can absolutely say that's the case. So I squeeze his hand, beaming at everyone.

"Pleasure to meet all of you," Willem manages, his tone conveying it is very much not a pleasure.

I suspect that's about as good as I'm going to get out of him. "Okay," I say brightly. "It looks like things are rolling! Where can we help out? Do you need me to wash? What can Willem do?"

Cody and Mary exchange looks. "Maybe help Derek with the cash box?" she says, and the look Mary gives me all but begs me to take over. "I think we're good on scrubbers."

"Excellent," Willem says before I can speak up. "You do that, my love, and I shall, ah, procure drinks." He leans in and presses another awkward kiss to the top of my head and disappears inside the burger joint. I move toward the small portable table and folding chair and find all the money has been tossed into the box in crumpled wads and there's no order to anything. As I glance over at Derek, he gazes out at the parking lot from under the awning, slurping his soda and, well, doing nothing.

They're lucky they have me to take over.

I get started organizing the money and quickly get absorbed in the work. There's change to be made for customers that come through, people that just want to donate to a good cause, and some of my fellow Fam that just want to talk. Willem emerges from the store with trays of drinks for everyone, earning him a few cheers, and he moves to my side, unbuttoning his sport coat and monopolizing the other metal chair next to mine as he leans over. "How much will it cost me to get out of this?"

"Hmm?" I ask, distracted by how close he leans in. He smells like cookies.

"This is a fundraiser, yes? Unless we want to be here all day, I'm willing to offer up some funds." He opens his wallet, pulling out a few crisp bills. "Tell me how much it would cost for us to leave early."

I stare at him, my jaw dropping. "That . . . that's not how this works?"

Cody saunters over, rubbing his hand down his wet shirt, and it plasters to his six-pack abs. "You trying to bribe us, bro?"

"I thought it might be nice to take my girlfriend out on a real date," Willem says, pulling a wad of money out of his wallet and offering it to me. "Rather than sit here in the sun and bake all day while her friends do manual labor." He gives Cody a chilling look. "And I am not, nor have I ever been, your 'bro.'"

Cody scowls at him, losing all semblance of an easy demeanor. Maybe Willem brings out the worst in everyone. I push the money back toward Willem and shake my head, determined to pull these two apart. "This is a team-building exercise and a mixer, not just a fundraiser, honey."

"Of course . . . dumpling." He gives me a challenging look, as if daring me to refute his endearment. "Just trying to help."

I pull out my keys and beam at him. "I love that you want to give money to the cause, though. Do you want to get my car washed?"

"Do I?" But he takes the keys and then pauses before he gets up. He lowers his voice, leaning in, and he's so close I can smell cookies again. "You're all right? Not too tired to do this? I haven't worn you out?"

Cody's still watching us and I feel my face heat. He doesn't know that we're casting together, so he's going to think dirty, lascivious things. Why does that make my thighs clench together again? It's sweet of Willem to be worried about me, though. Just when I think he's an impossible jerk, he says something thoughtful. "I'm okay," I breathe, my face hot. "Thank you for asking."

Willem leans in further. "You're going to owe me so many spells later," he whispers into my ear. "Just you wait."

Instead of being annoyed by his demanding words, I feel my pussy clench, hard, in anticipation of the spellcasting. Why am I being turned on? This is bad. This is very bad. I don't like Willem. I don't think he's likable in the slightest. I'm just getting caught up in the moment. That's all. I give him an overbright smile as he gets to his feet and heads off with my keys. *Focus*, I tell myself, sorting through the crumpled bills in the cash box. He's just doing this stuff to distract you. I simply need a few moments to myself without thinking about Willem, and then I'll be fine.

Cody immediately takes the seat Willem just vacated. He

slouches next to me, hot and sweaty, his man bun tousled and his shirt sticking to rock-hard abs. "You and that guy, huh? When did this happen?"

"It's been a secret for about a month," I say, determined not to make eye contact. I keep my gaze focused on the bills, smoothing them and lining them up. "We were hesitant to bring it out into the open because he's a warlock."

It sounds legit, even to my ears.

"Mmm. So I guess you and me aren't a thing?" He crosses his arms over his chest and gives me that lazy, flirty grin of his.

I freeze, my mind frantically moving through my last few interactions with Cody. We chat and find ourselves together on bar crawls with the Fam, but is it flirty? I can't help but think about how only a few days ago, he invited me to go home with him and I almost took him up on it, simply for a change of pace. It's not that I don't like Cody. He just doesn't do anything in particular for me. I'm sure kissing him is nice. I'm sure sex with him would be nice. But it doesn't fill me with anticipation. And thinking about sex makes me think about spellcasting and how I orgasm. I think I've had more orgasms in the last few days than I did with my last boyfriend.

I glance over at Willem, but he's driving my car to the back of the designated washing area. A quick glance at Cody shows he's still watching me, waiting for an answer. "Mmm, you and me?" I reply, oh so casual. "What about you and me?"

"I kinda thought we were vibing." He nudges me with his shoulder, friendly-like, and I realize how close he's sitting. It doesn't make me prickle with awareness like when Willem sits that close. It just makes me vaguely irritated.

The Willem thing has to be because of magic, though. It's certainly not his winning personality. I beam a friendly look at

Cody, because it's not his fault I'm in a secret agreement with a prick of a warlock. "Were we vibing? I'm sorry. I didn't realize I was throwing that out there."

"Don't be sorry," Cody says, and reaches over, brushing my bangs back from my eyes. "Just be happy. You look like you've been crying. Do I need to do something about him?"

I bark out a laugh, uncomfortable. Boy, Cody is touchy-feely today. Boy, am I in this mess up to my darn neck. "We had a bit of a fight earlier but I'm better now. I'm happy."

He doesn't look convinced.

"I love Willem," I choke out, and it takes everything I have to keep smiling. "Really."

"Well, I'm here for you if you need anything." Cody smiles at me. "Anytime. I mean it."

I really do have such good friends.

WILLEM

From afar, I glare daggers into the man-bun-wearing fool. I lean against the car, watching as he flirts with my fake girlfriend, reaching over and touching a lock of her hair and laughing with her. Does he think because she's claimed that now he has to stake out his territory? Because it looks as if he's trying to pull her into his lap. Penny smiles again, discreetly moving her chair a little farther away when the idiot leans in again. At least it's only one-sided. I'd be all kinds of pissed if she had a secret paramour . . . And then I frown at myself. Why does it matter? I just need her for casting, to be my power source. There's nothing personal about it.

Still, I don't like how friendly that man is. I glare in his direction as he throws his head back and laughs.

"So you and Penny, huh?" A woman moves past me, slapping a wet sponge on the hood of Penny's car. "I hope you realize how amazing she is."

I turn to glance at the woman washing the car. She's there with two small children, probably her brood, judging by the looks of them, and they're all rubbing sponges on the car itself. "Yes, she is my girlfriend," I state, using modern terms. "You are . . . ?"

"Katrina," she says cheerfully. "This is Kitty and this is Billy."

She gestures at the children, as if I care. "I've been part of the Fam for fifteen years now, though we just moved here last year."

"The Fam," I echo.

"Society of Familiars," she tells me. "The Fam. And Penny's a great catch. You're lucky to have her. I've never met someone with such get-up-and-go." She chuckles, shaking her head as she moves the soapy sponge over the car. "Not like that, Billy. Wash. Don't just spread the dirt around." Katrina squints up at me, lines creasing the corners of her eyes. "Lots of the guys kinda keep an eye on Penny."

"Yes, I see that," I say, voice dour as I glare at the man bun in the distance.

"Hell, I'd probably flirt with her a little myself, but I've already got a wife." Katrina chuckles at her joke. "So how'd you two meet again?"

"Work," I say, my gaze locked on Penny. She's still talking with Man Bun, but another fellow—this one with a curly beard—has just arrived and is chatting with her, and she's smiling up at him with that big, broad smile that takes over her entire face.

"Work?" Katrina asks. When I don't answer, she clears her throat. "Warlock dick must be special dick indeed."

"Mommy, that's a bad word," Kitty whispers.

"Mommy can use adult words," Katrina corrects. Instead of letting it die, the woman keeps talking to me. "If you don't mind me asking, you two don't seem like a fit. What made you fall for Penny?"

I turn and glare at the woman. She's dressed in a faded pink T-shirt, and her fried blond hair is pulled into a loose ponytail. She looks tired and weary, and strangely depleted. I compare her to Penny, who practically bubbles with vitality. Again, I'm surprised that another warlock or witch hasn't scooped her up if this is what the pool is to choose from locally. Man buns and soccer moms. "Penny fell for me," I say arrogantly. "I'm quite a catch."

"Mmm, yes you are." Katrina's voice turns purring. "You let me know when you get free from your ban. I'd be happy to work with you."

Alarmed, I step away from the car as she moves closer to me. Is she . . . hitting on me? Are all these lonely familiars oversexed? Dear Jove.

Penny is going to owe me so many spells by the time this "date" is done. I step away from the car, stalking toward Penny's seat. "If you'll excuse me, I have to go rescue my girlfriend."

✳ ✳ ✳

WE STAY AT the car wash for two more hours, until the sun grows hot overhead and Penny's energy visibly droops. I empty my wallet, tossing the dollars into the till, and loudly proclaim that I'm taking my girlfriend home. If anyone's going to drain her energy, it's going to be me and not a bunch of nitwits at a car wash. I keep a hand at the small of Penny's back as she says her goodbyes to the group and save a special glare for Man Bun and his bearded buddy.

I drive, since Penny is yawning and I want her to conserve her energy. "I'm sorry," she tells me. "I didn't realize I was going to get that sleepy."

"You're my familiar now," I snap. "It's going to drain you until you get used to it."

"Are you in a bad mood?" she asks, puzzled. "What happened?"

"Your Katrina hit on me," I enunciate, disgusted. "And the men were flocking around you like vultures."

Penny chuckles, leaning back in her seat. "Yeah, that was a little unexpected, but I shouldn't be surprised. I'm dating a warlock. In their eyes, I've suddenly hit the big time. I'm surprised no one asked me if your semen tastes different than regular semen."

The car swerves as my hands jerk on the wheel. "I beg your pardon?"

"Everyone wants to know everything," she continues. "Especially about sex. All the familiars speculate if it's different or not with a witch or a warlock. I mean, I get why they're asking."

I shoot her a look. "Why would it be different?"

"Because you have magic," she emphasizes, as if that explains everything.

"So these horny fools are, what, imagining that I'm ejaculating glitter and toadstools? And they think that's why you're with me?" I'm appalled. Here I thought apprentices were just quietly waiting for a witch, and they're these incredibly horny creatures. I give Penny a speculative look, then decide I'm not going to ask.

Penny giggles. "I mean, I don't think you're jizzing glitter, no. But I did get asked several times if we're casting together."

I'm not too surprised at that. "And what did you say?"

"I said you're in retirement and I have never seen a single mushroom in the bedroom."

I relax a little. "That's not funny."

"It's a little funny."

"Semen tasting different, indeed. I don't know where they got that idea." Is that why Katrina was giving me such intense scrutiny? Do familiars just start strange rumors about warlocks simply because they're bored?

"So it doesn't?"

"Doesn't what?" I frown over at her.

"Taste different?"

"How the fuck would I know?"

Penny claps her hands, howling with laughter. "Oh em gee, your face is so red right now!" She has a good laugh as I do my best to ignore her, then wipes tears from her eyes. "Seriously, though, is there a difference between witch sex and normie sex?"

"I don't believe in kissing and telling," I say, and I sound stuffy and proper even to my own ears. "Also, I've never slept with anyone that wasn't a witch."

"I'll have to ask Reggie," Penny says. After a brief silence, she blurts out, "Not that we're going to sleep together."

"I should say not." I'm dismayed it even came up.

12

PENNY

I fight back another yawn as I leave work, trying not to wince at the stack of neglected orders on my table. I haven't been able to keep up with things, no matter how hard I try. It's not like me. Vivienne, my boss, chided me on a Zoom call and said she was concerned that I wasn't meeting the needs of the store. I reassured her that I was just under the weather and I'd pick things back up again, but it's the first time I've ever been reprimanded.

I hate it. It makes me want to cry, knowing I've disappointed her.

The thing is, she's right. I am falling down on my job. I love working at CBD Whee! and love my job fulfilling component orders. I love touching all the ingredients and imagining what spells they're used for. I don't want to leave my job, but it's becoming clear to me that being Willem's secret familiar is more draining than I anticipated. The moment I'm home from work, he's meeting me at the door, ready to cast. We've set up a cot in his laboratory, and I crash there most nights because I don't have the strength to go back up the stairs. I'm not even learning anything at this point. It's like the moment he casts, I orgasm and conk out.

Poor Pip hasn't been getting much of me lately. I bring his cage down to the lab with me and Willem hasn't objected again, but I feel bad that I don't have the time to cuddle him while watching TV like I normally do.

As for Willem, well, he's thrilled. So far he's still "practicing," he says. He claims that he's rusty and wanting to get his thoughts together, so most of the spells we've been focused on thus far are scrying spells. He watches people through a crystal ball, muttering to himself and making notes.

That's been my week so far, and now it's Wednesday again and it's society night, and for the first time in forever, I don't want to go. Groaning, I lean my forehead against my steering wheel and wonder if I can tell everyone that I'm not feeling well. But that'll lead to pregnancy rumors, and that's the last thing I want. Bad enough that I'm dating a warlock and everyone's going to be all over me the moment I show up at the meeting.

With a sigh (that turns into a yawn) I pick up my phone and text Willem.

> **PENNY:** I had to work late to catch up on orders and tonight is SoF night. I won't be home until late. Can you go upstairs and let Pip out of his cage and throw in some nuts? I would really, really appreciate it.

Before I can put my phone down, he's texting me back.

> **WILLEM:** You're not coming home?

> **WILLEM:** I wanted to scry tonight.

I grit my teeth.

> **PENNY:** I told you we'd have to work around my schedule. Tonight's busy. I'm sorry. Please feed my squirrel?

No response. Why am I not surprised? If there's one thing I've noticed, it's that Willem is very focused on Willem and nothing else. We don't get along in the slightest. Everything turns into an argument, and he treats me like I'm a nuisance. He hasn't even introduced me to the staff at his house, telling me that it's not their business. That makes things so damned awkward if I need to wander around the house . . . Not that I have, because I am usually passed out.

Annoyed, I drive over to the regular meeting hall. It's a business meeting room we've rented out at the same hotel for years now, and when I head inside, I'm a little surprised to see that the meeting is absolutely full. Anyone that's a member seems to be here tonight, which throws me off. They're also early. "Oh, hi, everyone," I say, putting on a bright smile. "What an excellent turnout."

I go to my normal seat and pull out my laptop, making a log of all attendees. I'm a little irked to see that Cody has picked the seat directly next to mine, even though he's not an officer.

"If everyone can please quiet down, we'll start the meeting," Derek drones. His monotone voice lets me sink into the task of taking the minutes, and between that, I check off names in the attendance logs. I love busy work, and I pay attention to the meeting with half an ear, making sure that I note down anything important.

The car wash raised $800 for Abby, and I'm thrilled, even though I know most of it was Willem's money. Abby can use it, though, and Willem doesn't need it. He's made it quite clear that he's loaded. We discuss other fundraisers and when annual dues are needed.

"Now that we are discussing the car wash, can we say congratulations to one of our members? While she's not an official familiar, our lovely Penny Roundtree is officially dating a warlock."

Everyone claps, and I look up, startled. They're congratulating me on my boyfriend? All eyes are on me, though, and I shouldn't be surprised. I'd be eager for gossip if someone I knew was dating a witch, too.

"I got to meet him on Saturday," Katrina calls out, drawing attention to herself. She gets to her feet and gives everyone a smug look, enjoying the limelight. "He's very fancy. You can just tell looking at him that he's got money and breeding. He carries himself differently than the rest of us."

Oh god. I hope this doesn't get back to Willem, or his head is going to be enormous.

"He said Penny was special." Katrina nods, beaming at me. "That he'd never met anyone like her and he needed her around him constantly." She clasps her hands over her heart. "And the way he just looked at her, like he wanted to eat her up with his eyes."

He . . . did? That doesn't sound like Willem in the slightest. Maybe he had indigestion.

"So how did you two meet?" calls Abby.

I wet my lips nervously. "Through work. He needed a special order and I . . . helped him with it." I shrug. "We argued and . . . here we are."

A ripple of laughter moves through the group. I smile, feeling awkward, and then a leg nudges mine under the table. "You can do better," Cody tells me, his voice low and hushed.

Oh. Uh. This is awkward. I give him a friendly smile. "You're sweet, but I'm very happy with Willem."

Someone else in the audience stands up. "So is the sex different?"

Yikes. Maybe Willem's right and everyone is totally oversexed here at the Fam. "Oh em gee," I exclaim. "You don't really expect me to answer that, do you?"

More laughter, but at my side, Cody doesn't seem to be laughing. This is just getting more awkward by the second.

"Now, now," Katrina calls out. "A good familiar never kisses and tells on her warlock."

"He's not her warlock," Edgar corrects. "He's her boyfriend."

"*Retired* boyfriend," I pipe up, because this is getting way too close for comfort. My neck feels hot and my skin is prickling, my heart racing. Surely no one's going to guess what we're doing this quickly, are they? I want to touch my cuff and reassure myself that it still looks and feels like a society one, but I don't dare. It'd be a dead giveaway. "He's retired. And we're not discussing the kissing."

Why is it I'm suddenly thinking about how he kissed the top of my head and how perfectly I fit against Willem? It was all pretend. When I get home, I'm going to have to deal with a cranky warlock who wants to scry and is annoyed that I have a life other than him and his whims . . . but the pretend boyfriend Willem at the car wash was rather nice.

Luckily, someone brings up a rival at a nearby chapter who recently got tapped to be a familiar, and all discussion turns to that. Relieved, I go back to taking minutes and updating logs, my head down for the rest of the meeting. Before I even realize it, the meeting is over and Derek bangs his gavel on the table, startling me.

"Drinks tonight at the Alehouse," Derek calls out. "First round is on me."

God. Normally I love to go get drinks with my friends, but tonight I just want to go home and go to sleep. Then again, it's not like Willem is going to let me go straight to bed, either, but at least I'll be one step closer to sleep. I slowly put away my notes and laptop while everyone files out of the meeting room, laughing and chatting. I'll wait until the others are gone, and then I'll just slip out into my car and drive home. They won't even notice I'm not at the bar until I'm halfway home.

Everyone leaves . . . except Cody and Katrina.

Cody remains in his seat next to me, and Katrina sidles up to us. Uh-oh. I slide my laptop into my bag and pretend to just now notice them. "What's up, guys?"

"We just wanted to talk to you," Katrina says, pulling up a chair and sitting across from me while Cody leans an arm over the back of my seat. "Check if you're okay."

Cody plucks at my sleeve, the touch a little overly friendly. "You just seem a little stressed lately."

I manage a bright laugh. "Of course I'm stressed. I introduced my warlock boyfriend to all my friends, and they're asking if he jizzes glitter. Anyone would get stressed out."

Katrina leans forward, all interest. "Honey, just admit why you're with him. It's obvious to everyone. You don't have to pretend."

A huge knot feels as if it's forming in my throat. There is no way they know the truth. No way. We can't be that obvious. "I don't know what you're talking about."

"It's obvious you're with him because he's a warlock, duh," Katrina says. "You're getting that warlock D so you can climb the social ladder. No one's judging, honey. Certainly not me."

My jaw drops. "You think I'm fucking him for street cred? Are you *serious*?"

Now Katrina looks confused. "Why else would you be with him? He's not very pleasant. The money? He does look like he's loaded." She leans in, her eyes widening. "Does he have a big dick? Is that what it is? He's definitely got big warlock energy, but I could see big dick energy, too."

"Katrina!" I exclaim, horrified. "What the fuck?" I look over at Cody, but he's silent, his mouth pressed flat. "You seriously don't think this, too? That I'm fucking Willem to get ahead of everyone else here?"

Cody gives me an almost pout. "You do have to admit it seems sus, especially when we were vibing."

"We weren't vibing," I practically shout. "I was being *friendly*!" God, why do men suck so bad? Does Cody seriously think that somehow Willem got ahead of him in the (nonexistent) line to get between my legs, and that's why he's being so weird? How is it that in the space of a week I've gone from the only guy in my life being my absent dad or my squirrel to now swimming in a sea of toxic masculinity?

I snatch my laptop case, only to have Katrina slap a hand down on it to stop me.

"Here's the thing, my friend," Katrina says to me. Her voice is smug, her expression cool, and I get the impression that she's loving being in control of the conversation. Like suddenly she's found power and wants to wield it. "He's a decent liar but you're not. Every time he kissed you or held your hand, you looked surprised. So he might be in it for the right reasons, but you're not."

"You're wrong," I protest, but my face feels hot. She's not wrong. I am a terrible liar. I thought I was doing better than that. I glance over at Cody, but he's just watching me closely, his eyes half-closed and his chair still far too close to mine.

"Like I said, do what you want, but we want in on it," Katrina tells me.

That makes me pause. "Um, what?" I gesture between all of us. "Like, in the same bed?"

"No! God no." Katrina pauses. "Unless he's into that?"

"No! He is not!" I try to wrestle my laptop out of her grip again. "And this conversation is done—"

Cody places a hand over mine, making both of us pause. "Give it up, Penny. We know it's not love between you guys. You're using each other for some sort of mutually beneficial arrangement.

Maybe he gets off on fucking familiars. Who knows. What we're saying is we want in on the transaction."

"There's no transaction," I say frantically. "I don't know what you're talking about."

"Real talk," Katrina says. "Neither Cody nor I are at the top of any sort of familiar waiting list. We're going to be slogging it out in the trenches forever, and I work retail. Cody is tech support. Neither of us are swimming in money." She tilts her head, studying me. "And we don't know any warlocks. But now we know one, right?"

"Okayyy," I say slowly. "Where are you going with this?" I feel like I can't breathe. Panic is racing through me. To think we can't even go a week without being figured out, and now I'm being blackmailed—

"We need you to spy on him for us," Katrina says, exchanging a look with Cody.

Of all the things I expected to hear, that wasn't it. "I'm sorry, what?"

"You spy on him," Cody says. "You give us information about him. Information we can broker."

"Information," I repeat, dumb. "Information about my boyfriend? Like if he wears boxers or briefs?"

"Information," Cody says, leaning in uncomfortably close to me once more. "About him, and if he's casting anything. About his friends. Who he hangs out with. What sorts of things they're casting. You're going to be in higher circles now. You're going to be learning things about witches and warlocks, and that information can be sold to interested bidders."

I shake my head, practically wrestling my bag out of Katrina's grasp. "I'm not spying on my boyfriend, and I can't believe you have the nerve to even ask me such a thing. Now leave me alone."

To my relief, they let my bag go and I snatch it up from the table, clutching it to my chest. I glare at them both as I race out of the conference room and into the main part of the hotel itself.

"Think about it," Katrina calls after me lazily.

✳ ✳ ✳

WHEN I GET home, Willem is in an obnoxiously bad mood. He scowls at me as I head upstairs to grab Pip. "About time. What kept you so long?"

"Someone at the meeting wanted to stay and chat," I call back as he follows me through the house. "I told you we'd have to work around my schedule." I'm shaken by tonight. I can't believe Katrina and Cody did that to me. Worse, they've rattled me more than I'd like. They haven't guessed what we're up to, but they're close, and I don't like it. Still, what can I do? Quit the Society of Familiars? That would send up a red flag right away. The idea is to make it all seem normal, not to throw bull's-eyes on my back. If I get caught, I'll be banned forever. I'll lose my job. I'll lose the goal I've worked for all my life.

"You're my familiar," Willem says grumpily as he stands in the doorway to my bedroom. "We were going to cast, remember? I have someone I want to scry upon."

"Anyone I know?"

"Of course not." He squints at me as I turn, Pip clinging to my shoulder. "Are you all right? You don't seem like yourself."

I smile at him, faking ease. "Why wouldn't I be all right? I'm just tired."

"Is there anything we need to talk about, *dumpling*?" He stresses the pet name. "Some sort of festivity we need to attend to satiate the unwashed masses?"

"Are you offering?"

"Absolutely not."

That makes me chuckle. "Then don't bring it up. And no, I'm fine. Really." I decide I'm going to ignore Cody and Katrina. They're bluffing because they're jealous that I'm with Willem, and it's not as if they have anyone they can sell information to anyhow. I'm not telling them shit. I'm just going to live my life and not worry about them at all.

After all, if they think I'm dating Willem because he's a warlock, that's not against the rules. It's the casting that's against the rules, and they don't know anything about that, and they never will.

Time to get casting . . . and get another orgasm. My thighs clench at the thought.

13

PENNY

"We've got a buyer," Katrina tells me as she slides into the seat next to me at the next week's society meeting. She gives me a self-satisfied grin. "A buyer that wants any sort of information you can leak to them."

I give her a frantic look, flipping open my laptop so I can pretend like I'm preparing to take notes for the meeting, which won't start for another fifteen minutes. "Who?"

"That's secret. All you need to know is that you need to provide good, solid updates and we'll get paid a grand a week."

Katrina really expects me to sell out the man I supposedly love for a grand a week? Split three ways? "I'm not doing it. I love Willem."

She moves my hair off my shoulders, examining my neck. "For a pair of lovebirds madly into each other, you don't have any hickeys on your neck."

I brush her hand away, glaring. "Willem is old-fashioned."

"Or he's a phony. All I'm saying is that you can feed us information. It doesn't even have to be about Willem, though our source prefers that. They want good, credible details about the local warlocks and witches. If we give good information, we'll be bumped up the list. Did you know that right now I'm thirty-second nationally? I've been in the society for fifteen years, and I'm still freaking thirty-second," she hisses, a look of frustration on her face. Her eyes well with tears. "Do you know how many familiars were taken on this year?"

"How many?" I ask, though my gut is clenching. I upload data to the Fam national database. I know these numbers.

"Three. At that rate I'll be a familiar by the time I'm fifty-five. Maybe. Cody is sixty-seventh, and you're forty-fifth."

I wince, staring down at my laptop keys without seeing them. Forty-four people in front of me. I do quick math—almost fifteen more years of waiting. I'll be forty-five. The wasted years yawn ahead of me. Fifteen more years of stuffing magic components into envelopes for others. Fifteen years of running society meetings and doing car washes and bake sales and getting nowhere while I wait for my chance . . . and that's provided that the witches in need of familiars go down the waiting list. Some insist upon a certain type of familiar. Some want a guy. Some want someone young, or someone with a particular education. It could be even longer.

Both of my parents had to wait nearly twenty years, and they were lucky. I'll be waiting even longer.

I swallow hard, my feelings a mess. This justifies me working with Willem, even if it goes against every rule in the book. It's not fair to be forced to wait forever just because you weren't born to a witch or a warlock house. You were born into the bloodline, but not the right bloodline. It's unfair. "It sucks," I tell Katrina. "I know it sucks. But there's nothing I can do—"

"You can help us," she says, grabbing my arm tightly. "You can help us secure spots for ourselves! Sell information on your sugar daddy. I know you're not in love with him."

"It's wrong." I jerk out of her grip. "Just quit it! Leave me alone! I love him!"

"You need to play along," Katrina snarls back at me, grabbing my arm and giving me a smile with too many teeth. "I know you think you're so smart, but we're on to you, all right? You need to do this with us, or it won't take much for me and Cody to start a couple of rumors about you guys. That you were seen wearing a familiar cuff instead of this ugly thing." She grabs my wrist and shakes it, indicating the familiar bracelet. "He's not gonna be too fond of you when everyone's breathing down his neck for breaking the rules, and you're gonna be bumped even farther down the list."

My stomach churns and I break into a cold sweat. "That . . . that's not true."

"It doesn't matter if it's true." Katrina's face is hard and un-yielding, all pretense of friendliness gone. "All we need to do is start a few rumors, and suddenly everyone's going to be looking hard at you two. After all, it sure is strange that a warlock banned from having a familiar is suddenly dating one, you know?"

I hate that Willem is right—I never should have stayed in the society. I should have come up with some reason why I couldn't attend. Quit my job, pretend to leave the country . . . something. Because all of this is terrifying me. Katrina is absolutely right that all she needs to do is hint that we're pretend dating and everyone will be watching us too closely. Our plan will be ruined, and I'll be banned from ever practicing magic.

Nervous sweat pouring down my face, I take several deep breaths to calm myself. It's either that or throw up in Katrina's face. "You're all wrong about us," I whisper, and a new idea comes to me. "You want to know why I'm with him? It's not for magic. He's paying me to have his baby. That's why we're together. You can sell that information, all right? Just leave me alone. Please."

It's an absolute whopper of a lie.

I sell it, though. My pale, sweaty face absolutely sells it. Katrina's eyes widen, and she gives me a speculative look and then laughs. She wags a finger at me. "I knew there was something fishy about your relationship. It all makes sense now."

I put a finger to my lips, glancing at the door as other people wander into the meeting room. "Just . . . keep it between us, all right? He wants it to look like we're really together." Oh god, if Willem finds out the truth, he's going to straight up murder me. I've just told everyone he's paying a stranger for a baby, and I have no idea how weird that will seem for warlock society, which is hyperfocused on bloodlines. "Let's keep it quiet for the baby's sake."

"Just you, me, Cody, and our benefactor," Katrina says with satisfaction. "This is a good, juicy start." She rubs her hands together and gets to her feet. "Get us something new for next week, all right?"

"Wait," I call out as she heads away. "I'm not doing this, remember?"

She's not listening to me, though. She heads straight for Cody and sits down at the back next to him, and I can see them whispering together. I pull a bottle of water out of my bag and sip it nervously as Derek arrives and takes his seat at the head of the meeting room. When they both grin at me, I feel worse. I've just made the situation even messier.

Now they think I'm legit with Willem, at least. The downside? They think I'm being paid to have his baby. And I've got to come up with some sort of new gossip for them next week, or I have no doubt the threats are going to continue. Feeling sick, I get to my feet, my head spinning.

Derek looks over from the speaker's podium, frowning at me. "We're just about to call the meeting to order. Sit down, please."

I shake my head, staggering to my feet. "I need to use the

bathroom. Right now. I'm going to puke." That'll sell the baby thing, I suppose. The terrible thing is that I'm so anxious I really do think I'm going to puke. "Give me five minutes—"

I can barely get the words out of my mouth and take a step away from my chair before the ceiling in the room crashes in.

14

WILLEM

Penny's late again.

I glare at the clock on my desk, then restlessly check a few warlock message boards. I'm starting to really hate Wednesday nights. She's always exhausted after her meetings, and they keep her out far too late. I know it's selfish of me to want to monopolize her time, but everything between us is still very new. I've yet to shake all the dust off my casting muscles, and I worry I'm doing something that's paining Penny. Every time I cast, she looks uncomfortable and makes strange noises, her breathing strained. She says she's fine, but I'm concerned. If it hurts her, she can't work as my familiar . . . and yet I desperately need a familiar right now. I have to ensure that my wards around the house are strong at all times.

I keep thinking about the bird that Stoker left as a warning in my mailbox. The box is warded now so he can't leave any more messages like that, but he doesn't have to. I'm aware that he knows where I am, and he's testing the limits of where my wards have been cast. He's going to continue to poke and prod at me like a sore tooth to see where things flare up.

Which means I need to stay ready for him to retaliate over his books.

Which means I can't if my damned secret familiar keeps avoiding me.

My irritation continues to grow as the minutes tick past. Penny can't stay up late, because she has to keep her fulfillment job, and while I find it inconvenient, I do admit that I like the ability to send her texts of components I need so she can bring them home. She wants to visit her friends for "Friday-night cards" in a couple days, and she made me promise I would go so we can continue to "sell" our relationship. I don't like the idea, but I do agree we need to be seen together as a couple in order to keep up our cover story.

The garage camera chimes, indicating movement, and I click onto the program. Penny's car shows on the monitor, and I resist the urge to jump to my feet in relief. Having her is an opportunity I can't squander, and as I leave my study, I clutch the written list of spells I want to perform tonight. If we can get started right away, we should be able to clear three spells before Penny loses her energy. I can shore up with my own, but she's my reservoir for a reason.

Straightening my jacket, I smooth a hand over my hair and cut through the house, heading for her. She wanders into the kitchen, setting her keys down on the pale marble countertop. There's a dazed expression on her face.

"It's about time," I snap as she pauses at the counter. "I've been waiting on you."

"Sorry," she breathes, and doesn't grimace or make faces at me for scolding her like she normally does. Nor does she smile. She always smiles at the thought of casting, even though she's tired.

Narrowing my eyes at her, I approach, studying her face. She looks completely distracted, and there's an odd scent clinging to her that I pick up on as I approach. There's a strange pale powder in her hair and on her shoulders, and a scratch on her cheek. I dust off her shoulder with a flick. "What's this mess?"

Penny blinks slowly and looks over at her shoulder, thoughtful. "Oh. I believe it's plaster."

Plaster? "In your hair?"

Wide-eyed, Penny nods at me. "I think I almost died tonight, Willem."

She whispers the words fearfully. It strikes a chord of fear in my gut. "At the meeting?" When she nods, I grab her by the arm and haul her toward my laboratory, where I have a permanent obfuscation spell that will prevent spying ears from hearing anything we say. "Follow me," I say. "And then I want you to tell me everything in great detail."

My familiar is silent as I lead her down the stairs, my grip tight on her sleeve. I half expect her to protest or complain about her squirrel, but she's utterly silent, which tells me that she's far more rattled than she's letting on. I feel helpless, but I also know what lightens my spirits when I'm frustrated and down. I steer her toward the chair next to my workbench that's become more or less "her" chair. Penny sits in it weakly, shoulders slumping. I snag a blanket from the cot down here and immediately wrap it around her shoulders. "Wait here, actually. I need to retrieve something from upstairs."

She puts a trembling hand to her forehead and nods.

I race back up the stairs, grabbing a carton of milk and an entire plate of the fresh-baked cookies the chef service left out for me. I head back downstairs with the food and drink, and set them in front of her. "I want you to eat several of these and wash them down with milk. I have one more thing to do."

I head back up the stairs, and my mind races as I go to her bedroom. She's going to ask for her damned vermin, and holding the creature always seems to make her feel better, so I head into her room and grab the cage by the ring at the top. The rodent immediately fusses at me, chittering and pitching a fit. "Yes, yes. Shut up already. You'll see her soon."

I carry the cursed creature through the house, heading down to the laboratory once more. When I get there, I see Penny hasn't eaten the cookies or drunk the milk, but she does perk up when I bring the cage toward her. "You brought me Pip?"

And she promptly bursts into tears.

By all the gods, not more tears. There's nothing I dislike more than tears. I grab a cookie and shove one into her hand. "I told you to eat."

Penny pushes it into her mouth, sniffing, and then opens the rodent's cage. It immediately climbs into her arms and chitters at her, and she feeds it another one of the cookies. "You're being really kind to me. Thank you, Willem."

Am I? I'm just trying to ease the distress that her misery causes me. Flustered at her response, I button and then unbutton my jacket. "Yes, well . . . just tell me what happened."

She finally takes a sip of milk and hugs the squirrel to her as the creature turns the cookie in its tiny hands and nibbles on the corners. "It was so weird. We were about to have our meeting, and then I got up to use the restroom. The moment I did, it was like the ceiling caved in. The hotel staff said it was just a freak accident. Some sort of weakness in the ceiling or something. The scariest thing was that it fell apart just over where I was sitting. Nowhere else." She shudders. "Needless to say, the meeting died a quick death."

I rub my mouth. "That doesn't sound like a coincidence."

"It doesn't?" Penny looks up at me.

A piece of plaster has worked its way to the front of her bangs, and I absently pluck it from her hair. "No. It sounds like a classic curse. If it happened right after you got up, my assumption is that it was a spell designed to go off the moment you left your seat. One intended to frighten but not kill."

At least, I hope that's the case.

She tilts her head, confused, and automatically picks up another cookie, taking a healthier bite. "But none of the familiars that go to the meetings know how to cast. Even Ben Magnus's classes aren't showing them more than the basics of how spells are put together and things they might be asked to do for their witch. No one I know would be so cruel, would they? They said they were going to wait for my answer."

"I don't think it's one of the society," I admit, and then pause. "Wait, what do you mean by your answer?"

"What do you mean by you don't think it's one of the society?" Her eyes go wide. "Why would a witch target me? Me specifically?"

Hmm. "Is this a bad time to mention I might have a nemesis?"

"I'd be surprised if you didn't."

"You would?"

She snorts, and I'm glad to hear that small noise, because she's sounding more like herself. "You're not exactly the friendliest man, Willem."

"Mmm." Penny's right. I'm not warm and open like she is. I have a reputation for being less friendly to outsiders than Ben Magnus is, and that's saying something. "I'll tell you about my nemesis, but then you have to tell me what you're referring to when you mention answers."

"You won't like it," she says, her expression woeful.

"And you'll like hearing about my nemesis? Doubtful." I give her a look of scorn. "It sounds like we both need to come clean so an instance like tonight doesn't happen again." I nudge another cookie toward her and then take one for myself. "Did you notice anything out of place when you arrived at the meeting? Was anyone there before you? Did anyone cast or bring foodstuffs with them? Any strangers in the audience?" She shakes her head to all my questions. "So it's possible that the spell was either cast upon you or cast upon a location that someone knew you would be at regularly. Either way, it means that if it's who I think it is, he's aware of your connection to me."

Penny grimaces.

"What?" I ask.

"So our situation? Our you-and-me situation? It's messy." Her snub nose wrinkles up, and I refuse to find her expression charming. Absolutely refuse. "And it's getting messier by the day."

"So someone has found out that you're my familiar?" I watch her closely. "You're not sneezing, so you didn't tell anyone."

"I wouldn't. I made a promise and I intend to keep it." Her hand strokes down her squirrel's back as she watches it eat. "I want this. I want to learn magic. I don't want to wait fifteen years or more to move up the ranks. I'm tired of waiting for life to happen."

I completely understand that craving. Didn't I say the same things to Stoker when he plucked me from obscurity after my father's untimely death? I was willing to do anything to become a warlock and to gather power for myself. Anything at all. "I know," I say, keeping my tone low and gentle, because she's stopped crying and I don't want the waterworks to start up again. "That means that someone is targeting my paramour instead of my familiar. At least we have that edge."

"Paramour?" Her lips twitch.

"I prefer that term to 'lover.'"

"You could call me your bae," she offers.

"I don't even know what that means." I look down my nose, giving her my best quelling look.

But she only scratches her squirrel's ears as the rodent crawls off her knee and heads for the plate. Penny grins at me, a genuine grin that takes up her whole face, and the sight of it relaxes the tight, tense knot in my gut. "You're amazingly old-fashioned, aren't you, Willem?"

"I see nothing wrong with that."

"Can I call you Willie instead of Willem?"

"No." I give her a look of distaste. "I forbid it."

"Will, then?"

"Here's a wild idea," I say dryly. "How about my full given name, Willem?"

Penny purses her lips at me. "Fine, whatever. So someone's out to kill your paramour."

"Correction. Someone's out to frighten my paramour. If they wanted you dead, I can assure you that having a ceiling collapse over you is a very bizarre way to do it." I pause and then add, "Plus, death spells are generally not answered by the gods. They're considered very poor taste."

"Well, thank goodness for that!" Penny chuckles, plucking her squirrel off the plate and ignoring his chitters of protest. She sets him in her lap again, adjusting the blanket around her. "Okay, so someone's trying to scare me. Mission accomplished. Why would they do that?"

"He's sending a message to me, I'm afraid." I lean against my workbench, crossing my arms over my chest. "There's an old master of mine who has waged a campaign of scare tactics and petty spell mongering against me just to try and make my life miserable. He likes to remind me that I can't get away from him, that his hate for me is eternal. That I'll never be free of him, and that he'll always be around to destroy me by inches."

Her expressive eyes go wide. "Oh em gee. Seriously?"

"Yes, seriously. Why would I lie?"

"I don't understand. Why does he have such a hateboner for you?"

A laugh barks out of me. Hateboner? A charmingly appropriate bit of linguistics. She watches me, waiting for an answer, and I'm not sure how to sum up the relationship between myself and Stoker. How do I explain that I viewed him as a father, only to realize he viewed me as a bug that needed to be squashed repeatedly? That I trusted him with my life only to find out that he was constantly tearing me down in front of others as well as in private? That he shredded my self-esteem and made me think I was nothing and it took me years to figure it out?

But she wants an answer of some kind. "It's a very long story."

"Go on."

"He was my first master. I apprenticed under him when I was sixteen, five full years before I was of age. It's against warlock law to take a familiar that is underaged, because we're considered too young to make the appropriate decisions when it comes to casting. But I was being harassed by creditors. My father had recently passed and had spent the family fortunes on gambling. I was going to be a pauper, and no known warlock or witch would house me until I reached my majority. My father had a bit of a reputation for being unlucky, and being the suspicious lot we are, no warlock wanted a Sauer under his roof."

Penny reaches out and touches my hand. "I'm sorry about your father. That must have been hard for you."

I'm surprised at her sympathy, more so because she looks as if she genuinely means it. I grunt my thanks and continue. "A warlock named Ebenezer Stoker offered me an avenue. He agreed to pay off all of my father's debts and allow me to keep the family estates, as long as I agreed to be his *sanguis vitae*, his magic pool. His familiar, but in secret. He would show me the basics of casting, and I would be debt-free. I thought it was the best of all worlds, and so I quickly agreed."

"But there was a catch," Penny guesses, hugging her squirrel to her chest.

"There's always a catch," I agree. "Always." And I tell her about Stoker's manipulations. How he maneuvered himself into paying off my father's debts but had the estates put in his name. How he drained me of my magic constantly so he could cast and showed me no magic in return. How if I was weak and couldn't keep up with the casting, he would beat me to "improve my strength." How he would build me up with his words and then tear me down the moment I failed him. Living with Stoker as his secret apprentice was both the highest of highs and the lowest of lows. He made it seem that if a spell failed, it was purely due to my weakness. He made me feel like I was never enough, that I was stupid and foolish, weak in spirit, and that he was the benevolent one having to put up with my uselessness. Just talking about him makes my shoulders stiffen with old, remembered discomfort. I hate Stoker. I hate him so powerfully that a knot forms in my throat when I say his name. I hate that he would beat me for transgressions and make me glad for the beatings, because then I knew I would be forgiven, that I wasn't going to be kicked out and cast away.

"Gaslighting," Penny murmurs, a sympathetic look on her face. "I'm not familiar with the term."

She waves a hand. "Doesn't matter. Go on."

I bite back a sigh. I'm not sure what else there is to say. I could spend hours talking about Stoker's manipulations, how he made me feel unworthy and useless, even as he siphoned my magic from me. "Stoker was a terrible teacher and an even worse warlock. The only thing he truly excelled at was manipulation. I realized one day when an old school friend visited me and commiserated on the loss of my estates that Stoker had stolen my family's fortune out from under us. That he had lied and manipulated me, and after more than five years of this—because of course I'd stayed with him even after I came of age, just relieved to have a warlock to serve— all I had to show for his 'teachings' was a back full of scars and a belly full of anger. I knew no spells. No cantrips. No potions. I was too *stupid* to pick up on what he was trying to teach me, you see. It was *my fault* I hadn't learned these things, not his. But hearing that he'd stolen my legacy was enough to wake me up. I confronted him, and he laughed at me. Said I was an imbecile that had let it happen under my nose. Threatened to make me miserable if I dared to leave him."

"But you left anyhow?"

"I did." The words are bitter on my tongue. "Once I figured out that Stoker likes nothing more than to build you up until you rely on him, and then takes great pleasure in breaking you. I took off his cuff and abandoned him. He's never forgotten it, either. He doesn't like being the one that gets left."

Oh, Stoker was pissed, too. He tried to get me expelled from the Society of Warlocks, only to have my case taken up by Abernathy, who owed my father a favor. Abernathy is old and revered for his knowledge, and so Stoker wasn't able to touch him or take revenge on me. Instead, he resorted to petty aggressions for a long time. It's been slowly escalating in the last century, though. And with the Y2K disaster handicapping my ability to cast, he's gotten braver. Now when Stoker's name comes up, I know I have to be on the hunt for intense curse tablets, spells that could have career-threatening consequences, and humiliation in front of my peers. Stoker never lets anything go, and a few months ago . . . I snapped.

I stole all his books.

It wasn't easy. I watched his schedule obsessively for a year, with a private detective tailing him, since I didn't have the magical means. I found out when he was going to warlock conferences and planned around those. I created a massive curse tablet that was imbued with magic, and suffered through the months of exhaustion it took to create it. Once Stoker left for the conference,

I broke the tablet, negated the wards on his house, and paid a crew of petty thieves to go in and raid the place.

I stole his library out from under his nose. Every boring tome about mushrooms and pharmacology. Every book on spells and components. Latin plays. Old apprentice manuals. Didn't matter what it was about—I took it. Of course, this is why he's hopping mad, but I don't regret it. Sometimes I like to go into my laboratory and just touch the spines of those purloined books, knowing that their loss is driving Stoker absolutely up a wall.

It was worth the months of endless preparation. Months of fatigue-inducing casting that left me limp and pathetic and unable to get out of bed. Absolutely worth it.

"So you left him two hundred and fifty years ago and he's still mad about that?" She wrinkles her nose. "Is this a pissing war? Are you two annoying each other because you can? Willem, I almost had a roof collapse on my head!"

She sounds terrified, and I don't blame her. It's a bold move by Stoker, going after my theoretical girlfriend. "I know. I didn't think he'd act against you. I thought he was merely coming after me. I didn't realize that he'd view me having a personal relationship as something to sabotage."

She huffs at me, her expression incredulous. "Seriously? You didn't think that? What about how he acted in your last relationship? How did he handle things then?"

I'm silent. The truth is, I don't have relationships. I've had paid paramours in the past, courtesans that would agree to stop by, sate my needs, and then go about their business. I've never had a "girlfriend," as they call them in modern times. I'm not a likable man. Women don't fall for me. "There are no prior relationships for him to have focused upon. I have always dedicated myself to my magic."

Penny blinks slowly at me. "Are you a virgin? I mean, it's cool if you are. I'm just curious."

"I'm not a virgin. I have simply preferred more transactional relationships in the past."

Realization dawns on her face. "Aaaah. Okay. I mean, I've hit it and quit it before, too. Doesn't matter." She chews on her thumbnail, thinking. "But if I'm the first woman you've lived with, then of course he's going to be all over that. He's going to think you're in love."

"Then he's a fool." My ears feel hot as her gaze flashes to me. It occurs to me that I might have offended her, and I hastily add, "Not that you're a bad choice. You—"

Penny waves a hand at me, thinking. "I know what you mean. I'm not your type."

Frowning, I study her. She's not my type. Not in the slightest. But that doesn't mean she's unattractive or impossible to like. "That's not—"

"It's okay." She scratches at her squirrel's ears absently, the beast curling up in her lap, now sated on my cookies. "So, all right. Your old boss has held a grudge against you for a really long time. Did you recently do something specific to make him angry, or were you just your normal charming self?"

I'm relieved she's taking this so well, though it could be a delayed reaction. She might panic tomorrow. "I might have broken into his house when he was at a warlock conference."

Her brows go up.

"And I stole all his spell books." I wave a hand irritably. "But that's no reason to try to kill my girlfriend."

The look she gives me tells me I am an idiot.

"He's to blame," I retort. "Not me. He's the one that's been carrying this petty grudge against me for two hundred and fifty years."

"We'll talk about assigning blame later. For now, we have to assume he's hella pissed because you stole his books. Have there been any other instances of him swiping at you recently? Or is my attack out of the blue?"

"Out of the blue."

Her smile turns into a grimace. "Maybe we're wrong, then. Maybe it was just a freak sort of occurrence and he didn't have anything to do with it."

I shake my head. "I'm afraid it reeks of him. Plus, there's the fact that a dead bird was left in my mailbox—one of his signatures. Plus Abernathy said that he'd scried and trouble was coming my way."

"When were you going to tell me *any* of this?" She looks furious. "If he finds out what we're doing—"

"He won't. He can't move against me directly. It's against the warlock code. Nor can he instigate my death. I don't think he wants to anyhow. I'm too much fun to torture." I give her a faint smile. "In a way, attacking me indirectly is his hobby. I just counter him and keep an eye out and go about my life."

"Until recently," she reiterates.

"Correct." I allow myself a small grimace. "Until recently, when I snapped and broke into his house and stole a priceless collection of spell books. That might have pushed him over the edge of propriety."

She gives me a slightly disgusted look. "Do you have any allies? Other than Ben Magnus?"

My second master, Abernathy, comes to mind. But Abernathy plays his own games. He's more straightforward, but also less willing to join a fight. He's far more interested in books and knowledge, and if something becomes too complicated, he simply walks away. He's on my side, more or less, but he won't lift a finger to help with the situation. "I don't need any allies."

"Boy, you're impossible," Penny mutters. She shakes her head, stroking the squirrel, which snuggles tamely on her lap. "So what now?"

"This is why it's important that we scry," I remind her. "Information is crucial in our line of work. Knowledge is power. As long as we stay ahead of him, he can't touch us."

She flinches. "Oh no."

"Oh no, what?" I arch a brow at her. "Is this part of what you were mentioning?"

Lifting her hand, she makes a pinching motion in the air. "A little. I've got a problem with the Society of Familiars." She bites her lip and then gives me a guilty look. "I might have told them that you hired me to have your baby."

I bark out a laugh. "I'm sorry, *what*?"

"I can explain!" Penny launches into a retelling of the meeting, of how both Katrina and Cody are trying to blackmail her into giving them information about me that they can sell to another warlock in exchange for some sort of imaginary step up on the food chain. I'm amused, actually. It's not an entirely terrible idea, but they're going about it all wrong. Information is definitely transactional among witches and warlocks. We're secretive by nature, so finding out another person's coveted spell or secret component they use to ensure success? That's a gold mine. But selling random information on the internet? Foolishness.

As Penny continues talking, I'm pleased at her loyalty. I haven't been the most pleasant of masters to her, and yet she never considered betraying me for even a moment. Her sinuses are clear without a hint of a sneeze, and her expressive face makes it obvious that she was insulted that they thought she would turn on me. I don't know why that pleases me so very much, but it does.

"We're not fooling them," she admits, rubbing her neck. "Katrina checked me for hickeys and said if we were madly in love like we were supposed to be, that I'd have love bites of some kind. That I'd blush more when I talk about you. And I'm not a great liar, so I kind of panicked. I denied it all, of course, but she thinks I'm with you to social climb. So I said instead that I'm being paid to have your baby and that's why I'm living with you and why we're a couple."

I laugh again.

"I mean, come on. It makes sense," she protests. "That kid would be hella magical. And it explains why we're not as gaga over each other as we should be."

And here I thought we'd done an admirable job pretending.

She winces when I go silent after laughing. "Are you upset?"

"No, actually. I'm thinking." I consider all the angles. "This could work, you know. If they say they have a benefactor that wants them to feed them information about me, it could very well be Stoker. Since I'm aware of the situation, we can carefully craft a false narrative. You can give them the 'secrets' they're demanding, and we can both remain safe and secure, knowing that whatever they're leaking is absolute bullshit."

Penny manages a small smile in my direction. "Okay."

"As for you and me, we'll just have to step up our game." The more I think about this, the more I like it. "If they're not convinced of our dating, we'll just have to go further to persuade them."

15

PENNY

I study my dress in the mirror, getting ready for a Friday-night date with Willem.

This is such a weird moment. Maybe that's why I'm nervous. That, and the fact that I have dreams that involve ceilings falling on my head. But it feels like I'm about to go on stage tonight, and I'm not sure I like it. I'm anxious and jittery. As part of our "performance," we're going to go have dinner at a popular gastropub that's owned by a local witch. After that, we're heading over for Friday-night cards at Nick's place. Nick is Reggie's old roommate, and his boyfriend should be there, as well as Reggie and Ben. I'm bringing Willem, who doesn't know the first thing about playing, but it's all part of appearances. If someone asks Nick or even Reggie if they've seen us acting like a couple, they'll be able to answer yes. Anyone scrying on us will see us loved-up and all over each other.

So why am I so darn nervous?

I smooth my dress again, staring at my reflection. Too much, I wonder? It's a baby-blue floral midi that swings into a ruffle just above the knee. The waist is wrapped at my side, and the neckline is cut into a low vee but still casual. It looks like me, but it still looks dressy enough for a date, I decide. Maybe a bit overly dressy for cards but not out of character for me. I slip on a pair of chunky, heeled Mary Janes that match my outfit, snag my purse (my cards already inside), and head out to meet Willem.

He's waiting for me at the base of the stairs, dressed in an olive sport jacket and matching slacks, his collared shirt a creamy off-white. His hair is as gelled down and rigid as ever, and I frown at the sight of him. "You look like you're heading to an office meeting. Don't you have anything more casual?"

Willem glances down at his outfit. "I didn't wear a tie. That's casual, isn't it?"

I bite back a laugh, because for Willem, it is.

My phone chimes with an incoming text, and I grimace. I pull it out of my star-shaped handbag, and sure enough, it's a text from Cody.

CODY: Well?

CODY: You're supposed to feed us information, remember?
We need something to sell.

I give Willem an awkward look. "I'm being shaken down for information about you."

He rolls his eyes. "Your 'friends' are impatient."

"They smell money." I shrug. "Being in the Fam doesn't pay anything." I'm miserable at being their target, but at the same time, I understand it in a weird sort of way. Katrina and her wife fight a lot and don't make much money, and Cody waits tables. And . . . they're blackmailing me, so I'm not sure why I feel a twinge of sympathy for their money problems? I'm a dummy. "So what should we tell them? That I haven't found out anything yet? That you cry when you ejaculate? What?"

Willem snorts with amusement at my words. "Tell them I have

a diary you've caught me writing in for the last few days but you haven't been able to locate it yet. That should keep them busy for a while."

A diary. It's a good idea. "Can I tell them you cry when you write in it? And *then* you ejaculate?"

To my surprise, he throws his head back and laughs. It feels ridiculously good to know my attempt at stupid humor amuses him. I like that. "Tell them what you like, just hurry. I don't want to spend all night thinking about your blackmailing little Fam."

I type a quick response to Cody about a diary and Will getting emotional (just to season the tease), and then I put my phone on mute.

When I look up, Willem is holding up a piece of jewelry. "Ready for this?"

Nodding, I move to stand at his side, and I lift my hair up with my hands, exposing my neck. This was the product of last night's spellcasting. It's a tiny amulet on a chain, and if someone's scrying on us while we're out, it'll get warm against my skin to let me know. I hold my breath as Willem's fingers brush against my nape, sending shivers up my spine. It reminds me that I came as he was putting the finishing touches on this necklace, and now as I wear it, I'm going to think about sex constantly. Heck, I'm thinking about it right now. "Are we sure it'll work?"

"Positive." He finishes with the clasp and, to my surprise, squeezes my shoulder, his thumb brushing against my neck again. My body responds immediately, and I feel flushed and warm. After our big conversation, I feel like I understand Willem a lot more. He's prickly because it's a defense mechanism for him. I understand now why when we start to argue, he escalates and becomes impossible. He's doing his best to push me away because he thinks he deserves to be alone. Stoker messed with his head so much that he thinks he's awful to be around.

But I know that's not the case. Ever since I became his familiar, he's been a pain in the ass, true . . . but his actions have been
ones of kindness. Instead of leaving me to sleep on the floor when
I passed out, he carried me up to bed and then set up a cot for me
in his lab for next time. When he worries over me, he fusses and
pushes cookies and milk into my hands as if they'll solve my problems. He even got my squirrel when I was upset, just to comfort
me, and I know he hates Pip.

In short, he's thorny on the outside and an absolute mush inside. Anyone that knew him for longer than five minutes would
realize this. Maybe that was how Stoker was able to manipulate
him. He saw that Willem had a soft underbelly and attacked it.
But Willem has me now, and we're a team.

He's also still rubbing his thumb against my neck.

"Is something wrong?" I ask nervously, my pulse fluttering.
He's close enough behind me that I can feel his warmth.

Willem is silent for a moment. "It occurs to me that we're selling our relationship, correct?"

I can't guess what's going on in his head. I'm too distracted by
the light hand on my shoulder, the thumb grazing my nape. When
was the last time someone touched me like this? Willem never
has, but I find myself thinking about when he tucked the blanket
around me the other night, his gaze clearly distressed at how dis-
oriented I was. It makes me feel warm inside. Warm and rather
wistful that I don't have anyone in my life who wants to take care
of me like that. "What are you thinking about?"

"Perhaps . . . perhaps I should bestow a few of these love bites
on your neck so we can further sell our commitment to one another." Willem's voice is low and hushed, as if he doesn't want to
be overheard. Which is silly, considering we're the only two in the
house right now. All the servants leave at four, long before I come
home from work.

His words make me prickle. "You want to give me some hickeys?"

"I mean . . . simply to sell the relationship, of course. It would make us seem more committed to one another, do you not think?" A hint of an accent comes out, and his voice becomes more formal. Is he nervous at asking?

His anxiousness seems oddly sweet to me. I turn my head and smile at him slightly over my shoulder. "No, I think it's an excellent idea. Do you want to do it now? Should I keep holding my hair up?"

"Yes. Just stay still." Willem's knuckles brush down my neck and I close my eyes, tilting my head ever so slightly to give him more access. I can't believe I'm doing this. I can't believe I'm about to let Willem Sauer leave hickeys on my neck so we can sell our fake relationship. It seems weird . . . and yet I'm brimming with anticipation. I wonder what his mouth will feel like.

Then there's a gentle brush of his lips over my throat. He presses lightly against a soft spot on the middle of my neck, and then his teeth scrape against my skin.

I gasp, shocked at how good it feels and how it sends a tingle between my thighs, just like his casting does. "Oh."

"Should I stop?"

"No, I'm fine," I breathe. "I was just startled."

He kisses my neck again, and my body is prickling all over with awareness. I'm reminded of each and every spell we've cast, each one accompanied by a pulse-pounding orgasm. Arousal floods through me, and with it, embarrassment. This is my boss. My warlock. I absolutely cannot get turned on by his kisses. This is just for show, I remind myself. He's not interested. He—

Willem makes a frustrated noise.

"What?" God, I sound breathless and horny to my own ears.

"It's not leaving a mark."

"Are you sucking?" I ask. "Make sure you suck." Floor, please swallow me now.

"Sucking. Yes. Certainly." His accent is out again, clipping his words slightly. His hand is on my shoulder again, and then his mouth is on my throat once more. This time, he nuzzles at my skin and I jerk when his mouth clamps down, sucking on my throat. Oh god. Oh god. I squeeze my eyes shut, trying to think about anything other than what's going on, because it has been far too long since I've dated and my neck is sensitive and this is all making me want to climb into Willem's lap.

And that is a Very. Bad. Idea.

Willem lifts his mouth from my skin, leaving a wet mark that feels cool against the air. I shiver, wanting to look over at him. "Did it work that time?"

"Yes. Yes it did." He sounds thoughtful. Distracted. "Should we do another? Just to be certain?"

"Excellent idea." I'm in so much trouble.

His fingers curl against me again, and then his mouth is on my throat once more. It's a spot just below the last one, and when his tongue presses against my neck, I bite back a whimper. Oh, sweet lord have mercy, how is it that these "fake" bites can feel so much better than anything I've felt in a long time? My pulse is throbbing between my thighs, reminding me just how hard I come each time he casts. His teeth graze my skin and my eyes flutter, hot need racing through me. When he lifts his mouth this time, he gives my throat a subtle lick as if bidding it goodbye and then lets me go.

I'm ashamed to say I stagger. Just a little.

Willem clears his throat. "Shall we get going?"

I turn to look at him, and his aristocratic cheekbones are flushed, his mouth reddened, as if he's as affected by our playacting as I am.

"Ready," I manage. How am I going to sit through a dinner at his side and act as if everything between us is normal? The man just tongued my neck, and now my panties are sopping and I can't think straight. If he wants to cast later . . . I'm going to be an absolute puddle.

＊　＊　＊

TURNS OUT IT doesn't take casting for me to turn into an absolute puddle after all. We arrive at the restaurant, and after Willem turns over his keys for valet parking, he takes my hand in his, holding it tightly, like I really am his girlfriend. It turns me into goo, and I want to squeeze his hand and grab his face and kiss him like the oversexed, overstimulated woman I am. It's been a while since I've gotten laid. Maybe that's why I'm struggling to keep perspective right now.

The restaurant is packed, so we stand near the front, waiting for the maître d' to return. Willem holds both of my hands in his and keeps me tugged close, asking about my job and making small talk as if we're two people on a date. He even smiles down at me as he squeezes my hands, and I feel warm and giddy . . . and confused. Willem is my boss. We're working together. Nothing more, nothing less.

I'm relieved when we're seated by a smiley waitress. We're close to the front of the restaurant, visible to the windows outside, and I wonder if that's part of the plan. Our table is a half table with two seats on one side. I think a setup like this is supposed to ensure coziness, but I feel strange sliding in next to Willem. "Can I get an amaretto sour?"

"My love will drink water," he corrects me, and leans over and taps my nose. "Think of the baby. I should like hot tea with lemon, myself."

Shit. I scowl at him as the waitress walks away. "You don't have to pretend when it's just us."

"Au contraire," Willem practically purrs at me. He brushes a lock of my hair back from my shoulder, exposing the sensitive, bitten side of my neck. "A scrying spell can catch anything. How's your necklace?"

I resist the urge to touch it. "Cool. Also, don't tap my nose."

"But it is a charming nose," he tells me, grinning.

A flirty Willem? I'm not sure what to do with this. Was kissing my neck what brought this on, or is it more pretending? If so, I need to take part. I crook a finger, smiling at him. He leans in toward me, and I muss his tidy hair.

He sputters, trying to push my hand away. "What are you doing?"

"I'm being your girlfriend and fixing this. Hold still."

His eyes narrow at me but he does as I ask, and I tousle his red hair into a slightly more modern style. "You really need a woman's touch."

"Do I?"

Willem's voice is so husky and intense it sends a shiver through my body. "You do," I say, pleased at his disheveled look. It's actually quite sexy, like he's lost a hint of his control around me. The thought is so delicious that I have to cross my legs to press my thighs together.

The waitress returns with our drinks and a pair of menus, and he immediately flips to the back. I peek over his shoulder and notice he's studying the dessert menu with great intensity. "You've really got a thing for sweets, huh?"

He gives me a startled look, and I can tell he's embarrassed. He flips the page, going back to appetizers. "I was just . . . perusing."

I nudge him with my shoulder. "You don't have to feel weird about it. I was just asking. Every time I'm sad, you're shoving cookies into my hand."

Willem manages a small smile, flicking back to the desserts. "When I was very young, I had a nanny. She came from a baking family and was convinced that all ills in the world could be solved with a good bit of *Baumkuchen*. I guess it's a habit that's stuck with me."

How sweet. I make a mental note to bribe him with cookies when I know I'll be working late. "I'm not all that hungry. Maybe we'll just have some cake before going over to card night?"

"Cake sounds delightful. We can order two different kinds and share."

I laugh at that. "Can we? Or is this just an excuse for you to get two slices of cake?"

The grin he gives me makes me ache. He leans closer, and for a moment, I think he's going to kiss me, really kiss me. Like just brush his lips over mine and . . . Do I want that? I watch him, breathless. Things between us have been intense tonight, and it makes me wonder if we can't be more than just warlock and familiar.

My necklace pulses hot, and my hand flies to my neck. "Oh. I think we have a bite."

He keeps smiling at me, though it feels a little more forced now. "Someone's scrying on us, then. I knew it. The moment we left the safety of the house, he couldn't resist taking a peek."

"Safety of the house?" I ask, casually picking up my water and sipping it as if this were all normal. "Is the house warded?"

"All around the perimeter," Willem confirms. "I set them up the moment I bought the place. The laboratory has a silence spell on it, as well. No one can hear a conversation that's inside."

That worries me a little. "Can he hear us talking right now, do you think?"

Willem shakes his head. "A scrying spell in a restaurant would allow him to hear all speakers in the room we're currently inhabiting. Right now he is hearing a lot of voices talking over one another. We're safe, but when we get to your friend's house, it'll be different."

"Because only a few people will be talking," she agrees, understanding immediately. "I won't forget. So what do you think his purpose is right now, watching us?" My skin prickles with awareness, and it does feel as if we're being watched from afar. I have to fight the urge to look out the window . . . or touch my pendant again.

Willem shrugs and leans in, tapping the tip of my nose again in that affectionate way. "I imagine he's watching to see how we interact. To see where he can place something that will come between us. Like if we argued in public over who gets to drive, he would probably cast a spell that would ensure that your car would go twenty miles higher than the speed limit it showed, and cast a luck spell that would mean you'd get pulled over. It's small, insidious things that can't quite be traced back to him but nevertheless are completely and utterly irritating."

"So we don't give him anything to work off of, hmm?"

"Precisely." He studies me intensely, and I wonder if he's going to kiss me, this time for show. It won't mean as much, but I'm still awfully curious about what it'd feel like. But then the waitress shows up, and we order cake, and the moment is broken once more.

16

WILLEM

I knew us going out on a date would be too much for Stoker to resist.

The moment we left the house together, I expected him to start scrying upon us. Penny's handling it remarkably well, though. She's telling me a funny story about an order she got at work as we eat our cake and have our date, and . . . I'm actually enjoying myself. I enjoy her company, and after being in her presence for several hours, I don't feel the need to leave the room. She giggles at her own joke, and her nose scrunches up again, and it's just so damned adorable that I want to reach over and kiss her.

I don't, of course. She wouldn't welcome it. But the urge to maul her like some sort of churlish schoolboy has been on my mind all night long. Ever since I gave her those love bites on her neck, I've been obsessing over touching Penny. Over skimming my hands along that dress of hers and hiking up her skirts to grab handfuls of that curvy derriere. Over hauling her against me and leaving her neck absolutely ringed with bites so they would all know just how delicious she is and how hard it makes me when she does that happy smile that makes her all cheeks and teeth. I've grown addicted to that smile.

I'm an idiot.

She's my familiar. I know she is, and I know messing around with a familiar is bad news. That's why it's considered gauche to date one. It's not forbidden, but it is viewed as slightly absurd. A good familiar has to be on call for their witch or warlock at all times, and their energy is given over to their master. The moment Penny was scooped up by some other witch, I'd be expected to take a step back in our relationship . . . provided that she wasn't my familiar. The waters are murky now that we're mixing business with pleasure.

Except we're not. Not really. It's all business, and my head is just twisted around because I mouthed her neck and she made a few soft noises that got me hard. I'm distracted because she smelled clean and fresh and sweet and I want to kiss her even more. I want to tug her into my arms when she nudges her half-eaten slice of carrot cake toward me with a knowing look, as if we're sharing a secret. It feels good to be part of a couple. Far too good, and it's all pretend. I need to watch myself so I don't get all swept up into things that aren't real.

I frown to myself as a new thought occurs to me. Did Stoker cast a love charm on us from afar, perhaps? Is that why I'm so obsessed with someone that's completely wrong for me? Is that why I lie awake at night and wonder what she'd feel like if she was in bed beside me? A love charm would explain everything, and the thought's a disappointing one. Of course the attraction I'm feeling isn't real. He could have spelled her to seem like she's enjoying my company, when everyone in witch society knows that I'm an absolute nightmare.

When we return home, I'll scry and look for castings, I tell myself. Abernathy has notes on how to pick up residuals, and I should be able to see if she's been affected by some sort of enchantment.

Penny immediately snags my hand as we leave the restaurant and drive over to her friend's apartment. I'm unfamiliar with the game, but everyone greets me with knowing smiles and teases Penny, as if they're pleased she's found someone. Nick and Diego seem like a nice enough couple. Both of them are athletic and friendly and have zero knowledge about witches, which is obvious from the conversations. Penny declines her own chair and instead sits in my lap as if we're an old married couple. Maybe it's a test, but I take her up on it. I slide my arms around her waist and rest my chin on her shoulder and watch her play, and . . . it's fun.

I can't help but notice that both Ben and Reggie (who are playing cards as well) keep giving us curious looks. Penny ignores them, and I do, too. I also can't help but notice that when my chin is on Penny's shoulder, I can see straight down the front of her dress, past the tiny amulet, and into what looks like an intense bit of cleavage. I shouldn't look . . . but I do anyhow.

After all. I'm supposed to be her boyfriend. I gave her love bites all over her neck. I shared a fork with her at the restaurant. Surely I can peep at her lovely skin just a little.

Not that I should be noticing that it's lovely. Or that she fits perfectly in my lap, or that her hair smells fresh and clean and I have to resist the urge to bury my nose in it. I'm a warlock. She is my familiar. I remind myself of all the reasons, and yet it's difficult to concentrate on the card game, even when Penny is doing her best to show me how to play.

After the most recent round of cards, Ben Magnus gets to his feet, unfurling all six and a half feet of his massive body. He moves to the refrigerator and gets out two beers, then holds one out to me. "Come on. Let's go take a break between games."

I glare at the IPA bottle he holds out as if offended. "I don't drink craft beer."

"You do tonight." He nods at the front door to the small apartment. "Hallway?"

I consider that. Clearly Ben wants to know what's going on, but if I speak to him in the hall, there's a very good chance Stoker will be able to overhear it, especially if the building is quiet or deserted this time of night. "Outside," I say, and gesture at the balcony. "If we must."

"Oh, we must." He hands me the beer and gives Penny an apologetic look. "I'm going to borrow your boyfriend for a few."

"Okay!" Penny gives me a bright smile and kisses my cheek, then musses my hair again before she gets up out of my lap. "He looks cute tonight, doesn't he?"

"Adorable," Reggie announces, and I can feel my face heating. Surely Penny doesn't truly think I'm "cute." She's just play-acting for her friends, and I'm fool enough to be absurdly pleased by it.

With two fingers, I hold the beer that Ben gave me and follow him out to the balcony. Outside, it's dark, the sounds of traffic filtering through the city. Nick's apartment isn't in a particularly scenic part of town, and we have a lovely view of a trash-filled alley. I hold my beer by the unopened neck and stare out. "Ah yes. I can see why you wished to come out here. Truly spectacular."

Ben leans on the railing, taking a swig of his beer as he looks over at me. There's something different about him recently, I realize. It's not his clothing—he still insists on wearing nothing but black sweaters and jeans as if no other color is allowed to touch his skin. It's not his too-long, shaggy black hair, which scrapes his collar or his equally long face. There's something in his demeanor. He looks . . . relaxed. Content.

Happy.

I resist the urge to curl my lip at the thought.

"You want to tell me what's going on with you and Penny?" Ben asks.

I eye our surroundings. "Do you suppose someone could cast a scrying spell that could zoom in on this balcony?"

He arches a brow at me and then looks around, thinking. "Only if they were nearby, I suspect. If you mean a vague sort of scrying spell from a distance, no. This would be considered citywide. Outdoor versus indoor."

Then it's safe to talk. "I'm not sure where to start. Things are a damned mess." I hand him the beer I have no intention of drinking. "What do you want to know about first? I feel as if I've aged a lifetime in the last week or two."

Ben squints at me, holding his beer to his lips. "How about you start with Penny? I noticed the marks on her neck and the fact that your face was practically in her cleavage." His gaze lingers on my mussed hair. "And . . . that."

I run my fingers through my stiff hair, trying to smooth it down again. "Penny is a problem. Not with the casting, of course. So far she's a surprisingly good familiar. Very attentive."

"Even though you want to murder her," Ben retorts.

I glare at him, because perhaps I'd texted him about such a thing a while back, but things have changed since then. "I am no longer feeling violent toward her, though she is still insufferably cheerful." I shake my head, gazing out at the awful view of Dumpsters and alleys and a lone flickering streetlight. "The problem is the Society of Familiars. They don't believe that she's moved in with me because we're in love. Shocking, I know." I shrug, scuffing at a mark on Nick's balcony with my shoe. "They told her to spy on me. To get information about me or any other witch I gossiped about, and they'd sell the information to any buyer they could. She declined, of course. Her loyalty is commendable."

"Penny's a good sort," Ben says, then takes another drink of his beer.

"So they switched to blackmail. Penny told them she's being paid to have my child instead."

Ben spews his beer over the edge of the balcony. "I'm sorry, what?" The frothy liquid drips from his mouth, and he gives me a shocked stare. "Your child?"

"It did shut them up," I confess. "But the love bites and the . . ." I gesture at my lap and then at my hair. "It's all part of the act."

His brows go up. "It's a pretty good act. You two were believable in there." He pauses. "And you think Stoker is targeting her suddenly?"

I say nothing. If I tell Ben that I've stolen Stoker's vast library, he'll be furious that I took Penny on as an apprentice, all the while knowing that my mortal enemy would make a move at some point. In hindsight, it was poor judgment on my part. I just assumed, as ever, that relationships outside of magic—children, paramours, family—were not to be touched.

Then again, when has Stoker ever respected a boundary?

Even so, I can't tell Magnus the reason behind Stoker's fury. So I go with the old nugget of our long-term animosity. "He does like me miserable," I admit with a tight smile. "Chasing off my first relationship in a long time would be one way to do it. Other than pettiness, though, I'm not sure why he'd target her. She's innocent. For all that he knows, she's a random bystander. It's not like a witch or a warlock to attack someone that they have no quarrel with, and I don't think Penny could ever quarrel with anyone."

Well, except me. She frequently argues with me when I'm trying to cast a spell. She even broke one of my curse tablets on purpose once, determined to get the upper hand on me. It used to make me crazy, but I'm starting to look forward to her fiery commentary and the "are you sure you're supposed to use that much mushroom oil" snipes.

"You're sure he's actually targeting her?"

I nod. "When she was at her society meeting, she narrowly missed having the ceiling collapse on top of her. And then tonight at dinner, I picked up a scrying spell."

Ben doesn't look happy. "You need to end this pissing war between the two of you."

"And how am I supposed to do that when I'm not allowed to cast and defend myself?" I snap. "Are you going to step in, Magnus? Take him down on my behalf?"

"You know I can't do that. I'd love to help, but I've got Reggie to think about and you've got far too many enemies. If I went after everyone that had a problem with you, I'd be attacking all day."

I snort, amused. "You're putting a lot more faith in my ability to tick people off than I am. Besides, most of my grudges have been settled, more or less. I had to eat a lot of crow when I got banned from taking a familiar." I'm still bitter after twenty years, but I suspect I always will be. I don't like conceding defeat.

Ben just shrugs. "Penny's a good girl, and she's innocent. She doesn't deserve to get caught up in your bullshit."

I cross my arms over my chest, irritated that he (of all people) is lecturing me. "You should have thought of that before you volunteered her to be my secret, illegal apprentice, shouldn't you?"

He grunts. "Point taken."

PENNY

Willem's mood seems a bit sour after he returns from having a beer with Ben. I'm sure Ben gave him a "dad" sort of speech about our relationship, if I know Reggie, and I think it's sweet. I like that my friends are wanting to see me safe, even if it's from a fake relationship. I sit down in Willem's lap again, making myself comfortable, and his arms go around my waist. I don't know why I'm doing it. Ben and Reggie know we're faking it. Nick and Diego are a big pair of sweethearts and wouldn't mind if I sat *next* to my boyfriend while we played cards. But no, I had to shove myself into Willem's lap. Maybe since we're with my friends, I'm trying to assert my dominance? Or maybe I'm just feeling weird from the neck nibbling earlier?

Either way, I half expect him to shove me off his lap, but he just wraps his arms around me like I belong there, and I like it too much to get up. I'm tempted to fuss with his hair again—that would be a very girlfriend thing to do—but I don't want to make his mood worse. We stay at Nick and Diego's for a few more hours, and then I start to yawn.

"I've been keeping Penny up late recently, and I'm afraid I need to take her home," Willem says, his voice oh so courteous.

"Gross, man. You didn't have to go TMI on us like that," Diego teases.

I giggle. Willem turns almost as red as his hair as he realizes how his words are being interpreted. I snag his hand in mine and give it a squeeze. "It's all right. I like late nights with him. So . . . next week? On again?"

Nick nods, slinging his arm around Diego's muscular shoulders. "Your turn to bring snacks and drinks. Sound good?"

"Perfection," I sing out, and hug everyone one last time while Willem waits by the door. "Will and I will see you next week!"

We're in the car before he corrects me again. "Willem," he mutters under his breath. "My name is Willem."

"I think Will is better. Sweeter. It sounds more intimate between us." I yawn again, wondering if he's blushing in the darkness. It's late. Most card games go on until past midnight, but I've been a party pooper lately. "I'm sorry I don't have the stamina for casting tonight. I thought seeing friends and introducing you to them would help make this thing between us seem more normal."

"It's all right." Willem's look over at me is concerned. "Are you feeling well? Do we need to slow down? Have I been too hard on you?"

It's the first time he's ever expressed concern over my ability to keep up in a genuine, friendly way. Not in a "you're disappointing your boss with your ineptitude" sort of way. It makes me feel warm and soft inside, and I feel the strangest urge to reach over and tousle his hair again. Just because. It's probably got a lot to do with the constant spellcasting orgasms, but hey. "You just want me to succeed. And you're ready to cast a jillion things again. I get it."

He stares out at the road, his expression thoughtful. "Yes, but thinking about my old master makes me realize perhaps I'm not the most lenient of teachers, myself. He demanded a lot from me, and it filled me with despair when I couldn't keep up with his punishing schedule. It made me feel hopeless. Unworthy. I don't want you to feel the same."

That warm feeling grows. "You're sweet."

Willem huffs with laughter. "I can assure you, I truly am not. I just know I can be an impatient arse. I hope you understand I don't mean anything ill by it."

"I know." I reach over and put my hand on his knee, giving it a squeeze. I just feel like someone needs to touch him in this moment. To reassure him that he's really not as bad as he thinks he is. That he can be prickly, but I understand what's behind it. That I think it's incredibly sweet that he's trying to reassure me.

He stiffens, and I realize just how personal a touch my hand on his knee is. I immediately jerk away, face flushing. What is wrong with me? If someone like Cody had put his hand on my knee, I would have flipped out. Sitting on Willem's lap doesn't give me carte blanche to just manhandle him. Embarrassed, I turn to stare out the window at the nighttime city.

Willem clears his throat. "Just so you know what Ben and I were talking about, he thinks we should set a trap for Stoker. Snare him and catch him casting against me. He'd get sanctioned for sure."

"What happens if you're sanctioned?"

"Well, for starters, they take away your familiar." His laugh is bitter. "More than that is just frosting on the cake."

Right, because he was sanctioned. I chew on my lip, thinking. "If we're not supposed to get caught casting, how do we set a trap for him?"

"Once I figure it out, I'll let you know."

I'm relieved when the car pulls into the garage. Tomorrow is Saturday, which means I don't have to work. There's a Fam mixer this weekend, but it's easy enough to bail out on that. I'm looking forward to staying home for a couple days and just sleeping in. Maybe cast a few spells with Willem. Maybe he'll let me take the lead on one or two. Yawning, I follow him inside the house, my eyes growing heavy with fatigue. "So what did you think of my friends tonight? Nick is such a jock, but he's really—"

My words cut off as Willem places a hand over my mouth. He pulls me against him, his body stiff and alert. "Someone's broken my wards."

He whispers the words, and all the hairs on the back of my neck stand up. "What's that mean?"

"It means that my house is spelled to let me know if someone breaks in, and someone just did."

Willem holds me in place, gazing out at his empty, austere house. It seems undisturbed, and I pull his hand off my mouth to ask a question when we hear footsteps upstairs. I suck in a breath and look over at him. He grabs my hand and races toward his media room, dragging me after him. When he flips the switch and opens the secret panel that leads to the laboratory, I get it. We're going to hide.

He hauls me into the narrow tunnel and then swings the door shut behind him.

I breathe in huge gulps of air, alarmed. "Why—"

Willem covers my mouth again, hauling me back against him once more. My back presses to his front, and he leans in and murmurs in my ear, "We don't know how many people are breaking in. If they've broken one ward, they might have broken others. We need to stay quiet."

I nod, worried. It's dark in the hall with the door closed, and the lab isn't lit below. There are only the sounds of our nervous breathing, and Will doesn't seem as if he's going to let me go anytime soon. That's fine, because feeling his presence against me in the dark is comforting. If his house is being raided by warlocks or their apprentices, I can't do anything against them. He can't, either—he's not supposed to cast. If he did, I imagine the sanctions they'd level on him next would be far more intense than just taking away a familiar.

There's a scrape overhead, and Willem makes a frustrated noise in his throat. "They're in your room."

"How the heck are we hearing them down here?"

"Wards."

Of course it's wards. Magic. Naturally. "Pip," I hiss, terrified for my poor squirrel. "Do you think—"

"He's fine," Willem reassures me. "There's no reason they'd take him, and most don't do animal sacrifices anymore. He's looking for something else." But he doesn't let go of me. He keeps me locked against his chest, and I wonder if he thinks I'm going to bolt out of here.

Animal sacrifices? I bite back a whimper. If he says I don't have to worry, I won't. Pip will be fine. He will. I try to breathe deep, but I just end up whimpering again.

"I know," Willem murmurs against my ear. "It's going to be all right."

Strangely enough, hearing that does make me feel a little better. He rubs my arm in a reassuring sort of way, too, and I relax. We hear a few more scuffles, then some low voices talking as they head down the stairs. I count two distinct tones—both men—but there could be more. Willem's arm remains tight around my shoulders, and when all goes silent, we remain where we are in the darkness.

"Should we go out?" I ask, whispering.

"Not yet. We don't know that they've left. They might be returning for some reason."

"Why my room?"

His chin moves against my hair in the dark. "I wish I knew.

For whatever reason, Stoker and his goons have decided to target you. Once we know it's safe, we'll go up and cast to see what's been disturbed."

I lick dry lips. Okay, that sounds reasonable. We'll be able to figure out what they're up to (hopefully), and then we can prepare after that. Until then, we just sit and wait until we're comfortable that they're gone. "Should we cast?" I ask, because I feel I should throw it out there, just in case. "I'm tired, but I can manage."

"No." He rubs my shoulder again, his hand big and warm through the fabric. "If he's setting up some sort of ward of his own and we cast anything worth a damn, it'll go off, and he'll have enough to take me in front of the Council of Warlocks. We just need to wait this out." He rubs my arm again, and his thumb grazes my skin. "Can you manage?"

I nod, leaning back against him. I'm just tired. I would have thought the adrenaline of someone breaking into my room would be enough to keep me awake, but being wrapped in Will's arms in the darkness is actually really soothing. Combine that with my fatigue and I don't think I could move a muscle, even if I wanted to. "This Stoker guy really doesn't like the thought of you having a girlfriend."

Will's chuckle against my hair is low and heated. "No, no he doesn't."

"You think he saw me sitting on your lap?"

"Mmm."

I don't know if that's a yes or a no. For some reason, I'm thinking of my hand on his knee in the car and how he'd stiffened. He hadn't looked offended.

Will's hand slides from my mouth down to my neck, and his fingers trail over my skin, sending goose bumps over my body. Oh. Oh. He rubs the side of my neck with the pads of his fingers, the touch delicate enough that I wonder if I'm imagining it. "Are you sore here?"

I have to bite back a moan, but a noise slips out of me anyhow. My neck is incredibly sensitive, and him holding me against him as he grips my throat? It's far, far too sexy and oh so slightly controlling.

"That's not an answer, my familiar." His voice is soft and dangerous against my hair, and I could swear his lips brush along the curve of my ear.

"Not sore," I manage. His fingers stroke my neck again and I tilt my head, giving him silent access to anything and everything he wants to touch. "It feels good. I like it."

Will groans, and then he lightly nips at one of my earlobes. I whimper into the darkness, lost in a spiral of heat. God, that's amazing. When was the last time someone touched me like this? Actually, I take it back. No one's ever touched me like this. Like I'm a possession. A beautiful, fragile possession that has to be played with and teased. I love this.

And when his hand slides down the front of my dress and presses between my thighs, I moan with need.

"Shhh," he murmurs, and then his teeth score my ear again. "You have to be quiet."

I nod, frantic. "I'll be good."

I don't know why I just said that. Why I volunteered to be "good" even as he's holding me by my throat and teasing my ear. It just felt right . . . just like the hand that rucks up my skirts feels right. Just like when he finds my panties and pushes them aside, only to tease along the seam of my pussy with his fingers.

It feels more than right. It feels downright amazing. I moan again, and this time, his hand moves from my throat to cover my mouth. His lips are hot on my ear, and his fingers glide through my folds. Will's breath hisses as I spread my legs a little for him, and I know I'm wet. So very wet.

He groans low against my hair, pinning me in place as his fingers dance over the most sensitive part of my body. I thought he'd go straight for my core and start finger-blasting me like most guys do, but he doesn't. Instead, he trails his fingers up and down through my folds, and when he finds the bump of my clit, he pauses there and begins to trace little circles around it, as if figuring out what I need.

The breath hisses from my throat, and then I'm squirming against his hand, desperate for more sensation.

Will nips at my ear again. "Tap me on the arm twice if you want me to stop, little familiar."

Stop? I will lose my damn mind if he stops. I want him to keep going. So I press my hand over the one he's got in my panties and help him rub. He lets out a guttural sound, and then he's rubbing the sides of my clit harder, in just the way I like. I bite down on one of his fingers, rocking my hips against him. He whispers my name, working my pussy more expertly than I could have ever imagined, and it takes me no time at all to come. The release is hard and swift, and I make a keening sound behind my teeth as he keeps teasing my clit, not stopping even when I quake with my orgasm. In fact, he doesn't stop until I push his hand away, and then he lets out a little huff of amusement, as if I'm the bossy one.

I slump back against him as he nips at my ear again, then presses a kiss to it. I feel boneless and soft, and I'm drifting on pleasure. A physical orgasm under his touch feels different than the spellcasting ones, and I decide that I like the physical one more (though I certainly wouldn't turn down the others). I don't care that my panties are soaked or that one of my legs is cramping up from the strain of my release. It just felt so damned good that I want to float for a while.

"I think they're gone," Will eventually murmurs against my ear. He's still holding me, one hand on my belly, one caressing my face.

Oh.

Oh. I've forgotten completely where we are. Our dangerous situation. Apparently all I need to forget about everything in my life is a bit of ear nibbling and a really good pair of fingers against my clit. Jeez. "Should we go see what damage they did?"

"Mmm."

I'm going to assume that's a yes, as Will lets me go, and I have to hold on to the wall to stay upright. My knees are weak and wobbling, and I'm not sure I've ever come so hard, not even when he spellcasts. He opens the door a crack and peers out into his media room, then opens it wider and offers me a hand. "Come on."

I slip mine into his. It occurs to me that I have no idea where we're going with this thing between us. That fake dating is different than fingering in a shadowy nook. I'm not even sure the guy *likes* me half the time. Then again, it is just a bit of foreplay. Sex doesn't have to be a big deal if you're in the right mindset, and I did say I wanted a bit of adventure in my life.

That definitely qualified as an adventure, all right.

Willem leads me through the house, his steps slow and deliberate. We pause a few times, listening in, just in case someone shows up, but there's nothing. He heads to the front door and growls with irritation at the sight of it, the locks broken off and the wood splintered. "They didn't even bother to use magic. They just burst in like common thieves."

"Maybe they *were* common thieves?" I ask, curious. "Are we just assuming it's involving magic?"

He gestures at the expensive art on the walls, the delicate vases and statues that decorate his cold-feeling gray house. "If they were thieves, they missed everything obvious."

"Laptops?" I ask. But I know it's a long shot. We came through the media room, and nothing in there was disturbed. These men had a purpose, and stealing electronics or priceless art wasn't it. When he shoots me a look, I nod. "Maybe I'm just hoping for a simple answer."

"Oh, the answer is simple all right," Will says bitterly. "Stoker."

He shuts the front door and then snags my hand again, heading for his study. I'm not surprised to see that it's been trashed—every book has been pulled from its place and opened up. Torn pages litter the floor, and I remember what Will said about how he'd stolen Stoker's books. Stoker clearly is looking for them. But Will only grunts at the sight before him, as if amused, and then tugs on my hand, leading me up the stairs.

We head to my bedroom, and I'm relieved when Pip immediately starts to chitter indignantly. I drop Will's hand and race inside, freeing my poor squirrel from his cage. He immediately climbs up my arm, his little claws digging in, and then proceeds to scold me in squirrel-talk, digging into my hair and flicking his tail madly. I'm just so relieved he's all right that I don't even care. I pull out some of his food and scatter it on the table, then kiss his tiny head a dozen times. "It's okay, buddy. I'm here."

"Nothing looks disturbed," Willem says, drawing my attention back to him.

I glance around my room. Sure enough, the bed is still made, my clothes are hanging neatly in the closet, and even the paperback I have on the nightstand has my fuzzy unicorn bookmark sticking out of it, just as I'd left it. "I don't understand. Were they looking for something and they didn't find it? Or were they trying to kidnap me?"

"We need to scry. I don't trust this."

Shit. I don't, either, but I brace myself, nodding. "Down to the lab, then?"

I follow after him, trying to ignore just how tired I am. Post-orgasm, all I want to do is pass out, but I know that's a bad idea. If they've booby-trapped my bedroom, we need to know about it. I can sleep soon, I pep-talk myself as we head back downstairs. Soon. Soon. Soon. By the time we make it back to the lab, my eyelids feel heavy, and the word "soon" is a drone in my head. I plop down on my stool as Will moves to his table.

Instead of racing around to get components, though, he leans on the edge of the workbench and eyes me. "I know you're tired."

"I am," I admit, yawning. I give him a weak smile.

"But I need you to concentrate. Who would you cast to in this situation?" He gives me a focused look. "For a scrying spell."

Oh. That wakes me up a little. "Are you asking my advice?"

His mouth twists in a wry smile. "Of course not. I'm trying to get you to think it through on your own. You wanted to learn, right? So learn."

Do I have to learn tonight, though? At one in the morning? I rub my face, thinking. "Well, Mercury is the obvious one, right?"

"Let's say Mercury hasn't been answering our spells lately. Who else would you request a divination from?"

I blink, considering. It never occurred to me that we'd need backup gods, but of course you do. One of the things that's hammered into my head constantly by him is that the gods can be fickle. Maybe they don't like your offering. Maybe they're just tired of working with you. Maybe they don't like the way you say an incantation. There could be any number of reasons why they just don't answer you, and you can either take that answer and try again later, or you can try a different god. So I try to think of who else would be useful. "Maybe Apollo? He's the god of oracles. Or, um, Fortuna?"

"Not Fortuna," Will corrects, but his tone isn't mean. "She's best when you need luck on your side. Apollo isn't a bad one, but there are more appropriate gods to pray to. Vesta, for example, who is the goddess of hearth and home, and since mine has been violated, she might be amenable to helping out."

"Oh, okay. That makes sense."

"Let's try Vesta, since Mercury is the obvious choice and Vesta might be getting a little less traffic."

I nod, and when he looks at me expectantly, I get to my feet. "You want me to pick out components?"

"What would you use to contact Vesta?" he asks, curious. Will leans against the table, watching me. "Show me. You're knowledgeable with all kinds of components. What would you use to entice the goddess of the home to answer your prayer?"

Even though I'm tired, I'm having fun. It's thrilling, knowing that he's leaving this in my control. I head to his rows and rows of components, all shelved in watertight containers, all neatly labeled in alphabetical order. I don't know where to start. I glance back at him. "Is it wrong to want to consult a book?"

"It is never wrong to brush up on your knowledge," Willem tells me, and the look he gives me is one of approval. "You should honor the gods with an appropriate spell rather than casting something that might offend them."

Pleased, I grab one of his spell books from its place on the wall and return to his side. My eyes are tired, and I rub them as I flip through the pages, looking for Vesta-oriented information. And when I find the appropriate page, I bite my lip and look over at him. "This says augury and haruspicy."

"Augury is out," he agrees. "I'm not proficient in the deciphering of bird patterns, and I don't want to wait to figure out if one is trying to shit on my clothes or if it truly has a message." He shakes his head. "And haruspicy is out of practice now."

"That's . . . entrail reading, isn't it?" I swallow hard. "I don't think I'm a big fan of that."

"It's showy, but it's also a gods-damned mess." He shakes his head, flicking the book ahead several pages. "If you'll keep reading, you'll notice that Vesta—who is represented by flame—is honored with offerings to the hearth. We can create a fire and honor her by sacrificing some of our favorite foods to show our commitment."

Oh, thank goodness. "That sounds much better."

"You should have kept reading," he chides me, nudging me with his shoulder.

I give him a bleary stare. "Will, I am so tired I am about to fall over. You're lucky I'm able to read at all."

His expression softens as he gazes down at me. "Of course. I'll handle it. I just wanted you to be able to participate. I didn't want you to think I was . . . monopolizing things." He turns his attention to the book and runs his finger over the page, as if concentrating, but his ears are red and I can tell he's embarrassed. "I don't want you to feel you're not getting anything out of our partnership."

Is he panicking because he thinks he's going to turn into Stoker? Is that why he's letting me take charge right now? "You're nothing like your old master, and I would love to have a more hands-on approach in the future. Just maybe not right now, when all I want to do is sleep?"

"Of course." He buttons and unbuttons the front of his sport coat, a nervous twitch I've been picking up on. "I'll handle this. You just . . . close your eyes and relax, all right?"

That, I can do. I return to my chair as he heads upstairs to get food, and I'm not entirely surprised to see he returns with cookies and milk. I watch as he tosses a bit of tinder into the ceramic offering bowl, builds up a fire, feeds the cookies in one by one, then adds a sprinkle of milk. He opens up another spell book and begins an incantation, and I can feel the spiral of pleasure curling in my belly as he casts. His voice raises as he invokes the goddess, asking for guidance, and the louder he gets, the more turned on I get.

When the spell floods the room with the indolent, heavy feel of magic being worked, I come all over again, unable to resist making a small sound as it quakes through me.

That catches Will's attention. He gives me a sharp look. "You all right?"

I nod, biting the inside of my cheek so hard I taste blood as the pulse of pleasure rolls through my body, my legs tight and cramping with the heat of it. "Just . . . peachy."

He looks as if he wants to say something more, but the fire in the offering pot flares high and then immediately goes out. Will dumps out the ashes onto the top of the worktable, and they immediately fall into a pattern. It's a square, I realize . . . a square with legs. And another square at the top.

My bed.

I whimper. "What's he doing to my bed?"

"Excellent question," Will murmurs. "Stay right here, Penny. I'll be right back."

As if I have the strength to go anywhere? It occurs to me that I left Pip alone and unsupervised, and he likes to chew. I should get up and check on him. I should accompany Will into my room to see what the goddess is pointing out for him. I don't do any of that, though. I slump in my chair and try not to pass out. One orgasm made me drowsy. Two is just unfair.

I mean, they were both really, really good orgasms, but now I'm exhausted.

I must have drifted off, because the next thing I know, Will is touching my arm, a look of concern on his face. In his hand is a phallus-shaped sculpture wrapped with what looks like a twine mess of leaves and feathers around the base. "What the fuck is that?"

"This," Will announces, "is what was under your bed. This is what they broke in to leave behind."

"The world's creepiest-looking dildo?"

"It's a fertility charm," he says, flipping it on the side so I can see the word written along the shaft of the dildo. "Fecunditas. Someone apparently wants you to have a baby."

"Should we . . . thank him? I guess?"

Will tosses the thing aside and leans in toward me. "You're not listening, Penny. Someone told him you're having my baby. That means your friends are speaking with my old master. I find it difficult to believe that he would leap to the pregnancy conclusion on his own."

"Oh." I pause as the implications hit me. "Oh shit."

"Exactly." He rubs his chin, thinking. "Now we need to figure out precisely why Stoker wants you to have my baby. If he thinks it's something I'd want, he would do everything in his power to prevent it from happening. But the fact that he's throwing out a charm and breaking into my house to set it? There's something more afoot here, and I'm not sure what it is." He glances over at me. "I don't like it."

"Me either. My bed feels violated." Just thinking about lying in bed again with the dildo from hell under it makes me kind of queasy.

Will shakes his head. "You're sleeping with me until we figure this out."

I'm too tired to even be nervous. I give him a relieved smile. "Cool. Thanks."

WILLEM

Cool. Thanks.

That's all she had to say?

I watch her sleep across from me in my bed. Perhaps I should have volunteered to sleep on the floor, but the moment Penny got into her pink heart-covered pajamas, she was practically comatose. I put her squirrel back in its cage with some extra food and water and then took the cage into my room, just so Penny would have her beloved creature nearby. I even left the door of the cage open in case the thing wants to climb out, because it seems cruel to leave it in a cage all day long.

Truly, I have become soft and weak.

I glare down at the woman in my bed, her dark hair spilling over my pillows. I thought when I got another familiar, my life would go back to normal. Instead, Penny has turned everything upside down with her mere presence. The cleaning staff smirks at me when they see me walk past. I'm arranging my schedule to work with hers.

I'm touching a rodent. Worse, I'm *worried the rodent isn't getting out of his cage enough.*

Penny is all enthusiasm and color and happiness. She talks loud. She uses abbreviations instead of actual words. She's all the things I hate.

And I don't hate her. Not even in the slightest.

Instead, I'm using every excuse possible to get to touch her. She could be in her own bed right now. There's nothing wrong with it. Our scrying showed only the single object . . . but I liked the idea of her being in bed with me. I liked the idea of protecting her. Of being able to watch over her. Of Penny being so close that I could draw her against me while I slept.

Not that I would. I just like the thought of it.

Truly, this "dating" farce has addled my brains. I've had familiars before. I've had at least ten, several of them women. I like to think that I'm a fair master, even if I'm difficult to deal with sometimes, and I always make sure my apprentices learn as much as they can under me, because I know what it's like to have your warlock withhold knowledge from you. Even if I don't get along well with other warlocks, my apprentices have never complained.

I've also never kissed a familiar before. I've never left love bites all over her neck or had her sit in my lap. I've never shoved up the skirts of an apprentice and fingered her in the hall to my laboratory. I've never given much personal thought to my apprentices at all.

Clearly Penny is a problem. I'm no longer thinking about her as a familiar, but as a woman. I keep thinking about the muffled sounds she made as I stroked her wet pussy, and the way her legs clenched and she bit my fingers as she came.

Oddly enough, she'd made the same sort of sound when I cast. I need to ask her about that, if the spellcasting is hurting her. I've heard it works that way with some people, and it's not ideal. Most apprentices that feel the magic too keenly never go on to become full-fledged witches, because they can't handle the casting. That might be why she's never said anything to me. But . . . if it pains her, I want to know.

I don't like the thought of hurting her, which also irritates me.

She should be a means to an end, and instead I'm watching her sleep and taking care of her squirrel like some sort of lovesick fool. I know I should put an end to all of this. Relationships do not turn out properly with me. I'm too damaged, too unpleasant.

Too everything.

I know someone like Penny isn't interested in someone like me. She's caught up in this fake relationship, and maybe she likes the pretending. But for me, it's difficult. It's difficult to have her sit in my lap, with her neck covered in my bites and not . . . want that.

By all the gods, do I want that.

I look over at Penny. In sleep, her animated face is relaxed. There are no nose scrunchings, no wide smiles, no theatrics . . . and yet I like her like this, too. I like her soft and secure and safe in my bed. She deserves better than what she's gotten out of this relationship with me. So far I've gotten a familiar who has an intense wealth of innate magic, and I've gotten to maul her twice now.

And what has she gotten out of this? A ceiling nearly dropped on her head, the world's ugliest fertility charm shoved under her bed, and betrayal from those she called her friends.

I watch her for a moment longer, then get out of bed. The locksmith is coming by at dawn, but I've already cast a portal protection spell over the front door until then from my own pool of magic. It's made me fatigued and given me a migraine, but I can't sleep anyhow, so I get up and head down to my study, where I'm composing a missive to my old master.

Not Stoker, but Louis Abernathy. Perhaps he'll have some ideas on why Stoker is targeting Penny so very specifically.

Surely it's not just because he wants to see her pregnant. If it's something Stoker thinks I want, he'll move heaven and earth to ensure I won't get it.

There has to be something else in play, and I can't help but wonder what it is.

PENNY

Things between myself and Will—I'm not calling him Willem anymore, not after he's had his fingers up my skirt—are weird the next morning. His side of the bed doesn't look as if it's been slept in, and when I go downstairs in my pajamas, Pip on my shoulder, Will takes one look at me and promptly leaves the room.

That makes me feel . . . strange. Like I've done something wrong. Yet he was the one that instigated things between us. I mean, sure, I might have been moaning and rocking against his hand, but he was the one that touched me first. So why is he acting like this now? I fix myself a cup of coffee, nibble on some fruit that I share with Pip, and then head into Will's office to make a nuisance out of myself, because I hate things being left unsaid.

He's working at his desk, typing away on his keyboard with two fingers instead of using all of them. Even on a Saturday morning, Will looks like he's about to head into a corporate office somewhere. Today's sport jacket is a deep maroon (that doesn't look great with his coloring), paired with a black dress shirt. His hair is back to being glued down to his head again. Poor hair.

He glances over at me when I enter and then goes back to

focusing on his monitor. "I'm busy this morning. Did you need something?"

A bit of politeness, I want to snark at him. His ears are red, though, and he looks distinctly uncomfortable. It occurs to me that he's 270, and maybe he's a bit old-fashioned when it comes to sexual stuff. Plus, this is Will, I remind myself. Will whose old master made him think he was absolute crap at all times.

So I give him the benefit of the doubt, because I'm a nice person. "Thanks for bringing Pip into your room. I feel bad when he has to stay in his cage all day and all night."

Will squints at his screen as if it's full of very important things. "Yes, well . . . let us not make it a habit."

"Thanks for letting me sleep in your bed, too."

He grunts.

I'm starting to learn him, though. I know he grunts when he can't think of anything specific he wishes to say except for uncomfortable things. *Feelings* things. So I just study him, wondering how far I should push. "It's not a big deal for my generation, you know."

That gets his attention. He wrinkles his orange brows at me. "Excuse me?"

"Sex. It's really not a big deal for my generation. If you want to hook up, we just need to establish some relationship boundaries. If not, that's cool, too. I just need to know where we stand." I settle Pip in my lap and stroke his long tail. "It's just easier if we set expectations so no one gets hurt."

He's utterly silent. He stares at me, quiet, for so long that I wonder if he even heard me. Then he says, "And what do you think happened between us?"

Will's tone is weird. Tight. I shrug, scratching at Pip's ears. "Bit of diddling in a dark hall?"

His nostrils flare with distaste. It's kind of cute, actually. "Do you know what happened between us?" he says, his voice icy. "A mistake. That is what happened."

I flinch. In a way, I sort of expected the words from him, but they still hurt. "Or we could call it that, I guess."

He turns back to his computer, jaw clenched. "It shouldn't have happened."

Oh, I'm seeing that now. I stare down at Pip, who's snuggling against my pajama-clad legs. "You know, you can just say you didn't realize things were escalating between us and you want to de-escalate. You don't have to be a prick about everything. You can just say, 'I'm not into you like that, Penny.' I'll understand. I'm an adult."

Will stares at me rigidly, silent as ever.

Right. I get to my feet, holding Pip against me, and head for the door.

"Wait," Will snaps. "Just . . . wait."

I turn to look over at him.

"Things . . . escalated and they should not have," he grits out. Then he rushes on. "And speaking of escalations, I am concerned about Stoker and the fact that he sent his goons here to my house to plant a fertility symbol. I'm convinced that he's up to something, but I cannot seem to put the pieces together."

"So you . . . want my help?"

He gives me another cool look. "I've reached out to my former master Louis Abernathy."

Oh. Right. He'd probably be more helpful than me. "What did he say?"

"Nothing, yet. Abernathy eschews modern technology. He's a monk from the Norman Conquest. When one of his familiars retrieves my message, they will convey it to him and he will write me back."

"What, like snail mail?" When he nods, I sputter with a mixture of amusement and horror. "Seriously? Snail mail? To contact a warlock?"

"He'll answer soon enough." Will sounds peevish. "And if you've got a better idea, I'm willing to hear it."

"I don't, actually." Heck, I'm still confused about what happened between us. Calling it an "escalation" and then not explaining to me how he feels isn't exactly making me feel better. Does he hate me? Is he grossed out that he made out with me? What? I want to ask Reggie if Will's hinted at anything to Ben, but I doubt he has. Will seems like the type to keep a tight lid on his shit. "I guess I'll go in to work, then. See you tonight."

I head out of his office and down the hall.

Immediately, I hear Will's loafers smacking on the marble floors. "Wait, what? You're going in to work again? It's Saturday."

"Yeah, and I'm so far behind on orders that Vivi's going to absolutely have my head unless I catch up soon." I give him a wry look. "Those spell component envelopes don't pack themselves, you know."

He pauses, his expression thoughtful. "And . . . you'll return?"

I'm not sure why he thinks I wouldn't return. "Of course. I live here now."

Will flushes, and I have a feeling I missed something very specific. But he just nods at me, turns on his heel, and heads back into his office. Huh.

* * *

I GRAB AN iced coffee from a drive-through and head into CBD Whee! for a day of overtime. There's a stoner kid that works at the storefront on the weekends who vapes all day and makes the place smell like bubblegum. He's nice enough, though, and he knows the back office is off-limits. But when I go in, he's not behind the counter.

Vivi is. And she looks unhappy.

I quake inwardly even as I put on a bright smile. "Oh em gee, Vivi! I didn't expect to see you here this morning."

"Kenneth called in sick," she says in a sour voice. She looks far too intimidating for the tiny storefront. Vivi loves a power pantsuit in a somber color and equally dark lipstick to set off her bright blond coif. It makes her appear regal and slightly menacing at the same time, which I imagine is the look she's going for. "I'm displeased with him. And you've been unreliable lately, so what was I supposed to do?" She arches an elegant brow at me.

Ouch. I step behind the counter next to her. "Well, I can man the desk. I was coming in to finish off the workload that I didn't get to this week, but I can take care of the front, too."

Vivi gives me a long, scrutinizing stare. "Is something going on with you, Penny? You've been such a good employee for years now, and then all of a sudden, you fall to pieces. Do I need to worry?"

I cringe. "Of course not. I just had a bit of a bug the last week or so. That's why I'm behind."

"And the week before? And before that?"

"Food poisoning," I say swiftly. "It really has been a heck of a month, hasn't it?"

"I'm not buying it," Vivi says, and my heart stops. "Do I need to worry about you setting up your own business on the sly?"

"What? Oh my god, no." I shake my head. "Vivi, it's really nothing like that. I swear. I would never cut into your business. I wouldn't even know where to begin." She doesn't look convinced, so I decide to spill a little truth. "If I'm being honest—"

"Please do," Vivi says, crossing her arms over her chest.

"—I started seeing someone." I give her what I hope is a dopey, besotted sort of look. "And we've been getting together and staying up late at night, and I guess I didn't realize how much it was interfering with my work. I'm really sorry, but I don't want you to think I'm working against you. It's just . . . new-relationship stuff."

Her fierce expression softens. She reaches out and squeezes my cheeks like I'm an infant, pinching them. "You sweet little thing. You have a man now? That's wonderful. Here I thought you were waiting for some witch to scoop you up. It's good to move forward in your life. You never know how long it's going to take to get an apprenticeship." She jiggles my face. "Is he good to you?"

The comment about how long it takes to get an apprenticeship doesn't have the sting it normally does. I smile up at her. "He's great. We just have conflicting schedules, and it's difficult trying to figure it out."

Vivi beams at me and then taps my cheek in an almost slap. "Well, figure it out, my dear. My clients are waiting. You'll catch up on orders today?"

"Absolutely."

She lets go of my face and scoops up her purse. "Then I shall head out." She pauses, glancing back at me. "Since we're close, would you like for me to give you a charm of some kind? Male enhancement?" She wiggles a finger at me. "It makes for a fun date night. I'll sell you one cheap."

"I'll think about it," I chirp, knowing I'll do no such thing. "Thanks, Vivi."

With a careless wave, my boss is off, leaving me alone in the store. I sit on the stool and catch my breath, stressed. Okay. I need to stay on top of Vivi's orders, because I don't want her fishing around the whole Will situation. I can't give her any reasons to worry about me. The last thing I need is both Vivi and the entire Society of Familiars up my ass, trying to find out about me and Willem.

Not that we're a thing. Other than a casting thing. I frown to myself, hating that I have to designate between the two. He's made it clear that he's not into me sexually, even though he was the one that grabbed me and fingered me. Maybe it was a power play of some kind and I'm reading more into it. The thought makes me glum. I grab my iced coffee and head to the back room, turning on the wards that will monitor the front of the shop in case a customer comes in. It'd probably be easier to install a bell on the door, but . . . well, witches like to do things their way and I've learned not to argue.

I settle in at my station in the back, pulling out printed requests and gathering components when the door spell chimes a notification. Racing back into the main room, I'm surprised to see it's Reggie. She's wearing an old T-shirt and jeans, and her hair is pulled into a sloppy bun atop her head. "Oh em gee," I say, beaming. "Hey, you! What are you doing here?"

A look of relief crosses her face. "Penny! I didn't know if you were working today, but I had to run a few errands and thought I'd stop by anyhow. This is perfect."

"It is?"

She nods, stepping behind the counter to join me. I don't mind—Reggie and I hang out all the time. "Yes, I'm afraid I've used up all of Ben's mugwort and he wants some for lessons on Monday. I don't suppose you have a supply of it in the back?"

"We have a supply of everything," I promise her. "Come on."

I take her into the back with me, and her eyes grow a little wide at the sight of the stacks of unworked invoices and the envelopes all over the counter. I know what she's thinking. I'm normally so very organized. This chaos is not a normal Penny Roundtree trait. I'm usually the one on top of things, and I just feel awkward and a bit foolish when she gives me a curious look.

"It's been busy," I say defensively. "I'm a bit behind."

"Is everything okay?" Reggie asks, sitting next to the table.

"More than the mugwort, I wanted a chance to talk to you and see how things are going, F-word to F-word."

F-word? Oh, *familiar*. I shrug, feeling a little mopey after my dressing-down from Vivi and Will's cruel indifference this morning. "I honestly don't know. I thought they were going pretty well, but then Will made it clear he wanted nothing to do with me last night after the incident, and I guess I read things wrong."

Reggie's brows go up. "Incident? Did I miss something that happened? Because last night you two were not looking like master and apprentice. You were looking more like lovers."

"Oh." Was that just last night? It feels like a million things have happened since then. "Well, there was an incident in a dark stairwell where he fingered me until I came."

"What?" Reggie shrieks, her jaw hanging open. "Willem Sauer? Tell me *everything*."

I do. I tell her about our date and how we were scried upon, but how it still felt comfortable and fun. I tell her about our plan for the hickeys and how it wasn't supposed to be sexual. I tell her about the break-in and the subsequent making out in the dark, and then me sleeping in Will's bed . . . and then I tell her how cold he was to me this morning.

Reggie has a thoughtful look on her face. She taps her chin with a finger. "I don't buy it."

"Which part?"

"The part where he says it was a mistake and he's not into you. Ben has known him forever, and he says that Willem would never let a girl sit in his lap. That he's never seen Willem act like that with anyone. And last night at cards? After you left? Nick and Diego wouldn't stop talking about how utterly besotted Willem seemed with you. He was practically staring down your dress all night and hovering over you like he didn't want anyone else coming close."

"Yeah, but that's just for show." I shake my head, glum. "He made that very clear this morning."

"Bullshit," Reggie says. "If he was just fooling around with you, he would have planted a hand on the top of your head and tried to get a free blow job out of you. Instead, he made you come. He *likes* you."

My heart squeezes in my chest. "Do you really think so?"

"I do. Ben is convinced of it, too. He says Willem is an absolute boor to everyone. Everyone. And that's to people he likes. Last night he was a different sort. And he couldn't take his hands off you." She raises her brows at me as if to say, "See?"

"But this morning—"

"This is Willem Sauer," Reggie reminds me. "I've never met someone as uptight as him. You think he's going to be totally fine with casually admitting he likes someone?"

"I thought the same thing at first," I admit. That Will's been a little damaged by Stoker undermining him all the time. "I guess I just doubted myself when he rebuffed me."

"Of course you did," Reggie soothes. "Anyone would. They're a jillion years older than us, and so we assume they know a lot more about relationships. Turns out no, they've just had several hundred years to grow shittier in them." She snorts, leaning over to grab one of the invoice sheets. "But I think if you want to pursue something with Willem—something beyond the fake dating—you're going to have to let him know you're interested. You're probably going to have to take the lead."

Normally I'd be fine with that. I'm still stinging after this morning, though. He was so very cold when he icily told me it was a mistake. "And if I'm wrong and he really doesn't want something with me?"

Reggie looks at me from over the edge of the paper. "Curse him with something that will make his balls shrivel off."

I have to admit, I have a good laugh at that.

* * *

I CONSIDER REGGIE'S advice as I pack component orders and sell vape cartridges to walk-ins. It's a lot to think about, and I have a lot to lose if things get weird. What if I hit on Will and he's repulsed by me? I'm not pretty like Reggie. I like ultra-girly things and ruffles and pink. I'm a little doughy instead of sporty. My face might be cute on a good day, but never sexy. A powerful, wealthy warlock—even one as cantankerous as Willem—could probably get anyone he wanted. There's no reason he'd want me other than magic.

And that's another thing. If he rebuffs me again and we still have to work together, that's going to make things really awkward.

So I'm not sure what to think. I need to figure him out. I need to find out if he has feelings for me and is just fighting them, or if he genuinely thinks touching me is appalling and is only doing it for the cover story.

I ponder this, but I don't come up with an answer. How does someone like me, who doesn't have a sexy bone in her body, seduce a buttoned-up warlock that has centuries on her? Maybe I shouldn't ask at all.

Maybe I should just demand.

WILLEM

I pace restlessly around the house all day.

There's work to do—there's always something to investigate and document—but I can't concentrate. It'll be days before I get a response from Abernathy, if I get one at all. He could be deep in his research and won't answer until he feels it's appropriate. If it's never appropriate, well, then he simply won't respond. That's expected, though.

What's making me restless is Penny.

Penny and the breathless noises she made when I touched her. Penny, who I fondled in the darkness like some sort of rutting beast. Penny, who's been unconditionally loyal and giving since the moment she arrived. Who decided to make jokes about what we did in the hall as if it were some sort of lark.

It's not a big deal for my generation, you know.

Bit of diddling in a dark hall?

Not only did her words make me feel foolish, they made me feel old. Out of touch. Far too old and dated for the likes of someone as vibrant as her.

I didn't want to hear her make excuses for me, and so I lashed out. Of course, I'm regretting it now. Even if things become highly awkward between the two of us, I still want her as my familiar. That means any kind of sexual hanky-panky is a rotten idea. I should simply take myself in hand and forget all about the way she felt pressed against me. The last thing I need is a romantic entanglement, not when Stoker is rearing his head and attacking those around me.

The best thing I can do for Penny is leave her alone. Unfortunately, since I need her as my familiar, I can leave her alone in every way except that.

I should ask her to move out, perhaps. While it's convenient to have a familiar under one's roof, if it's placing her in danger and distracting me from my work, it might be wiser to go about this in a different way. Perhaps we could schedule time for casting and work in the time she needs to recover afterward. Maybe Tuesdays and Thursdays, with a bit of extra casting on the weekends . . .

So I storm up and down the main hall, trying to figure out the best way for things to move forward. Hands clasped behind my back, I pace, my thoughts full of Penny and Stoker and the predicament we're in. I'm still not sure why he wants her pregnant. There has to be some sort of advantage he would get if she had my child. Why isn't he against it if it's something I supposedly want? In the past, if I grew close in friendship to a familiar, he would try to bribe them out of my service. If I grew to enjoy a particular restaurant or a blend of tea, Stoker would buy it out. If I purchased a house with a scenic view, he would buy the land across from my house and put in an ugly shopping center. If he found I was bullish on a particular stock, he would try to take over the company. There's always something he's doing to make me quietly miserable. I'm used to it.

I'm fucking tired of it, but I'm used to it.

But Penny isn't. And I feel a need to protect her. I turn, pacing back down the way I came. Perhaps I need to take a long trip somewhere. Since I'm theoretically in retirement, I could do such a thing. Maybe pause on the spells I'm casting with Penny, just long enough to let Stoker think she's no longer a factor in my life. I'd hate to, but I've waited over twenty years. I suppose I can wait another ten if it means that she's safe. So then, where should I go that Stoker wouldn't be able to reach me? I ponder, turning and striding down the hall again. It would need to be someplace resistant to magic. Somewhere vaguely inhospitable.

I wonder what sort of accommodations Antarctica has for a long-term tourist . . . Antarctica seems extreme, but warlocks are an extreme type, and I daresay that even Stoker would hesitate to partake of the bitter winds of the Antarctic. It's a thought. It . . .

I turn and Penny is standing there.

She, as usual, has not listened to any of my requests about her wardrobe. Her dress is a sky blue with pale, filmy sleeves that billow as she moves. The bodice ruches over her breasts, amply outlining them, and her skirt seems to be made of flowing panels that float around her legs and end just below the knee. Her hair is pulled into a ponytail, two big yellow teardrop earrings dangle against her neck and draw attention to the marks I left there, and her shoes are just as yellow as her jewelry. It should look gaudy. Ridiculous. Like something a child would wear.

Instead, she looks . . . like Penny. Lovely and bright and charming. My cold heart gives a shuddering thump in my chest at the sight of her.

"Oh good," she breathes, her gaze fixing on me. "You're here."

"Where else would I be?" I ask, cranky.

She shrugs. "You and I need to talk. We've got to discuss how we're moving forward. You want to do this out here, or should we head to your study?"

I rub my mouth, worried. Her expression is calm. Very calm.

She's not doing that bright smile that entrances me, which tells me there's a problem. Is she going to quit? So soon? Have I pushed her away already? Panicked, I shake my head. She's not allowed to quit. "Now is not a good time."

Penny frowns. "Oh. Okay. After dinner, then?"

"I'm going to be busy," I declare, making my tone imperious as I gaze down my nose at her. "I have a great deal of research that needs to be done."

"Oh, okay, then." She gives me a thoughtful look, as if trying to determine my mood, and then heads upstairs, pulling her earrings off. I don't breathe until she's out of sight, and even then, there's a burning in the pit of my stomach. She's right to leave, of course. But that doesn't make it any easier.

I head off into my formal study, sitting in my reading chair by the window. I've recently been rereading Reginald Scot's *The Discoverie of Witchcraft* just to get ideas. He doesn't know what he's talking about through most of it, of course, but even in the most insane rantings there's always a kernel of knowledge, and I like to try to apply it to what I actually know. I can't concentrate, though. I set the book in my lap and stare at the pages, but instead, I keep thinking of Penny.

Penny, and the way she'd gently tugged her earrings off her lobes. The way her skirts swayed as she moved up the stairs. Penny, whose breath hisses between her teeth when she's coming . . . or when I'm casting.

Penny, who is no doubt abandoning me. I close my eyes and rub my mouth, frustrated at myself. Why is it so difficult for me to tell her that I have feelings for her? That she makes me absolutely crazy and yet her smile is the best thing I've ever seen? Why is it so hard for me to admit that I might be besotted and it hurts my feelings that she just wants a quick fuck? There are parts of me that are interested in that, of course, but the larger part of me feels . . . wounded that I am still not enough for more than a mere physical encounter.

I'm so lost in thought that I don't hear the swish of skirts until she's right next to me.

No sooner do I open my eyes than I see Penny, standing right before me. Her earrings are gone, along with her shoes, and she wastes no time in plucking the ancient, valuable book out of my lap and tossing it aside, then straddling me.

"What the devil?" I sputter, alarmed. Is she possessed? Has there been another charm left somewhere that's cursed her with something?

"I think we should talk," she tells me, sliding her hands to the back of my neck even as her thighs frame mine. She's facing me, the cradle of her legs pressing down against my pelvis, and my body is reacting. I freeze in place, because if she realizes just how hard this quick move has gotten me, she'll be revolted. "Actually, scratch that," Penny continues. "I think we should kiss."

"Kiss . . . ?"

That's all I get out before her mouth is on mine. Penny presses her lips to my face with single-minded determination, and I taste cherry-flavored gloss and a hint of vanilla, and then I forget about tasting anything, because she's kissing me with soft, delicate, sweet kisses that fill me with yearning. Her mouth is warm and seductive as she gives me small kiss after small kiss, peppering my mouth and chin with delightful nips that make my cock jerk with each one . . . and make me hungry for more.

"You're trying to push me away, aren't you?" she says between kisses.

"I don't think I could push you away right now if you were on fire," I admit, my nose brushing hers. I follow her mouth when she leans away, hungry for more kissing.

Penny giggles, the sound as sweet and effervescent as her. "I meant in general, Will." She tugs on my lower lip with her teeth, sending sensation pricking through my body. "You get nervous when you get involved, don't you?"

I swallow hard. I don't want to speak and ruin this moment. "I . . . never get involved," I confess. "No one likes me enough."

"I like you," she breathes, one hand resting on my chest while the other plays with my hair. "I like you but you are trying to shove me away."

She's not wrong. "I don't want you to feel trapped. Nor do I want you targeted by Stoker. You should be safe. You deserve better than this."

"Better than you, you mean?" She runs a finger along the line of my jaw, and it's hard to focus on anything other than her fascinatingly pink mouth and how close it is to mine.

"Mmm." I lean in to try to kiss her again.

Penny pulls back, a teasing expression on her face. "Will, I chose to be your familiar. I knew it could be dangerous. I knew it could fuck up both of our careers. I took the risk, just like you did."

"You chose to be my familiar, not my . . . paramour."

"I can't be both? We can have sex, you know. I'm not averse to it." She strokes a hand down my chest. "It's just sex, not world peace. There's no need to get worked up over things."

I draw back, stung. "So that's what you want, then? Just a cock to service you?"

She pulls back, too, her head tilted, and gives me a strange look. "No. I want to have sex with you because I like you. What on earth are you talking about?"

"You want to be with *me*," I enunciate, still not entirely sure I believe her. "Willem Sauer."

"Yes."

"The warlock you said you hated."

"I never said that." She leans in again and gives me another one of those featherlight kisses that send streaks of pleasure all through my body. "And even if I did, that was weeks ago. A lot has changed between us, don't you think?" She kisses me again and then starts to get up. "But I can leave—"

I lock my arms around her waist, holding her down. "No. Stay."

She smiles and wriggles against me, then grinds her hips over my cock, and her eyes widen in surprise. "Oh."

Grimacing, I try to adjust my weight so I'm not pressing against her. "Apologies—"

Penny grips my chin and kisses me again. "Do you want me to get off you?"

I want her lips to linger on mine is what I want. "No."

"Do you want me to stop being your apprentice?"

"Never. You're an excellent pupil and an even better familiar." She practically preens with the pleasure of my words, and it makes me wonder why I'm such a fool. Why have I been lashing at her with sour words when the sight of her joy is so delightful? Why am I such a bloody arse when it's clear I should be complimenting her at every turn to let her know how much I like her? "You are . . . amazing."

She smiles, that gorgeous, charming smile that nearly swallows her entire face, and I want to just kiss the hell out of it. So I do. I drag her closer to me and slant my mouth over hers, this time taking on the role of the aggressor. I don't kiss like she does. My kisses aren't light, sweet, breezy things. Mine are hungry, obscene, devouring sorts of kisses. I slick my tongue over hers, wanting her to realize just how much I need her, how much she arouses me even though she's the opposite of what I always thought I'd want. I'm so gods-damned hungry for her that I don't even care that her lip gloss is all over my face or her hands are in my crisp hair, lifting it from the careful part I've made. Her tongue tangles with mine, and she tastes so damned sweet that I could lick her for all time—

Her backside buzzes, her skirts shivering.

Penny groans, pressing her forehead to mine. "People really do have shitty timing."

"Then ignore it," I tell her between kisses. I hold her tight against me, rocking my hips up against the vee of her thighs, hungry to claim her. "Ignore it and we'll stay like this forever."

But she only chuckles and presses a quick kiss to the tip of my nose and then fishes her phone out of her skirts. She flicks a finger over the screen to activate it, and her face falls.

I don't like that look. "Oh no. What?"

She sighs, giving the phone a thoughtful look. Her thumbs move over the bottom of the screen, typing quickly. "It's my parents. They want to know where I am. They probably finally noticed I haven't made sandwiches or done the laundry recently. I guess I should probably tell them I moved in with you."

Perhaps it's the hundreds of years I have on her that makes me old-fashioned, but I'm utterly aghast. "Wait a moment. They don't know you moved in with me?"

"Nope."

"But you've been here for weeks," I sputter, realizing what this means. "They're just now noticing you've been gone?"

She bites her lip, and I can tell Penny is uncomfortable with my questions. She tucks the phone back into her skirts. "It's not like that. They both have witches that they are familiars for."

"So?"

"So they get caught up in what their witches are working on. Sometimes they don't come home for days on end. They know I'm self-sufficient. I can handle myself. I am thirty, you know."

Thirty, and yet no one checked in on her for weeks? That

seems wrong to me. I arch a brow. "And how long have you had to be self-sufficient for?"

"Oh no," she teases, her brilliant smile returning. "You don't get to judge them. This is how our business works and you know it. A witch takes priority over the familiar's life. Didn't I drop everything to come and be your familiar?"

"Actually, no," I point out dryly. "You kept your job and your circle of horrid friends, and that's precisely why we had to pretend to start dating, remember?"

She chuckles. "Well, our situation is a little different. But you know as well as anyone that when a witch takes you on, nothing else matters, because what you're gaining makes up for the time you're losing with family."

Does it? I think about my father, gone when I was too young, and how I'd have given anything for a few more days with him. I think about the mother that died in childbirth who I never knew. I think about brilliant, sweet, loving Penny, who is so eager to please . . . and the neglectful parents that don't remember she's alive. I don't like it. I don't like them, either. I would have noticed Penny was gone within an hour. It's been weeks and all they're doing is texting her? That seems wrong to me.

Her phone buzzes again, and she pulls it out, tucking her front against my chest and settling her face in the crook of my neck. I slide my arms around her. It can't be the most comfortable position for her, seated sideways in my lap and leaning against me, but I like holding her like this. She fits in my arms perfectly as she reads her phone's screen and then chuckles. "My parents want to meet my boyfriend."

I shouldn't be surprised by that. It's the very least they could do . . . and I do mean the very least, considering she's been living with me for a while now. "And is that what I am? Or are we pretending?"

Penny sits up, facing me. Her expression is serious. "Do you want to be my boyfriend, Will?"

"Yes." My foolish voice is hoarse with how much I want to be her "boyfriend." "I should like that very much."

She smiles sweetly at me and then leans in to give me another kiss. "I like it, too. Come on, then. Both of them have tonight off and they're at the house."

Penny hops off my lap and holds a hand out to me, and it takes everything I have not to adjust the hard bar of my cock in the front of my trousers. I sit up and take the hand she extends to me, frowning. "Right now?"

"Right now," she agrees. "I don't know when they'll have time again. Their schedules usually conflict."

I sigh. For her, I'll do this . . . but I'd much rather go back to the part where she was straddling me and kissing me.

PENNY

I'm nervous as we drive over to my parents' house. I shouldn't be. Up until a few weeks ago, I lived here. My parents are very sweet people but also very busy ones, and I have no doubt that our meeting won't last long. Even so . . .

I look at the man in the driver's seat of the car. Will's mouth is still flattened into that disapproving line as he drives, as if he's ready to yell at my parents the moment he sees them. He doesn't get it, though. I've grown up in apprentice society. I know what it means to finally get that witch to make you her familiar. I get that nothing else comes first anymore. I've grown up expecting to see my mom snatched up for her potential, or for my father to finally get to start casting on his own. My grandmother on my father's side served her witch until she got pregnant with Dad, and returned to service after he was born, only to pass away in a car accident. My mother's mother is still serving her warlock, into her sixtieth year of apprenticing, with no intention of ever leaving. Grandma Rosa looks like she's thirty and travels the world with her warlock. I've met her twice, and I was stunned both times by how young and powerful she seemed for an eighty-year-old. But that's just how it is when you grow up in a family full of familiars.

Will doesn't understand, probably because he's from one of the old families and he was expected to move directly into casting after a very short apprenticeship. He doesn't know the endless waiting the rest of us with "lesser" bloodlines get to experience. He doesn't know what it's like to be passed over, year after year, waiting for your chance.

So I don't begrudge my parents anything.

Both cars are in the driveway when we pull up, and my heart flutters at the sight. Will parks behind Mom's family van (so she can drive Aurelia's kids around). He turns and looks over at me, his tone icy. "Their names?"

"Margie and Doug. Roundtree."

"Mmm. And their witches?"

"Aurelia Snowthorpe and Diana Sabinus."

One of his brows goes up. "Old families?"

I nod enthusiastically. "They both got really lucky." Both Aurelia and Diana are friendly and come from close families that know each other well and have kept the old bloodlines pure, trying to marry for magical benefits rather than love. Aurelia is a thousand years younger than Diana, but Aurelia is the stronger caster. "Mom says both of Aurelia's children are brimming with magic and that they'll make incredible witches someday."

"Lovely" is all Will says, and it's hard to read his mood. He gets out of the car and moves to my side as I open the door, holding a hand out to me. Surprised, I take it, and when he tucks my hand in his arm, I realize he's back in boyfriend mode. Of course. He's going to make sure that everyone thinks we're wildly in love so our cover isn't blown.

We walk to the front door, and I wince at the overgrown front yard. It looks bad, and I really need to see about getting a lawn service set up to handle things. I'll put that on my list for tomorrow. Will pauses on the doorstep, glancing down at me.

"What?"

"You look nervous."

"Of course I'm nervous," I exclaim. "You're meeting my parents!"

He lifts a hand to my chin, tilting my face up. "Yes, but you shouldn't *look* nervous. I don't care for it."

Before I can sputter out a response as to how he thinks I should look, he leans down and kisses me. Will's mouth is soft and somehow demanding as he kisses my upper lip, sucking on it gently and making my insides turn to mush. He turns his attention to my lower lip next, and the front door opens just as he's releasing my lower lip from his mouth with an audible groan. I don't know if the groan is mine or his, just that it's needy and full of yearning.

"Well now," my father says, in full dad mode. "Not what I expected to see on my doorstep."

"Hi, Daddy," I say brightly, my face bright red.

My father taps his mouth and then steps back, inviting us in. Will glances over at me, and I notice he's got my lipstick smeared all over his mouth. Oh. I reach up and wipe it off with my thumb, and all the while, Will gazes down at me like he wants to devour me. It's making me a little nervous, because this isn't "safe" boyfriend mode. This is obsessed boyfriend mode, and I'm not sure if he's acting or if it's because we were making out in the chair in his study earlier.

Either way, it's really turning me on, and I hope it's not all pretend on his end.

We step inside the house, and I'm a little chagrined to see that there's laundry everywhere. There's piles of it in the hallway, and when we pass by the kitchen, there are dirty dishes piled in the sink and the flowers I left in a vase are dead and dried out. It's clear they've been home, and it's also clear that they haven't bothered to clean up after themselves. Immediately, I start grabbing some of the towels that are in a pile, giving Will an apologetic look. "Why don't I just start a load of laundry while you get comfortable—"

Will immediately plucks the towels right back out of my grasp and tosses them back on the floor. "Leave it. You're visiting, remember?"

"Oh, but—"

The look he gives me is scathing Willem Sauer. Right. Okay. I abandon the towels and give him a nervous look, and he puts a hand on my shoulders, guiding me forward.

Mom's in the living room, wearing her favorite pink sundress and heels. I got my love of girly dresses from my mother, who loves a thrift store find and an old-fashioned vibe. She's texting on her phone as we enter and looks up, beaming. "Why, hello! You must be the boyfriend. I'm Margie."

I try to see my mom through Will's eyes and realize that she looks only a few years older than me at this point. Has she stopped aging now that she's a familiar? I glance over at my dad, and he's got very little gray in his dark hair, too. How is it that we all live together and don't notice the basics about one another? I'm so used to seeing them as my parents that it feels like this is the first time I'm seeing them as fellow apprentices.

Of course, they don't know that I am one.

"It is a pleasure to meet you both," Will says, his hands going behind his back, his pose stiff in that formal way of his. Immediately, both of my parents turn back to their phones and start texting, and I inwardly cringe. I know from experience that even when they're home, they're still attached to their witches at the hip, so this isn't surprising. Nor is it surprising when Will continues with a too-pleasant tone of voice, "Penny has told me nothing about either of you."

I wince, but they don't seem to notice. Dad doesn't look up

from his phone, no doubt texting Diana. "Yes, well, we wanted to meet the man who'd swept our precious kitten off her feet."

"Yes, I can see how precious she is to you," Will murmurs, glancing over at me.

I swat him with my hand, scowling. *Stop it,* I mouth.

My mother glances up from her phone, smiling sweetly. "How did you two meet again? Sorry. Aurelia has a question about the kids' project for school, and I was helping her." She wiggles her phone. "I promise I'm paying attention."

I clutch Will's arm, beaming at them. "We met at work. I work at the component shop, remember? CBD Whee!"

My mother chuckles. "Yes! It's about as close as you're going to get to magic for a while, isn't it, sweetie?"

For some reason, that stings. Why are they acting like I'm a ten-year-old instead of a thirty-year-old? Or am I prickly because Will is here and they act as if they couldn't care? Because the house I normally take such great care of is filthy? Don't they care? But my mom simply beams up at us, and I feel like a jerk for thinking salty thoughts. They're just busy. "Will is a warlock," I announce. "Temporarily in retirement, but a warlock. We met when he came in to pick up an order."

Both my parents look up at that. My mother blinks, her smile a little frozen. "I'm sorry, what did you say your name was again?"

"Willem Sauer," the man at my side says in a cold, distinct voice. "I'm certain you've heard of me."

"Absolutely," my father says, exchanging a look with my mother. They both immediately bend over their phones again, typing away.

I bite my lip, and I can feel the tension brimming through Will. I'm just imagining what they're texting their witches about him. That he's dating me? That he's "retired"? What? But my mother gestures at the sofa. "Please sit down, Willem. Would you like some tea?"

"I sincerely do not know," he says in a cranky voice.

"He would love some tea," I chirp, kissing Will's cheek and giving his hand a squeeze. "Be right back."

"I shall be here, *dumpling.*" Oh, he says the pet name very dangerously, and I can just imagine what he's thinking. Nothing good.

Fighting back the urge to cringe, I hustle into the kitchen after my mother. She holds the teakettle, giving the stove a confused look. "Is this a gas range? You know I never cook here."

"I've got it." I move forward and turn the burner on, then put the kettle on with it. The gas range was installed seven years ago, but hey. "You and Dad been busy? I haven't seen you in forever."

"Oh my goodness. *So* busy," my mom says with a chuckle. "It's just about football season, and you know how involved Aurelia is with the local team. And the kids have so many practices that I drive them to back and forth every day. My schedule is a mess, darling. Truly a darn mess." She sighs happily. "And your father and Diana are taking on a new project, you know."

"They are?"

Mom nods. "Something about her family's heritage and transcribing all of their spell tomes into multiple languages or some such. I admit I tuned it out." She waves a hand. "I just know that he's going to Rome for a few months starting next week and he'll be out of pocket quite a bit. That's why I'm delighted we get to meet your young man tonight."

I return her beaming smile, a little disheartened that no one told me my father was leaving the country soon. "He's two hundred and seventy, Mom. He's not that young. As for Dad—"

"Young for a warlock," she says, as if she's even a fraction of his age. "And speaking of clothing, I don't suppose you know where my lime-green A-line dress is, do you? I was looking for it and I can't find it."

But . . . we weren't talking about clothing? "It might be in the laundry."

My mom purses her lips. "Oh dear. Do you think you could wash it for me? I'm running low on clean clothes."

"Of course. Just watch the kettle." I pat her arm and go to grab some of the laundry out of the hall. I fill the washing machine and then start dusting because there's a bit of mud in the foyer, probably from Dad's shoes. I head back to the kitchen and start doing the dishes while my mom tells me all about Aurelia and her kids and what they're up to at school. I hate that I feel bitter about it. I hate that Will's presence is showing me that my parents have lives that don't involve me, and they love those lives. As my mom chatters on, she texts her witch, and I want to smack the phone out of her hands.

What is wrong with me? They're my parents. I know them. I understand them. It's only getting to me tonight because Will's here.

I'm relieved when the kettle finally whistles, and I pour several cups of tea and head for the living room. The moment I head out there, my dad gets to his feet. "Well, it's been great, sweetie, but I really have to get going. Diana has some casting that can't wait, and she needs me at her side."

"But—"

He plants a kiss on my forehead and smiles absently at Will. "You'll take good care of our little girl, won't you?"

"I'll spank her every time she's naughty," Will agrees, arching a brow in my direction. "You have my word."

My father laughs, and I know he wasn't paying a bit of attention. He's already staring at his phone as he heads out the door. Now I won't see him again for months because of Diana's stupid project, and I fight back another wave of irritation. It isn't like me to be bitter. I'm supportive of my parents' careers. I know how hard they work and how much it means to them. And I don't know that I'd be any different if I were in their shoes. So why is it bothering me so much tonight?

My mother sits down with her tea in one hand, her phone in the other. "So tell us about you, Willem. What's keeping you busy right now?"

"Why?" Will asks, practically bristling. "What does Aurelia want to know? Just ask and I'll say it. Let's not pretend, shall we?"

Mom gives me an uncertain look, smiling, and I move to Will's side, squeezing his thigh.

He glances over at me and his expression softens slightly. He puts his hand over mine and gives it a return squeeze. "Since I cannot cast and no spellcasting firms will hire me, I've taken to research. I'm trying to think of my time as less of an exile and more of an enforced break." He lifts my hand to his mouth and kisses my knuckles. "The company is good, at least."

And the look he sends my way is very heated. I think about being in that chair on top of him earlier, and my heart flutters.

"Any particular sort of research?" my mom asks, setting her tea down and now typing one-handed while she pretends to pay attention. It's pretty obvious that she's texting her witch and sending back information about Will, and it's embarrassing.

"Nothing exciting. Curse subversion. Componentless divination. The usual." He shrugs. "Tell me about you and your family. How did you meet your husband?"

Mom actually sets her phone down, smiling over at me. "We met in the society, actually. I sat next to him at meetings for two years before he asked me out. We've been married thirty-five years now."

"And Penny is your only child?" Will asks politely, lifting his tea to take a sip.

"Oh, gods, yes," my mom says with a laugh. "Now that we're both familiars, there's no way I'd let myself get pregnant again. I'd have to stop being an apprentice." She wags a finger in my direction. "A baby drains your energy, and that belongs to your witch."

"Gross, Mom. You make it sound like you're a battery and not a person." I'm a little disgusted.

"Besides," my mother continues, "I'm helping Aurelia raise her children, and it's been very fulfilling. By the way, how long on the laundry, sweetie?"

And there goes that stab of jealousy again. I smile, but it feels frozen on my face. "A bit longer."

"Of course." She beams at Will. "So tell me about yourself."

WILLEM

I'm an idiot.

Well, I'm less of an idiot than Penny's self-absorbed parents, but I still feel foolish as her mother prattles on about how meaningful her work is and how amazing Aurelia is. I've met Aurelia many times, and the word I would use for her is "self-important" and not "amazing." But at least one good thing has come out of Mrs. Roundtree's careless blathering, and I can't wait to share it with Penny later.

As it is, we can't escape quite yet, so I continue pretending to be invested in what Penny's mother says about Aurelia and how her evil-eye charms are more potent than anyone else's. It takes every ounce of my strength not to roll my eyes at such claims, but I just sip my tea and mumble platitudes while Penny does a load of laundry and straightens the kitchen. I keep trying to stop her, but Penny's mother acts helpless, and the next thing I know, Penny is back on her feet again, scrubbing something.

I don't like it.

I also don't like her parents. It's obvious they're taking advantage of her positive nature and cheerful energy. I don't think they're doing it out of a place of maliciousness, of course. I simply think they're incredibly self-centered and involved in their jobs and have decided those are more important than the daughter they treat like a servant.

I still haven't forgotten that it took them weeks to notice she was gone. She deserves better than that, and I won't forgive it, no matter how brightly Mrs. Roundtree smiles in my direction and gushes about how proud she is of her daughter "landing" a warlock, even if it's one as "unfortunately" retired as myself.

After Penny puts the laundry in the dryer and her mother starts texting again, I get to my feet. I'm tired of this, and I want to talk to Penny about what I learned from her mother's careless words. I know what Stoker is up to now, and I want her feedback on it. So I smile and button my jacket. "I thank you for your company, Mrs. Roundtree, but Penny and I must be going for the evening. We have plans early in the morning and shouldn't be out late."

"Of course," she enthuses. "And call me Margie. Mrs. Roundtree makes me feel old." She winks at me as if we're bosom companions. "I should be heading back to Aurelia's anyhow. We've got some casting to do this weekend that had to be put off for Taylor's spelling bee competition—that's Aurelia's oldest—and you know what an ordeal those are."

"I don't, actually." I glance over at Penny, but her expression is frozen, her smile not reaching her eyes.

My protective streak rears, and I want to grab her and hug her against me until her mother's flighty carelessness stops hurting her. I move to Penny's side and slide an arm around her shoulders, hugging her against me. "We really must be going."

"Oh! Did you finish the laundry?" Margie asks, glancing back at the kitchen. "Or do you think you have time—"

"We are leaving," I insist, smiling to take the sting out of my words. If Penny so much as touches one more dirty towel, I'm going to bury a dozen curse tablets in this yard, and Taylor is going to lose every spelling bee for the rest of her days and Margie will get a flat tire every time she leaves the fucking house.

Penny doesn't protest, letting me urge her out of the house and back into my car. The moment she's seated, I hurry over to the driver's side and put the car in reverse, watching as Margie waves from the porch. At my side, Penny looks ready to cry.

"Are you all right?" I ask, even as I back into the street.

"I don't know."

I want to ask her more, but the way that Margie is watching the car as we leave pings my senses. "Is your necklace warm?"

Penny touches the charm between her breasts. "Oh. Yeah. You think—"

"I think your mother and Aurelia are being nosy," I say, pulling up to a stop sign. I glance over at Penny, and she looks so damned sad that I immediately lean over and turn her face toward mine, then kiss her. Just to wipe that sadness off her face.

She gives me a dazed look, blinking in surprise.

"We'll talk later, yes?" I murmur, letting my lips linger over hers for a moment. Even now, Penny tastes like vanilla and cherries. *Is there anything about her that isn't achingly sweet?* I wonder. Of course, the thought of tasting her everywhere is now in my head, and my cock hardens in my pants.

I'm uncomfortably aroused as we drive home, and Penny is silent in the seat next to me, fingering the charm. Once we get back inside my house and safely behind my wards, I want her to tell me everything. Until then, I have to bite back how irritated I am with her parents and the situation there. I don't like that they hurt Penny's feelings and we can't even talk about it until we get back behind the walls of my house. I immediately try to think of what will improve her mood. Cookies and milk, obviously. She will want to hug her squirrel. Perhaps a back rub . . . ?

Or is that my cock thinking for me?

I park the car in the garage and all but leap out of it to take Penny inside. "Go into my study," I tell her. "I'll meet you there and we'll talk."

It's a sign of how distressed she is when she doesn't protest, just nods and heads in that direction. I grab cookies and a bottle of milk from the kitchen, then race up the stairs and snag her creature in my arms. "Come on, you," I tell him, shoving a cookie in his direction so he doesn't bite me. "Your mistress needs you."

To my relief, the rodent doesn't fight, though he does try to climb up my jacket and makes me spill cookies out of the sleeve they're in. Sputtering, I try to pick them up, only to step on one, and I have to set the milk aside and clutch her squirrel with one hand while I retrieve cookies with the other.

"Will . . . what are you doing?" Penny's voice comes from behind me.

I turn around, startled. "I'm getting things to make you feel better." Her squirrel chitters and nips at my hand, and I curse and release the hated thing onto the bed. "Little beast wants to be the object of my next *haruspex* spell," I mutter. "Just you wait."

Penny moves forward and snags her creature. She hugs him to her chest and sits on the edge of the bed, staring at me in a mixture of wonder and amusement. "More cookies and milk?"

"I didn't like your sadness—"

"Will, you're incredibly sweet," she says, and looks for a moment as if she might cry. "Thank you."

"Don't thank me," I mutter. "I just ground them all into the carpet because your animal made me drop them."

"He'll eat them," she promises, setting her squirrel on the carpet in my bedroom. Sure enough, the creature goes to the first mashed cookie and starts picking up the bits, eating them. She pats the spot on the end of the bed. "Come sit with me?"

It takes everything I have not to immediately grab a vacuum cleaner. I kick aside some of the cookie bits, hand her the tightly sealed bottle of milk, and sit down at her side. "It should be safe for us to talk now. Are you all right?"

She sets the milk down on the floor and takes my hand in hers, lacing her fingers with mine. Like the rest of her, Penny's fingers are small, and her nails are brightly colored, but I like the sight of our hands entwined. "I think I'm cursed, Will."

"Cursed?"

She bites her lip. "Yeah. I've never resented my parents before tonight, but today, everything they said and did just made me so unhappy. I've never felt like that before. It made me wonder if something happened."

I snort. "You mean other than your eyes are open to their self-ishness?" She flinches, and I ease my voice down from an indignant snarl into something gentler. "Penny. It took them weeks to realize you weren't there, and I think they only noticed because of the laundry. And instead of worrying over you, they asked you to come home and clean up. They didn't put their phones down the entire time we were there. I could have been a serial killer, and they would have never noticed anything amiss."

"I know, and that makes me feel worse." Her eyes get shiny. "They're not bad people. It's just . . ."

"They've chosen the lives they want and haven't left any room for you," I speculate. "And it hurts you."

She shakes her head, and a tear spills down her cheek. "Fucking Taylor and her fucking spelling bee. Do you think my mom ever took me to competitions? Never. They missed my graduation, both of them. They were never there for me when I needed them, and I told myself it was fine, because they were living out their dreams. But right now it just sounds like my mom's raising Aurelia's kids, and it makes me angry."

"You're allowed to be angry over that. Do you want to curse them?"

Penny chokes on her laughter. "God, no. I just wanted them to care a little more." Another tear slips down her face. "I can't even be mad at them . . . I'm disappointed that all I am is an unpaid housemaid. Reggie checks in on me more often than they do. Hell, Nick checks in more often."

I fight back a surge of jealousy. "Does Nick text you a lot? Do I need to curse *him*?"

She looks over at me, her expression thoughtful. "No. I think you need to kiss me again."

That, I can do. I reach over and cup her round cheek, stroking it with my thumb. I love her expressive face, her button nose and her sweet smile. Penny gazes up at me, worry in her dark eyes, and I just want to make her happy. This doesn't feel like me, and yet at the same time, it feels absolutely right that I should put myself in charge of her tender emotions. I should look out for her, because she needs someone to look out for her. She needs a champion . . . and unfortunately, she's stuck with someone like me.

But I'm going to fill that role, because Penny deserves the best.

I lean in, stroking my thumb along the edge of her lower lip. "Are you sure you want me? You can do better."

Penny huffs a small laugh. "Are you kidding? You're a warlock. Everyone in the society would fall all over themselves to get to be your girlfriend."

I don't know how to take that. "And is that why you want me?"

She shakes her head and gently nips at my thumb with her teeth. "I want you because I feel *seen* with you."

I groan with need, unable to resist sliding my thumb between her lips. "You're more than seen. I can't look away from you. Perhaps I should, since the last thing I should do is touch my familiar, but I can't help myself. You're the most frustrating, intoxicating woman I've ever met."

Penny sucks on the tip of my thumb, and I can't look away from the sight. By all the gods, I need to touch her. I slide my other hand to her hair and grab a fistful of it, tilting her head back. She gasps, her mouth opening and freeing my thumb, and I trail the wet digit down her chin and throat. She's gorgeous like this, panting at my touch, her breasts heaving as if begging to be touched.

I flick the pendant between her breasts. It won't work inside the house, as we can't be scried upon here. Still, I like the thought of someone seeing me kissing her—claiming her as my own. I've never thought of myself as an exhibitionist, but I want everyone to know that she's mine. *Everyone.*

She makes a needy little sound, gazing up at me with hungry eyes. I trail my thumb over her mouth again, teasing her, because the tease is part of the enjoyment. I love the way she parts those pink lips for me, her lashes fluttering, and I brush her lower lip again. "You need to be kissed, do you?"

"Desperately," she breathes.

"And do you want soft, gentle kisses where I taste your pretty mouth?" I drag my thumb over her top lip, my words a caress. "Or do you want hard, deep kisses where I claim you as mine?"

Penny whimpers, transfixed. "I have to choose?"

Greedy, sweet thing. "You want both?" I lean closer, my breath mingling with hers. "Should I—"

I never get to finish the statement, because Penny's mouth is on mine. She closes the distance between us, wrapping her arms around me as she pulls me to her. I forget all about teasing. Instead, I cup the back of her head, and my tongue delves into her mouth, claiming her as my own. I want to kiss her hard enough that she forgets about everything but me. No one gets to hurt her.

No one gets to make her feel sad. She's mine to protect, and if it means kissing her until she sees stars, then that's absolutely what I'm going to do.

At least, that's the intention I start with. As I claim her mouth hungrily, I forget about everything except Penny. Penny's tongue slicking against mine. Penny's cherry lips and her eager kisses. The little moans she makes every time I taste her. Gods, kissing her is a pleasure.

She drags a hand across the front of my jacket, her mouth frantic on mine, and then her hand slides between my thighs, rubbing at my shaft.

I break off with a hiss of surprise.

"Too much?" Penny asks, drawing back. There's a look of uncertainty on her face. "I wanted to touch you."

"I . . . I just wasn't expecting that," I stammer. Has anyone wanted to touch me in the past? I can't recall. It seems like even when I was with partners in the past, I took all the initiative. They never reached for me with greedy, eager hands like Penny is, and for a moment it makes me feel bashful. "I only want you to do what you want to do, Penny."

"Great, then we're on the same page," she says, and reaches for my cock again, palming me through my pants. "I want to touch you."

I have to bite back a moan as she outlines my cock in my pants with her fingers. Gods, her eagerness is going to kill me. It's going to be impossible to control myself. But if she doesn't want control, then I'm going to touch her back. I kiss her fiercely, claiming her mouth even as my hands roam up and down her back. She makes a little sound of excitement in my mouth, stroking me through my trousers. Fuck. I slide a hand to her front, seeking out one of her breasts, desperate to touch her and excite her like she is me.

She squeals against my lips when I find her nipple and pinch it through the fabric of her dress. "Will. Do it again."

"As if you can stop me," I growl, and pinch the tight bud of it again, loving the noises she makes. Of course Penny is noisy when she's aroused. She's always noisy. I like this, though. It tells me that I'm pleasuring her. That she wouldn't simply lie back and endure my touch. That she wants it as much as I want her.

I rub that tight little nipple as we kiss, practically mauling her as she drags her hand over my cock. I nip at her lower lip, and when she makes another one of those sexy whimpers, I want to fling her skirts over her head and lick her until she screams my name. And now that I have that visual in my head, I won't settle for anything less. "Lie back for me, Penny."

With a moan and a wriggle, she flings herself back on my bed, her skirts floating around her before settling again. "Oh, please tell me you're into pussy-licking," she pants, her hand pressing between her thighs. "That would make you the perfect man."

"I am very into the idea of licking your pussy," I agree, shoving her skirts up as I move between her legs. "Are you sensitive?"

"Does a witch like mugwort?" She drags her skirts up, revealing hot-pink panties with a little ribbon bow at the waist. "Actually, I don't know if they do. It's pretty popular at the store, but it also smells really bad, and I'm not sure—"

She chokes off in a whimper as I drag my thumb up and down the gusset of her panties, outlining the seam of her pussy. Her legs flail, bent at the knee, and I slip one over my shoulder, settling down between her legs so I can enjoy this thoroughly. "It's been a long time since I've done this," I warn her, my breath fanning over her skin. "I might be a bit rusty."

"How long?" she pants, unable to lie still underneath me.

"Couple decades. Is it really important?" It might also be twelve decades, but it doesn't matter. She's here, she's excited to be with me, and she smells so good I might lose my mind. I bury my face against her panties, and when she gasps, it's the best noise in the gods-damned world. I push the fabric aside, revealing her folds, and of course she's gorgeous here, too. A trimmed thatch of dark curls covers her puffy folds, and I can't resist. I drag my tongue down her slit and love the trill of excitement that comes out of her.

"Oh god, your tongue!" Her hands go to my hair, mussing it. "Do that again!"

With pleasure. I lap at her, teasing at first, then growing bolder. I use the tip to explore the folds of her body, learning how she is made. No two women are alike, and some enjoy a different touch than others. I know that much. I also know that when I find her clit, it's practically begging to be touched. She's swollen and flushed here, and I lean down and take her into my mouth, sucking with enthusiasm. She cries out, her legs arching into the air. I grab on to her thighs and hold her down as I tongue her, licking and sucking until she starts bucking against my mouth. When I can sense she's close, I press a finger into her, teasing with slow, careful motions. She's slick and ready, and I crook my finger inside her, seeking out that slightly roughened spot on the inside of her—

Penny cries out, arching up.

Found it. Tickling at that spot with my finger, I drag my tongue over her clit in repeated circles. She's got fistfuls of my hair in her grasp, panting hard and whimpering my name as she rocks against me. When she comes, it's with that strangled little sound that seems *so* damned familiar, and I press kisses onto her flushed skin while she comes down from her orgasm.

"Oh my god," Penny moans, panting. "You're a unicorn."

I lift my head, frowning up at her. "I'm a what?"

"A unicorn," she says dreamily, the look she gives me utterly sated and content. It's so damned sexy I can't help but press more kisses along the inside of her thigh. "A good-looking man that likes to give head *and* knows where my G-spot is. Like I said. A unicorn."

"I'm not certain if that's a compliment or not," I point out, licking my lips. I press another kiss to the inside of her knee and then sit up, trying to finger-comb my destroyed hair back into place.

"Oh god, is it ever a compliment." She stretches on the bed and sighs, reaching for me. "You're the best, Will."

"Willem."

"Will," she insists, and when I lie down next to her, she cuddles against my chest. "My Will."

I . . . guess I don't hate it. I slide an arm around her, realizing that it's rather warm in my bedroom. Of course, I am still fully dressed. Mentally, I make a note to have my suit dry-cleaned to get the smell of pussy out of it. Then again, maybe not. I do like the smell of her. I wouldn't mind going around just breathing in her scent all day long.

"Mmm," Penny moans, the picture of contentment. She strokes her hand down my side, making me twitch. My cock is throbbing painfully, but I'm an expert at self-denial. I don't want to ruin this moment for her, not when she's had such a stressful night and I've gotten to put my mouth all over her.

Our relationship can progress later. For now, I'm just quite pleased that she's no longer melancholy.

23

PENNY

I lie against Will's chest, listening to his heart beat, and wait for it.

Every girl knows that moment. It's the moment when you're getting cozy with your man and not moving fast enough, so he decides he's tired of waiting and puts a hand atop your head, trying to ease you down to his crotch for a blow job.

But it never comes. I just remain still and he drowsily runs his hand up and down my back, contented. And while it's quite lovely, it's also a little confusing. I know Will is prickly at the best of times. Is it possible he doesn't like to be touched? I suddenly feel guilty that I had my hands all over him, rubbing his cock and grabbing at his hair like an absolute trash bag of a human. I didn't even ask if that was okay.

"Hey, Will?"

"Mmm?" He traces a finger down my spine, making me get all shivery and turned on again.

I sit up and look at him. Oh em gee, he looks so stinking adorable with his carroty-red hair sticking out from his head like that. "I didn't ask what you liked in bed. Do we need to talk about it?"

I could swear the man blushes. He reaches for the front of his jacket to button it, and I snag his hand to stop him. As I do, I notice that the front of his trousers are still tented and there's a wet droplet staining the front. "What is there to discuss?"

"Do you like it if I touch you?" I ask. "Or would you rather I not?"

His eyes are dark with heat as he gazes at me. "Of course I'd like you to touch me. Why wouldn't I?"

"I wasn't sure. This is the second time you've touched me, and I haven't really done much for you." I shrug, feeling a little silly at the scowl he sends in my direction. "I thought it was polite to ask! Don't look at me like that. You're the one still fully dressed while I had my skirts over my head five minutes ago."

"A very pretty scene, too," he murmurs, and the heated look he gives me makes me squirm. "If I'm not showing the proper appreciation for you, my love, I apologize. You've had a trying day, and my only thought was to make you feel better, not to score pleasure for myself." The accent is back in his words, a sure sign that he's feeling uptight and slightly anxious about something. "If I've sent the wrong message—"

I hold up a hand. "Can I suck your dick, yes or no?"

I love that his eyes practically bug at my crass words. I wait for him to scold me in that slightly accented, aristocratic voice. Instead, he swallows hard and gives me another steamy look that conveys so much more intensity than his clipped words do. "You may do anything to me that you would like, Penny. My body is yours to enjoy."

"Cool. And just to be clear . . . we enjoy a dick-sucking? Because some guys don't—"

"I do," he says quickly. "Yes. I do."

I bite my lip to keep from smiling. Is all this bluster because he's shy in bed? Why do I find that so achingly sweet? He really is a gosh-darn unicorn. "I'd like to suck your dick."

He groans, closing his eyes. His hands fist into the blankets, as if he's afraid to touch me. "You make it sound so obscenely filthy when you say it like that."

"Is that good?"

"Gods, yes. Yes it is."

I smile and slide down his body just a little, settling near his thighs. I feel good. Languid and wonderful. For all that he's stiff and proper, god, Will can lick a pussy like there's no tomorrow. It's been a long time since I've had anything that felt that good, and I'm willing (and eager) to return the favor. I move to his belt and undo it, glancing up at him to see his reaction. His hair is still disheveled in that adorable way, but the look on his face is hungry and raw and makes me shiver, my core clenching all over again. I carefully unzip him once the belt is out of the way, checking for underwear. Something tells me he's a tighty-whities sort of guy, but I'm surprised to see vivid green boxer briefs with a designer logo at the waist. I should have known. He does love his designer clothing.

I peel his pants back a little more, and then the bulge of him is revealed. There's a wet dot on the front of his boxer briefs, right next to the crown of his cock, which is quite firmly outlined against the tight material. My goodness, he's very thick. I pull down his underwear, mindful of the elastic, and come upon another surprise.

He's not circumcised. That's . . . new.

I glance up at him. "You're my first hooded dick."

"Hooded . . . dick?" Will blinks, as if not quite certain he hears me.

"Do I do anything special with it? Peel the foreskin back? What?"

His hand slides down to cover the tip of his cock. "You do not *peel* anything! Good gods."

"Okay, okay, no peeling." Now that I've seen him, I'm eager to experiment. He's thick and juicy-looking, with a flushed tip that manages to look bulbous despite the extra skin all around him. And adorably, I'm not surprised to see that his pubic hair is immaculate and just as red as the hair on his head. "Is the foreskin sensitive, then?"

Willem sits up on his elbows, watching me with a look of consternation. "I'm almost afraid to tell you."

If he's not going to tell me, then I'll figure it out for myself. I slowly curl my fingers around the base of him, and yup, he feels like a big, hard cock. Other than the extra bit of skin gloving him, everything else seems to be the same. I'm fascinated as I give him a squeeze. "Feels jiggly."

"Do *not* tell me that," he hisses, eyes closing as I give him another squeeze.

"It's not a bad jiggly. Just different. Let me figure you out." I slide my hand up his shaft, and as I do, I notice there's a lot more movement involved. Oh, okay. It's like a slippery glove covering his length, with only the tip and a bit of skin underneath protruding. I squeeze and stroke, and he hisses again. "Ooh, I bet this makes an awesome hand job."

His only response is to pant.

Right. I'll save the hand job for some other time. Blow job now. But still, this helps me figure things out. If I had to guess, I'd focus on the head and give the foreskin a li'l jiggle as I work him. While the foreskin isn't the prettiest thing I've seen, the head of his cock is fat and gorgeous and beaded with wetness, making my mouth water a little. I lean down and lick him, and I'm pleasantly surprised at the taste. Maybe all those sweets that Will is shoving into his mouth help things along, because he's not nearly as bitter to the taste as most pre-cum is.

Will sucks in a breath the moment my tongue touches him. I swirl it over the head, peeping up at him, and notice that he's got his eyes open, watching me with that hungry, hungry stare. Oh, I like this. Squirming with pleasure, I give him an obscene, deliberate lick and then give his shaft a squeeze and gentle tug.

The breath escapes him with an "unh" that tells me I'm doing well. I repeat the motion and then twirl my tongue along the head of his cock, trying to figure out what he likes best. I slide my other hand to his balls, because a girl knows what to do with those. I tease and toy with them, gently tugging every now and then as I slurp on the head of his cock and work his shaft with my hand.

"Penny," he grits out, the sound slightly desperate.

"Feels good?" I ask between licks. "Am I missing something?" I tease the tip of my tongue on the underside of his cock-head and glance up at him.

His head goes back and his breath hitches again. New pre-cum blooms on the tip and his hips jerk. "Need to—"

"Do you want to come on my face or my tongue?" I ask, tugging him into my mouth and sucking gently on the tip again.

"Ah!" As if my words triggered his release, he comes a split second later, flooding my mouth and dribbling down my chin as I squeeze and work his length. His face looks downright tortured when he comes, his eyes squeezed tightly shut and sweat beaded on his brow as the release overtakes him. I don't stop, even when his seed covers my hands and chin, and he collapses back on the bed with a gusty heave of breath.

Will groans after a moment and glances up at me. My hand is still on him, though I've stopped pumping, and I lick one finger, my face and the front of my dress a mess. "You're obscene."

"You love it."

"Jupiter help me, I really do." His hard mouth twitches with the barest hint of a smile, and I feel like I could conquer the world right now.

* * *

SOME TIME LATER, after we've both cleaned up and changed into pajamas, I snuggle against Will's chest. I'm not entirely surprised to see that his pajamas are a matching striped pair in a designer brand and look so stiff they could wrinkle. But his hair is still slightly disheveled, and the looks he sends my way are soft and affectionate as I curl up against him. He plays with my hair and trails his fingers over my arm and back, as if he's content to just touch me for all time.

A girl could get used to something like this.

"Well," I say after a while. "I guess we won't have to try very hard to convince anyone we're dating anymore." I play with one of the buttons on his pajamas. "I can just tell everyone at the society meeting that we're trying to get pregnant but nothing's landing."

His hand pauses, and then he wraps a lock of my hair around his finger. "I don't like you going back there."

I don't much like it, either, considering they're blackmailing me for information on him. It does hurt, given that they're supposed to be my friends. How much time in my life have I devoted to the society, and this is the thanks I get? I know not everyone is like Cody and Katrina, but it still bugs me. "I can't leave. That would make people more suspicious than anything. It really does need to seem like business as usual. I'll keep going, and I'll keep showing up to my job."

"Doesn't mean I like it," he grumbles. "We're going to have to charm the hell out of you."

"Charm?"

"Protection charms. Evil eyes. Wards against scrying. You name it, we'll do it. I want you to be safe, and since it's probably a bad idea for me to hover at your shoulder, this is the next best thing." Will pauses. "Unless you want me to show up and hover over your shoulder? I could, you know."

I smile at that, mentally picturing the scowl on his face as he glares at everyone in the meeting. He'd intimidate the hell out of everyone there. "No, it's not necessary. I can manage them as long as we come up with a decent lie or two, but I hate playing into their games. What if they're feeding information back to Stoker?"

His hand stills on my back. "Actually, about that . . ."

I sit up, worried. "What?"

Will gazes up at me. "Your mother said something earlier that made me pause."

I wince. "Oh?"

"Nothing bad. Just . . . remember the charm we found under your bed, and how I told you it was dedicated to a fertility god to ensure pregnancy?"

"It's a good thing you came in my mouth, then, huh?" I tease.

His cheeks flush with color, which I find adorable. "As I was saying," he continues in a dour tone, leveling a stern look in my direction, "it was a fertility charm, and I couldn't figure out why Stoker would break into my house in order to ensure you got pregnant. It didn't make sense to me, because if it was something I wanted, normally he would do his best to ensure it wouldn't happen. But then your mother commented that familiars try to avoid getting pregnant because they can no longer assist their witch or warlock. It's too much of a drain on their resources."

Oh, he's right. I remember Reggie telling me that Dru—Ben's aunt and a powerful witch—initially hired Reggie because her old familiar was very pregnant and couldn't assist with casting. "So Stoker thinks we're casting together and wants us to stop?"

"It would seem so."

I chew on my lip, considering. "So he's afraid of you casting anything big. Why doesn't he want you to be able to cast?

What's he afraid you're going to do? That you'd move against him?"

"Hardly." Will's hand plays at my hip. "If I did, the Society of Warlocks would immediately expel me. I'd be hunted down as a traitor by everyone with an ounce of magic in their blood, and they wouldn't stop until I was dead. So no, I'm not making any moves against him."

Goose bumps flare over my skin. "Wait . . . what?"

He tilts his head on the pillow, looking up at me thoughtfully. "What?"

"They'd kill you if you're caught using a familiar?" I feel sick to my stomach. "I . . . I just thought you'd get in trouble, Will."

"At this point? No. They'd kill me." He shakes his head. "It's nothing for you to worry about. I know the dangers in casting. Everything we do will be very quiet and under the radar."

I feel the sudden urge to rip his bracelet off my arm. I don't want him dying because of a stupid scrying spell or whatever piddly shit we're casting. "This is serious, Will. I don't like the thought of you risking your life to cast a couple of spells with me. We should stop."

"We're not stopping. Not until we figure out what's going on with Stoker and why he thinks he should take you out." He shakes his head. "You being with me has put you in danger. Or did you forget about the roof he tried to have caved in over your head? He wants you out of my hands, and I need to determine why. If we stop casting, that gives him all the advantages."

"Yes, well . . . I don't like it." I shake my head. "I think we should stop."

"You think I like you being in danger?"

"All the more reason," I say, moving to the edge of the bed and away from him. "Maybe we should stop working together entirely."

Will jerks upright, staring at me in shock. "Are you . . . leaving me?"

It's probably the smart thing to do. I'm already catching feelings for him, which is a bad idea. Add on top of that the spells we're casting that could get him killed? I should take his bracelet off right now and call it a day. Chalk this up as a bad idea and leave.

Let someone else be his partner. Just the thought feels as if it's gutting me, but maybe I need to walk away for both of our sakes. I look back at him, and his expression is angry, but his eyes are so damn wounded. It's those eyes that make me hesitate. "You could probably find a better apprentice—"

He grabs my hand and tips me backward until I bounce flat onto my back again. In the next moment, he covers me, pinning my hands above my head and glaring down at me so fiercely that it takes my breath away. "I don't want better. I want *you*."

"I want you, too," I whisper. "Which is why it really bothers me that you're risking your life."

Will leans in and kisses me, his mouth light and flirty against my own. It sends a ripple of hunger through my belly. "I assure you, I don't want to die, either. Not when certain things in my life are better than ever."

"Certain . . . things?"

"Mm-hmm." He buries his face against my neck, nuzzling at my throat.

"What things might those be?" I ask, fishing for compliments.

Will lifts his head, looking playful. "Well, I don't like to brag, but my stock portfolio has really taken a leap—"

With an outraged squeal, I fling my arms around him and push him over. "Double-yew tee eff, you jerk! You'd better be teasing!"

He laughs, and the sound is so happy and so rare that it melts my heart. Maybe Will doesn't see himself as lovable in the eyes of the rest of the world, but that doesn't matter. All he needs is me.

My phone chimes with an incoming text, and I groan. That's what I get for turning it back on.

Will glances over at the nightstand, where I've left it. "Your blackmailers again?"

"Probably." Reggie wouldn't text this late at night, and my parents are usually too busy to text much at all.

"Ignore it," Will says, leaning in to nip at my ear. "We'll come up with some sufficiently ridiculous lie for the morning."

* * *

IT'S SO QUIET for the next few days that I almost forget that Will's being targeted. Cody and Katrina did want more information about Will—specifically his books in his library—but I play stupid for a few days.

I'm back on track at work, I'm less tired after castings, and best of all, I get to come home to Will. We spend our evenings curled up on the sofa together, watching Netflix and eating cookies that I split with Pip. Will actually really enjoys period dramas and loves to tell me all about how they get things wrong, and I just love snuggling on the couch with him and listening to him talk. We do some spellcasting, but not as much as before. I think it's because Will wants to make sure he doesn't tire me out. He watches me closely, a worried look on his face each time my legs spasm and kick out from the orgasm rippling through me. I haven't told him yet that I'm coming with every spell. I don't know if it's normal or not, so I don't say anything at all.

Mostly, though, I'm just full of emotions that Will is thinking of me and not himself, and it makes my heart flutter even more. It's like we really have become a team.

Well, mostly.

Sometimes we bicker over spells.

"I just think if you're going to sabotage the new guy at Atticus & Partners, you should do it in a nicer way," I point out as he etches words into a curse tablet. Each slice of the stylus into the soft lead sends a bolt of pleasure through me, like a finger stroking over my clit. "Make him late to work. Don't make him mess up his cases."

"For the record, I am not sabotaging him," Will says as he marks on the tablet. "I am simply enhancing his luck." He pauses. "In the opposite direction from what he would probably want." He makes one last mark and then straightens, gazing down at his tablet. "There, I think it's done. Now to cast."

Here it comes. I wiggle on my seat by his lab table. I clench my thighs tightly together and wait. Sure enough, Will starts casting, and the moment he does, hot pleasure glides through my core, heightening every sensation.

I suck in a breath as he invokes Jupiter's name, waiting for the inevitable pulse of orgasmic pleasure that will rocket through me the moment the spell is completed.

Will turns toward me, stopping midcast, a look of concern on his face. "Are you all right?"

"I'm good," I answer, voice tight. Oh god. He needs to keep going. I'm so close.

He frowns at me, and I'm embarrassed that I can't hold my shit together. How do other familiars handle this? I need to ask, but it seems so personal. So I just give him a wobbly smile and a thumbs-up.

"Should I stop casting?" Will asks.

"Oh, god no," I blurt out, and then blush at how urgent that sounded. He's going to think I'm a horny freak. Clearing my throat, I cross my legs (tightly) and try to look composed. "You should absolutely finish."

So I can finish, too.

And when he does, it's glorious.

✳ ✳ ✳

WEDNESDAY ROLLS AROUND, though, and my happy, contented feeling turns into a knot in my stomach. I'm nervous all day at work, and even texting Will doesn't make things better. I keep my phone constantly with me as I fill orders in the back room, checking for texts between pulls.

WILL: Are you coming home after work, dumpling?

I snicker-snort at the moniker. He's started to use it unironically lately. He says I'm short and plump like a dumpling and that I make his mouth water. I decide it's a good nickname, because I am short and plump, and he looks at me like he wants to devour me. That, and because he always goes down on me after saying something like that. I've never met a guy that liked to eat pussy as much as Willem Sauer, but he loves it. We make out every night before bed, drowning in kisses and touches, but never going further than third base. It's like he's a little worried about that fertility charm after all . . . or maybe it's the old-fashioned part of him that doesn't want to push all the way to consummation. Whatever it is, I'm happy to play it slow.

Well, mostly happy. Sometimes I whine when he doesn't give me a good dicking, but he makes me come hard enough that I forget, at least for a little while.

PENNY: I wish! I have Fam tonight.

WILL: You remember our conversation from this morning?

I do indeed. We talked over what to tell them as we ate Pop-Tarts. I sat on his lap and squirmed while he nibbled on my neck. Somewhere in all that, he told me that the best thing to use was a piece of the truth—that I had a fertility charm under my bed and he was trying to make me pregnant.

The pregnant part isn't true, of course, but the rest should hold them off until next week.

PENNY: And you're sure this is a good idea?

WILL: If he's their buyer, he'll know we're on to him. It'll make him have to consider his next move.

PENNY: No more roofs collapsing over my head I hope.

WILL: I doubt he'll try that again. If he does, tell them I made you a charm and it took me a week to pull it together. That'll sound about right.

I touch the charm at my neck. He did make me an evil eye to go with my scrying charm, and both of them hang between my breasts on the same chain. I hope he knows what he's doing. Any time we bring up Will casting anything, it makes me nervous. But he didn't want me to go to the meeting tonight unprepared, so the evil eye it is. It's actually not evil at all—it's supposed to force evil to "look the other way," and keep me protected. It sounds creepier than it is, and I play with it all day, touched that he fusses over me so much.

No one ever fusses over me. It's a really nice feeling.

PENNY: I'll come home straight after. Can you feed Pip for me?

WILL: I already have. That rodent actually scolded me as he ate. It was insufferably rude.

PENNY: You're such a good boyfriend!

WILL: I am the best boyfriend you will ever have, dumpling.

Oh god, just him calling me the pet name in a text makes me horny. I squeeze my thighs together and hope the day passes quickly.

* * *

TO MY SURPRISE—AND pleasure—Ben and Reggie are the special guests at the Society of Familiars meeting that night. Most everyone gives poor Reggie displeased looks and ignores her as Ben takes the podium and begins to speak. I hate that the Fam is so snobbish to her just because she apprenticed from outside, so I snag her hand and sit at a table in the back with her instead of my usual spot at the front.

"How are things going?" Reggie whispers, her gaze locked on her tall, pale boyfriend as he argues with Derek. She's ridiculously in love with Ben and it's adorable.

"He met my parents the other day," I whisper-confess. "He got all growly and protective over me. It was the cutest."

Reggie beams at me. "I love that. I knew you'd be good for him." She leans in. "How is the *other* stuff going?"

As in, the stuff with Stoker. I wrinkle my nose at the thought. "He doesn't like to admit it, but I think he's stumped." I touch my charm to make sure it's cool, and when it is, I continue with "He might need help."

"Say no more," Reggie tells me, an excited look on her face. "I have the best idea."

"Oh?"

"Double date!"

Oh em *gee*, that is a great idea.

* * *

"A DOUBLE DATE," Will grumps as he fusses in the mirror the next evening, adjusting his tie. "I don't see why it has to be a double date. Can't they just come over and cast with us? Why must we parade ourselves before the locals?"

"Oh my god, listen to you." I sit on the counter in front of him and loosen his tie, then remove it. "First of all, they're your friends and it's nice to see them. Second of all, it's good to have allies in this. Third of all, we're supposed to look like we're dating, right? A double date makes sense." I artfully pop his collar and consider the look, then reach up and muss his hair.

Will bats my hands away, giving me an indignant look. "I'm going to look like a boybander if I'm left to your devices."

"That'd be hot," I tell him, curling one ankle around the back of his leg.

He pauses. "It is?"

I nod. "Totally makes me want to sit on your face."

Will leans forward, his cheeks flushed, but he lets me tousle his hair into a more modern style. When I'm done, he kisses me, a thoughtful look on his face. "I'm going to hold you to that later, dumpling. You know that, right?"

I squeeze my thighs tightly. "You absolutely should."

✳ ✳ ✳

WE MEET REGGIE and Ben at a cozy Italian restaurant. I immediately recognize the place as one where several of the Fam wait tables, and bite back a groan. Sure enough, Cody shows up with a notepad and a sanctimonious smile on his face, and I want to hide under the tablecloth with frustration. His man bun is in full swing tonight, and he arches his brows at me as Will pulls my seat closer to his and settles his arm across the back. I don't know if he's recognized Cody or if he's just in boyfriend mode, but either way, it's effective. Cody looks at us. "What can I get for you folks?"

"Wine," Ben says. "The best red you've got."

"Water for me," I chirp.

Will puts a finger under my chin, tipping me up for a kiss. "That's right," he coos, and I realize in that moment he absolutely recognizes Cody. "We're trying to make my little dumpling pregnant, so no wine for her."

"Of course," Cody says unctuously, and gives a little bow. "I'll return to take your orders."

Reggie grimaces at me from across the table. "Anyone know a spell to check for pubes? Because he's totally going to put pubes in your food."

"He won't," Ben states, somewhat arrogant. "Two warlocks at one table? He'll be afraid of retaliation."

"I don't know." Reggie shakes her head and fusses with her napkin. "That look he was giving Willem wasn't an 'I'm afraid of warlocks' look. It was the 'you stole my girl' look."

"It was?" I echo, surprised. "That's exciting. I mean, he did offer to be my fuck buddy, but I never took him up on it."

"He what?" Will turns to me, indignant.

I reach over and pat his thigh. "It was before we got together, baby."

"That doesn't make me want to murder him less." Will's nostrils flare, and he pulls me slightly closer to him. Hell, if he pulls me any closer, I'm going to be in his lap, though maybe that's the goal. I shoot a look over at Reggie, and she gives me a subtle wink. Ooh, she's devious. I love the way her mind works.

Cody returns with the wine, and we order our food. Over salads, Reggie and I gossip about Nick and Diego, and if there will be wedding bells there soon. "I don't know," Reggie says, swirling her wineglass. "I've known Nick for years, and I would say he's not the type to commit, but he's a different person around Diego. They're already pretty serious. He told me the other day that Diego combined his cards with his."

"Monster," Ben says in a dry voice.

"You don't just combine cards!" Reggie gives her boyfriend an indignant look. "What if you both want to play the same ones? That's why you keep your collections separate. It just doesn't make sense to combine. Madness!"

Ben's lips twitch as Reggie rants.

"I take it you haven't combined your cards?" Will asks, amused.

"Never," Reggie retorts. She stabs her salad passionately. "It's just not done. The Spellcraft: The Magicking community is *very* clear about such things."

Will looks down at me. "And do you share the same feelings? Or would you let me combine my cards with yours?"

"I'd let you combine your cards with mine, of course." At Reggie's horrified stare, I add, "I don't have any good ones anyhow. And he doesn't know how to play."

Reggie just shakes her head at my traitorous ways. "You're supposed to teach him. You're coming to cards again, aren't you, Will? The group always needs fresh blood."

"If I must." Will shrugs. "Whatever Penny wants to do. I'm game to follow her lead."

He's far too good at this boyfriend thing. When we're like this, it feels like the real thing and it makes me ache. I rub his leg with my foot under the table, and I'm rewarded with a flush of his high cheekbones. It makes me want this to be permanent.

The realization that this could all be temporary on his end takes some of the pleasure out of the evening. What Reggie and Ben have is real—it's evident from the little smiles they share and the way Reggie sticks her fork in his plate and steals an olive. Ben Magnus is supposed to be the scariest warlock imaginable, a man capable of murdering his family in cold blood, but the man at the table with us is just a normal guy (admittedly a little goth-looking) who happens to adore his girlfriend.

I asked Will if he wanted to be my boyfriend, but I never clarified that I wanted him to be my real boyfriend. That it wasn't just more teasing about our weird fake relationship. I don't know if we're legit or if I'm just a familiar playing pretend so we can keep casting in secret together. Thing is, the feelings I've developed for him are real, and I don't know if his are.

I poke at my fettuccini, no longer all that interested in it.

"So have you heard from Abernathy recently?" Ben asks as he drinks his wine.

The question is quiet and posed in a normal conversation, but Will immediately stiffens, as if on the defensive. He glances over at me and I touch my pendant. It's cool, and I give him a nod to let him know it's all right. Will pushes his plate away, tossing his napkin on it. "Not recently. Such is the nature of my old master. He might answer right away, he might answer never. The choice, as always, is entirely up to him."

And Will gives us a tight, bitter smile.

"You think he'll know anything?"

"Hard to say." Will shakes his head, his gaze trailing over to the dessert cart at a nearby table. "Abernathy has always been a bit peculiar, even when I served under him."

"If you need to speak, I'm happy to reach out on your behalf," Ben offers. "A simple spell of communication would work. And we have all the components here." He gestures at the food on the table. "We could get a new loaf of bread, some olive oil, and I could cast before they bring dessert."

"Wait, what?" I squeak, shocked. "You'd do that right here?"

Everyone looks at me in surprise.

"Is that a bad thing?" Reggie asks, her gaze curious. She sets down her wineglass. "It's not like anyone knows what we're doing. And the other tables won't pay any attention." She tilts her head in their direction, and she's got a good point. The other tables are a few paces away from ours, and we're tucked into a nice, shadowy corner full of ambiance. And since Will isn't casting, there's no harm.

Even so . . . *right here?* And I'm going to have to watch Reggie come? *At the table?* I'm scandalized. I mean, I like to think that I'm fairly open to a lot of stuff, but that might be too much even for me.

I lean in toward her. "This isn't . . . weird for you?"

"Weird?" She blinks at me and then looks at Ben. "Not . . . really?"

I must be missing something here. I shoot a look over at Will, who looks equally puzzled. "Okay, uh, never mind."

"Oh no." Reggie leans in. "Now you have to say. You're not getting out of this that easily. What's going on?"

I squirm a little, swallowing hard. "I just must be mistaken about something. Don't worry about it."

"Mistaken about what?" Will insists.

Playing with my fork, I stare down at it as I admit, "Well, every time he . . . you know . . . I . . . *you know.*"

Everyone's quiet. I look up and see three equally confused faces. Reggie frowns. "I'm really lost now."

"You don't . . . get a little, um, sexually excited when he casts?" It feels like I'm shouting the words across the table.

Ben's eyes go wide and he looks over at Reggie. "*Do* you?"

Her jaw drops. She looks equally shocked. "No! And now I feel like I'm missing out! You seriously come every time he casts?"

Furtively, I glance over at Will. He's staring at me, too. I give a nervous little laugh. "Okay, so it's just me. Never mind. Forget I said anything."

"Oh, I'm not forgetting," Will murmurs, and he puts a possessive hand on my thigh that makes me clench all over. "I can't believe you've been keeping this a secret."

I wince, giving Reggie an embarrassed look. "I dunno, I kinda thought that was one reason why you two got together. She was casting with you, and the next thing you know, boom. Throw in a few orgasms and I totally understand it."

Reggie gives me a horrified look. "Penny, I was Aunt Dru's familiar first. You think I was . . ." She puts a hand up and closes her eyes. "You know what? I don't actually even want to finish that sentence."

Ben coughs politely into his napkin.

Will just keeps watching me, his fingers rubbing circles onto my thigh. "So every spell I cast makes you orgasm . . . I thought you were in pain all this time."

"Nope," I say brightly. "A good spell is better than the best vibrator." I pause and then add, "But not as good as your mouth, Will. I prefer that."

"Glad to hear it, *dumpling*."

My thighs clench at the nickname, and I could swear his hand moves higher.

"I've honestly never heard of such a thing," Reggie admits.

"I have, actually," Ben interjects. "I've heard in the past that those with an intense connection feel magic more physically than others do. I just didn't realize it meant . . . that."

"Mmm." Will gives me another speculative look. "I'll have to keep that in mind." He teases another circle on the inside of my thigh with his thumb and then turns to Ben.

"And I do appreciate the offer to contact Abernathy, Magnus, but for now I prefer not to bother him. He'll respond if there's urgent need. If there isn't, I'll figure something out." He shrugs casually, but the hand on my thigh gives me a light squeeze and then slides under my skirt.

I wonder if it's possible to spontaneously combust at the table.

✳ ✳ ✳

TALK STEERS TOWARD normal things, and I toy with my necklace and try not to wriggle in my seat as Reggie and Ben tell us all about Drusilla's adventures island-hopping. Dru is Ben's aunt, a very old, esteemed witch, and she's taking a hiatus while her familiar, Lisa, raises her own child. I feel a pang of envy for that child, thinking about my parents, but then Will's hand slides to the inside of my thigh and his fingers trail back and forth against my skin. It's like he's deliberately trying to distract me.

It's like he's trying to make me come right here at the damned table. I'm getting so aroused that it's hard for me to concentrate on the conversation, and I get quiet, pretending to listen as Will's hand creeps higher and higher up my skirt, until his fingers are brushing against my panties while he takes a bite out of his tiramisu.

"Do you want a taste?" he asks me, holding the spoon over to me. As I lean forward so he can feed me, his finger presses against my clit, and I nearly come off the chair.

At Reggie's surprised look, I get up and shake my leg out. "Cramp. Not used to sitting down for long periods of time."

Will manages to look completely unbothered, eating another bite of tiramisu. Well, two can play that game. I plot my revenge as Ben and Will argue over the bill for a bit, and it feels like a normal double date, right down to the part where I hug Reggie at the door as we part and promise to text her later. Then Will and I head off for his parked car, and Ben and Reggie head in the other direction. Will opens my door and I slide inside, and then the moment he's behind the driver's seat, my hands are on his cock, frantic.

He grunts.

The next thing I know, Will jerks the seat release, and his seat slides back another foot. He hauls me into his lap, and we're kissing uncontrollably. His hands push at my skirts, desperately seeking bare flesh under my panties even as I work at his belt buckle. "You little minx," he purrs at me between kisses. "Sitting in your chair like a good girl and quivering. Here I thought you were tired, but you were coming every fucking time I cast. Do you know how hot that is?"

I whimper as he strokes his fingers through my folds. I'm sopping wet and so darn ready. "Let's fuck tonight, yes? Right here? Right now?"

He groans, and for a moment, I think he's going to turn me down. But then Will's hand is on his belt and he's impatiently tearing at it. I try to help free his cock, and the moment his erection is uncovered, I lift my hips and pull my panties aside and then use my hand to guide him into me.

We both hiss the moment our bodies make contact.

"Oh fuck," I whimper, clinging to his neck. "You're so big."

His hips slap against mine, his face contorted with pleasure. "We shouldn't be doing this—*fuck*." He drives up into me, and then I'm rocking over him, riding his cock as he bounces me atop him, our bodies crashing together. It's messy and urgent and I can't stop myself. I press my forehead to his as I move faster. My legs are cramping, and I'm pretty sure one is trapped against the door, but I can't stop.

Will buries his face in my neck, dragging me down even as he surges up, and then I feel him trembling as he comes inside me. He holds me tight, the breath gusting out of him as he comes and then hisses out an angry curse. A moment later, his hand is where our joined bodies meet, and he's rubbing my clit until I come, too.

That was . . . fast. Far too fast.

But good. I let out a breathless little moan and lean back.

The car horn honks, shocking us both. I jerk, gasping, and Will's head goes back again as my pussy clenches around him. "Fuck," he mutters. "We can't do this here. Later . . . We need to get home, Penny. Home."

"Right," I breathe. "Home."

"Home and then I'm going to fuck you for hours," he promises, and then leans in and sucks on my neck until pleasure ripples through me again, and I know he's left a mark.

"Yes please."

WILLEM

That got out of hand.

I've always prided myself on my restraint. My control. So fucking much for that. The moment I found out my casting was making her come, it reminded me of every spell we'd cast, every time she'd made one of those little gasps or gotten red in the face, and I never realized what she was up to. She never said a damned word. To think all those times she'd had a wet, aching pussy and never told me. I want to bend her over my knee and spank her.

She'd probably love that, though. Gods know I would.

But I'm not supposed to touch my familiar. We're supposed to be a professional pairing, no matter how it looks to the outside world. Instead, since the moment she arrived, she's been turning my life upside down. Now instead of the composed, aristocratic warlock I try to present myself as, my hair is disheveled, my pants are sticking to my legs, and my car smells like sex.

And I've never felt so damn good.

I glance over at her, at her flushed, rounded face and the love bite I left on her throat. Penny looks disheveled and well fucked, and just the sight makes me all the more possessive. There's no way on earth that she is ever going to serve another warlock or witch. Not when she's as responsive as she is. Not when magic makes her come. I was already obsessed with her, and now I fear I'm over the edge.

"You're looking at me weird," she murmurs sleepily from her side of the car.

"I'm trying to decide if you'll come harder if I cast a bigger spell, or if even a small spell will set you off like a rocket."

She shivers. "I think it's just the magic culminating. Doesn't matter the size of the spell."

I bite back a groan, because now I'm imagining casting while I'm inside her, bending her over my lab table and working as she pushes back against me and . . . yeah, she's never serving another warlock. Ever. "We're going to test that," I tell her, and I love the hot look she sends back in my direction. "When we get home, you and I are going to cast and then . . ."

Trailing off, I stare at the unfamiliar cars lining the long drive-way that leads up to my house. Three shiny black sedans with tinted windows are waiting for us, and a cold clench settles in my gut.

Stoker has finally made his move.

"Penny," I say carefully as I pull into the driveway. It's too late to back away now. They'd have seen us coming. Even now, as I watch, a man emerges from one of the cars and waits. "I want you to stay in the car. No matter what happens, stay in the car, all right? Until they're gone. The car is warded to protect its occupants."

"What's going on?" She sounds afraid.

I put the car into park a short distance away from them and touch her thigh. "Just do as I ask, yes?"

She nods, her eyes full of worry for me. "What are they here for? Who are they?"

There won't be enough time to tell her everything . . . mostly because I'm not certain of it myself. They could be here for any number of reasons, and all that matters is protecting Penny. They shouldn't harm her, but I can't be too careful. "Once they take me away," I continue calmly, "I want you to contact Magnus and tell him what happened. Contact Abernathy as well. They'll help you figure out how to move forward." I pull her hand to my lips. "Promise me you'll do all that."

"But . . . but . . ." She looks helplessly at the cars and then at me. "Will, let me help you—"

"No. If they find out what we've been doing together, your life is ruined, too." I shake my head. "Let me shoulder everything. If anyone asks, you know nothing about anything. I'm retired. Understand?"

Tears brim in her eyes. "I don't understand, actually. I don't understand any of this."

"I know." I brush my mouth over her knuckles, wanting to touch her more, wanting to devour her, wanting to pick her up and squeeze her tight. "Just . . . know that I love you."

"What?" she chokes.

I get out of the car. Immediately, an unnatural silence falls, and I know they've cast a spell on our surroundings to hide what they're doing. I hold my wrists out in a mocking gesture, daring them to cuff me. More warlocks emerge from the cars. Titus, my old enemy. Marcus Ruiz, who lost a spell book to me more than fifty years ago and has held a grudge since. George Greenwald, a very old rival of mine. Enforcers for the Society of Warlocks, I'm guessing. Well now, this has to be important. "To what do I owe this honor, gentlemen?"

"The Society of Warlocks has heard that you have attacked another warlock with intent to kill," Titus says, his tone gleeful as he moves to my side. "Come with us quietly and we won't cast against you."

"Oh, I'm very quiet," I sneer. "And what warlock is it that I've attempted to kill? Let me guess. His name rhymes with 'poker'?"

"Do you deny it?"

"Does it matter?" I eye Titus as he approaches with a pair of warded cuffs for my wrists. "You're going to arrest me anyhow." I'm irritated more than anything. I knew Stoker was going to move against me at some point, but I thought I'd have more time. I glance back at the car, where Penny's tearful face is lit up by the interior. "Just leave my girlfriend alone. You can cast a truth spell on me. She doesn't know anything about this."

"Already done, and we have no interest in her."

I try not to show my relief. As long as Penny's safe, nothing else matters. Whatever story Stoker has concocted against me won't hold up in a tribunal. I simply have to wait to get out.

Unless things go like they did with Y2K. If that's the case, then I'm well and truly fucked.

PENNY

I don't know what to do.

I watch in horror, tears streaming down my face, as they cuff Will and take him away in one of the black sedans. He told me to stay in the car until they were long gone, and I do, weeping in the darkness and thinking about how wonderful tonight had been. How we'd been all over each other in the car and had furtive, messy sex and how he'd told me he loved me.

And now everything is shattered.

I clutch my purse to my chest as I sit in the passenger seat.

Just . . . know that I love you.

How the fuck am I supposed to get past that? How can he say something like that to me and then let them cart him off? Probably to execute him? Didn't he say if he got caught again, he'd be killed for violating warlock law or some shit like that? I can't let this happen. Scratch that. I'm not *going* to let this happen.

Maybe most familiars would sit back and let their warlock be imprisoned, but I'm Will's girlfriend, and I'll be damned if I'm going to just do nothing.

I get out of the car after they leave, and head for the front door. I have Will's keys, and when I step inside, nothing goes off or blares, the wards accepting my presence without him. It feels strange to be here when he's not. There's a hard lump in my throat that won't go away as I look around his empty, austere house, checking to see if anything was moved out of place. Everything looks as bare and gray as it always does, though.

I don't know why they've arrested him and not me as well. They would have come for both of us if it was casting related, so I have to assume that it's not.

I head up to Will's bedroom and check under the bed for weird-ass fertility statues. Nothing. Pip chitters angrily at me from his cage, so I get him out and head down to the kitchen to feed him fresh veggies and nuts, and as I do, I stroke his back and think. Will claims he doesn't have allies, but he's wrong. Ben Magnus will help him. And Ben has a very influential aunt, Drusilla. Even the greenest familiars in the society have heard of the legendary Drusilla Magnus.

There's Will's old master Abernathy. From what Will has told me, he's on good terms with Abernathy. It's just that Abernathy is strange and flaky. I need to let him know what happened so he can speak on Will's behalf.

I can reach out to my boss, Vivi, too.

Hell, I can reach out to my parents and ask their witches to intercede on Will's behalf. He's not alone in this. He's got me, and I'm not going to give up on him.

Despite the late hour, I immediately start texting people.

✳ ✳ ✳

MORNING.

I groan, exhausted, as Pipstachio nibbles on my hair and scolds me with a series of squeaks and chitters that tells me he's hungry. I sit up, rubbing my face, and look around me. I'm in Will's lab. It's a mess, as I've pulled out every single spell book he has, drafted several curse tablets, and basically taken the place apart looking for hints as to why Will is in so much trouble that the Society of Warlocks hauled him away.

It has to be something with Stoker. With the books. Yet he stole them months ago. Surely they would have acted upon theft like that quickly if it was a problem? Vivi has mentioned in the past that petty theft is rampant among warlocks and witches. That's why all the components are kept in a locked, warded room at the back of the store. It's almost expected for someone to lightfinger things.

So . . . not the theft of the books. But if not, then what? Yawning, I check my phone.

BEN MAGNUS: On it. I'm reaching out to see what's going on.

REGGIE: Are you okay, Penny? Do you need me to come over?

REGGIE: That does it. I'm coming over with donuts at 8 in the morning.

REGGIE: Be ready for me. We'll figure something out.

REGGIE: Ben's going to be making a million phone calls this AM.

VIVI: The timing definitely seems suspicious. I've been hearing his name pop up on my social networks lately. Let me see what I can find out. You won't be late to work on Monday will you? XOXO

MOM: I am so mad on your behalf! Let me talk to Aurelia!

DAD: Will speak to Diana. Kisses.

DAD: Diana says check in with Abernathy.

DAD: Let me know if I can help, Pen. Dad loves you.

The flood of supportive messages makes me feel all weepy. Will's not alone in this. We're going to get things figured out. Sniffling, I flick over to the time and wince. I still have a half hour before Reggie arrives with donuts. Absently, I get to my feet and scratch at Pip's ears. "We'll eat in a bit, buddy. I just need to straighten up down here."

I pick up a spell book and then pause.

Will was showing me how to cast. I wonder if I can cast something on my own? Or am I still too new for the gods to pay attention to me? Will has said before that the gods dislike inexperience and look for any reason not to grant a spell, but it's worth a try, isn't it? I flip through the books, looking for one about sending messages. Mercury would be the obvious god to request from, but what components would he like? Parchment paper? Bird feathers? Food?

I ponder all of this, and as I do, a bird chirps somewhere upstairs.

Alarmed, I grab a knife off the table. Will doesn't have a bird. He doesn't like animals and barely tolerates Pip (though I think he's getting used to him). "Stay here," I tell my squirrel and head upstairs with my weapon.

When I slip out of the secret passageway and into Will's media room, the bird chirps again. It sounds much closer . . . and it also sounds fake. That's odd. I follow the sound into Will's study and notice that there's an open mailbox over the fireplace, and an envelope is sitting inside. As I reach for the letter, the mailbox chirps again.

Fascinated, I pull out the piece of parchment. It's been sealed with wax and a symbol on the back that I don't recognize. Will's name is the only thing on the front, with no address or return address of any kind. I hesitate for a moment, then break the seal. If Will were here, he'd want me to open it, right?

My apprentice,

I have done several spells to guide me upon this and I can assure you that the answer you seek is in your books. The gods will not tell me more.

—Abernathy

I cluck my tongue in frustration. Not only is Abernathy's timing crappy, but his guidance is useless. The answer is in the books? The books Will stole? His spell books? Or is Abernathy being coy? What fortune cookie shit is this? Why not just tell him that a positive attitude will solve everything? Frustrated, I fold the letter again and then peer inside the mailbox to make sure I didn't miss anything. It's empty, though, and I feel vaguely cheated. So much for Will's helpful mentor.

It doesn't matter, I tell myself. I'm going to get answers for Will.

✳ ✳ ✳

EIGHT HOURS LATER, I'm full of donuts and milk and sick at heart.

I flip listlessly through Will's grimoire of *defixiones* and glance over at Reggie. "I haven't seen anything that would be the answer."

"We just have to keep looking," she tells me, eating another donut. "It has to be a spell. That's the only thing I can imagine it would be, unless there's a curse tablet or a scroll tucked somewhere in the pages?"

I shake my head. "I thought the same thing and shook them all out before lunch."

"Hmm." She licks her sugar-coated fingers and plucks another book off Will's shelf, skimming through the pages. "We need

Ben. He said he was going to be on his way soon, but I'm not sure what's keeping him. And of course, Aunt Dru is in Fiji, and I swear she only checks her phone once a week." Reggie shakes her head. "So she's not going to be helpful just yet. But Ben will help."

"I hope so," I say softly. Some of my initial determination is flagging. I just feel in over my head with this situation. I'm barely a familiar, and now I'm supposed to figure out how to tell what's going on with a bunch of secretive warlocks that have kidnapped my boyfriend? "I don't suppose they post meeting notes or anything online, do you think?"

Sitting across from me, Reggie snorts and peers down at a star chart in one of Will's books. "Are you kidding me? Some of them still have beepers and consider that cutting-edge technology. If anything, I'm guessing their notes are in a nice, musty old book at their equally musty headquarters."

I heave a sigh in frustration. "Someone has to be able to tell us what's going on."

"Ben," Reggie agrees, checking her phone. "Ben will have our answers. Don't lose hope." She flicks through another page. "Also, these books of Will's are incredible. He's got a collection to rival Aunt Dru. This is really something."

"They truly are." I wonder if I should keep biting my tongue about the fact that they were stolen, and then decide to confess it all. "Some of them are Stoker's, by the way."

"They are?" She looks up at me in surprise.

I nod. "Will got pissed about Stoker needling him and stole them from him. From what I can tell, most of them are just boring stuff and a lot of apprentice primers." I shrug. "No personal spell books of Stoker's. I get him being angry, but I'm not sure if he's angry enough to have Will imprisoned over a few spell primers from old familiars of his."

Reggie thinks for a moment. "Huh. Yeah, I have a spell primer myself, and it's just got baby witch stuff in it. Nothing important. But it feels like there should be a connection." She pauses and then points at another volume. "Did you know there's an entire book on moonlight excretions as components and the effect on a spell versus sunlight ones?"

"I know," I say softly. "Lots of books and no answers, though." I bite my lip. "Do you think they have Will in a dungeon? Do you think they're torturing him?"

She gives me a firm look. "You need to stop that line of thinking, Penny. Remember to be positive."

"I'm positive they could be torturing him," I manage, and sniffle. "I'm positive he deserves better help than a familiar who doesn't know any spells. I'm positive that I'm useless!"

Reggie gets up from her seat and moves to my side, sliding an arm around my shoulders. "You've had a very long night, all right? Give yourself a break. From talking with Ben, the last time a warlock was arrested by the warlock council, it was for crimes against his fellow warlocks and it was in the Inquisition. They held him for a month and then had a public trial, and all the warlocks voted if he was innocent or guilty."

"And was he innocent?"

Reggie rubs my shoulder a little harder. "Oh no, he was very guilty. I believe they dipped him in boiling oil and then tossed him into an iron maiden. But that's beside the point!"

I moan in horror. My poor Will. "Don't tell me that!"

"Sorry, sorry." She pats me awkwardly. "Just . . . don't worry, okay? Will's not popular with a lot of the warlock community, because he comes across as aloof and a bit of a snob, but I can't imagine he would do something of such magnitude that they would want to destroy him. We have to figure out exactly what charges they've brought up against him, and then we refute them. It'll be easy."

She's right. We can do this. It has to be trumped-up charges against Will. "I'm just . . . panicking." Especially at the thought of a group of his peers being the ones to decide whether he's innocent. If Abernathy's "help" is anything like what he can expect, we're in trouble. And Will *is* pompous and arrogant. But he's also sweet under all that prickliness, and it's a sweetness only I get to see.

No more doubts, I tell myself. We're going to do this. We need a place to start, and then everything will fall into line. Determined, I pick up another one of Will's spell tomes and open it up. *Treatise on the Efficacy of Cave-Grown Fungi and Best Practices for Fertilization.* Right. That sounds boring as hell and not at all useful, but I dutifully pore over every page.

Just in case.

* * *

REGGIE HAS PIP in her lap, petting his chest as I read through *Augury: For the Birds.* "Oh! Ben's here and we need to get the door for him. He's got something for us."

"Right. Of course." I close the useless book in front of me and get to my feet. I head upstairs with Reggie at my heels, and when I get to the front door, I'm a little shocked at the sight there.

It's Ben Magnus, an enormous dead pig in his arms. "Quick," he says, stepping over the threshold. "Let's get this in the kitchen before it starts to drip."

"Drip?" I ask, worried as I follow him inside. "Why do you have a dead pig?"

"Oh no," Reggie moans. "We're not . . ."

"Oh yes," Ben replies. "Haruspicy, my sweet. There's a reason why so many elders use it."

"Because they're gross?"

"Because it's effective," Ben corrects her, and glances over at me. "Where is the best place to set this down?"

"At a butcher shop?" I say faintly, and then shake my head. Haruspicy is reading entrails, I remind myself. If Ben went to the trouble to get and kill a pig to help Will, I want to be part of this. "Come on downstairs. We can clear off a lab table down there."

"How the heck did you get a pig?" Reggie asks as she follows behind her large boyfriend. "Did you go to a butcher?"

"I went to a farm that sells to witches, and they charged me an exorbitant amount," he admits. "But they didn't ask questions and they killed it humanely without opening it up, so that's the best I can hope for. Now come on. They're supposed to be alive when sacrificed, but I figure with the right spells we can still use this pig as long as he's relatively fresh."

"Of course," I murmur, trying not to be grossed out. This is just part of the job. I move ahead of Ben and Reggie, pulling books off the tables they've been scattered on. I make sure everything is moved aside and then gesture at a bare table for Ben, who plops the thing down with a very heavy thump. I swallow hard at the sight of it. "I, ah, really appreciate this, guys."

"Will is a friend," Ben says. "The least I can do is cut a pig open for him. Get some aprons and gloves so we can get started— there's no time to waste."

PENNY

Watching Ben Magnus prepare to root around in the innards of a freshly dead pig is a horrifying experience. I force myself to pay attention, because this is for Will. I can't get sick, though the thought of watching him cut open and poke around inside a dead pig makes me want to vomit.

"This is going to require my concentration," Ben says in that dour, deep voice of his. "Before I get started, I wanted to let you know what I found out from the Council of Warlocks. It seems that Stoker has reported his latest apprentice as having gone missing. Stoker claims that Willem would have motive to destroy his familiar and leave him defenseless, and cited past disappearances of his familiars as further proof. He claims to have found a recent curse tablet that shows Willem's plans."

"But that's all bullshit," I exclaim. "Will's been with me constantly the last couple weeks. I would know if he's cast that kind of curse tablet. I don't think he even knows who Stoker's assistant is!"

"I know that, and you know that, but Willem doesn't have many friends on the council and Stoker does."

"Then we need to prove he's full of shit." I put my hands on my hips. "They can't do anything to Will without proof, right? They can just cast to make sure that Will wasn't the one that made whatever tablet that Stoker drags up, and he'll be free, right?"

"That's the thing." Ben looks miserable. "I'm not certain anything has to be proven for Willem to be found guilty. If it goes to a trial, people simply vote on it. It'll be a popularity contest no matter how flimsy Stoker's evidence is. And Willem isn't well liked by many."

I want to vomit. If it's a popularity contest, Will will lose, just because he's an asshole to people that don't know him. Because Stoker fucked with his head when he was younger and made him doubt himself. I'm so angry I could spit. "Then we can't let this go to trial."

"My thoughts exactly," Ben says. He looks over at Reggie. "Ready for this, love?"

Reggie nods, blanching as Ben reaches for the pig. He pulls out a knife and I look away, because I'm too squeamish to watch. I lock eyes with Reggie, who winces when there's a wet splat, and I hug Pip to my chest. "Don't look, little buddy."

A few more wet sounds, and then Ben begins to chant. It sounds like Latin, so I can't understand a lot of the words said, but I do catch the word "Jupiter." My skin prickles as the weight of magic fills the room, and it feels strange to be in the presence of so much magic and not have it affect my body. It makes me miss Will and the moments we shared casting. I need those back.

I need him back. He can't go to trial. He just can't. I'll figure something out.

As the spell goes on, Reggie looks positively green at the gills, but she gives me a thumbs-up as if this is very normal. I remind myself that it's all for Will, and if watching Ben play with intestines while murmuring prayers to Jupiter will get us somewhere, then I'm all for it.

But at the end of a very long hour, Ben only says "Hmm" and tosses the innards down. "Well, that was a bust."

"It was?" I ask, biting my lip and clutching my squirrel against my chest. At my side, Reggie yawns, exhausted from Ben's casting. I peer forward, wondering if anyone can make out anything in the innards or if it requires special training. To me, they just look . . . well, rather gross. "What do you see?"

"Nothing. And that's the problem." He pauses, wiping his hands on the towel Reggie hands to him. "Either the gods aren't answering us, or we're being blocked."

All of that for nothing? I swallow hard, trying not to hold poor Pip too tightly. "I don't understand. Why wouldn't the gods answer us?"

"It could be a variety of reasons." He stares down at the pig, frowning. "Perhaps someone is unhappy with the sacrifice presented. Perhaps the gods feel as if they've already answered the question we're posing and aren't inclined to answer again. It's hard to say. I didn't feel as if we'd been blocked, though. I'm more likely to chalk it up to the gods being fickle . . . or they just don't like Willem in this particular instance."

I make a wordless sound. "How can they not like Will? He's amazing! And dedicated! And I've seen the offerings he gives. He goes above and beyond to make sure the gods are given the right sorts of spells and that the components used are of the highest quality. He's so thoughtful and devoted to this craft. It doesn't make sense that they'd hate him."

Ben turns and gives me a faint, almost amused smile. "Are you talking about the same Willem Sauer I know?"

"Yes," I retort, indignant, and raise my chin. "You can say what you want about Will, but you can't call him careless or indifferent."

"I agree." He turns to Reggie, caressing her with his gaze. "You okay?"

She yawns again and gives another thumbs-up. Her eyes are tired and her shoulders slumped, but she straightens and gives herself a little shake as if to wake up. "So what now?"

"We know it's Stoker," I say desperately, clinging to Pip. "We know it's bullshit. How do we prove that?"

Ben glances over at his girlfriend. "Perhaps that's a problem that can be solved in the morning. Reggie needs her rest."

Oh. Frantic, I squeeze Pip tight. It feels like I'm failing Will if I don't get an answer for him soon. Tonight. There has to be more I can do. Maybe I can cast something on my own, appeal to Jupiter myself, cry buckets of tears—

"Maybe . . . ," Reggie begins, noticing the frantic look on my face. "Maybe we look at the note Abernathy sent again? Maybe Ben will have more ideas."

"Yes," I squeal, excited. "Thank you, Reggie! Let me go get it!"

Reggie gives a tired smile to her less enthusiastic boyfriend. "Of course. Anything for a friend."

I race back upstairs, making a beeline for Will's study. The letter is in its spot on the mantel mailbox where I left it, and I snag the parchment and unfold it, reading it again to make sure I didn't miss anything obvious.

My apprentice,

I have done several spells to guide me upon this and I can assure you that the answer you seek is in your books. The gods will not tell me more.

—Abernathy

Biting back a frustrated sigh, I fold it up again and turn. And then I hear the front door rattle.

27

PENNY

Someone's breaking into the house. Panicked, I consider racing back to the hidden tunnel and hiding in Will's lab with Ben and Reggie. They'll know what to do.

The moment I think that idea, though, I immediately discard it. Instead, I'm angry. I'm so mad I could spit, because whoever this is hasn't even waited a day after Will's imprisonment before coming in to raid Will's house again. What the hell does Stoker want? Is he coming after me now?

I'm tired of this shit and I'm going to send a message, I decide.

So I tiptoe back over to Will's study, just down the hall from the front door. I grab the well-used cricket bat that he keeps in the corner, and then I head back to the front door. I can hear the jiggle of locks as they try to figure out how to get around the dead bolt, so I press myself to the wall next to the door in the darkness and I wait.

There's a bump and a snick, and then the dead bolt clicks. A moment later, the door swings open and a man steps inside the dark house. He clicks on a flashlight and shines it down the hall, taking a few steps.

I raise the cricket bat over my head and bring it down on him as hard as I can with an angry screech of rage. It crunches into the back of his head, and he jerks, then goes down like a light, falling flat on his face.

Panting, I stare down at the average-looking man sprawled on the floor. I don't recognize him, but I know he has to be involved with Stoker. There's no way that he's just some run-of-the-mill thief that happened to hit up Will's house tonight. The timing is far too coincidental. I glance at the door, but there's no one else coming in, so I shut it quickly and lock it again and then put a finger under the man's nose to make sure he's breathing.

Once I'm satisfied that he's not dead, I go through the man's pockets. He doesn't have a weapon with him, just lock-picking tools and what look like some spell components. His wallet shows that his name is Roger Turlington, but the name means nothing to me. He's got two twenties in his wallet and a plane ticket to LAX for tomorrow, and that's it.

I sit back on my heels and contemplate him. What do I do now? Call the police? Shove him out of the house and have Ben and Reggie reactivate Will's wards? I chew on my lip, thinking. Rope, I decide. I need rope. I glance around me, but there's nothing that could be used to tie up anyone. Will's house is spare and austere, and there's not even a drapery to be seen, just miniblinds. I move to one of the blinds and grab a cord thoughtfully. This could work. I just need to cut it off.

Racing back down to the basement for Will's big knife that he uses for casting, I run into Ben and Reggie, who are heading back up.

"You were gone for a bit," Reggie says, worried. "Is everything okay?"

"Totally fine. A man broke in, so I hit him over the head with a cricket bat," I babble. "I need rope now."

"Wait, what?" Reggie grabs at Ben's arm, her expression alarmed.

Ben's eyes narrow. "Where is he?"

"At the front door," I tell them. "Be right back." A knife, I repeat to myself. I need a knife. I find Will's favorite and caress the handle, then race back toward the front of the house, waving it as I go. "I need to cut the blinds for a rope!"

I return to the foyer, only to find Reggie passed out and snoring next to the unconscious man, and Ben using his pinky and some blood to write runes on the door.

"Did I miss something?" I ask, confused.

"Reggie's tapped," Ben says. "I'm redoing the wards so no one can enter without your permission."

"Oh. Okay. Good idea." I pause. "I don't suppose you know who this asshole is, do you?"

Ben snorts and turns to look at me. "I'm pretty sure that's Stoker's familiar."

"The one that's supposed to be dead?" I squeak.

"The very one." He focuses on the door again, making another rune. "Ballsy move."

I'll say. It makes me want to punch both Stoker and his assistant. Or maybe get the cricket bat and give the familiar another good whack in the face and then the balls. I'm feeling a little violent. "Stoker must really think we're idiots if he's sending his familiar over to the house of the man that's just been arrested for supposedly killing him."

"He's arrogant," Ben agrees. "Most of the older warlocks are. He's confident he won't need to prove anything in order to ensure that Will is brought down. Even if he's freed, Will's reputation will be so tarnished no one will ever want to work with him." He continues to focus on the door. "But we can use Stoker's arrogance against him."

I hope Ben's right. "Just as long as we're on the same page."

"Of course."

"I'm thinking torture." I cross my arms over my chest, gazing down at the man. "Get him to confess everything he knows."

Ben drops his hand and turns to look at me, utterly confused. "Did . . . you just say 'torture'?"

"Were we both not thinking torture?"

"I was thinking we keep him hostage until the time is right to reveal he's alive." He squints at me. "I'm not sure you're the type to torture."

"Why wouldn't I be?" I gesture at Stoker's unconscious apprentice. "This man and his warlock have tried to get my boyfriend killed. Why wouldn't I be contemplating doing awful things to get him to speak up?"

"And . . . what sorts of awful things did you have in mind? Bamboo under the fingernails? Waterboarding?"

Yikes. Now that he mentions it, maybe I'm not the best sort for that. My version of torture isn't exactly the same as his. "I was thinking more like . . . tickling."

"Tickling," Ben echoes.

I nod. "Just getting a feather and tickling him until he spits it all out. And if that doesn't work, we find the worst videos on You-Tube of people who think they can sing and force him to watch them on loop. And pepper."

"Pepper?"

"Pepper on everything," I agree. "And jalapeño juice under his nose! And we hide all the toilet paper in the house! And—"

Ben puts up a hand. "While I appreciate creativity as much as the next man, perhaps we go with my idea first. The whole hostage thing."

"Right," I say cheerfully, snapping my fingers. "I'll get the rope."

He just stares at me thoughtfully. "You know, when Reggie

and I first suggested that you work with Will, I thought he was going to eat you alive. Now I'm thinking the two of you might be more suited than I realized."

I'm choosing to take that as a compliment. Knife in hand, I head to Will's study to butcher his miniblinds.

WILLEM

I lean back against the wall of my cell and try not to feel bitter about my situation.

It's difficult. On one hand, I'm exceedingly grateful that the charges trumped up against me are for me and only me. That means Penny is safe and no one knows she's my familiar. Not even Stoker's long arm has touched her, and for that, I'm pleased. But the fact that I've been dragged away from my house and my lover and treated like a criminal? The fact that I've been sitting in this empty, bland room for two days while others of my kind plot against me?

It's hard not to be pissed about that.

There's a clatter of dishes on the other side of the door, and I sigh heavily. I'm in Titus Ragonius's basement. Of course I am. Titus has long been my enemy, back when it was just fun to have a nemesis. We feuded for two hundred years because feuding was popular, but I'd forgotten all about it in the modern era. Apparently I'm the only one. Titus was eager to lock me up, and since warlocks are generally not arrested by their own kind, there was no official sort of prison to house me in. Therefore I'm sitting on a cot in a damp, musty basement filled with boxes of holiday ornaments and lawn decor tomfoolery. There's a stack of old magazines at my side, and Titus's idiot familiar is my jailer.

The dishes clatter again at the top of the stairs, and I get up from my cot and move to the bottom of the staircase. "You can just come in the damned room, you dolt. It's not as if I'm going to break free." Last night Morgan (Titus's familiar) tried to convince his boss that he needed a prison door complete with a food slot in order to properly guard me.

I'm not going anywhere, though. Not if my presence here keeps their attention focused fully on me and off Penny. I imagine how hurt she is. How she's coping. Is she wearing a black dress with a fluffy skirt in my honor? Crying into a pink handkerchief as she comforts her squirrel? I hope Reggie and Ben help her get on her feet again.

I wonder if they'll let me will my estates to her. I don't have property like the Sauer family did once upon a time—Stoker took care of that—but I do have a decent-sized fortune. I'll have to insist upon talking to my estate lawyer prior to whatever farce of a trial they put me through. We all know it'll be a popularity contest, and I absolutely won't win one of those.

There's another clank of dishes at the top of the stairs, and I run my hand down my face in frustration. "Morgan, you absolute cretin—"

The door opens and Penny steps inside, holding a tray for me. My jaw drops.

She turns her head and winks at Morgan, who doesn't look too happy. "We won't be long, I promise. No one needs to know I'm here."

"I don't like this, Penny," Morgan whines.

"I know. Which is why I won't be here long," she affirms cheerily, and then heads down the stairs toward me. "Hello, Will darling."

My mouth goes dry at the sight of her. She's not dressed in black, of course. I don't think Penny owns a stitch of black clothing. Her dress is a vibrant green covered in pineapples, with straps that tie behind her neck and leave her shoulders enticingly bare. The skirts are full and fluffy with a hint of a yellow crinoline underneath and bounce with every step she takes toward me. Her hair is pulled up in a flipped ponytail and her earrings are a pair of matching pineapples, and she looks so damned perfect and effervescent and *Penny* that it makes me ache.

I just stare as she descends the stairs, then holds the tray out to me. "Your lunch?"

"What are you doing here?" I ask, taking the tray from her. I immediately set it aside atop a box, because I'm not hungry. I'm far more interested in what my damned familiar is doing showing up in my prison when I'm doing everything I can to keep her safe.

"Visiting you, of course," she says gaily, and then flings her arms around my neck, pulling me down into a heated kiss.

Startled, I flail for a moment and then recover. I immediately pull her to me, loving the feel of her hot, eager mouth against mine. By all the gods, if this is the last time I get to see her, I need to make it count. I kiss her relentlessly, tonguing her sweet mouth with all the need that's been building inside of me. She's been on my mind constantly the last few days, the need to keep her safe rising above all else.

If I bring Penny down with me, I'll never forgive myself. I'll do whatever it takes to keep her free of my entanglements, and if that means letting Stoker win, then that's exactly what I'm going to do. I kiss her a dozen times, peppering her round, cheerful face with one quick peck after another. "You shouldn't be here."

"Nonsense. I found out where they were keeping you and decided to pay my lover a visit." She pats my cheek sweetly and then looks around. "I wanted to make sure they're treating you well."

Treating me well? Does she not realize how serious this is? "Penny . . . they mean to execute me."

She shakes her head, as if my words are somehow incorrect. "If it goes to trial. Surely you'll figure something out before then."

What exactly does she think I'm going to be able to do from down here? I can't cast unless she's nearby so I can draw from her energy. I open my mouth to protest, and she puts a finger over my lips.

"I didn't come here to talk about your trial," she whispers. She pushes on my chest. "Sit down."

I thump onto the cot and stare up at her.

Penny immediately wiggles her eyebrows at me and moves forward, straddling me and mounting my hips. Her fluffy skirts pool around us, and she settles in over me, rocking against my pelvis. "You comfortable?"

"I should be asking you." I slide my hands to her waist. "It seems you're always climbing on top of me."

"Are you complaining?"

"Not in the slightest."

"Good. Because I missed you." She plants her hands on both sides of my jaw and leans in to kiss me again. Her tongue flicks against mine, and when I touch hers, she moans and I'm reminded of our brief interlude in the car and how we never got more than that. "I missed you so much, Will. And I was so scared for you."

She trembles against me, and I realize not all this sunshine she's projecting is real. As strange and terrifying as this has been for me, it's been a nightmare for her, too, and I'm unable to be at her side and protect her. "I know, love. The charges against me are lies, though."

"I know. You've spent all your time with me. It's not like you've had time to hunt down someone else's familiar." She leans in and presses another hungry kiss to my mouth, her nose brushing against mine. "I hate how empty my bed is at night."

My cock surges in my pants and I groan. My hands slide to her hips, and when she rocks lightly over me again, I press up against the cradle of her thighs. "I miss you, too. How did you get here? How—"

Penny shakes her head and kisses me again, her mouth covering mine. "Let's just say," she breathes between kisses, "that Morgan owed me a favor." She captures my lower lip in her mouth and sucks on it, sending a bolt of heat straight to my groin. "I once helped him write a very convincing essay on why he should be selected as Titus's familiar. He's repaying the favor by letting me spend a few minutes with you."

"Just a few?" I pant.

"A very few," she agrees, pouting. "Just enough for a quickie."

A what—

Penny shifts on my lap, moving her pooling skirts aside, and then her hand is on my cock. She gives me a saucy grin and rubs me. "Looks like you're in the mood."

When she leans in to kiss me again, I murmur a protest against her sweet cherry lips. "Spells . . . We're being watched . . ."

"I figured," she whispers back to me. "But it's a good thing I have skirts, hmm?"

She reaches down between us again, her lips on mine, and as her tongue flicks enticingly into my mouth, I give up trying to protest. If she's into this, I sure as shit am. "Penny," I groan. "Amazing, gorgeous, perfect Penny. I'm so glad you're here."

"I'm gonna make it all better for you, Will, I promise." She strokes my cock again, and then something hard and flat is pressed against my shaft. She kisses me again, nipping hard at my lip as if to give a warning, and then presses the item farther down in my pants, shoving it against the outside of my thigh. "My poor Will," she coos. "I didn't bring a condom. Is that all right?"

She really wants to do this? Right now?

"Maybe you can still give me your baby," she breathes, a silent message in her eyes. "Fill me up and give me everything you've got."

If this is some coded message, I'm not getting it. All I can think about is how gorgeous she is, how her wicked fingers are back on my cock and stroking me again, and when I kiss her, her lips are the best thing I've ever tasted. "Penny."

"Push my panties aside, Will," she tells me, her hands on my nape as she presses her forehead to mine. "I want you."

I search her face, her lovely, dark eyes, but I don't see any hesitation there. She's already passed me whatever bit of contraband she came here to give me, so there's no need to pretend. But she also isn't stopping. She's all over me, her mouth warm and soft and hungry, and when I slide a hand under her skirts, her panties are soaked. The breath hisses from between my teeth. "This little pussy did miss me, didn't it?"

"So much," she whimpers. "Please, Will."

As if I can refuse? I shove the soft material of her panties to the side and run my fingers over the folds of her sex, just to be sure that I'm not imagining things. Penny is wet, all right, and when I glide my fingers over the entrance to her body, she tries to bear down on my fingers, her teeth digging into my lower lip.

"Someone might be watching us," I warn her. Titus has this room covered in spells, and I know whatever I say and do down here is going to be reported back to him.

"Let them watch," Penny purrs, rocking against my fingers. "Just make me come hard before I go."

Ah, gods. She's killing me. I slide a finger inside her, my thumb moving to find her clit, and I stroke her, fascinated at the wet sounds her body makes when I touch her. "How is it you get so fucking soaked for me so quickly, Penny? How am I so lucky?"

She moans, her arms going around my neck, her face buried

against the crook of my shoulder as her hips desperately drive against my seeking fingers. "Missed you," she whimpers. "Missed you so much."

"I know." I turn my head and find her ear, toying with her earlobe with my mouth even as I pump into her with my fingers. "We didn't get to have our second round, did we? Seems like every time I turn around, you're climbing on me in public and giving me everything, and I'm giving you nothing but empty promises."

"Will," she cries, driving down against my fingers. "Baby. You'll give me a baby."

"You want my baby?" I know it's pretending, but why is it so gods-damned sexy when she says that? "You want me to fill you up with my release and remind you that you belong to me?"

"Yes," she whimpers. "Please, do that."

I slide my fingers away and she whines a soft protest. I take my cock in hand—hard as a fucking poker—and drag the leaking tip through her slick folds. She immediately tries to bear down on me, and I tsk. "Greedy girl," I murmur. "You have to ask for it."

"Will," she cries out again, biting at my neck. Her hands are dragging through my hair, making a mess of it as her eager hips rock over me. "Please, please, please."

I press my mouth against her ear again, just because I have to be certain. "You sure that's what you want? Even if we're being watched?" I whisper it so low that I hope no spell can pick it up. Even if they do, I don't care. I just need Penny to be okay with this. I need her to be all right with the realization that this might not be private. "We can stop now—"

She lifts her head to my ear and captures my earlobe, sucking on it even as she grinds down against the head of my cock.

Right. Penny's not shy. She makes a hungry sound in her throat, and that's all it takes for me to commit. I push into the hot well of her body, and I nearly lose my mind at how good she feels. She's so damned tight and sweet, wet and warm, and I love the way her breath shudders out of her even as I drive my way in.

"Good?" I ask, my voice strained.

"So good," she whimpers back. "Oh god, so good."

Penny clings to me as I jerk my hips. Her skirts rustle with every movement, and I'm tempted to roll over and pin her underneath me and just drive into her body, but that would expose her pretty backside to anyone watching. At least with this, she has the modesty her skirts allow. Her mouth moves to mine, hungry and insistent. "Ride me," I murmur. "Take your pleasure, love."

She moans and does just that. With slow, fluid motions of her hips, she starts to rock on top of me once more, pulling up and then sinking down on top of me again. Her body is so slick and wet with arousal that we're making obscene noises as my cock drives into her, but the rustle of her dress drowns almost everything out but the sexy little whimpers she makes in the back of her throat every time I bottom out inside her.

I need her to come. I need her wild on top of me. I lick my thumb and slide my hand between us, gazing up at her. I drag my wet thumb over her clit, and I'm pleased when her body clenches around my cock, her eyes fluttering in response. She rocks atop me harder, and I keep my thumb pressed there, letting the teasing pressure of it build up. "My greedy girl," I murmur as she rides me frantically. "My gorgeous, greedy girl. I fucking love you."

"Will," she pants, and grabs a fistful of my hair in her hand, her face scrunching up as her release climbs. "Oh fuck, Will—"

"Inside you," I growl. "Inside you and filling you up. Don't you fucking forget that."

Her pussy clenches around me, hard, and then she makes that gaspy, breathless moan that I fucking know so well, and she's coming, her pussy fluttering around me. I groan and drive up into her, gripping her hips and using her to bring myself to the peak I need just as badly as she does. I come with a shudder, choking out her name, and then I'm filling her up with my seed, so much of it that our bodies are a sticky, joined mess. I take several deep, gasping breaths of air as she circles her hips against mine, making soft little noises of contentment in the aftershocks of her pleasure.

"Someday," I pant, "we're going to have sex in genuine privacy."

Penny chuckles, kissing my jaw. "I'm just happy to be able to touch you right now. Are you okay? Are they treating you well?" Her knee squeezes against the hard object she pressed against the outside of my thigh. "Do I need to scold someone?"

I shake my head, leaning back against the wall. "I don't want you talking to any of them. This is warlock business, love. You're not a part of it."

"But I want to help you," she protests, and squeezes the object against my leg again. "Let me help you, Will."

I kiss the tip of her nose, admiring her sweaty face. She's so fucking beautiful after she comes that I can't stand it. It makes my heart ache. I love how dark her eyes get and how the tip of her nose flushes pink. "You're helping me just by being here, Penny. I promise you."

She rests her cheek against my shoulder and I hold her, running my hands up and down her back. "I'm still wearing the necklace you gave me," she murmurs, her voice all sleepy sex. "I never take it off. It makes me feel close to you."

Penny presses it to my chin and it feels hot. Very hot. Clever minx. She's warning me that we're being watched. I have a million things I want to ask her about, but I don't dare say them aloud. It might not just be Titus who's listening. For all I know, Stoker is, too. I rub her backside and give it a light smack. "Good. I want you thinking about me all the time."

Squirming, she wriggles atop my cock and sends a bolt of heat through my body. I'm tired, but given a few minutes, parts of me might rouse again.

Her expression goes from playful to soft, and she takes the necklace off and slips it over my head. "Now you can think of *me* all the time."

Gods, she's smart. With the necklace, I'll be able to know when I'm being watched and when I'm not. I need it more than she does right now, and I could kiss her for being two steps ahead of me. She's perfection.

There's a knock at the door above and Penny freezes. "Oh no. Has it been fifteen minutes already?"

"Either that, or he's tired of watching the show." I give her a little smile to take the sting out of my words. "Please be careful, Penny. The only thing that makes this bearable is knowing that you're safe. Promise me you'll watch out."

Her eyes get suspiciously shiny. "You promise me that you'll be careful. I'm the one worrying about you."

I run my knuckles along the curve of her jaw. "Alas, I'm not going anywhere anytime soon."

Penny leans forward and gives me another hard kiss. We separate, and I hastily stuff my wet cock back into my pants and zip things up. She grabs my hand and squeezes it, then gives me a longing look as she heads for the stairs. "I'll try and come back again soon."

"Not if it's dangerous," I chide. "Remember what I said about staying safe."

"I love you," she calls out, her voice hoarse. "I love you, Will."

That makes my chest clench up. She's never said that to me before. I know I blurted it in the car shortly before being arrested, but it was simply because I needed her to know, not because I was demanding to hear it back. The words are like a balm, though, and some of the frustration eases from my shoulders. "I love you, too."

She blows me a kiss and then heads up the stairs, and I hear her talking to Morgan once more. The lock on the door rattles, and I know I'm trapped alone again. I glance over at the tray of food, but I'm not interested in eating it. I want Penny to come back. I want to be free. I want Stoker to walk off a fucking cliff.

But none of those things are going to happen, so I reach over and flick off the lamp that's at the head of the cot—the only light in this dark, dank basement—and pull the blankets over my head. Let it look like I'm sulking—that plays into my needs perfectly. I carefully unzip my pants again and extract the smooth, cold object. A phone. My phone.

Penny, you little minx genius, you.

The battery is full, and I run my finger over the switch on the side. Mute. Perfect. I unlock it and glance at my messages. The most recent one is, of course, from Penny. It's from a few hours ago, which proves to me that this was all part of a plan she's been putting together to free me, and my heart swells with fresh affection.

PENNY: Let me know when you're ready to talk and I'll get you up to speed.

WILL: I'm here now.

For long minutes, I stare at the phone in the darkness, under the blankets, until my breath starts to steam up the screen. There's no response, no read receipt, no nothing, and I start to worry that someone upstairs has realized what she's done and has captured her. That they're punishing her even now.

But then three gorgeous, beautiful dots appear.

PENNY: Sorry about the delay.

PENNY: Morgan is a real talker, whew. I finally had to tell him your leavings were dripping down my leg so he'd get the picture.

PENNY: BTW I LOVE YOU

PENNY: I needed to say that again.

WILL: I'm certainly glad to hear it again. I can't believe you risked yourself to bring me a phone.

PENNY: I figured you wouldn't be able to talk freely and there's a lot I need to say to you.

WILL: More declarations of love?

Why am I smiling down at the phone like a besotted fool? Love should be the last thing on my mind right now. It's just . . . I like hearing it. I matter to someone. I'm important to her, and for the first time in a very, very long time, I feel as if I've got someone truly on my side and at my back. It's the best feeling in the universe . . . even if it's a little too late to save my neck. I'm allowed to savor it for now, though.

PENNY: Actually no. Though those are important too!

PENNY: I wanted to update you with everything that's happened since those jerks arrested you.

PENNY: Btw I thought about going to the police and reporting it as a kidnapping, but then I figured they'd retaliate and I could do a lot more to help you on the outside.

A flurry of texts follows, and Penny fills up my screen with description after description of everything that's been happening since I left. Her search through my spell books, contacting everyone she knows to find out details about my charges, and Ben's and Reggie's tireless help. I'm a little surprised to hear that Magnus went to the effort of bringing a dead pig to my lab and casting haruspicy spells on my behalf. All this time I thought we were frenemies and rivals who grudgingly worked together from time to time. Reggie truly has softened him . . . just like Penny has softened me.

> **PENNY:** And of course, we now have Stoker's apprentice being held captive.

I stare down at the phone in shock.

> **WILL:** I'm sorry, what? Is that a typo?
>
> **WILL:** You have his what?
>
> **PENNY:** We stole Stoker's apprentice. 😈
>
> **PENNY:** I was getting to that part.
>
> **PENNY:** He tried to break into your house last night after dark. Bumped the dead bolt and everything. No spells, just a good old-fashioned break-in. Before he could get more than three feet, I whacked him on the back of the head with your cricket bat. When I searched his wallet I found his name and Ben says he works for Stoker.
>
> **WILL:** This is perfect! I can't very well be convicted of killing him if he's alive. What was he doing at my house? What was he seeking? Surely it wasn't another fertility charm?

PENNY: I'm getting to all that. As for your conviction . . . I'm going to need you to trust me a bit longer.

WILL: . . . You know I'm rotten at trust.

PENNY: But do you trust ME?

I stare down at the phone. Something tells me whatever she has in mind, I'm not going to like it. I want to get out of Titus's fucking basement. I want my freedom. I want them all to realize they've made a mistake. I want to get out of here and bend Penny over my desk and fuck her for hours. But the fact that she slipped me a phone instead of telling the world that she has Stoker's supposedly dead assistant tells me that I'm not going to get any of that.

I rub my mouth with my hand and contemplate. Trust her. Trust her to get me out of this mess instead of taking care of things myself. Trust her to get involved with dangerous people instead of letting me handle it.

Trust the woman I love to continue to have my back.

PENNY: You sure got quiet.

WILL: I'm just contemplating all the ways this could go wrong. Remember what I said about you staying safe?

PENNY: Fuck that. I'm helping you. I don't care if it's risky.

WILL: Stoker is dangerous. You're playing with fire.

PENNY: 🔥 🔥 🔥

WILL: I'm serious. I don't find this funny. I'm trying to keep you safe.

PENNY: Funny, that's what I'm doing. 🐶

WILL: Quit sending me pictures. I'm serious, Penny. I don't want you anywhere near Stoker. He's got a long reach and an even longer memory.

PENNY: And you're just going to have to trust me. Now, do you trust me AND love me or do you only love me? Because if it's the latter I'm not going to tell you my plans.

WILL: Gods damn it, woman. You're impossible.

PENNY: You can spank me when you're free.

PENNY: (I mean that, too. I'd totally be into a naughty spanking.)

WILL: This is not helping. And yes, I fucking trust you. And yes, I'm going to give you a naughty spanking when I'm out of here. You can count on that. In fact, I'll be thinking about that constantly.

PENNY: Me too.

PENNY: We probably shouldn't sext, you need to save your battery life.

WILL: Just tell me what's going on before I lose my mind! Am I getting out of here?

PENNY: Not yet.

PENNY: We need to know what Stoker is up to.

PENNY: So we're going to set a trap—me as your girlfriend, and Ben and Reggie.

PENNY: We'll play it safe, I promise.

Play it safe. She doesn't know who she's dealing with. Stoker has been playing these games since her ancestors were in diapers. I'm worried she's going to get in over her head far too quickly. I don't know of anyone that's gone up against Stoker, spell to spell, and won. He's an old, crafty bastard that knows every trick in the book.

WILL: I can't tell you no because you're headstrong, but I'm just going to ask you to please be careful and if you get in over your head, call on your parents to pull in their witches to help. I beg you. I don't want both of us dead.

PENNY: I don't want either of us dead!

PENNY: Oh and we heard back from Abernathy finally.

PENNY: But it was useless.

WILL: Wait, what?

WILL: You didn't lead with that? What did he say? Scan in the note!

PENNY: I could scan it in but it's quicker to just type it. He said you already have the answer you seek. That it's in your books.

I gaze down at the phone, frowning. Abernathy does love a vague sort of prophecy, but normally when I've asked him for help in the past, he's been pretty concise. I don't understand why he would deliberately be obtuse when I need help . . . and it's disappointing.

WILL: That's all it said?

PENNY: That's it. So I'm guessing he's pointing us toward a spell but won't say which one. I've been reading through your personal spell books and Stoker's apprentice ones looking for answers, but I haven't hit on anything yet. If you can think of something, I'm all ears.

WILL: It wouldn't be something obvious. Let me ponder it.

PENNY: Ok.

PENNY: Are you mad that you're going to have to stay a few more days?

PENNY: It's just . . . if we get you out, who's to stop Stoker from pulling this shit again in a month? A year? You're never going to be free of his harassment.

PENNY: But if we show everyone he's deliberately targeting you, then we win.

PENNY: And I want you to win against him. MORE THAN ANYTHING.

PENNY: So please don't hate me.

PENNY: I'll send you pics of my tits to pass the time.

WILL: I don't hate you, you wildly inappropriate creature. I love you.

WILL: I just don't like the thought of you risking yourself.

WILL: But . . . yes. Go ahead and send pics of your tits.

WILL: Please.

PENNY

It takes everything I have not to text Will constantly or send him endless pictures of my girl bits. I love him, and I hate that he's trapped and worried while I'm on the outside. I need him to realize that I'm in this until the bitter end. That nothing else matters but his freedom—not only from these trumped-up charges, but from Stoker himself.

And he needs to trust in my plan.

Just as soon as I get one, anyhow. But I'm sure I'll come up with something.

Reggie's over again today, while Ben has a few client meetings. I'm supposed to be working, but Vivi called in her part-timer, Kenneth, and got him to work instead. I appreciate the effort, even if I'm just sitting at home reading through Will's books for the hundredth time and eating more donuts.

"Can I have one?" Roger whines from the corner. "I'm starving."

"You had one earlier," Reggie retorts. "These are all filled and you said you didn't like filled."

"I changed my mind. I'll eat a filled one."

She looks at me and rolls her eyes but gets to her feet and moves forward to hand a donut over to Roger. His hands (and feet) are bound in front of him with zip ties, and the rest of him is vel-croed to a kitchen chair that we've pulled downstairs. I should feel guilty that we're holding a man hostage, but Roger seems kinda . . . unbothered by the whole situation? Which is weird to me.

I turn and watch him as he scarfs down the donut, and then Reggie hands him the last bottle of milk. "You know, this would all go a lot easier if you'd just fess up and tell us what your master wants."

Roger shakes his head, his wispy hair floating around his ears. He's pale, and his hair is blond and downy like a chick's, and his face is smooth and unlined. His eyes are old, though, and it makes me wonder if he's 30 or 130. "Oh no," Roger says. "I'm not falling for that. Stoker would have my hide if I confessed anything, even under pain of torture."

"No one's torturing you," I point out.

"What about last night, when I had to pee and you were gone for six hours?" he asks, giving me an indignant look.

"You should have thought of that before you drank three sodas in a row." We're treating Roger decently. We're keeping him fed and hydrated and giving him regular trips to the bathroom. Maybe that's why he's not turning on Stoker. Ben says to be patient, that eventually he'll let something slip, but it's hard when I know that every day that passes is another day that my Will is stuck in Ti-tus's basement, waiting for a trial.

"I'm going to tell everyone how awful you both are," Roger declares. "And that you're casting without supervision. I saw it with my own eyes. You'll both be fired as familiars."

My heart pounds.

"Now you're just making shit up," Reggie says, picking up an-other book and flipping through it. "Penny isn't casting—she's reading. That's not against the laws of any familiars or warlocks. You can cast a divination spell to determine if I'm lying or not, but we both know I'm not lying. And besides, Penny's allowed to look for solutions on her boyfriend's wrongful imprisonment, you absolute jerk."

"Yeah," I chime in. "So ess tee eff yew."

"You're both hopeless." Roger finishes his milk with a chug and then tosses the bottle on the ground in the lab. "Good luck trying to outsmart my warlock with those two female pea brains of yours."

Oh, so he's a chauvinist to boot? Ugh. I get up from my chair and cross the room, then turn his so it faces the wall. "Trust me, we don't want you here any more than you want to be here. But you're not going anywhere until my boyfriend is freed."

"Good luck with that—"

"If you don't learn to shut up," I snap, at the end of my patience, "I'm going to find a dirty sock and shove it in your mouth."

Roger gets quiet, and I bite back a sigh of relief. Turning to Reggie, I give her an exasperated look and shake my head. It's been two days since I saw Will. Two days of us endlessly poring through Will's spell books, looking for any sort of connection. Abernathy said the answer would be in the books, after all. So we're looking for whatever spell he thinks will solve our problems.

Even Ben hasn't been able to help. "It's a needle in a haystack," he told Reggie last night. "Any spell can be modified for the right situation. I'm not sure what Abernathy wants us to find out, but we could be looking for years and still not find it."

It's not an encouraging thought.

I return to my seat and pull open another book. And another. All the while, my eyes water with unshed tears. Will's counting on me, and I have to figure something out. He needs me.

"We'll figure it out, Penny," Reggie says in a low, gentle voice. "Don't give up."

"I just . . ." I draw in a ragged breath, trying to control my tears. "I wish I knew what the big deal was with these stupid books. He has to be coming for them, right? That's the only thing that makes sense."

"Maybe he's a fan of gray furniture and ugly Cubism paintings," Reggie jokes, pulling open another book and spreading it in front of her. "I've never seen a man that hated clutter so much. Other than this lab, you'd think he's a Spartan."

"He's too young to be a Spartan," I admit, but Reggie's comments have me thinking. She's right. Will's decor is simplistic but pricey. He likes everyone to know he has money, and he likes a clean, uncluttered house. It has to be the purloined spell books. It can't be anything upstairs. Each time someone has attempted to break in, they didn't go for the art. They were looking for something specific.

Something they didn't find.

Which means it's most likely in the hidden lab.

Chewing on my lip, I stare at the surroundings of Will's lab. Spell book after old, battered spell book line the walls. Some of them are much, much older than Will is. *I might have broken into his house when he was at a warlock conference*, I hear his proud, aristocratic voice saying in my head. *And I stole all his spell books.*

Is it the books, or is it something more? They've sniped and fussed at each other for 250 years, but things have escalated dramatically, according to Will, especially after he stole the books.

I grab the nearest book and flip through it anxiously. "Did Ben say if there were any rare, special spells in Will's books?"

"I don't think so," Reggie says thoughtfully. "He said most of them were boring research. That Will likes the tried-and-true spells and refining them versus experimenting with new spellwork."

"Because the pride is in a traditional spell done to perfection,"

I agree absently, turning pages. Will's a traditionalist. He's not going to break the mold. So . . . what then?

I pick up another book—the one on fucking mushrooms again—and immediately put it aside once more. And then I pause, staring. Each of the spell books has a very traditional binding to it. Some of the books are red with gold lettering, and some are black with gold lettering. Some are brown, and all are bound in leather. They look a bit like a law library from the outside, and it's only the contents that are arcane-seeming. I practically know each one by sight now, so it's strange to me that I never noticed before that some of them have a different-colored interior board. I pull out the mushroom book again and run my fingers over the inside of the cover. It's a creamy off-white and feels like parchment, thick and slightly gritty. I pull out Will's favorite spell book on divination and compare it. This one has a thin white cloth glued to the inside.

Fascinated, I pick up another book. Parchment on the inside. The next one has parchment, too, but the third one I pick up—on augury—has the cloth binding on the interior. I know it's not Will's book but one he's stolen—he has a lot of derision for augury in general, and so I don't feel too guilty picking at the glued edge. The book is so old it uses *F* characters in place of where an *S* would go, but I don't care if it's priceless.

What I care about is getting answers.

I flip the book again, looking it over. It's an apprentice's primer, a spell book for baby witches. These tend to be a slender kind of book, Will told me, and has only very basic spells that any witch or warlock would know. It's useless to a highly skilled witch. Definitely useless to Stoker, but he wants it back for some reason.

I peel a corner of the backing away, and to my surprise, there's a name underneath.

ſamuel Davieſ, London, 1663.

"Who's Samuel Davies?" I ask Reggie, showing her the interior. "Does that ring a bell to you?"

She moves over to my side, glancing at the book and the name I've uncovered. "I don't know. Want me to ask Ben?"

I nod, and I immediately pull out my phone, too, using any chance to talk to Will.

PENNY: Hey boo

PENNY: Does the name Samuel Davies ring a bell? London? 1663?

WILL: It's one of Stoker's old apprentices, actually. Why?

PENNY: His name is in one of your books. Did you know him?

WILL: Nope. He died in the plague of London in 1666.

PENNY: Ok. Just curious. Love you!

WILL: I'm going to turn the phone off for a few hours. My battery is getting low. I'll check with you in the morning.

WILL: I expect to see tits on my phone in the AM.

WILL: XOXO

My heart melts. Did he just text me *X*s and *O*s? The man is turning positively soft and I'm loving it.

"Well?" Reggie asks, curious.

I lean over to her across the table, whispering. "It's one of Stoker's old apprentices. Will didn't know him. Said he died in a plague in London."

"That man has bad luck with apprentices," she mutters. "He loses a lot of them."

A prickle goes up my spine. "What do you mean?"

She shrugs, running her fingers over Davies's name. "Ben commented once that he's had a lot of apprentices die on him. That's all."

I blink. Then I pull out another book with the cloth binding on the interior. "Do you think we're going to find other names on the insides of these books? Names of other apprentices?"

"It's worth a shot," Reggie says. "Why?"

"I'm curious to know what happened to all of them." My Spidey sense is tingling. Stoker has taken it really badly that Will walked away from him. What if he didn't handle it well when others tried the same? What if he did something . . . terrible? I glance back at Roger, who seems to be trying to listen in on our conversation. "I don't suppose you have headphones in your purse?"

"Actually," Reggie says, and pulls out a tiny box with her Air-Pods. "Shall I give our friend some mood music?"

✳ ✳ ✳

A FEW HOURS later, Roger is asleep, slumped in his chair as whale sounds play in his ears. Reggie and I have pulled the bindings off every single spell primer and uncovered twenty-three different names from the last five centuries. I can't ask Will about them, but Reggie asks Ben.

He knows three of them, and all of them met bad endings.

"This can't be right," I tell her when she gets off the phone with him. "Three familiars dead by lightning strikes, all of them Stoker's familiars?"

"They're centuries apart, though." Reggie shrugs. "Maybe spell-casting makes them vulnerable to storms? I don't know."

Something about it strikes me as odd. In fact, all of this strikes me as odd. It's too many coincidences piling up. I grab my laptop and open it up, immediately heading for the Society of Familiars website login.

"What are you doing?" Reggie asks, leaning over my shoulder.

"I'm in charge of the Fam's records," I tell her. "We might not have information on some of these oldest cases or what the men died of, but we'll have records of them leaving the society and who they went to apprentice to."

"You want to cross-reference?" she asks, excited. "That's a brilliant idea."

I type in the first name and start searching records.

* * *

A FEW HOURS later, both Reggie and I are quiet with our grim discoveries. Each name we've uncovered comes from a different branch of the Society of Familiars, and each one apprenticed under Ebenezer Stoker. Only a few have death records—a couple of drownings, one plague, two carriage accidents—but the most disturbing thing is when the names are put into a timeline, they show that Stoker's been going through apprentices far too quickly for any warlock. Ever.

They're all meeting terrible ends, and then he requests a new apprentice from across the country, and that one meets another sort of terrible end in twenty years.

"He really has some rotten luck with apprentices," Reggie comments. "A little too rotten."

"What if these apprentices aren't unlucky?" I ask Reggie. "What if Stoker's killing them?"

"And these books are the evidence," Reggie agrees, excited. "That's why he wants them back so badly. It's not a spell in the books, it's the books themselves!"

I touch one of the books, the name that's been covered up in the binding. The handwriting in the book is different, too. I don't know why I didn't see it before. I thought maybe it was Stoker's handwriting that had changed over time. But it's not. It's almost two dozen different people that have worked for Stoker and vanished mysteriously. "What if we're wrong?"

"Ben's going to do some research in the warlock society archives," Reggie says excitedly. "And when he comes over tonight, we can scry and see what else we can find out. I think this is it, though."

"I think so, too." I glance back at Roger, his head tilted in sleep, the whale songs drowning out our conversation. "You think he knows anything about this?"

She makes a face. "Hardly. If I was a mustache-twirling bad guy who'd destroyed two dozen—or more—of my own apprentices, do you think I'd tell the next apprentice? My guess is that Roger's probably clueless."

I clutch the book in my hands to my chest. "Okay, so let's think about this. We have Roger. We have the books. They're both proof that he's lying but not necessarily proof that he's done anything bad. Even if we had more proof, I don't know that anyone would listen to us if we went to them with this. We need more." I shake my head. "Someone else higher up needs to realize that they're being played. We can show them the books and bring up the names, but that doesn't solve the long-term problem."

"How do we get more?" Reggie asks.

My phone buzzes with an incoming text. Will? I pick it up automatically . . . and then freeze at the message on the screen.

It's from an unknown number. You have things that are mine. Perhaps we can come to an agreement in exchange for Will's life.

"It's Stoker," I tell Reggie, and show her my phone. "I think he wants to meet."

"That's a terrible idea," she protests.

Is it? Because an idea is forming in my head, and I smile. "Actually, I think I'm going to do it." At her look of horror, I grin. "You're right. He *is* a mustache-twirling bad guy. And if that's the role he wants to play, I'm going to let him twirl his mustache at me and do himself in."

30

WILLEM

I'm roused out of a deep sleep by the sound of the basement door opening. I sit up, squinting at the light that pours down the stairs. I don't know how long I've been down here now. I've been keeping the phone off to preserve battery life, resorting to checking it only when I can't stand it any longer. It's been days since Penny passed it to me, and the battery bar is deep into the red.

As I watch, Titus strolls down the stairs, a particularly gloating look on his irritating face. He adjusts the cuffs on his suit—a cheap suit, I might add—and smirks at my disheveled appearance. "Today's your lucky day, Sauer."

It's bait. I know it's bait. And yet I can't help but rise to it. "And why is that? You're going to be hit by a train?"

He gives me a thin smile and stops at the base of the stairs. At the top of the landing, I can see his familiar hovering in the doorway, watching his master and no doubt blocking my escape if I try anything. As if there's a point to that. Penny wants me to stay here and I'm trusting her, even though the worry of it all is driving me slowly mad. Penny doesn't even have fifty years under her belt, much less a full month of spellcasting. How is she going to go toe-to-toe with someone like Stoker, who's made my life a misery for over two hundred years? It's terrifying to think about.

"You should know," Titus begins, his voice pitched dramatically for the greatest effect, "that your nosy little girlfriend is meeting with Stoker today."

I jerk to my feet and don't have to feign my horror. "She's what?"

Titus shrugs. "She's a fool, what do you expect? He offered her a compromise or an exchange of some sort, and she jumped on it. Doesn't seem to understand that it won't have anything to do with the charges that the society has laid against you. Those are separate from any personal vendettas, of course."

And he gives me a thin, self-satisfied smile.

Surely this isn't Penny's grand plan? To meet with Stoker and try to arrange my release? There's got to be more to it than this. *And you're just going to have to trust me*, she insisted. *Now, do you trust me AND love me or do you only love me?* And then she sent me obscene, filthy pictures as if to prove that she does indeed trust me.

I take a deep breath. Then another. I said I would believe in her, and I will. Even if this makes my skin crawl, I'm going to leave it be. I wish to all the gods that I'd kept my phone on this morning to see if she'd texted me about her plans, but I've been saving that sliver of battery life for emergencies. Looks like the emergency arrived, though, and I wasn't prepared.

"What's she meeting with him about?" I ask, trying to remain calm. If she is in his presence, he could get a strand of her hair or something that she's touched and curse her, or . . .

"All I know is that it's an exchange." He smirks at me again as if he knows something.

Why all the bragging and prancing about if it's just an exchange? "So why are you so fucking excited?"

Titus raises his chin, arching an eyebrow at me and looking pathetically ridiculous. "Because I can't wait to hear Stoker put the girl in her place."

31

PENNY

Like my mother, I've always believed in dressing the part. Today's no different. I sit at the Starbucks we've designated for our meeting, the carefully wrapped book on the table in front of me, and my dress ready for action. I picked something that hopefully screams business. I'm wearing a navy-blue dress and heels, with a sailor collar and matching anchor earrings. Okay, so it's not the most businesslike outfit I have, but it's a somber color, and that counts. My purse sits atop the table next to me, and I sip a coconut-milk chai latte as I wait for my lover's mortal enemy to appear. I glance around the quiet coffeehouse, but I don't see anyone that looks like a dastardly warlock of many centuries.

"No spells or wards?" says a scratchy, wobbly-with-age voice. "You're a trusting little one, aren't you?"

I ignore the "little one" crack, even though it riles my temper. I keep my expression sweet instead, because I need to keep him off guard. "I thought you might try something, which is why we're meeting here."

It's the most public spot I could find, trafficked at all hours of the day. Even now, the café is full of writers with laptops and a group of moms sitting on couches in the corner. My heart feels like it's in my throat, though.

My first thought is that he looks old for a warlock. I've seen them come into Vivi's store from time to time, and I've met both of my parents' witches on several occasions. I've had dinner with Reggie, Ben, and Ben's aunt Dru. They all look healthy and vibrant, and Aunt Dru is the oldest at two thousand years, and so she's silver-haired and tiny but still spry. Stoker just looks . . . weathered. His skin is papery and thin, dry with age and covered in liver spots. His hair is silver and wispy, tied back in what looks like an old-fashioned queue, and he's wearing a sweater and slacks that could have been taken from Mr. Rogers's closet. He gives me a smile that's supposed to be benign, but all I see are big yellow teeth that could use a good whitening.

He's not aging well, this guy. To me, that's a red flag.

But I play it cool, gesturing at the seat across from me. "Hello, Stoker. I'm here, just as you suggested, and I came alone."

"Did you cast anything?" he asks, sitting down across from me. "Anything to nullify magic in the area or compel anyone?"

"No. I can't cast. I'm in the Society of Familiars." I'm careful with my words in case he's cast a truth spell, and I hold my cuffed wrist up into the air.

He leans on a cane as he sits down and studies me thoughtfully. "So it would seem. Why are you so invested in Mr. Sauer, then?"

"He's my boyfriend. Why wouldn't I be invested in his safety?"

"He's a pompous twit who thinks very highly of himself," Stoker retorts. "If you're seeking a warlock to date, I'm sure I can introduce you to a few that are far more highly known."

"I don't want any warlock. I want Will," I say stiffly. "He's the entire reason I'm sitting here, and I'm not going to let you bully him any longer."

Stoker gives me a faint, wintry smile. "Speaking of bullies . . .

you have my familiar, don't you? He would have returned to me had he been capable. Since he hasn't, I assume you're responsible."

"Roger is safe," I state loudly. "You know, the Roger that you claimed Will had targeted and murdered? He's safe and he's alive back at Will's house. Where, I might point out, he showed up the day after Will was arrested, and broke in, looking for something."

Stoker just sighs heavily. "If you want a job done right, you have to do it yourself, I'm afraid. It was a mistake to send him." He shakes his head as if beleaguered. "It's so very difficult to get good help these days, as I'm sure your Mr. Sauer knows."

"Don't compare yourself to him," I snap. "You lied about your familiar being dead! Just to get Will arrested!"

"You're new to our games, little one," Stoker says. "It's best if you don't get involved."

"I should call the police and tell them you had my boyfriend kidnapped," I retort.

The look he gives me is pitying. "Warlocks and familiars don't concern themselves with mundane laws, child. We play by an entirely different set of rules."

"Rules that are crooked. You had Will set up. Do you deny it?"

"Why would I deny it? The truth of it is that it doesn't matter." He gives a papery, thin chuckle. "No one likes Sauer. I trumped up some charges against him and let his enemies do the rest. It won't matter what he proclaims at the end. The Council of Warlocks is run by fools, and they're going to vote to execute him simply because he's irritating."

"You can say something and have him freed," I persist. "He hasn't done anything to you. He's been forbidden from taking a familiar for over twenty years now. Why won't you leave him alone?"

"Why should I?" Stoker chortles again, and it occurs to me that he really is completely and utterly arrogant. He's delighted with himself and the situation he's put Will into. "It's so delightful to see him struggle when the noose tightens around his neck." The look he gives me is utterly self-satisfied. "Here's the thing about being a warlock. It's more of a popularity contest than you'd think. Like when Willem got in trouble for that whole Y2K business? Do you really think anyone feels Willem is threatening enough to murder a business partner? Or do you simply think that they were just looking for an excuse to punish him for being arrogant and all they needed was a gentle push in the right direction?"

"Did he even do anything? Will says he barely knew the guy."

"Does it matter?" Stoker raises an eyebrow at me. "If you're well loved, you can get away with anything. If you're not, then, well . . . it looks like you're Sauer."

That bastard. My nostrils flare with anger, and it takes everything I have not to lose my shit on him. "So he shouldn't even be in trouble. You're the reason he got banned from taking a familiar in the first place. Will didn't kill anyone. He never could figure out why they'd thought that. I guess I'm looking at what happened. Or more accurately, *who*."

Stoker chortles with delight, as if he's having a great time. "Are you sad that you can't be his apprentice? Is that what this is about?"

"It has nothing to do with apprenticeship. I'm determined to help the man I love get free from a bully."

"The whole 'I love Willem Sauer' part," he says, waving a hand at me. "I know him well. He was my familiar for a few years. He's a hard one to love or to even like."

"Really?" I cross my arms over my chest. "Then why were you so upset that he chose to leave your service? Because it sure seems to me like you've been punishing him for the last two hundred and fifty years for that one action."

Stoker's expression is no longer so amused. "No one leaves me," he hisses at me. "*I* am the warlock. I say whether or not anyone can leave my service."

Now we're getting to the good stuff. "Which is actually why I wanted to meet with you," I tell him, unwrapping the old book in front of me. "I know your secrets."

He rolls his eyes. "You know absolutely nothing."

"Really? Does the name Samuel Davies ring a bell?" I pull the book open and show him the name at the front.

"No. Should it?" His expression grows shuttered.

I pull out the piece of paper tucked at the front. "You should, since he was your familiar that died in the plague in 1666. According to warlock records, you were very distraught and immediately sought out another familiar. How about the name Guy Averil?"

"Don't know it."

"He was Samuel's replacement. Served you for five years and died in a house fire. Bad luck, huh?" I run my finger down the list. "Or Arthur Cooper? Drowned. Six years after he started working for you. Edith Dare? Her coach was robbed, and she was supposedly never seen again. Or how about—"

He interrupts me. "What is the point of all of this?"

"My point is that in the library of books that Will liberated from you, we found the names of twenty-three different familiars. All twenty-three were once apprenticed to you. That's quite a few, isn't it? An average of a new familiar about every twenty years. That's barely enough time to train them, isn't it?" I cluck my tongue. "And each one seems to have died horribly, and of course those horrible deaths were reported to the Society of Warlocks so you could then get a new familiar immediately after the demise of the last one. I cross-referenced each name with the Society of Familiars, because we keep records, too. And sure enough, each one was pulled from the Fam's records, and all from different locations. I assume that was so no one got nervous that so many familiars were disappearing under the same warlock."

Stoker watches me with narrowed eyes.

"It's almost like they were being bumped off by their master," I coo. "But gosh, that'd be too obvious, wouldn't it?" I flip the book open again. "At least, that's what I thought, until I ran across this necromancy spell that gives the life force of a volunteer to their warlock. Permanently. Just a little at a time, of course, so no one realizes what it's for. It's a pretty terrible spell. I'm sure that's against the rules of the Society of Warlocks, isn't it? To drain your familiar to the point of causing their death?"

"I've never cast such a thing," he says stiffly, his eyes glaring hate at me.

"See, that's the wild thing. I'm friends with a bunch of warlocks and witches, and so I had Ben Magnus—you know Ben, right? Kinda tall, kinda grumpy, long family history? I had him cast a truth spell on Roger. That's your current familiar, by the way. And we ran the spell components past him and asked if you'd ever cast anything with those particular components." I point a finger at the list. "You know, they're such specific components. A tooth from a young elephant. A naturally doubled egg yolk. Two pieces of cloth from a dead man's shroud. Ashes from—"

"Get to the point," he snarls.

"My point is that your familiar, Roger—who I would like to point out again is not dead and has not been accosted by my boyfriend, Will—knew all about these spell components. He says that they're for a scrying spell that you like to do on the full moon. Ring a bell?"

Stoker is silent.

"Right. Crazy thing about scrying spells. See, I work at a spell component dispensary. My boss is a witch. Vivi Hastings. You've heard of her, right? I asked Vivi what sort of spell components are used in scrying, and she said it's blood and just a little bit of food. And it just seemed odd to me that Roger dear wouldn't know the basics of a very simple scrying spell. So then I pulled records at work to see what kinds of orders you'd had fulfilled in the last couple of years." I wrinkle my nose at him and give a fake smile. "That's the neat thing about modern computers—they can pull up a customer's history in such a jiffy. And you won't believe just how many elephant teeth we've sold you in the past few years."

He glowers at me.

I lean in. "It's in the hundreds, Stoker. And the shroud threads. And everything else. You're casting these spells. You're draining your familiars of magic, and then you're tossing them aside when they're used up." I fold the paper up again. "It's really incredible what you're able to get away with right under the noses of everyone else in the business. But like you said, it's a popularity contest. And you've been skating by all these years by not being on anyone's radar, right? You wear your Mr. Rogers sweaters, and you keep a low profile, and you let louder people take the fall for you. People like, say, Willem Sauer."

And I wait.

Stoker is silent.

"Well?" I say, unable to resist poking the bear. "What do you have to say to any of that?"

He shrugs. "So?"

Of all the answers I'd expected, casual indifference wasn't one of them. "So?"

He shrugs again. "So what? A familiar is unimportant. So a few of mine have turned up missing. So some of my components look suspicious upon first glance. So what?"

I'm disgusted with him. "So you should apologize to Will! Have him freed, or I'm going to expose you and your crimes to everyone in warlock society. You'll be the one imprisoned, not him."

Stoker laughs. "You are *pathetic*. What do you think you can do?" He leans forward, hissing his words at me. "I am a warlock. I am esteemed. I come from a very old line of warlocks, and my blood is full of the blessing of the gods. And you think you have a chance against me?" He laughs again, the sound cold and oh so arrogant. "You should be asking me for forgiveness. Give me my books, give me my familiar, and we'll forget all about this."

"And Will?" I ask. "What about him?"

"Willem will pay the price for crossing me." He says it all smugly, as if he's had control this entire conversation.

I hate that he's rattling me. I know I shouldn't worry, but it's hard when he's pointing out so many things that are correct. He is hundreds—maybe thousands—of years old. He does have a reputation among warlock-kind. I'm not even a familiar, not according to anything official. But I'm determined to play it cool. *You have all the cards*, I remind myself. *Draw him in and let him hang himself.*

"So let me make sure I'm hearing this correctly," I say slowly. "You want Will to give you back spell books that aren't really yours but belonged to a bunch of your old familiars who you also had murdered."

"'Murdered' is such a strong word," Stoker purrs unctuously. "I prefer 'disposed of.'"

"Okay. You used them up like tissue and disposed of them. But I've got that part right?" I blink wide eyes at him, trying to seem guileless.

He laughs, as if my choice of words delights him. "I think that sounds quite right."

"And you accused my boyfriend of murdering your familiar without any proof. And then said familiar broke in and I had no choice but to defend myself against him. Now you now want me to turn him over to you instead of turning him over to the authorities, so you can finish draining him like some sort of magic vampire. And in exchange . . . I get nothing?"

"You get to walk out of here," Stoker says coldly. "I should think that would be a priority for you."

"What about my boyfriend? Because it sounds like the only crime he has committed is that he's kind of a dick. He didn't do this Y2K shit, and he didn't murder your familiar, so he did . . . nothing wrong. Have I got that right?"

Stoker just laughs. "And he'll die for it. It's a perfect plan."

"I mean, it's a decent plan," I agree. "But you are your own worst enemy, because you're an arrogant sack of shit, and it's time someone took you down."

He arches an overgrown eyebrow at me and laughs. "And you think you're the one to bring me down? *You?*"

"Me," I agree, a giddy, nervous feeling in my belly.

Stoker laughs. "You're not even a familiar. You have zero training in magic. Your bloodlines are marginal at best. You cannot possibly cast anything that can harm me."

"You're absolutely right about that. But I've got something you don't."

He looks utterly delighted at my gumption. He leans in, his expression mocking. "Oh, is that *so?* What, pray tell, is that?"

I pull my phone out of my purse and wave it at him. "I've got speakerphone, bitch. You've been on a conference call with the Council of Warlocks, and they've heard everything you've said."

Stoker goes silent. He blinks.

His gaze slides to my phone. To the black screen that shows the minutes that the call has been going on. I can tell that a million things are whirling through his mind. He's been so amped up, so ready for me to try to cast something against him, that he's forgotten about the tools a perfectly normal person can use. He wanted to twirl his mustache at me and I let him. Now he's implicated himself in a hell of a lot of trouble.

It was a gamble. A gamble, and it involved pulling a lot of strings, but it's about to pay off.

Stoker's bony throat swallows. He waves a finger at my phone, looking old and feeble. "You . . . It's against the law to record someone without their permission."

I give him my most dismissive smile. "Warlocks and familiars don't concern themselves with mundane laws, remember?"

WILLEM

The next day, when Titus comes into the basement, he removes my cuffs. He doesn't look me in the eye, either. Confused, I rub my wrists, and when he gestures at the stairs, I give him a wary look. "Is this a trap?"

"No. This is an apology." Titus's florid jaw clenches, and he looks rather revolted at the words but manages to spit them out anyhow. "We were wrong about you, Sauer. It's not a crime to be a prick, and it sounds like that's the only crime you've committed." He gestures at the door again. "Please follow me into my office, and we'll work on your release paperwork."

I don't believe it.

Titus Ragonius, one of my many mortal enemies, just apologized to me. I'm being released. Somehow, Penny managed to pull this all together. I'm utterly bewildered, but I can't seem to stop laughing, either. I think the entire world has done a disservice to Penny Roundtree by underestimating her. No longer.

An hour later, I stand in Titus's study with a certificate proclaiming my innocence and a second one revoking the ban on my ability to take a familiar. I also received a video conference call from the council, who apologized for the misunderstanding. "It seems we've been misled," Amalia Haverford said in an austere voice. It's not quite an apology, but knowing the snobbish Amalia, it's all I'm going to get. "I do hope there are no hard feelings. Rest assured Stoker will be taken care of."

"Taken care of?" I asked, because I had to.

"He has turned himself over," Titus told me, hands clasped in front of him, the very picture of penitence. "With a little convincing, of course. And while his crimes are being investigated, we thought it best to transmogrify him so he cannot continue to cause harm as we research the precise depths of his transgressions. Due to the scope of things, we anticipate it will take several centuries for us to research and facilitate the precise nature of said transgressions. I hope you understand."

Oh, I understand. Basically the council doesn't want to deal with it, so they're passing the buck—so to speak—to future generations. I don't care, though. Any transmogrification spell will alter a person's mind, and after centuries of transmogrification, there won't be much of Stoker left. "Should I ask what he was transmogrified into? Just to be on the lookout?"

"I'm afraid we cannot give more details than we have already," Amalia said haughtily.

"Quite so," Titus agreed, and then touched an ugly, misshapen paperweight on his desk.

I stared at the paperweight. It looked, if you squinted hard, like a face. Stoker's face. "I see."

"He said that he had a particularly aggressive cancer he was trying to stay ahead of," Titus explained. "Hence his malicious and transgressive castings against his own familiars."

"So?"

"It doesn't excuse it," he told me. "Just in case you were looking for . . . clarity of some kind." He shrugged. "Apparently he's been going after you because he suspected you were the only one with enough information to bring him to justice."

I'm not sure I care. All I care about is that I'm free. Free after more than twenty years of being hobbled. Free because Penny refused to let "good enough" be enough. She wanted to free me from Stoker completely, and I can't stop thinking about how amazing she is. She made this happen. That's all that matters to me.

And I need to tell her just how amazing she is.

As I turn to leave, Titus clears his throat. "You know . . . I'm good friends with Atticus. I've spoken to him about the position you applied for recently. I'm told it's still open. The warlock he hired didn't quite work out."

I'm sure he didn't, as he was an idiot. I pause. "Is he offering me the job? At Atticus & Partners?"

"Are you interested?"

I don't even pause to consider it. "I'll discuss it with my girlfriend."

His lip curls. "Your girlfriend? You're going to let her decide your career for you?"

Is he kidding? "My girlfriend is everything to me. She has my back at all times. I trust her with anything and everything, so yes, I would absolutely let Penny decide my career for me."

Titus narrows his eyes at me, and I can't tell if he's annoyed by my declarative words or just waiting for me to leave. I turn to go again, and he clears his throat one more time.

Biting back a sigh, I turn back. "Yes?"

"There is the issue of Stoker's apprentice. He's had Stoker's apprentice cuff removed, but he's rather distressed at the realization that he no longer has a warlock to serve."

"I would think he's more distressed over the fact that his warlock has committed major crimes with his assistance," I reply caustically.

Titus grimaces. "I thought the same. Yet Roger has asked if he could apprentice to you."

"Absolutely not. I'm not touching anything Stoker has had his hand in." Besides, that position belongs solely to Penny. I can't imagine anyone else casting with me. I also can't stop thinking about the little catches of her breath when I cast, which I now know are orgasms. I can't wait to see that in action once more. "Tell him to find someone else. Better yet, tell him to hit up the Society of Familiars. I hear the local chapter is fantastic."

With that, I nod and head out of his study.

Morgan, his familiar, meets me at the door to Titus's sprawling house. "I assume you're going to drive me home?" I ask, trying to straighten some of the wrinkles out of my jacket in vain. I look absolutely dreadful, I'm certain. I'm vain enough to hate that I might look as if I've been sleeping under a bridge . . . or in a basement for the last week. Which I have. I might not have personality, but at least I can cut a sharp figure in a nice suit. I smooth my hand over my hair, wincing at the tufts sticking up. "I shouldn't like to go out in public like this."

"Actually, sir, I've already arranged for your ride." He gestures out at the drive.

My car is out there, and Penny waits at the base of the stairs. She's a vision in her nautical dress and ridiculous earrings, her eyes bright and shiny. The moment she sees me, she wiggles like a puppy and then surges forward, a high-pitched squeal in her throat.

Before I can even take two steps down the palatial stairs that lead to Titus's front door, Penny flings herself into my arms, wrapping her legs around my waist. I hold her against me, pressing kisses to her face. "You crazy, insane, wonderful woman," I growl into her ear. "To quote you, double-yew tee eff. How the fuck did you pull this off?"

She laughs, excitement bubbling over as she clings to me. "Oh, Will, you look like such a mess. God, you're so cute." She's babbling, her hands gripping my jacket tight. "I've missed you so much."

I squeeze her tight, closing my eyes and breathing in her fresh scent. She smells like cherries and vanilla, and my cock decides those are the most erotic scents ever. It's that or the fact that Penny's rubbing all over me that makes me stiffen. Either way, I don't care. I'm going to enjoy this moment. So I bury my face in her hair and hold her close, hugging her for far, far too long. I'm not going to take her for granted. Every time I get to grab her and squeeze her against me, I'm going to do so. I rub my nose over her neck. "Penny. I don't know how you did this, but you're going to tell me every detail, and then I'm going to smack that sweet bottom of yours just like you wanted. Been dying to do that for days now."

"Ew, TMI," cries a familiar voice.

I lift my head and look over at both Ben Magnus and his horrified familiar, Reggie. They're waiting for us, Ben in the driver's seat of my car and Reggie in the front passenger, with the windows down. I guess they heard about me wanting to spank Penny. My ears get hot, but I can't find it in me to care all that much. "Don't listen in if you don't want to hear it."

"But you guys are so loud," Reggie complains. "Can we please just go?"

I don't need to be asked twice. I give Penny's rump a squeeze, and she detangles her legs from around my waist. The moment her feet are on the ground, though, she grabs my hand and hauls me after her. I stuff the now-crumpled papers in an interior pocket of my jacket. I'm framing these fuckers when I get home, just so no one messes with me ever again. Penny pulls me to the back seat, and the moment I buckle in, she's in my lap and all over me again.

"I hope you don't mind that I asked them to drive us," she says, showering my face with kisses. "I wanted backup in case Titus was a dick to you."

"Titus offered me a job," I admit, running my hands all over her. Gods, it feels good to touch her. "I told him I had to ask my brilliant girlfriend what she thought."

She gives a low, mischievous giggle. "Did you really?"

"Hell yes. I'm still not sure how you pulled this all off."

Penny snuggles into my chest, and I'm grateful she's a small human being, because she fits against me perfectly, tucked into my lap with my arms around her. "It's taken a few days of planning. But Stoker contacted us, trying to make a deal, and I realized that I needed to get him to confess everything he's done. So I thought, he was such a braggy, pompous ass that he'd probably confess everything if I confronted him. I called in every favor I could to Vivi and to my parents' witches, asking to get the council on the phone for five minutes at a scheduled time. They were not enthused and thought I was pulling something to try and save you, so I offered them a deal. They only had to listen for five minutes, and if I was wrong about Stoker, I'd take over running the Society of Familiars permanently in Derek's stead."

I'm appalled. "You what? Why would you do that?" It takes a moment for me to absorb what she's saying. "And wait. Who's Derek?"

"Derek is the current head of the Society of Familiars, and he likes to contact the council with lots of fiddly requests. I think he drives them crazy, because the moment I suggested it, they were all on board." She smiles brightly at me.

"I'm shocked you'd risk such a thing, Penny. You shouldn't have." I know how much she wants to be a witch in her own right, and how it would kill her spirit to remain as a familiar-to-be forever. "I would never ask that of you."

"Then it's a good thing I volunteered, huh?" She gives me a sweet smile. "Besides, I knew the risk but you're worth it. I also was pretty convinced I was right."

"I still don't like it."

"You don't have to like it, because it's done." She sighs happily. "You're free now, and you even get to have a familiar again. Isn't that amazing?"

Ben looks over at us from the driver's seat. "By the way, you're welcome, dick."

"Glad to see you, too," I call to him. "And thank you." I bury my hands in Penny's hair and pull her down for another deep, scorching kiss. It's good to have friends, I'm realizing, but it's even better to have someone like Penny. She's changed everything for me.

I hold her tightly through the long drive, and it feels as if I don't draw a deep breath until I'm back inside my own home, with the wards safely in place. The locks on the doors have changed, and it's a bit messy inside, but I don't even care. I'm home . . . and I'm free. There's no more Stoker hanging over my head. No more disapproving council. I can have a familiar openly.

I want to fling myself to the ground and just roll around like a puppy with the sheer giddiness of it.

Instead, I grab Penny in my arms and swing her about. "You are the most marvelous woman I've ever met, you know that?"

She gives me a shining smile, so broad that her eyes crinkle and disappear, and my heart melts at the sight. Gods, I love this woman.

I growl low in my throat and lean forward, hauling her over my shoulder like a caveman. With a glance at Reggie and Ben, I give them a nod of thanks. "You have my undying gratitude, but I owe this woman a spanking and several other filthy activities. Please don't expect to see either of us for at least a week or two."

Penny lets out a wicked giggle, and I swat her ass playfully.

"Oh my god," Reggie moans, turning and burying her face against Ben's black sweater. "We've created a monster by pairing these two together."

"It's appalling," Ben agrees, smirking at me. "Utterly appalling. Come on. Text us if you need anything." He puts an arm around Reggie's shoulder and leads her toward the door.

I don't stop to see if they're staying or not. I don't care if they are. I just know I'm personally not going to stick around and entertain them. I carry Penny to my bedroom, my hand on her bouncy, adorable little backside. It's messy in here as well, with Penny's discarded laundry everywhere, along with several books. "Did you ransack my house while I was gone?" I tease, setting her down on the bed. "Because it looks like it."

She chuckles, leaning back on her elbows. "Our priority was getting Stoker taken down, not housecleaning. And I couldn't pay the maids, so I told them not to come by until you were back. I hope that's okay."

As if I care about the maids. I move to the bed and crawl over her, kissing her again . . . and then get a whiff of my scent. Dear gods. I smell like I haven't bathed in a week, probably because I haven't. "Ugh." I get off her again. "I should shower before anything."

Penny reaches for me, making a noise of protest. "I don't mind how you smell."

"I do. I'll take a quick shower, and then I'll come back and spank you properly."

She shivers, her eyes bright with excitement. "I hope you know all I want is a pretend spanking that leads to a very naughty fingering and at least two orgasms."

The mouth on this woman. I bite back a groan. Part of me is always scandalized at just how open Penny is about her sexuality, but a much larger part of me likes it. I always know where I stand with her, and if I'm not pleasing her in bed, she'll make sure to tell me so. I like that she's just as bold, open, and fearless under the covers as she is above them. "If that's what you'd like, then I shall strive to provide."

Penny gets comfortable on the bed, flipping to her side. "Okay, go shower, then. I'll wait right here."

The urge to grab her and fuck the hell out of her wars with my personal fastidiousness. In the end, fastidiousness wins out, though. I really do smell rank, and I want to have clean hands when I touch her all over. I head for the bathroom and shower quickly, pausing only to comb my hair down into its usual hairstyle, but I skip the product. Penny likes to touch my hair for some reason, and, well, I want her to do a lot of touching.

I emerge from the bathroom in nothing but a towel wrapped around my waist. Penny is gone from my bed, and I frown, wondering if I've missed yet another opportunity to make her mine. She returns a moment later, though, hair down and dressed in a filmy pink nightgown with spaghetti straps over the shoulders and a feathery edge that dances against her thighs. It's entirely see-through, and I'm dumbstruck by her small, dark-tipped breasts and the neat tuft of hair between her thighs. She waves a pink bottle at me. "I was getting lube for us."

"Lube," I echo. "I've never used lube." In my experience, a male needs lube when he cannot get his female sufficiently wet to take his cock. "Is there a problem?"

"Oh em gee," Penny sighs, a dreamy expression on her face. "Lube is just bedroom crack, baby. Sex is good, but sex with lube is next level. You'll like it, trust me." She pauses. "Oh, and while I think about it, we should talk about birth control."

"Birth control." It's terrifying to realize that I've been in her twice so far and we haven't used any. "Yes. We need to work on that. Unless . . . you want a baby?"

"I'm not opposed to a baby, but I'd rather be your familiar first." Penny shrugs. "I'm only bringing up the birth control because we've barebacked it twice now, and while it feels great, we might be testing the odds if we go for a third time." She bounces over to the bed, and I watch her tits jiggle in that sheer nightie. "Do you have condoms?"

"I . . ." I swallow. "No, alas. I haven't had any relationships in several decades."

She looks utterly delighted at this revelation. "You really are the cutest, you know that? All right, we'll raw-dog it one more time, and then in the morning, we are raiding a pharmacy."

Raw-dog. Good gods. "You know your vernacular is terrifying."

"You love it."

"Gods help me, I really do." I stalk toward her, moving across the bedroom, and then pause. A quick glance over at the far side of the room, where she's kept her squirrel since she moved into my bed, shows that the cage is gone. "Where did your mongrel go?"

"Pip isn't a mongrel," Penny exclaims, giving me an exasperated stare. "He's just a squirrel. And he's staying with Nick and Diego since things have been weird. He can't stay with Reggie, because Maurice tried to eat him."

Maurice. The name sounds familiar. "Wasn't he someone's assistant at some point?"

"I believe so. Long story." Penny wiggles the pink bottle enticingly at me again. "Are we going to talk about familiars, or are we going to have incredible sex and shake the bed all night long?"

When she puts it that way . . . I move to her side and put a finger under her chin, tipping her face up. "We should talk about familiars anyhow, shouldn't we?"

Her smile is as bright as ever. "As if it was ever a question? I'm obviously taking the job. You don't even have to ask."

"Mmm." She's been teasing me so much that I feel the need to tease her back. I pinch her chin between my fingers and pretend to examine her face. "I don't know. I'm not sure I'm supposed to fuck the hell out of my familiar, and I plan on fucking the hell out of you."

I love the way her eyes flare with heat, her pupils growing dilated. She takes a deep, shuddering breath, gazing up at me. "I mean, it works for Reggie and Ben."

"So it does," I agree, and run my thumb over her full lower lip.

She immediately takes the tip between her teeth and flicks her tongue against it.

I groan. Naughty, wicked thing. I slide my hand to her hair and grab a fistful of it, tilting her head back. I keep my grip light but firm, because I don't want to hurt her. I simply want to challenge her for authority in the bedroom . . . because I plan on being in charge between us. She might speak boldly, but I'm still the warlock around here. "And do you want me to fuck the hell out of you?"

"Yes, please," Penny says breathlessly.

Taking the bottle of lube from her, I eye the label. Strawberry-flavored. How did I know? "And is this for you or for me?"

"Both of us," she immediately answers. "I thought I'd coat your cock and suck on it for a while, and then we could switch and you could go down on me. And then more lube, and some really wet, nasty sex and—"

I cover her mouth with mine before she can finish her breathless, filthy statement. With every kiss and sweep of my tongue, I show her just how much she means to me. She makes me absolutely crazy, this woman, but I love hearing the things that come out of her mouth. I love the sighs and whimpers. I love the noises she makes when—

Aha.

An excellent idea hits me and I break the kiss, leaving Penny blinking up at me. "I think I want to cast a spell."

Dazed, she gives me a confused, aroused look. "You do? What for?"

To make you come. I don't say it aloud, though. "More wards," I say. "We need to make sure they're secure."

"Right now? We do right *now*?" She practically whines the words, glancing back at the bed meaningfully.

"Right now," I agree. I adjust the towel at my waist, ignoring the tent in the front, and hold my hand out to her. She takes it automatically, her frown evident as I lead her out of the room. "Won't take long, I promise."

"Okay." Penny doesn't sound thrilled.

I lead her through the house and back down to my lab, which looks equally as wrecked as the rest of the place. Every single book has been taken from its home, and I'm appalled at the ones that lie open, the backings ripped up. I know it was to save me, but it just wounds my ledger-loving soul to see them treated so callously. "I see you made use of my lab while I was incarcerated."

"Don't be mad," Penny says with a squeeze of my hand. "We worked down here while we tried to figure out how to free you."

As if I could be mad about that. I'm humbled that she put so much on the line for me. But I lead her through the mess and then pause at my favorite workstation. Books are stacked everywhere on the table's surface, and I release Penny's hand, then push the books aside, clearing off a space. "Bend over the table for me, please."

She lets out a tiny squeak of surprise. "W-what?"

"You wanted a spanking? I'm going to give you a spanking for making such a mess."

Penny whimpers, and my cock twitches so abruptly that I nearly lose my towel. The little sounds she makes are incredibly sexy. I watch, fascinated, as she puts her hands on the edge of the table and slowly leans forward. It makes her short little nightie ride up, revealing the rounded curves of her ass, and the damp pink folds between her thighs.

"Spread for me," I murmur, fascinated at the sight. I can't look away.

She makes a little moaning sound and then does as I ask, revealing everything to my hungry gaze. Oh, I love the sight. I run a hand over one plump ass cheek and then give it a light tap, appreciating the jiggle of it. She wriggles against my hand, glancing over at me and panting. "That's all you've got?"

"I haven't even started yet, Little Miss Sass." I give her ass a harder tap, and I'm fascinated with the ripple of her backside. I love that she's all roundness and curves. I love the dimples on her buttocks and the soft jiggle of her thighs. I love all of it, and I want to watch it for hours as I touch her.

My towel falls to the floor with a soft thump, and she giggles.

"Are you laughing at me? Your warlock?" I fake outrage and give her ass another tap, this one hard enough for her to yelp in surprise. I immediately pause, rubbing the offended cheek. "Was that too hard?"

"It's fine," she says. "I like it."

"I'm not sure I do," I mutter. If it's what she needs, I'll give it to her, but I'm not keen on hurting her. Not when I'd rather worship between her thighs. "This won't help me cast anyhow. Go ahead and flip over."

"Flip over?" She straightens, no longer bending over the table, and gives me a confused look.

I pick her up by the hips and seat her atop my table, then push her thighs apart again. "I need to cast," I tell her, and my cock is as hard as stone, jutting out as I move between her thighs. I pick up the bottle of lube as if I've used this sort of thing all the time and squirt a healthy dollop onto my hand. "And while I cast a spell, my pretty familiar is going to show me if she really comes when the magic hits her."

"I'm not lying," Penny protests as I make a fist, slicking my fingers. "It's not something I'm proud of. I—ooh." Her eyes widen and flutter shut as I push my slippery hand between her thighs and stroke down her cleft.

"You're right," I murmur. "That *is* nice."

She's wet, but the lubricant adds a slippery layer to things that just makes it better all around. I slide a finger into her with ease, and she's hot and slick around me. I add a second finger and love the obscene noises her body makes as I work her pussy.

Penny whimpers, leaning back on the table and bracing her hands, spreading her thighs wider for me.

"Look at how pretty you are," I say as I work her. My fingers stroke in and out like melted butter, and I decide that we're going to have to use lubricant all the time if it adds this much fun to things. I slide my thumb through her folds, seeking out her clit, and rub it in time with the movement of my fingers.

"Will," she pants, her eyes closed and her nose scrunching up. "Oh god, that feels so good."

I'm entranced by the contortions of her face as she approaches her climax. There's nothing about Penny that's subtle, and that's one of the things that I love about her. Every emotion shows on her face, and I can tell when she's about to come . . . and I slide my fingers back out of her and stop. "Let me find my book—"

"Will!"

I grab the first book close by. I have no idea what I'm going to cast. Just that I want to cast something and sexually torture my pretty familiar just a little bit more. Penny grabs my hand and drags it back between her thighs, but I make a fist, robbing her of my fingers. With my other hand, I flip through the book. It falls open to Tempestas, and a request for a sudden rainstorm. Fine. We can use the rain. "This is perfect—"

"Will," Penny beseeches me, her hand on my wrist. "Come *on*."

I lean over and give her a hard, possessive kiss. She moans against my mouth, her hips bucking eagerly when I stroke through her folds again. I seat two fingers deep inside her . . . and then stop moving. "Hold still for me."

She squirms. "W-what are you doing?"

"An incantation for rain, love. Now be good and hold still, like I said." I pretend to focus on the book, but I'm really focused on every twitch Penny makes, every squeeze of her channel around my fingers, the warmth and wetness of her body. "I'm going to cast this, and we'll see if I really do make you come when a spell pops off."

Penny moans, her thighs tightening around my hand. "Oh god."

"Hmm. This looks rather simple. I need a feather from a bluebird, a bit of rainwater, and a drop of honey." I glance around the messy laboratory. "Where's my casting bowl?"

She whimpers incoherently, her body squeezing around my hand. Her eyes are tightly shut, and I can feel her clenching around my fingers deep inside, as if trying to work herself over the edge.

"Right. You're focusing. I'll get them. You wait right here." I press a kiss to her forehead and free my hand again and win another frustrated protest from my familiar. All right, this is actually rather enjoyable. I love the sexual element added to the casting, and though I normally sway toward the prudish line of things compared to Penny, I don't even care that I'm naked and striding around my laboratory, choosing components with lube-slickened fingers and humming to myself.

By the time I return to the table and kiss Penny again, she claws at my shoulders, desperate to come.

"Did you miss me?" I purr at her.

"Will," she pants, kissing me hungrily. "I need your cock. I need your hands. I need something—"

I return the kiss, teasing her with my tongue, and rub my fingers through her slick heat once more. Then I push two fingers deep in her body again and pretend to turn my attention back to the spell. She moans as if pained, her pussy clamping around my fingers desperately.

"Please move," she begs me. "Please move your fingers. Your thumb, anything."

"Shh. I'm concentrating."

She makes a pained sound, clenching tight again.

The spell is thankfully straightforward, as I'm having trouble concentrating. With the use of only one hand, I add the components into the offering bowl, murmuring the incantation to Tempestas. Magic builds and hums in the air, and Penny's body flutters around my fingers, her whimpers growing more intense as I continue invoking Tempestas to grace us with just one small little thunderstorm, just enough to make the spell—and my familiar—pop off.

When thunder cracks overhead, Penny sucks in a breath, and her channel constricts around my fingers. I'm fascinated, turning to watch as her face flushes, her eyes fluttering and her tits heaving as the orgasm rocks through her. She soaks my hand, and I decide to be a good warlock to my poor, sweet, suffering familiar and stroke her with my fingers. She immediately cries out, and her body starts clenching up all over again, as if another orgasm is about to work its way through her.

Suddenly, I'm tired of playing. I want to be inside her, and I want it now. I pull my hand from the tight clasp of her body, and Penny wraps her arms around me, clinging to my shoulders. I press a kiss to her soft, parted lips and pull her down from the table, only to turn her around again. "Back on your stomach, love."

With a shaky little sigh, she does as I say, pushing her bottom up into the air for me. I grip her by the hips, shoving her nightie up, and then seat myself to the hilt inside her. She makes a sound of intense pleasure, and I groan, echoing it. Nothing feels better than being deep inside her, and with Penny twitching and squeezing around me, I won't last long. I slide a hand to her shoulder, anchoring her in place, and fuck her in earnest, pounding deep into her as she cries out for another release.

This time, when she comes, I'm there with her.

Afterward, I slide off her trembling body and press a dozen kisses onto her shoulders, running my hands all over her sweet self. "Was that too much? How do you feel?"

She moans, her eyes closed and her body collapsed against the table. "Boneless. Good. Really good. Can we do it again?"

I chuckle at that. "Down here or upstairs?" I grab my towel from the floor and shake it off, then wrap it around her hips. "Would you like to shower? Do you want a cookie? Some milk?"

Penny turns and presses her cheek against my chest. "Just tell me you love me."

Her words make me ache. I wrap my arms tight around her, fighting the ridiculous knot of emotion in my throat. To think that when she appeared on my doorstep, I wanted nothing to do with her. She was too cheerful, too enthusiastic, too everything. Now I want to grab her and squeeze her cheeks. I want to kiss her until she smiles. I want to see her cast her own spells at my side, and the look of delight on her face when one works. I want to share every fucking day with her.

She's the best person I've ever met, the most loyal and unselfish, and I've never felt for another person what I do for her. "I don't deserve you," I whisper, my voice stupidly ragged. "I love you, and I'm humbled by you, and I don't deserve someone as wonderful and clever and determined as you."

Penny hugs me back, her arms around my waist. "Don't say that."

"Say what?"

"That you don't deserve me. Maybe I'm exactly the person you deserve." She turns her face, kissing my chest. "Maybe we both deserve each other. You annoy people because you're a snob, and I annoy people because I'm too excitable. But maybe that's what makes us perfect for one another."

"Worst superhero team-up ever," I agree.

She giggles, and the sound makes me smile. Damn, it feels good to smile. It feels good to just be with her, period.

"I don't care what anyone else thinks," Penny tells me. "We can annoy the rest of the world as long as we're happy together, right?"

"Are you happy with me?"

"You even have to ask?"

"I do, because I'm a rotten prick who's too used to being hated by everyone." I stroke my hand through her soft, dark hair. "Just as long as you happen to like those qualities in a warlock, I'll be happy."

"As it happens, I *love* a good prick," Penny teases.

Then it's good for her that I have *and* am one.

Her expression grows thoughtful as she gazes at me. "You're sure you want me as your familiar? Registered with the Society of Warlocks and everything?"

"I'm positive. I'll send an email right now if you want." I gesture vaguely upstairs at my phone. "I'll tell the world. I . . ." I pause, my eyes watering and my nose itching.

Then I sneeze. And I sneeze again.

"Oh shit," Penny breathes, her eyes going wide as she realizes what this is.

"Tablet," I wheeze, realizing it, too. "We need to get that curse tablet and break it."

She giggles hysterically, clutching her sides. "We didn't make allowances for a real partnership!"

I just sneeze again.

Epilogue

PENNY

DEREK: When it says 3 strands from deer ...

DEREK: Does it mean 3 strands from the same deer, or one strand from 3 different deer?

DEREK: Also can I put them all in the same bag?

DEREK: When do you come in again? I have more questions.

I make a noise of quiet rage at my phone. "Why did I think this was a good idea? Why?" I turn to Will. "Why didn't you talk me out of this?"

He doesn't look up from the lit magnifying glass in front of his face, carefully brushing an illuminated letter onto a piece of parchment. "If I recall, dumpling, I did tell you it was a terrible idea. You said you felt sorry for him and wanted him to have something outside of the Fam."

"Ugh. That does sound like me," I say dramatically, moving to the plush chair that now sits in the corner of Will's lab. It's my chair, hot pink, overstuffed, and full of bright cushions. It doesn't look like it belongs in his austere laboratory, so it makes me doubly happy that he's including me in his spaces. I have an office upstairs, as well, and I've taken the liberty of slowly starting to redecorate parts of the house, but I know his lab is his kingdom. I rub my hands over my rounded belly and lift one foot into the air. "Are my ankles swelling again?"

That gets his attention. Will puts down his paintbrush and gets to his feet, moving to my side. He kneels in front of me, taking one of my multicolored flats off my foot and rubbing it with his hands. "They do look a little swollen. How do you feel?"

"Sleepy," I admit. This baby's taking a lot more out of me than I thought it would.

"Do you want something to eat? Drink? A foot rub?" His hands move over my ankles.

I wave a hand at him. "Go back to your book, Will. I'm just going to sit here for a moment and ignore Derek's messages. I need to space out replying to them so he lowers his expectations. That's on me."

Will gets to his feet, kisses my forehead, and runs his knuckles down my cheek, then returns to his spot at his workbench.

I rub my stomach as I watch him work, deliberately avoiding my phone. It's been hard for me to detangle myself from the Society of Familiars. It's been such a big part of my life for the last nine years, and I'm the type that has to take on a bit of everything. Well, okay, more than just a bit. While Derek's been the figurehead in charge, I've been the one running things behind the scenes, and now that I'm a full-fledged familiar, it's hard for me to pass off all the details of the job to a new secretary. The person taking my place is a sweet girl named Elissa who's a college student majoring in accounting. She enjoys paperwork and wants to have a "mundane career" if being a familiar doesn't take off for her, so she's perfect for the role. Best of all, she can tolerate Derek and his rambling.

Poor, poor Derek. Actually, poor Society of Familiars. It's been a mess in the seven months since I officially left. Derek stepped down after some not-so-subtle nudging from the Council of Warlocks. Cody and Katrina were both expelled and added to the "do not familiar" roster, and rumblings from upstairs compelled Derek to put in a new leader. It's a nerdy middle-aged man named Larry. He's not great at the job, and Derek has been moved to treasurer, which he's also not very good at. A few of the newer members have left after seeing where they were ranked on rosters, and enrolled in Ben Magnus's ongoing classes, content to dabble in minor magic and nothing more. It's been a time of turmoil and upheaval for the Fam.

It's also not my problem any longer, I remind myself.

I scrub my face with my hand and peek at my phone again. There's a wall of text messages, and I bite back a moan, because I know it'll make Will upset. It's my own fault. I told Vivi when I officially signed on as Will's familiar that I couldn't work for her any longer, and Vivi panicked. She didn't want to be involved with the shop and liked that I ran things. So I'm on part-time as a consultant, and I've been training the team that I have working there to fill my shoes. It's taken three employees to handle what I once did, but I hired all of them from the Fam. I want them to have experience with witches and components, even if they can't use them yet.

And I hired Derek because I felt sorry for him. I wanted him to have a bit more to his life than just running the Society of Familiars. He's not great at it and he overthinks everything, and I remind myself that he's elderly and means well, and he's got no one else. So I pick up my phone and reply to his text messages, making sure to end each of mine with a smiley face so he doesn't realize I'm annoyed.

I finish texting and glance over at Will. He's the picture of concentration, carefully working on the illuminated page spread out on the drafting table before him. His lab has changed slightly in the past few months. Ever since we found out that I was pregnant— turns out raw-dogging it three times in a row is one time too many—we've had to change our plans. I can't cast much and Will is terrified of harming me or the baby, so I suggested he work on spell books. He made a custom one for Reggie as a thank-you for her help, filling it with a few basic spells and drawings, and etching a protection spell onto the edges. It's nothing a far more experienced witch or warlock wouldn't have in their library already, but Reggie was so touched that she brought it up constantly and showed it to people at parties. The next thing I knew, Will was getting custom orders to create more spell books for people that didn't have the time or inclination to create their own. The books take a ridiculous amount of time because Will tailors them to the owner, but he loves doing it and I love how happy it makes him. He's done the last several for free, and word has been getting out in warlock society about how thoughtful and generous he's been with the books.

Will wanted to charge, of course. But he's already rich through investments and getting richer all the time. It was my idea to give them away as goodwill presents. After all, Stoker was right about warlock society being a popularity contest, and I'm determined to turn around the perception of Mr. Willem Sauer.

They're going to love him as much as I do, damn it.

"You have that look on your face, dumpling," Will says from his worktable.

"What look?"

He peers over at me, grinning. "The scary one. The one that says you're thinking about how to conquer the world."

"That's your favorite look," I tease. But . . . he's not wrong. I'm planning all right. "I was thinking about having a house party."

Will arches a brow at me. "For cards? Aren't we going to Nick and Diego's on Friday as usual? I just made a deck." He's finally sat down to learn the rules of Spellcraft: The Magicking, and it turns out that my boyfriend is really, *really* competitive. It's adorable.

"I was thinking more like inviting all the local warlocks and witches over for a mixer. And of course, their familiars, too. It'd be nice to see everyone. You have a great wine collection, and we can put out some charcuterie boards, maybe mention the upcoming wedding and fish out if anyone wants to be invited . . ." I trail off, looking over at him.

Will has straightened in his seat, his brush down again. "You're determined to make me popular, aren't you?"

"I am."

"You know this is a terrible idea."

"I think it's a very good idea," I say loftily, sliding a hand over my rounded belly. "I mean, since we can't cast much right now, we might as well mingle, right? You can show off your spell books, make a few connections. It'll be fun."

He sighs. "Remember when you sent the fruit basket to Titus, dumpling?"

"What, like I was supposed to know he would think it was poisoned?" I frown over at him. I still have Morgan's frantic messages in my voicemail, of him asking what he'd done wrong and to please consider him if we were trying to assassinate his warlock. "I don't know why everyone thinks you're going straight for the murder route, seriously."

"Because I was Stoker's only familiar to escape his clutches? So they think I'm as ruthless as him?"

"Not his only familiar. At least they don't think you're like Roger?" Poor Roger. He's now working at Vivi's store, too. No other warlock or witch wanted to touch him after the mess with Stoker, so he's been added to the pool of "in-waitings."

The look Will shoots my way is incredibly fond. "Love, you can't make them like me."

"I can too." I lift my chin. "It's just that you're amazing and smart and talented, and I need them all to realize it." I tap my belly. "And I want our family to be part of the community. You said you wanted to get married before the baby was born, and I said yes. Let's have a party to celebrate our engagement, then. It doesn't have to seem fishy. It can just be about our love." I give him a wicked, calculating grin. "And then we make them realize how amazing we are and how foolish they've been to look down on you. They'll be begging to be our friends . . . and begging for your books."

He points the blunt end of his brush at me. "You're terrifying, you know that? Under that bubblegum-and-glitter exterior is the calculating heart of a true tyrant."

"You love me and my tyranny," I tease.

Will grins over at me. "Gods help me, but I really do."

Keep reading for an excerpt from
another exciting Jessica Clare romance

GO HEX
YOURSELF

REGGIE

When I pull up to the location of my job interview in Nick's borrowed car, my first thought is that I've made a mistake. I peer up at the ominous-looking building, a black-brick Victorian tucked among several more-brightly colored neighbors, and consult my phone again. No, this is the right place. After all, there's only one Hemlock Avenue in the city. With a worried look, I glance up at the building again, then find a place to park a few streets over that's not too close and not too far away. It's a corner store, and I check the parking lot lines to ensure that I'm perfectly within my space, and then repark when I'm not entirely satisfied with how close I am to the yellow line. It takes a little more time, but it's always better to be precise than to be sloppy.

Ten minutes later, I'm down the street with a freshly fed meter running, and I've got my CV in hand. Am I really going to interview at someone's house for an assistant job? I'm a little uneasy at that, but it's for a gaming company, and those sorts of people are notoriously quirky . . . I think. I check the address one more time before I move up the steps and ring the doorbell, smoothing my skirt with sweaty hands. Up close, the building seems a little more imposing, with dark burgundy curtains covering every single window and not letting in a peep of light. The stairs up to the door have an ornate black iron railing, and even the door knocker looks like something out of a horror movie, all vines and animal heads.

Someone has a goth fetish, clearly.

The door opens, and I'm startled to see a woman about my age in jeans and a T-shirt proclaiming her favorite baseball team. Her hair's pulled back into a bedraggled ponytail, and she's not wearing a stitch of makeup. She's also about twenty months pregnant, if the balloon under her shirt is any indication.

"You must be Regina," she exclaims with a warm smile, rubbing the bulge of her stomach. "Hey there! Come on in."

I'm horribly overdressed. I bite my lip as I step inside, painfully aware of the clack of my low-heeled pumps on the dark hardwood floors. I'm wearing a gray jacket over a white blouse and a gray pencil skirt, and I have to admit, the feeling that I'm in the wrong place keeps hitting me over and over again. I don't normally make these mistakes. I like for things to go perfectly. It's the control freak in me that needs that satisfaction. I researched what one wears to an assistant interview, so I don't know how I flubbed this so badly. I want to check the ad one more time, but after rereading it over and over for the last three days, I know what it says by heart.

SPELLCRAFT EXPERTISE WANTED
Assistant required. Excellent pay for familiar.

I mean, I've been a fan of the card game Spellcraft: The Magicking since I was a teenager. I have thousands of dollars of cards and even placed second in a local tournament once. Sure, I was playing an eight-year-old . . . but he had a good deck. Heck, I've even brought my favorite deck with me in my purse, in case they think I'm bluffing about my love for the Spellcraft game.

So am I qualified? Fuck yeah, I am. I can be an assistant to some-one that works for the Spellcraft: The Magicking company. It's kinda my dream job. Well . . . my dream job is actually to work on the cards themselves, but I'm not experienced enough for that, so being an assistant would be the next best thing. But I'm smart, I'm reasonably educated, I'm good with spreadsheets, and I'm exces-sively, excessively organized.

(Some might say "obsessively," but I ignore haters.)

I smile at the pregnant woman, suspecting she's the one I talked to on the phone. "You're Lisa?"

"That's me!"

I hold out my CV, tucked into a fancy leather-bound folder. I pray that the nice packaging will hide the fact that my detailed CV is kinda light on office jobs and heavier on things like "Burger Basket" and "Clown holding sign in front of Tax Masters." It's all about enthusiasm, though, right? I've got that in spades.

Lisa takes the folder from me with a little frown on her face, as if she's not quite sure what to do with it, and then gestures at the house. "Want me to show you around Ms. Magnus's house? She'd be the one in charge day to day."

Er, that's kind of odd. Why do I need to know about my em-ployer's house? Maybe she's just really proud of the place? But since I'm interviewing, I paste on a bright smile. "That'd be great."

Lisa's smile brightens, and she puts her hands on her belly, wad-dling through the foyer. "Follow me."

I do, and I can't help but notice that the interior of the place looks much larger than the exterior suggested. Inside, the ceilings are incredibly high, and the rooms seem airy despite the dark col-oring. The walls are the same burgundy red, and several of them are covered in reproductions of ancient Roman murals. "Your boss must like Roman stuff."

"Oh, she's Roman. All the big names are," she calls over her shoulder.

"Ah." Funny, I researched the game and thought the CEOs were from Seattle. Maybe she's an investor? Who just likes to talk about the game? That might be kind of fun. My enthusiasm brightens as Lisa shows me through the living room and the modern, elegant kitchen. She heads down a long hall and looks over at me again. "This way to the lab."

"Lab?" I echo. "Oh, you mean office?" I beam. "It's so charming that she calls it a lab."

"What else would she call it?" Lisa opens a large symbol-covered door, and I think Ms. Magnus must be a huge nerd to decorate her office like this. When we step inside, though, I'm a little stunned. There's a large desk, all right, but instead of a laptop and paperwork, there are beakers and bottles. An old book is spread out on the table itself, and the walls are lined with jars and more books. The ceiling is hung with what look like dried herbs.

It's an absolute nightmare. Every iota of my organization-loving heart cringes at the sight of this. It's clear that Ms. Magnus needs me. I'd never let a place of work get this disorganized. The books are all over the place, there's no computer to be seen, and I'm pretty sure under the stacks of loose paper and piles of nonsense, there's a bookshelf. Somewhere.

It all needs a guiding hand, and that's what I do best. Guide. Or . . . control. Whatever. I'm good at this kind of thing.

"So this is the lab," Lisa chirps. "I hope you're up to date on your herbs, because a lot of Dru's favorite spells are plant based. She's more of a traditionalist, unlike her nephew." Her hands go to the small of her back, and she stretches uncomfortably. "You'll see him around here from time to time, by the way. He lives in

Boston, but when he's in town, he stays with Dru. And he might ask you to assist him with some minor stuff. Mostly running errands."

"Sorry, what?" I ask, peering at a jar that really looks like it's got a pickled frog in it, of all things. These props are really incredible. It looks like something out of a witchy movie, all right, except there are no cobwebs or cauldron, and I'm definitely not at the apex of some fog-covered mountain, being chased by a hero. I poke another jar, but it just looks like it has wizened berries of some kind in it. "This place is amazing. Does she use these props to help her get in the mood? Sort of like method acting?"

"Method what?"

I turn to look at Lisa, and as I do, I suck in a breath at the sight of a glowering god standing in the doorway to the room. The man there looks . . . intense. He's impossibly tall, with broad shoulders that would put a linebacker to shame. He's dressed in a black suit with a black shirt underneath, complete with black tie, and his hair is dark and just brushes his collar. The long, solemn face is unsmiling, his expression stern, but his mouth is full and pink and shocking against the paleness of his skin.

"Who are you?" he asks bluntly, ignoring Lisa and looking right at me.

"Hello," I gush, extending my hand and moving forward. "I'm Reggie Johnson, here about the job. I'm such a big fan of . . ."

The tall man gives me an up-and-down look and then dismisses me as if I'm unimportant. He turns to Lisa and holds out a piece of paper. "I need these books from the library. Today. And did you file those requests I asked for?"

"I'll get to them," Lisa says tersely. She deliberately rubs her belly and glares at the man, who glares back.

Well, this is awkward. I tuck my hands back down to my sides and glance between the two of them. I truly hope that this isn't going to be my boss, because yikes. Hot but pissy.

The man casts another imperious look in my direction and then points a finger at Lisa. "Get it done, today." He turns on his heel and leaves without acknowledging me, and then he's gone.

Lisa sticks her tongue out at his back. "Such a dick."

My mouth has gone dry. "Is that . . . Mr. Magnus?" If so, my boss has a stunningly handsome (and stunningly dickish) husband.

"Sure is."

I divert my attention to what looks like a stack of bills shoved under a book, and my hands twitch with the need to clean up. "Does Mr. Magnus work for his wife?"

Her eyes widen, and then she chuckles. "Oh no. That's *a* Mr. Magnus, but he's not married to Dru. He's her nephew and between assistants himself, so I'm having to fill in." She leans toward me confidentially. "No one likes him. Can't keep anyone in his employ."

My smile returns. "I'm good at multitasking." I'm also a huge suck-up.

Lisa snaps her fingers and then pulls out her phone. "While I'm thinking about it, I had a few questions for you."

"Oh, of course." I read a book last night on interview questions one could expect for a fast-paced job, so I'm more than ready for this. I do wonder when we're going to get to the sit-down part of the interview, but maybe Lisa's just doing introductions before I meet her boss. That makes sense, and I give her a practiced "I'm very interested" look. "Ask away."

She flicks through her phone with her thumb. "Any allergies, food or otherwise?"

"No." Weird, but maybe I'd be in charge of getting coffee or grocery shopping or something. Some assistants do that, don't they? "Do you need to write this down? Should I take notes for you?" I dig in my purse, pulling out a notepad and pen. "I'm happy to do so."

"Not necessary." Lisa taps something on her phone, and I'm pretty sure I hear game music. She stares at the screen for a moment and then looks back at me. "Star sign?"

Getting weirder. "Taurus."

"Ah, a hard worker and stubborn." She dimples, nodding. "She'll like that. Tauruses are great employees. Very easy to work with."

"Thank . . . you?"

"Too bad Mr. Magnus is a Cancer. Very moody." She makes a face, still locked onto her phone. "Here we go. Any particular crystal affinity?" She gestures at one of the shelves, and I notice for the first time that there are rows and rows of crystals of all shapes and sizes in glass containers. Not in any sort of order, of course, but I'm sure I can help with that, too.

"Um, I don't think so?" This is definitely verging on fully weird territory. I'm starting to get a little uneasy, but I glance around the office again. Maybe this woman is some kind of new-age hipster that needs inspiration to work on the game? "What do crystals have to do with the position?"

"A lot. Blood type?"

"Is that really important?" I ask finally, resisting the urge to show my frustration.

"Not necessarily," Lisa admits. "But Ms. Magnus likes to know."

"I'm an O."

"Wonderful." She types with her thumb. "Any physical ailments? Do you work out at a gym? Eat healthy?"

I'm torn between pointing out that those are extremely inappropriate questions and just answering, because I really want the job. "I count macros," I say after a long moment. "For my nutrition." And because it feeds my obsessive need for control to hit the numbers perfectly.

She tilts her head. "I guess that's pretty good. Come with me, and I'll show you into Ms. Magnus's personal offices."

I follow behind her, glancing backward at the "lab" we're leaving. If that's not the office . . . Nope, Reggie. Don't ask questions until they mention the pay. You've had weird jobs before. As long as it pays well, you can put up with weirdness. I paste a smile on my face and follow Lisa's slower steps down the hall and toward the stairs. As we cut through the house, I glance over at the kitchen. Mr. Magnus is in there, with a glass of water in front of him on the counter. He's leaning over it and staring intently in our direction, practically scowling.

I can't help but notice that the kitchen is in complete disarray, with dishes on the counter and several cabinets hanging open. Maybe he hates the mess as much as I do, and that's why he's cranky.

"Just ignore him," Lisa continues. "He doesn't like strangers. Remember. Cancer sign."

Right. Moody. That fits him. I cast a brilliant smile in his direction, and I'm pleased when he gives me a startled look and turns away. I could swear he's blushing. Suck on that, Magnus.

We walk down the hall, and it seems the house gets bigger the deeper I go into it. The hall branches off into two others, both of them lined with doors, and there's a high ceiling with a crystal-covered chandelier above the stairwell. I gaze around me in awe as Lisa leads me past a glorious-looking library filled to the gills with all kinds of old books. There are portraits on the walls, most of them old, and I realize that the Magnus family is old, old money. No wonder they're eccentric. Lisa heads toward a pair of double doors and opens them. "Just have a seat, and I'll let Ms. Magnus know that you're here."

"Thank you," I murmur and step inside.

She turns and goes to leave and then pauses in the doorway. "Actually, before I go, I should give you a bit of a warning about

Ms. Magnus." Lisa gives me an apologetic little look. "She can be a bit of a . . ." She hesitates, clearly choosing her words.

Oh boy. Here it comes. "Hard-ass?"

Lisa clears her throat. "Ding-dong."

I blink.

Of all the things I expected to hear, "ding-dong" wasn't one of them. This whole place has a weird vibe, and the more Lisa talks, the more I'm not sure this is a good idea. I think about the weird nutrition questions, and my Spidey sense tingles. "You know what? Maybe I should go—"

"No! You're the only applicant so far!" A panicked look comes across her face. "You read the ad, so you're clearly more than qualified. Please, Regina, just stay a little longer. I know Ms. Magnus can be a bit eccentric, but that's why she pays her assistants so well."

I bite my lip. "Exactly how well?" I feel like a bit of a heel for asking, but since she's calling her employer a ding-dong, I guess politeness is out the window, right?

Her expression relaxes. "Twenty-five thousand."

I blanch. "A year?" I do some quick math in my head. That's a little under five hundred a week, and I'm pretty sure the local coffee shop pays more than that. Maybe I should apply there instead. Oh, but the tables there are always so damned messy. It'd drive me crazy to see customers leaving the place like that.

"Oh no." Lisa giggles. "A month. It pays twenty-five thousand a month." She leans forward and puts a hand to her mouth, whispering. "She's loaded. Absolutely no clue of what anything costs these days."

My mouth goes dry, and my knees feel weak. "A m-month?" I stammer. That's insane. That's three hundred grand a year.

"To put up with an out-of-touch ding-dong, yes." Lisa raises her eyebrows at me. "Still interested?"

I nod wordlessly. She closes the door after me, and I'm left alone in the room, trying to catch my breath. Twenty-five thousand dollars a month. Good god. The things I could do with that money. I wouldn't even have to work here long, I reason. Even if Ms. Magnus is completely unbearable, a month or two and I can pay off all my bills and get a down payment on a decent place to live. I can put up with any sort of bullshit for twenty-five grand a month.

I could . . . I could pay off some of Mom and Dad's debt.

No, I chide myself immediately, squelching that line of thinking. *They are not your responsibility. They got themselves into that mess.*

With a little sigh, I look around the room. It's a study, all right, with books along one wall and all kinds of creepy dead stuffed animals along another. There's a stuffed ostrichlike bird standing in the corner, and several other dead animals in various stages of taxidermy are scattered about the room. Blech. Absently, I reach out and turn what looks like a stuffed ferret on its stand so it faces the right direction. Someone likes dead critters. I wrinkle my nose as I move toward a big glass case laid out upon an antique table, and I'm not entirely surprised to see it contains hundreds of dead bugs, all neatly pinned. Because of course.

I move over to the bookcase, wondering if this lady likes the classics. The organizer in me reads the spines to see if they're in any particular sort of order, but as I try to read the lettering, it fades and I can't make it out. Odd. I pick up a book. It's written in some sort of scrawling, scribbly language I can't understand, and the binding feels cool to the touch. I put it back and glance around, and as I do, I notice the door is open. Is it the hot jackass again? As I frown at the door, an elderly woman steps in, cane in hand. She's wearing a floral muumuu and a bright purple turban on her head that looks as if it went out of date a hundred years ago, and she's so old that liver spots cover her paper-thin golden skin. She is way, way too old to be the auntie of the hot dickbag downstairs, and I smile at her.

"Hi there."

She looks up at me, and her eyes are sharp even as she sits down in one of the chairs for guests. "Far too many stairs in this house," she says disapprovingly. "Whoever made this place never had to walk a day in heels in her life."

I can't disagree. I smile, nudging a statue that looks slightly out of place. I notice that the woman's feet are bare, and her cheeks are round like a cherub's and bright pink with rouge of some kind. "Are you here for the job?" I ask.

I look around for Lisa, but she's nowhere to be found. The woman is a bit old, but she's got a sweet expression on her face, and my heart hurts at the idea that she needs to find employment at this stage in her life.

The woman nods. "I suppose I am."

"Did you . . . forget your shoes?" I smile politely. "Your feet are bare."

"Was I supposed to wear shoes?" The elderly woman looks puzzled. "Is that a requirement?"

"Perhaps not." I don't want to make her feel bad. Why is she here, though? Shouldn't the interviewers be more cognizant of this sort of thing? Maybe Lisa didn't see the woman's feet with her big pregnant belly in the way, though. I decide friendliness is the way to go. Older players of Spellcraft aren't that uncommon, though perhaps not this old. "Big fan?"

She glances up at the ceiling. "Is it big?"

I fight back a giggle and pick up another book, flipping through it. More gibberish, this one with all kinds of hideous drawings in it. Again, I can't read the spine, which is frustrating. How does anyone keep anything organized in this place? Maybe that explains some of the utter chaos. "I meant the game. Are you a big fan of the game?"

"Is it a game?" she asks, musing. "Some would say it's more of a lifestyle."

I think of the sheer dollar amounts I've spent on rare cards and the weekend conventions I used to drive to with my college friends. "Well, you're not wrong about that."

Lisa rushes in a moment later, all smiles. "Oh good, you've met." She moves to stand next to the tiny woman, and when she struggles to stand, Lisa helps her up. "That saves me some time."

Boy, this place is really unprofessional. I hesitate and then put the book down, moving over to Lisa's side. "Are we really supposed to meet if we're interviewing for the same position?" Part of me wants to leave, but the small greedy part of Reggie deep inside is screaming, *TWENTY-FIVE THOUSAND A MONTH!* "It seems . . . a little unfair to pit us against each other."

"Same position?" Lisa says blankly. She turns back to the elderly woman and helps her behind the desk. "What? No, she's the witch."

That makes me pause. Hard. That . . . seems rude. "I'm sorry. Did you say '*bitch*'?"

"WITCH," the elderly woman clearly enunciates as if I'm deaf.

"Witch," I repeat.

"Yes. This job is for a witch's familiar." Lisa rolls her eyes. "Though I suppose the modern term is more like 'executive assistant' or some such. Whatever it is, she is the witch." Lisa gestures at the wizened old woman. "This is Ms. Magnus of the House of Magnus." The door opens, and the tall, dark man steps in. "That is Ben Magnus, her nephew. Also of the House of Magnus."

"A witch house," Ms. Magnus adds brightly. "Fine, rich magical bloodlines run deep in my family. Have for millennia. Though I do like 'bitch,' too."

I make a noise that might be a protest or just kind of a squawk. Now they're all frowning in my direction. Lisa squints at me. "What exactly did you think this job was about?"

I sit down weakly in the chair across from the desk. "A card game?"

New York Times and *USA Today* bestselling author Jessica Clare writes under three pen names. As Jessica Clare, she writes contemporary romance. As Jessica Sims, she writes fun, sexy shifter paranormals. Finally, as Jill Myles, she writes a little bit of everything, from sexy, comedic urban fantasy to zombie fairy tales. She lives in Texas with her husband, cats, and too many dust bunnies.

CONNECT ONLINE

Jessica-Clare.com

 AuthorJessicaClare

 _JessicaClare